THE BANISHED OF
MUIRWOOD

Books by Jeff Wheeler

The Covenant of Muirwood Trilogy
The Banished of Muirwood
The Ciphers of Muirwood
The Void of Muirwood

The Legends of Muirwood Trilogy
The Wretched of Muirwood
The Blight of Muirwood
The Scourge of Muirwood

Whispers from Mirrowen Trilogy
Fireblood
Dryad-Born
Poisonwell

Landmoor Series
Landmoor
Silverkin

THE BANISHED OF
MUIRWOOD

THE COVENANT OF MUIRWOOD

Book One

JEFF WHEELER

47N●RTH

Text copyright © 2015 Jeff Wheeler

Published by 47North, Seattle

www.apub.com

Amazon, the Amazon logo, and 47North are trademarks of Amazon.com, Inc., or its affiliates.

ISBN-13: 9781503945326
ISBN-10: 1503945324

Cover design by Ray Lundgren
Illustrated by Magali Villeneuve

Printed in the United States of America

To Tom, Jordan, Dale, and Steve
(and Madge)

NAESS

BAMBURG

NORRIS-YORK
KRUCIS
TINTERN
Bridgestow
The Myntlas
Billerbeck
Forshee
SEMPRINGFALL

ROSTICK

HAUTLAND

VIEGG

PRY-REE

COMOROS

HOLYROOD
MUIRWOOD
Winterrowd
Comoros
CLAREDON
AUGUSTIN
Caspur
CEASTER
Doviur

ANTIMO

PAEIZ

Watzholt Mtns.

RIVAULX

Peliyey Mtns.

SUMEELA

FENTON

LISYEUX

CRUIX

The Spike

DAHOMEY

Bried

MON

DOCHTE
Vezins
Roc-Adamour

Peliyey Mtns.

CASINUM

Argus

LOST ABBEY

Cursed Shores

AVINION

AVINION

• Towns
✠ ABBEYS

TABLE OF CONTENTS

Before your great-grandfather and I boarded the Holk *and left the forsaken shores . . . Before the Scourge destroyed every living soul save one . . . Before the waters of a new land lapped against the hull, or our skiff crunched into the sand . . . Before the first boot plunged into the mud . . . Before all of these things happened, great-granddaughter, I made a Covenant. I promised the Aldermaston that my posterity would return and rebuild the ruins of Muirwood Abbey. I made a Covenant that the Apse Veil would be restored and that his soul would finally find rest in Idumea. With the Apse Veil closed, the abbeys are shut off from one another and the dead are stranded on this world, unable to return to their rightful home. But I made my oaths before the visions began. It was only later I foresaw that another people would claim our country before our posterity returned. There is much I must explain to you. The Covenant must be fulfilled, or all is lost. I lay this burden on you.*

—Lia Demont, Aldermaston of Muirwood Abbey

CHAPTER ONE

Kystrel

Maia watched from the window seat as Chancellor Walraven's eyes turned silver. The councillor reposed on a stiff wooden bench against the wall, lanky and relaxed, his aging body covered in the black cassock of the Dochte Mandar. Incongruously, he wore brown leather clogs over his dark stockings. A golden tome sat open in his lap, and one of his hands stroked the gleaming aurichalcum page; the other hand rested crosswise against his breast, just under the kystrel that hung from a chain around his neck. His wispy gray hair was askew, and a thin trimmed beard adorned his jaw.

As he invoked the magic of the kystrel, whispers of the Medium swept through the tower cell and filled the turret. Maia felt a shudder shoot through her, the sensation tinged with excitement and fear. Every time she watched him use the kystrel, that same nervous feeling squirmed to life as she stared into his glowing eyes. His gaze was fixed on the corner of the turret, where several books bound in leather had been stacked haphazardly. Aisles and aisles of books, tomes, chests, and urns cluttered the circular space. The only window in the tower was above her seat, and she could feel the dusky light bathe her small shoulders as she looked on with utter fascination.

Maia was nine years old and she was a princess of Comoros, the only child of her parents. On her name day, she had been bequeathed the name Marciana after a distant ancestor related to her Family, but her father had taken to calling her Maia, and it had not bothered her in the least.

Scuttling noises sounded from the stairwell. Maia shivered involuntarily and kept her legs tucked tightly underneath her, despite the pinpricks of pain that shot down to her ankles from staying in the same position for so long. She gazed in wonder as the first arrival appeared from behind a worn leather book, drawn forth by the kystrel's magic. Dark beady eyes and twitching whiskers announced the arrival of the mouse. Then another appeared. And another.

As Chancellor Walraven sat idly, absently stroking the tome, the rodents began to flood the turret floor. The air jittered with squeaks and rustling as the mice began to file toward the chancellor, sniffling around him as if he were a piece of sweetmeat. Soon the floor writhed with gray fur and twitching pink ears. The feeling of power lingered in the air, thick and palpable, and the chancellor's silver eyes focused on the doorway, his expression weary yet firm. He shifted on the bench, and the wood groaned softly beneath him.

"Do you sense the Medium, Maia?" he asked her in a soft voice. "Do you feel its power holding them in thrall?"

"Yes," Maia answered in a hushed voice, the hairs on the back of her neck prickling. Part of her feared that some of the mice would leap up onto the window seat, but she knew that she needed to control her fear or else they would. She sat stone stiff, eyes watching the mass of mice in fascination.

"The mice *must* obey the summons from the kystrel. They cannot help themselves. They are drawn to it. They cannot think right now. All they can do is *feel*. If I asked you to open the window, I could fill them with fear and make them rush off the edge and plunge to their deaths. And they would, Maia. They would."

"Kara Cook would thank you for it," Maia said, a twinkle in her eye. She shuddered with revulsion at the teeming mass that only continued to grow. A few rats began to appear, their whiskers even longer, their front teeth like saws.

The feeling in the chamber began to ebb as if it were water draining from a tub. As the Medium dispersed, the spell broke. The mice and rats scrambled with chaos and fled the turret down the steps, cascading over each other like pond waves. Maia started when several tried to leap onto her lap, but she shooed them back into the avalanche.

Maia tried to calm herself, touching first her heart and then the jeweled choker around her neck. She gulped down huge breaths of air, waiting for her nerves to calm.

"To use the Medium, one must be able to control their thoughts and emotions," the chancellor said. He shook his head. "You are not ready yet, Maia."

A pang of disappointment stabbed her, and she tried not to grimace. "Not yet?"

He scratched his cropped whiskers, making a scratching sound. "You are still young, Maia. Years of turbulent emotions lay ahead of you. Wait until you are say . . . thirteen, hmmm? Turbulent emotions aplenty then! No, I will let you read the tomes, even though it is forbidden, but I cannot *trust* you with a kystrel until you are much older. The old Dochte Mandar failed because they used the kystrels' power unwisely. The maston tomes have taught us the proper way to use the Medium, and we must ensure that kystrels are only wielded by those who will not abuse them, whether intentionally or not. You, my dear, are not yet ready."

Maia sighed deeply. She wanted a kystrel. She wanted to prove she could be trusted with one. Many maston families could still use Leerings to invoke the Medium, but for reasons no one understood, mastons had grown weaker with the Medium over the centuries. The only way to channel real power through the Medium was by using a kystrel, and kystrels were only used by the Dochte Mandar. Still, Maia was not ungrateful for her rare position and her treasured secret.

None of the girls of the seven realms were allowed to learn the secret art of reading and engraving. That was a privilege only allowed to boys and men. Because of something done in the past, something related to the Scourge that had destroyed so many people, women were not trusted to learn how to use the Medium by reading ancient tomes, and it was absolutely forbidden for a woman to be given a kystrel. Some women, because of their lineage, were strong enough in the Medium that Leerings obeyed them, and that was considered acceptable. Those women could become mastons. Women could be trained at abbeys to speak languages, learn crafts and music, but nothing more. Except for Maia, and she knew that it was because her father was the king, and he made his own rules.

Maia uttered a Pry-rian epithet about patience.

Walraven scratched his beard again. "You must have inherited the Gift of Xenoglossia from your ancestors, child. How many languages do you speak now?"

"Dahomeyjan, a little Paeizian, and our language, of course," Maia replied, sitting up straight and smiling broadly. "I can read and scribe them all. I wish to learn the language of Pry-Ree, my mother's homeland, next. Or the language of Naess. Which would be better?"

"You are only nine, child. I find Naestor particularly excruciating. There are too many runes to memorize." He tapped his finger on the polished golden tome in his lap. "You must never let on that you can read, Maia. I would be put to death if my brethren of the Dochte Mandar discovered our secret."

Maia twirled some of her dark hair and gazed at the chancellor with concern. "I would never betray you," she said gravely.

He smiled. "I know, child. The Medium broods on me. You are destined for great things. I think it is quite probable that you will become the Queen of Comoros someday."

Maia felt a spasm of dread. "What about my mother's confinement? Do you have a premonition of evil about the baby, Lord Chancellor?"

Walraven combed his fingers through his wiry gray hair. "I will always tell you the truth, Maia. You were the firstborn, a daughter. By law and custom, you cannot rule even if there are no male heirs. Your mother has had three stillborn children after your birth." The words sent another shudder through Maia, and a terrible surge of guilt nearly strangled her. Still, she did not cry. Her father had once boasted to an emissary from Paeiz that his daughter, Maia, never cried.

"Was it my fault?" Maia asked in a calm serious voice.

"Who can say for certain? Perhaps it is the Medium's will for your mother to bear no other children. Even now, we await the word." He waved his hand toward the mounds of parchment on his desk. "I have missives to write, instructions to send, curiosity to sate. Every ruler of every kingdom wishes to know the sex of the child and if it is born living. Do you see that pile on the edge of my desk? It is an offer of marriage from the King of Pry-Ree if the babe is a boy. A vast sum. The King of Dahomey has several daughters, quite old already, and you can be sure he would send a parchment and a cask of jewels to secure an alliance with the young prince, just as he did for you." A wise smile split his mouth. "He may still begrudge the past, but he is clever enough to value a relationship with a stronger kingdom."

Maia smiled ruefully at the thought of her marriage. When she was two years old, the King of Dahomey had sired his heir and promptly made an alliance with Comoros, binding the two children with a plight troth. The troth was retracted years later after a trade agreement fell apart between Dahomey and Paeiz, a conflict that had ended in a brutal war.

Maia had always known her marriage would be political. Even at nine, she harbored no illusions about that. However, she trusted Chancellor Walraven and knew him to be a shrewd man . . . and a caring one. He was her father's closest advisor, her personal tutor, and a prominent Dochte Mandar even outside their kingdom.

Maia smoothed the front of her dress over her aching knees. "Do you have any plans for me . . . to marry?" she asked him, trying not to betray her conflicted feelings on the subject.

"Hmmm?"

She saw that he was cocking his head, his ear angled toward the open door.

"Are there any negotiations underway for . . . my marriage?"

"Not presently," Walraven replied. "You are a handsome lass, if a bit shy. There are certainly no shortages of offers for your hand. But it would not be politically prudent to finalize anything until it is clear whether or not your mother will give birth to an heir. As your father's advisor, I must steer the ship the way the winds are blowing, not where I wish them to blow. If I judge them properly, you will one day rule this realm even though no woman ever has. That will make a difference in who I select as your consort, do you not think?"

Maia could hear shuffling feet coming up the turret stairwell. Chancellor Walraven stood and hefted the tome onto his desk, shoving aside a stack of parchments to make room. He frisked the front of his cassock and gazed through the window pane, out over the mass of shingled roofs and belching chimneys. The sky was a soot stain outside.

It was one of her father's knights who breached the threshold. Carew. His face was damp with sweat, his eyes haunted with emotion, and Maia knew just from looking at him that the babe was dead. Her stomach shriveled at the thought, and she felt the ache press against her heart. She wanted a sibling, even if it meant losing her chance of becoming Comoros's queen one day. She had always enjoyed the company of other children, but though she never lacked for playmates, every other child in the kingdom was inferior to her in rank and station. She knew the other children had all been trained to agree with her. To let her win at their games, to fawn over her ideas and her desires.

She hated that.

To her mind, it was nothing more than luck that had made her a princess. She considered everyone her equal unless they proved themselves not to be. Maia was competitive by nature, she wanted to win on her own merits, not because someone else let her. As a result, she did not have many friends her own age. Most, like the chancellor, were much older and wiser.

"The babe . . . is stillborn," Carew said between gasps. He

hung his head and shook it. "A boy. You must come down and console my master. He is beyond himself with grief."

"I will come presently," Walraven said gravely. Maia watched him as he peered out of the window again, steeling himself for the encounter to come. His jaw muscles clenched, and his hands fidgeted, but he took a calming breath and then turned toward the knight. "Come with me, Maia."

She was shocked and pleased that he would invite her on such an errand. She clambered off the window seat and felt dagger slashes of pain shoot down her legs. Rubbing her calves, she began hobbling down the steps after the chancellor.

Maia's heart was on fire with conflicting emotions. Her little brother was dead. Or perhaps he had never truly been alive, though she remembered pressing her palm against her mother's abdomen and feeling his gentle kicks. The memory seared her heart, threatening to destroy her composure. Her mother's previous miscarriages had happened long ago, when she had been too young to feel them keenly. This burden was much harder to bear without breaking, but she had to be strong for her parents. Yet there was a slender, guilty part of her that was almost . . . excited. For the last year, the chancellor had been preparing her to be her father's heir, but his training had been more discreet lately given her mother's pregnancy. Would she be given the chance to rule on her own right and not as a result of whom she married? The idea of becoming queen one day was sweet on her tongue, sweet as crispels, and it conflicted with the bitterness of the moment. She wondered if she was truly a wicked child for having such thoughts.

When they reached the main corridor, they marched vigorously. Moans and wails were already starting to echo throughout the castle as news spread. Her parents' grief would be shared by everyone. Maia clutched her stomach as an awful, constricting feeling clutched at her chest. She kept close to the chancellor's heels and together they mounted the steps to another turret. Leerings began to illuminate the way as they climbed, bathing the steps in cool, smokeless light. Around and around they climbed, and soon Maia could hear voices. The handsome knight shook his head and refused to go any farther. He crumpled into tears. Still Maia did not weep. She merely followed the chancellor as he walked around the man.

When they reached the landing at the top of the turret, Maia could hear her father's voice. That he was suffering was obvious—his voice was husky and ferocious.

"Why did I even marry you?"

Her eyes went wide with shock as she took in the meaning of the words. She had never heard him say such a thing, and was stunned silent.

The chancellor paused at the threshold, his eyes narrowing with anger. His face became a mask of calm, his lanky body stiffening with resolve as he held out an arm to prevent her from entering the room.

Maia could hear her mother's sobs. "Forgive me, Husband. Forgive me. It . . . I . . . please . . . forgive . . . me. My child! My son!" There was a torrent of tears, gulping and swallowing and hissing breaths.

"To see you in such pain!" her father moaned. "It would have been better if we had never . . ." His voice trailed off and he coughed violently. "How could the Medium fail us . . . again? My thoughts were fixed. So were yours. It begins . . . with a thought, that is what they say. And all the vigils that were held to strengthen our connection to the Medium . . . the whole city was holding vigil!" His voice rose like thunder. "How could it fail us like this? What, in Idumea's name, does it expect from us?"

"No . . . no . . . it is not . . . no . . . the Medium . . . it is not . . . the Medium's . . . fault, Husband." Her mother was babbling.

Maia shrunk, experiencing a dread that she had never felt before. Her parents had always made her feel comforted and safe. Hearing them so distraught, so wild, frightened her.

"I thought," her father said venomously, "that if we obeyed the will of the Medium, our line would be secured. This is the *fourth* stillborn! It must be a sign that our marriage is cursed."

"No!" came the pleading voice. "We both felt it, Brannon. We felt the Medium consecrate our marriage. This is a test. To see . . . if we will be faithful."

Her father let out a hiss of anger. "Another test? And what then? Another? What if we were wrong? What if we should never have married? We are being punished by a mistake from the past."

"Hold me. Please, Husband. Hold me. To hear you say such things . . ."

Maia heard only muffled words after that. Chancellor Walraven's hand pressed against her shoulder now, squeezing it firmly enough to cause a flinch of pain. She stared up into his glowing silver eyes. The emotions from the chamber were draining away, drawn into the kystrel hanging around his neck. Walraven's face twitched with agony, his fingers digging into her flesh so painfully that she nearly cried out, but she chewed on her lip and endured it, seeing the calming effect it was having on her parents.

He was taking their emotions into himself, drawing away their pain. She saw the snake-like vine of a tattoo crinkle along his neck, poking out from above the ruff of his collar. He had warned her that the use of a kystrel painted the flesh of the chest with strange tattoos. It was a residue of the magic that marked the one who wielded it. He had shown her his own whorl mark once, half hidden beneath a thatch of gray hairs.

The storm of emotions was passing. The chancellor's eyes filled with tears and he brushed them away with his wrist, releasing the painful grip on her shoulder. She knew there would be bruises in that spot later.

Walraven gave her a fierce look. "Never repeat what you heard here," he whispered. "Your parents' grief is private. When husbands and wives suffer blows such as these, they say things they may later regret. I have helped them through the worst of it. Remember the lesson, child. Even the deepest griefs can be governed by a kystrel. Above all, you must learn to control your emotions."

"I will," Maia said solemnly.

Together, they entered the birthing chamber where the smell of blood made her sick.

CHAPTER TWO

Corriveaux

A rough hand shook Maia's shoulder, waking her. She blinked rapidly, still lost in the fog of the childhood dream. The whine of mosquitoes barely penetrated her thoughts and she struggled to remember where she was. The forest was thick and impenetrable, damp with soggy vegetation that clung to her tattered gown and frayed cloak. She sat up, wincing with pain from her festering wounds and bruises, and tried again to remember where she was and how she had come to be there.

It took her several moments to orient herself. When the memories finally came flooding back, she almost wished they had remained elusive. She was camped in the cursed forests of southern Dahomey. In a desperate attempt to find a solution for the troubles that had beset Comoros after his banishment of the Dochte Mandar, her father had sent her to this land with a kishion—a hired killer—and a few soldiers as protectors, on a mission to seek out a lost abbey that contained secrets of the order.

The way to the abbey had been lined with terrors, and a giant beast had scattered and brutalized her father's men. Only she and the kishion still lived. They had at last found the abbey, and there, in a dark pool bathed in mystery, Maia had learned that her journey had only just begun.

It was a nightmare, and yet it was all real.

"You have a faraway look in your eyes, Lady Maia," the kishion said, coming around and squatting in front of her. Sweat dribbled down his cheeks—his coarse hair was damp with it. Rags encrusted with dried blood bound wounds on his forearms and legs. His eyes surveyed her warily, his gaze flashing surreptitiously to the kystrel hanging loose in her bodice and the whorl of tattoos staining her upper chest and throat.

"I was dreaming," she mumbled hoarsely, shaking her head to try and clear the memories that clung to her like spiderwebs. Her dark hair was a nest of twigs and nettles. She arched her back, trying to loosen her muscles, and rubbed her arms vigorously. The world was syrupy and slow, the edges not quite real.

The childhood feelings of anger and pain still churned inside her from the dream. Slowly, she kneaded circles into her temples. That long-ago day when the babe was lost was the first time she had witnessed a hint of the man her father was to become. She shuddered and bile rose in her throat as she thought about how young and naïve she had been. The memory of what it had felt like to be a princess of the realm glimmered brightly.

Well, she was no longer that young naïve girl of nine. She was twice that age now, and a princess no longer.

"What troubles you?" he asked gruffly, his face livid with scars. Part of his ear was missing.

She squinted up at the kishion. "It was a sad dream. One from my childhood." There was a stitch of pain in her side, and she kneaded it with her fingers to relieve the sensation. "Another stillborn babe. My mother's grief. My father's callousness. It was long ago." She paused. "Before my father sent me away."

"You mean before you were banished," the kishion said flatly.

Maia shook her head. "No—he sent me away first, to the town of Bridgestow on the border of Pry-Ree. I was ostensibly there to help manage the border disputes between Pry-Ree and Comoros."

"Ostensibly," the kishion said with the twinge of a chuckle. It was the closest he ever came to laughter. "And what am I to make of such a word, my lady? I am a killer, not a scholar."

"Forgive me. My thoughts are still muddled from the dream. I was only nine years old when I went to Bridgestow. It was at the chancellor's suggestion. Do you remember Chancellor Walraven?" It earned her a curt nod. "After my mother's last failed birth, he advised my parents to send me to Bridgestow so I could begin learning my duties as the heir to the throne. I lived on the border of Pry-Ree for three years. That is where I learned to speak Pryrian." She smoothed the wrinkled mass of her skirts. "Beautiful country. My mother's Family is from there. I think my grandmother is an Aldermaston at one of the small abbeys. The trees are ancient. Have you been there?"

The kishion shook his head no but said nothing.

She gazed at the swarm of gnats that surrounded them, seemingly attracted to their voices. Waving them away with a stroke of her arm did little. She was tempted to use the kystrel to disperse them, but she needed to be sparing in its use. Already the tattoos were nearly climbing up her throat, and soon they would be visible to any keen observer. Once she was discovered, someone would tell the Dochte Mandar, and she would be executed immediately.

Of course, she was going to her death anyway.

The quest she had been given in the lost abbey had sealed her fate. She was to go to Naess, the seat of the Dochte Mandar, to seek the High Seer of the mastons—a woman—and learn the history of the Myriad Ones and how they had once infested and destroyed the kingdoms. It was the only way to save Comoros. But how could she possibly travel into the very heart of the place that had outlawed women to read or use the Medium?

Maia stared at the bark of a fallen redwood, the trunk slender and stricken with lichen and moss. Noises and clicks filled the gap in the conversation. She and the kishion were hurrying westward, trying to return to the shores of Dahomey, where the ship that had brought them, the *Blessing of Burntisland*, hopefully awaited. Though the kishion was as harsh as the unforgiving terrain they had wandered into, their journey was still beset with woes. Each night brought hordes of insects to torment them. Serpents were common—dangerous and poisonous. Clean water was scarce, but thankfully a path of Leerings had been left as waymarkers to the lost abbey.

Maia turned to the Leering she had slept beside. It was a tall, rounded stone, almost her height when she stood fully erect. There was a ravaged face carved into it, a face that had nearly been rubbed away by the centuries. All Leerings had faces carved into them and could channel the power of the Medium in some way, providing water, light, fire, heat—along with many other arcane powers. The Leerings had eased their journey.

Their rations had already vanished, but the kishion was adept at living off the land, even though the fare was not to her liking—lizards and rodents and sometimes bats for meat. She was starving for a decent meal and hoped they would reach the ship within the next few days. Sailing to her doom in Naess would almost be a relief so long as she had a bed to sleep on for the voyage.

"Let me check for bites," the kishion said, motioning toward her ruined gown.

The front of the garment had been torn when the soldiers her father had sent as her protectors attempted to snatch the kystrel from her neck and choke her to death. She clenched the fabric tighter around her throat and shook her head. "When we reach the ship," she said. "I don't feel any bites."

He snorted, shrugged, and rose, surveying the Leering and rubbing his bandaged hand across the rippled edges of the stone. He sniffed at it, his expression one of disgust or superstition, and waited for her to summon water for them to drink.

Maia brushed a mass of tangled hair behind her shoulder and bent at an angle next to the Leering so that the gushing waters wouldn't soak her. She invoked the kystrel, and the fire-coal eyes of the Leering ignited instantly. Water began gushing from the slats where the mouth had once been carved. Maia rinsed her filthy hands first, scrubbing away the dirt and muck, feeling the cool clean water play across her fingers. She cupped water into her palms and gulped it down, coming again for another drink. Then a third. The excess water dribbled onto a small bed of silt at the base of the Leering.

The kishion took his turn once she was through, burying his head under the stream of cold water before tipping his scarred lips up to the flow and gulping down deep swallows. Maia rested her palm against the Leering.

When her skin touched the stone, an image burst into her mind so sharp and clear it was as if a window to another place had opened and she could see both places at once.

Who are you?

The thoughts came from a man—a man kneeling in front of another Leering, another of the waymarkers leading to the lost abbey. She recognized his surroundings instantly, a grove of dead bones and rusted armor. It was the graveyard of some vicious battle where the participants had all slaughtered one another. The man's hair and beard were ash blond; his countenance was tired and stained with grime. His black Dochte Mandar tunic was splattered with mud, and he clenched his own kystrel in his left hand.

Who are you, girl?

His fierce thoughts snatched at her mind, gripping her in a vise that bound her to the Leering. She could not move. She could not breathe. Soldiers wearing the uniform of Dahomeyjan knights scuttled around the man. Panic began to churn inside her. These men were also in the cursed woods . . . and they were hunting her. She could sense the blazing intensity of the blond man's thoughts.

Maia tried to release the Leering, but her hand would not move. A surge of piercing power cut through her marrow and sinews, binding her fast.

I have her, the man thought to someone else. Another Dochte Mandar loomed into view and he put his hand on the stone next to the blond man's. His thoughts joined the fray. *She slept by the gargouelle last night. Orlander is almost there. I will try and hold her until they come. We have her! She is the one we seek.*

Maia shoved at his thoughts with her will. The vise-like grip of the power that had her pinned groaned, and she tried to pry free. Some of her memories leaked through the bond.

She is strong, Corriveaux! the second Dochte Mandar thought, almost admiring.

Not as strong as me, the blond man snapped. She could still see him . . . the bearded one, Corriveaux. His thoughts began to intrude into her mind. His will was like a bar of iron, and he used it to bludgeon her resistance, his jaw clenched with fury.

Yes, you are *Marciana Soliven,* Corriveaux thought to her. *We seized your ship and crew. Whilst you slept, I sent soldiers ahead with two hunters. Do not think you can escape me. Yield, Lady Marciana.*

Maia's whole body trembled with fear and rage. She flexed her will against theirs and felt the resistance start to budge. Corriveaux scowled, his brooding look turning darker. *I see you. You cannot outmatch the resources of the King of Dahomey. We will hunt you down, my lady. Trust that. You cannot escape. When the soldiers arrive, you will surrender to them. You will instruct your protector to hand over his weapons. You will . . .*

Maia squeezed her eyes shut, trying to blot out the Dochte Mandar's thoughts. Despite her best efforts, they embedded themselves into her consciousness like runes carved into a rock. He was forcing his will on her, commanding her to obey his instructions. A raw compulsion gripped her, and she knew that if she saw those men, she would obey.

"My lady?" the kishion asked, looking up at her, at last sensing something was amiss.

She could not speak. Her tongue clove to her mouth. She looked down at him, her eyes pleading.

Leave me alone, Maia thought in desperation. *Do not interfere.*

I cannot hold her, the second Dochte Mandar thought with a groan of mental anguish.

We have her, Corriveaux thought. *With both of us, we can tame her. Do not slacken your thoughts!*

The grip on her mind tightened further, sending a piercing shard of agony into her skull. She began to moan, feeling her will crumble. Her knees were shaking, and the rest of her body started to convulse. She hunkered inside herself, summoning reserves of strength and determination. She would battle them off. There was no choice. She was willing to die in her quest, but not this soon.

Lady Marciana, you will surrender. You will surrender. You will surrender!

Her breath gushed out of her as the kishion tackled her away from the waymarker and landed on top of her. With her connection to the Leering abruptly broken, she felt herself free of the torturous grip on her mind. She was soon hyperventilating, gasping for breath.

"They found us!" she gasped through chattering teeth. "The Dochte Mandar are in the woods!"

"Where?" he asked, getting up quickly and pulling her with him. He unsheathed a blade and whirled around, staring into the dark woods.

"The way we came," she said, pointing west. "I saw them in my mind. They said they have our ship and crew. They knew we were camping by the boulder, so they sent men ahead, including two hunters. We must flee, but where? Now we have no way of crossing the water."

Her heart pounded with confusion. This was a foreign land. It was the land where death was born.

"If the ship was taken, then the west is closed to us. We have no choice—we must go north and cross Dahomey on foot."

Maia knew he was right, though she dreaded it with all her heart. An ancient rivalry existed between Comoros and Dahomey. The ruler of Dahomey was an ambitious and ruthless young king who had sworn to humble her father and subdue Comoros, not only for daring to expel the Dochte Mandar, but also for breaking the long-ago plight troth binding him to Maia. What the King of Dahomey did not know was that her father's kingdom was already rife with violence and unrest. And now its fate rested on her shoulders, the banished daughter her father had disinherited.

Grabbing their supplies, Maia and the kishion started away from the Leering and plunged into the woods. There was no use running and tiring themselves needlessly. Their pursuers had traveled all night in the dark—they would be weary and confused. An oily black feeling swirled in Maia's mind as they made their way, an imprint of the Dochte Mandar's intentions. She had never encountered a person with such a forceful will before, let alone two. Worse, there might well be more of them traveling with the soldiers. If the Dahomeyjans knew they were facing a woman with a kystrel, they would have sent sufficient men to bind her powers.

Maia swatted at a tree branch, her heart pounding with the effort of hiking. She had always been fascinated by maps of the known kingdoms and had studied them all her life, memorizing the names of cities and provinces, tracing mountains and forests with her finger. What she remembered from her childhood studies was that more than half of Dahomey was still uninhabitable. Nature itself had turned against the kings and queens of this land, and the Blight that had destroyed all the kingdoms still reigned. Deadly serpents and poisonous spiders had proliferated in the cursed part of the kingdom, making it impossible to settle. There were communities throughout the northern part of Dahomey, but very few in the southern hinterlands. She could not remember a single name of any of the villages or towns.

She realized, with dread, that there were three other kingdoms blocking her way to Naess, the seat of the Dochte Mandar—Hautland, Paeiz, and Mon. The latter was a coastal kingdom that could probably be avoided, but there was no other way, except by ship, to pass around the other kingdoms. And all had been hostile to her father since the day he drove the Dochte Mandar from Comoros.

They walked with determination born of desperation. Maia was sturdy and had survived the dangers they had faced thus far. With each slogging boot step, she pushed herself hard, not deigning to complain or utter curses. There was too much to do. They had to outdistance their pursuers, find supplies, and race toward their goal as quickly as they could.

Her stomach cramped with the strain of the pace they kept, and her throat seared with thirst as the sun climbed and arced across the sky, filtering through the dusky leaves and moss-ridden boulders scattered throughout the way. There was no sign of any habitation. No waymarkers to guide the path.

They paused to rest briefly; Maia needed to preserve her flagging strength. Her legs itched from the continuous scratches and slashes from the poking undergrowth. Her ankles were swollen. She breathed hard, feeling her heartbeat pound in her ears.

"How far do you think they are?" Maia said with a wheeze.

The kishion shook his head, gazing ahead, not behind. "They will need to stop and rest eventually. But let us keep walking, even if we walk all night. It will be harder to track us, which will slow them down. They do not know our destination, do they?"

Maia shook her head. "They cannot. And Naess is the last place they would ever expect us to go."

He grabbed her arm, signaling the rest was over, and they continued to plunge through thick woods and dense scrub. Thirst was a continuous torment. Neither had dared to drink from the bracken ponds they encountered, knowing the water would be as poisoned as the land they traveled through, and Maia could not take the risk of seeking another waymarker. Not when Corriveaux could be lurking by one again, waiting for such an opportunity. No, they had to blind the Dochte Mandar to their presence and their path. Make them trudge in the dark and jab sticks into every bush.

What they needed was their own hunter, someone who could disguise their trail. Someone who knew the land and its secret places. Someone who could be trusted. The greatness of their need pounded through Maia as they continued to forge their way. She fixed her heart on it, pushing the fierce, focused thought into the aether: *I need a hunter. I need a guide.*

A gust of wind blew into her eyes, almost as if in response to her pleading thoughts. She did not know if it was the Medium.

Before nightfall, she realized that it really was.

When I was a wretched living in Muirwood Abbey, a strange fellow named Maderos told me a tale about the hill near the abbey, the one we called the Tor. A crew of warriors from the north came. Not men from the seven kingdoms, but from a land of dark pools and steep firths. These warriors came on painted boats to conquer our lands. They massacred a small village along a lake near the abbey and came marching to Muirwood itself. The Aldermaston raised his hands, and a hill from a surrounding area lifted from the ground, hovered over the enemies of the abbey, and then plummeted down, smashing them into oblivion. Some of the attackers survived, great-granddaughter. They fled back to their dark land and warned of the inhabitants of the seven kingdoms and the awful power of the Medium when provoked. What you need to understand is that these people, the Naestors, came and inhabited the lands that we forsook. They are a cunning, warlike people. When the mastons return again to the seven kingdoms of Comoros, Pry-Ree, Dahomey, Hautland, Mon, Avinion, and Paeiz, they will discover an eighth kingdom has claimed all that we abandoned. Though they will feign friendship, they will not trust you. They will fear you. They will bring back the Dochte Mandar. Be wary.

—Lia Demont, Aldermaston of Muirwood Abbey

CHAPTER THREE

Argus

They smelled the chimney smoke first, just the hint of it on the air. Before long, the plumes became visible and directed their course. With Maia's tired legs aching from the rocky climb, they crested the snow-spattered ridgeline and gazed down at a village nestled along the shores of a small lake. The crags of the mountains were steep and full of cracked shale and broken stone, making the footing treacherous and difficult. The sky held wisps of fleecy cloud that passed over them, blocking the sun for moments as they gazed down at the tiny hamlet. Maia noticed that many of the pine trees along the crest and down the slope were dead, the bark turned to silver with little protruding stubs. She rubbed her hands on the smooth, graying bark and gazed down at the village. Her stomach growled enviously at the thought of the provisions they might find there.

The kishion looked back the way they had come, watching for signs of pursuit, then returned his gaze down the slope to the hamlet.

"No more than twenty stone hovels down there," he said disdainfully. "Not much by way of help."

"Yes, but my legs are weary, and we need water and food," Maia said. She winced, her knees aching from the arduous climb. "Even if we sleep in the brush, it is better to move forward. Maybe someone down there knows the land. They could help us find the way."

"Or give us trouble instead," he said gruffly. "The village is too small for a garrison, so we need not fear meeting the king's men. At the least there are fires to keep warm. The ground is treacherous, Lady Maia. Hold my hand as we descend."

She was grateful she did, for several times her boots slid on the crushed shale, causing rocks to patter down the winding trail or scatter off the edge of the cliffs. Her heart pounded with fear and exhaustion as they traversed the winding switchbacks into the valley.

She admired the seclusion of the place, the rugged privacy that kept it away from the rest of the land. There were no obvious roads in or out, but as they walked down the ridge, they encountered a small footpath that had been trampled amidst the brush and debris—proof that the villagers below were used to climbing up to the peaks. The sun was beginning to set, and the gusts of wind were violent enough to chill them to the bone, causing Maia to grip the kishion's hand more firmly as she maneuvered her way down.

They had encountered a number of strange plants and wildlife along the trek into the mountains, but the feeling in the air had begun to change as they painstakingly made their way downward. Since landing off the storm-ridden coast of Merohwey, the land *had* felt cursed and inhospitable. But the feeling was beginning to dwindle now that they had crossed this cracked range of gray, shattered rock, and the normal signs of deer and fox began to present themselves. The music of birds chirping came as a welcome sound to her ears. There was a subdued feeling, a quiet hope in her heart. Even though the Dochte Mandar were chasing them, she did not feel quite so desperate.

"We are in the midst of Dahomey," the kishion said as they stopped to cup water from a small brook with their hands. It was their first water of the day, and both gulped it down eagerly before filling their waterskins. "I do not speak this tongue very well, so you must be the one to talk with the villagers. Say little. Men's tongues wag when they see something strange, or a pretty face." He wiped his mouth on his gloved hand. "Even our clothing marks us as foreigners. Try to barter for information. If they prove reluctant, I will make things *simpler* for us."

She stared into his eyes. "I do not want to be troublesome to these people. They are innocent."

"You said you would trust my judgment, my lady. Believe me, in towns like this, they will respond to fear more than they will coins. There is no one here who can face me, not even all of them together. I will not harm them if I do not have to, but we must be quick and to the point. We need the supplies to cross this land into either Paeiz or Mon. A guide if we can persuade him. Otherwise, he will guide us unwillingly."

"Very well. Let me do my best to convince him first."

The kishion stood and brushed twigs from his sleeve, gazing back up the trail, and then nodded. Maia knelt and sipped again from the water in her palm. It was cold, clean, and delicious. She sighed, her joints aching from the long journey. Her gown was stained and splitting at the seams, so she fastened her cloak more tightly around her throat and raised the cowl to conceal her face. Daylight dwindled quickly, and they hurried their pace to reach the town before darkness would force them to stumble blindly. Huge pine trees swayed in the stiff winds that whipped her cloak out behind her and threatened to tug loose her cowl.

As they reached the shelter of the trees stationed along the lake, the winds struggled to pierce their clothes. Large boulders hunkered all around, some twice the height of a person. Other boulders rested in the shallows of the lake, and Maia realized that many had cracked off the edge of the mountain and tumbled down.

There were ramshackle stone huts throughout the grove of trees, many of which had small chimneys radiating the smoke they had seen earlier. There were enough fallen trees around them to provide almost an unlimited supply of firewood. Her boots crunched in the gravel and needles as the two maneuvered through the small hamlet without encountering a soul. Voices could be heard emanating from one structure—an inn or tavern of some kind that seemed to be a gathering place for locals. The walls were made of sturdy stone slabs, each cut by nature and not by hand, fastened around the buttress of an enormous boulder as if it had been the ruins of a great castle. It had a timber roof that was in danger of sagging under the weight of dead pine needles.

The kishion nodded toward the structure, and they approached the only door. As the kishion pulled on the iron-ring handle, the door opened, sending out a blast of warm, fragrant air. Maia smiled in spite of herself, very willing to lie down on the dirt floor and sleep right there.

The room was full of mostly men, though there was a handful of hardy-looking women who were lean and weather chafed. Three hearths circled the room, and a skewered stag was roasting on a spit in one of them, the smell of the sizzling meat making Maia's mouth water.

As they entered, a man approached who was balding and very tall, probably the tallest man she had ever seen. He waved them in and greeted them in a deep bass voice, speaking Dahomeyjan with a slight accent.

"Hail, travelers!" he said with a warm smile. "Some bread and wine? Come and sit by the fire. Emilie!" he boomed. "Rest and I will fetch you some victuals. You look weary."

"Thank you," Maia said, trying to match their accent. They seated themselves by the raging flames, and she felt the heat sink into her bones quickly, making her cheeks pink. The tall man was middle-aged and he had a long, lanky stride. A woman—his wife?—piled food on a tray, while the rest of the patrons gazed at them for a long moment before continuing their conversation.

One man's voice caught Maia's attention amidst the din of the roaring flames and chuckling voices.

"And what do you expect we found, by Cheshu, with the bear scat? A hand. Bitten off and chewed to bits. Naught but the bones were left. Wander these mountains before the snows, and you are asking to become a meal yourself!"

Maia blinked with startled surprise and turned her gaze. The talker was a barrel-chested man, shorter than her, but wide enough to be two people. A thinning thatch of curly copper hair sat atop his balding head, and a bristly beard that was more brown than copper pointed from his chin like a cone. Beside the wide chair in which he slouched, an enormous pale boarhound rested on the floor, its head resting on its front legs as it stared at her with its big eyes.

What had struck Maia so forcefully was the epithet the man had used along with his accent, which was unmistakably Pry-rian—not at all what she had expected to hear in the hinterlands of Dahomey.

"No, no, no—you have to realize it. I have been walking these mountains for years, and you cannot believe how ignorant people are. Especially the wealthy. Does a blizzard care how much coin is in your purse? I once saw a man blasted by lightning as we walked the trails. He was no farther from me than that tun of wine, close enough to raise the hair on my arms. I jest not! By Cheshu, I had a struggle to keep Argus here from feasting on the corpse. I do not quibble if he has a taste for bear meat, but I would rather he not get a taste for one of us!" He patted the dog's head and then held his own belly while he laughed, joined in chorus by the others gathered around him.

Maia watched him closely, noting how he had become the center of attention in the room by the way he projected his voice. Copper-colored hair was also rare in Dahomey. There was no denying it, the man was Pry-rian. He looked to be a dozen or so years older than her, and the good-natured smile on his face told her he was comfortable in his position. She noticed in her observation that he had two throwing axes and a long knife in his belt and seemed to be quite unfamiliar with starvation.

The tall man approached with a massive tray of bread, nuts, cheese, and some wild berries. "I will cut some meat when it is finished cooking," the man said. "Are you warming up now, pretty lass?"

Maia nodded and thanked him again. "How much can I pay for the meal?" she asked.

The man waved her off and shook his head. "You are hungry and must eat. Why should coins exchange hands for that? We are simple people who live off the land. What we have, we share."

The notion startled her even more. Was it a maston village? "That is very kind. Thank you. Who is that man in the chair by the other fire?" she asked him.

The tall man's grin broadened. "The best tracker and hunter in Dahomey if you ask him. I thought you might be here to find him. He provided the stag roasting on the spit. His name is Jon Tayt. Are you seeking a hunter? Most who travel up to this village seek him."

"Can you introduce us then?" Maia asked, feeling a prickle of warmth that had little to do with the fire. She knew instinctively that her need had brought them to this quaint hamlet. It was the work of the Medium.

The tall man nodded and approached the man, bending low to whisper in his ear. The hunter's gaze did not shift or change. He simply nodded and made a motion to shoo the others away. Some cast furtive glances at her and the kishion, but they filed away without argument. Jon Tayt eased up off the chair and walked toward them, his heavy boots thudding on the dirt floor. The boarhound raised its head, its ears going on the alert, but it did not follow its master.

Maia was secretly starving, but she refrained from enjoying the warm bread and nuts as she waited for the hunter to approach. His hazel eyes seemed to size her up, taking in the sight of her torn bodice, the rugged look of the kishion, the hunted expressions on their faces. He grabbed another chair and spun it around and sat in it, resting his meaty arms on the back of the chair.

"Well, you came over the mountains," he said in a slow, deliberate voice. "Ach, you came from the *other* side. And you survived it. Incredible." He gave a nod to the kishion. "Wolves? The scars on your hands . . . you ran afoul of a maddened pack. And the scabs on both of your skins. I know the insects that made those. Little buggers burrow into your skin. If you do not burn them out or cut them out, you go mad with disease." He chuckled with some amusement and shook his head. "Obviously you did not come here wanting me to lead you *inside* that foul domain. So what brings you here tonight, I must wonder?"

Maia felt a spasm of excitement inside, but she tried to calm it. This was exactly the sort of person they needed to guide them. Still, she would need to be very careful about what she revealed.

She tried a subtle tactic. "I was not expecting to find one who speaks Pry-rian," she said in that language. It rolled off her tongue, and she watched as his eyes widened with surprise. A twitch on his mouth started, and then he was grinning fully.

"Nor was I, lass," he replied in kind, bowing his head to her. He slammed his fist onto the table, jarring the tray and scattering some of its contents. "By Cheshu!" he roared, laughing so hard it shook the room. "When I awoke this morning, I was the only man within three hundred leagues who could speak my mother tongue. How I miss hearing it! Who are you, my lady?" He leaned forward in his chair, his eyes piercing hers. "You do not have the look of Pry-Ree, though you speak the tongue true as any lass born and bred there."

She stared into his eyes and took his measure. If she wanted to earn this man's trust and respect, she decided, she needed him to understand the fullness of her plight. Threats would not work. While she had wanted to keep her identity a secret, she felt that trusting another foreigner, a man from Pry-Ree, might be possible, particularly since the Medium seemed to have brought them together.

She decided to trust him.

"I am Marciana Soliven," she announced softly, causing the kishion to hiss in surprise and alarm. He grabbed her arm, his fingers digging into her muscle.

"Are you now?" Jon Tayt said, clearly astonished by her candor. He started to chuckle again, shaking his head in wonder.

"Lady Maia of Comoros. The banished princess." His words were spoken softly, with an echo of sympathy. He shook his head again, leaning back away from his chair, and folded his arms. "I barely recognized you, you look so terrible."

"Have we met?" Maia asked, her interest piqued.

"You would not remember me, as you were just a little wisp of girl yourself at the time. Your father sent you to settle border disputes between Comoros and Pry-Ree when you were a wee child. Everyone knew of you by reputation, but I also saw you occasionally. At the time, I was often surveying lands *for* those border disputes . . . or helping *enforce* them afterward, sometimes with an axe or an arrow."

"So you were a hunter for the King of Pry-Ree?"

He snorted and waved his hand. "No, I work for hire. Usually for lesser nobles or people with means. I cannot guard my tongue. I say the truth regardless of who it hurts, so no king ever secures my services for long. Most noble folk are pure and utter fools, and I tend to despise them."

"I value loyalty and someone who speaks the truth."

"Yes, but even the best men grow weary of my stories," he said with a smile free of self-consciousness. "As I recall, you settled those complaints fairly, if a bit ignorantly. At least you were equal in your treatment of Pry-rian claims and those of your own countrymen, who lied and tried to deceive you as much as we did. It was never clear which side you would favor, but you did gain a reputation for fairness, my lady." His eyes narrowed. "When your father . . . when he did what he did, those border disputes became tangled again. I pitied you. I grew sick of the whole business and ventured away."

"This is quite far from Pry-Ree, Jon Tayt. Why did you come?"

32

"I told you I am a blunt man. I wanted nothing to do with intrigues or broken oaths. I traveled about as far away as I could imagine going and ended up in the hinterlands of the civilized world. Welcome to Argus hamlet, Lady Maia! I named it after my hound over there. The lazy cur."

"After your hound?" Maia asked, a smile beginning to stir on her lips. He was a gruff and opinionated fellow, but already she liked him.

"Seemed a suitable name at the time since we were the first ever to live here. I built this hovel and most of the others when others chose to join me." He leaned forward and placed his hands flat on the table. "You realize that Dahomey is not a safe haven for one of your blood. Your kingdom is at war with every other nation that upholds the doctrines of the Dochte Mandar."

"I am very aware of that fact, yes."

"And yet here you are."

"Yes. Here I am."

"How can I serve you, Lady Maia?" He leaned forward and the chair squealed under his weight.

"I am not looking for a servant, Jon Tayt. You said yourself you want nothing to do with kings and intrigues."

"Where are you bound, lass?"

Somehow, Maia felt she could trust the hazel eyes that stared down at her. The Medium had brought her to Argus. It had led her to this man.

She leaned forward, her eyes boring into his. "Can I trust you, Jon Tayt?"

He stroked his pointed beard and then scratched the fleshy underside of his chin. It made a raspy sound. His eyes turned stormy as he rested his hands on his belly. "I have no love for your father. I have no love for any man. Whether or not you choose to trust me is entirely up to you."

She wanted to look at the kishion, to read the expression in his eyes, but she worried it would be interpreted as a sign of weakness.

"I will ask again. How can I serve you, Lady Maia?" the hunter repeated, his voice sincere.

"I need you to bring me safely through Dahomey. It would be best if we traveled through roads less frequently used by others."

"Easily done. Dahomey is a large, broken kingdom. You want me to take you back to Comoros?"

Maia shook her head. "Just to the borders of Paeiz or Mon. That is all I will ask of you."

"Ack," he chuckled gruffly. "If we are going to travel that far, you will need some new clothes to survive these mountains. It is my trade to guide folk through these mountains safely. I have the gear and plenty to spare. The mountains do not care figs whether you were born of noble parents or what kind of fancy boots you wear. They only respect those who come prepared. And right now, you are not." He eased up from the chair. "Better come with me. Bring the tray. Argus. *Chut*."

The boarhound rose from its position and sidled up next to the hunter. As Jon Tayt shoved the door open, the wind bustled in and made the fires all leap and dance. Excitement burned inside of Maia. She was grateful for finding the hamlet, grateful for the knowledge and expertise that might make the challenge before her possible. She held the door for the kishion, who exited silently behind her and followed them.

Jon Tayt stopped them on the other side of the massive boulder. He raised his arm and pointed toward the jagged cliff face silhouetted against the sky. Stars painted the sky with their profusion of jewels, but as Maia followed his arm, she saw other spots of light descending slowly down the mountainside.

"You did not mention, my lady, that you were being followed." His expression hardened.

"I am. By the Dochte Mandar," she said softly.

Jon Tayt cursed under his breath. "Ack, that is a fine kettle of fish," he muttered. "They are not easy men to kill. Best we hurry then."

CHAPTER FOUR

Mountain Storm

Jon Tayt flung open a heavy wooden chest and began tossing different garments out of it haphazardly. The boarhound sniffed at several, its stout tail wagging vigorously as its master grumbled under his breath.

"Fetch the tallest bow sleeve," he barked to the kishion, gesturing to several hanging from pegs on the wall. "Several quivers as well. This is a good wool cloak." He shoved it to Maia and continued rummaging. "Ah, a scarf, some gloves. You would be shocked to hear how many people lose fingers and toes, wandering these mountains. I knew a man who scratched his earlobe during a blizzard, and it came right off. By Cheshu, I do not jest you! Let me see." He dug around some more and withdrew a long wool gown, dark burgundy in color. He snorted. "May even fit you. Put it on. We cannot waste time."

Maia looked around the tiny stone hut. It was hardly big enough for the three of them to remain standing upright in.

Rather than a bed, there was a nest of bearskin furs shoved against one wall.

Feeling ashamed to undress in front of the men, she turned around and began fussing with the lacings on the back of her gown, but the hunter rebuked her. "Put it on *over* your other gown, my lady. You will need more than one layer in these mountains. You can doff one of them later when the sun is blazing. Two cloaks is fine. If I could fit your feet into two boots, I would. Quickly now!"

The kishion had fetched the bow sleeve from the wall and clutched two quivers. Jon Tayt scowled as he glanced around the tiny hut. "You have water flasks already. Dump the food platter in that sack over there. There is a large cheese in the cold barrel. Take it." He went to the wall and grabbed two more hand axes, another long knife, and a sling with a pouch of pebbles. He snapped on two leather hunting bracers and a shooting glove. For a short, squat man he moved with efficiency and speed.

Argus's ears went straight up, and a low growl emerged from his throat. He stared at the door.

"It's either a bear or strangers afoot," Jon Tayt groused. The kishion slid a knife from his sheath.

"If you fancy a stronger blade, take what you can carry," the hunter offered, nodding to the assortment of weapons suspended from the wall. He went over to a pack and began stuffing one of the bearskins from the floor inside it. He shoved it all the way in before grabbing a length of rope, a small iron skillet, a tinder stick, and several other strange devices that Maia did not recognize.

The hound's growl increased in pitch.

Maia was securing the belt on the gown when Jon Tayt's voice muttered, "*Fffft.* Douse the candle."

The kishion squeezed the burning wick and darkness enveloped them instantly. Only the glowing end of the snuffed candle remained, like a tiny Leering's eye, and then it too was gone. The sound of the hunter's boots was muffled by the packed dirt floor as he approached the door and pulled it open a sliver.

Moonlight cut a slit down his wary face, his gaze staring into the darkness of the trees beyond. He waited cautiously, standing still, listening to the hiss of the wind through the door.

Something heavy slammed into the door, shoving it all the way open. The hunter jerked away just in time as a body came crushing into the stone hut. It was a soldier, by the looks of his tattered tunic and sword as he sprawled onto the ground. The kishion knelt and knifed him soundlessly. The figure's leg twitched once and was still.

Jon Tayt stepped into the cool night air through the open door, hefting an axe, which he suddenly lifted and hurled. It spun end over end, and the blade struck another soldier in the chest, felling him instantly. Argus snarled and charged into the woods, launching himself at another soldier and bringing him down with a single bound.

The kishion fled the stone hut next and sent his knife spinning through the air, into another of their pursuers.

Jon Tayt went to the body of the man he'd killed and drew the axe away, stepping on the man's leg to free it. Maia blanched, but she steeled herself and followed her protectors, raising the cowl as she went.

"This way," the hunter whispered. An arrow lanced by him, the shaft clattering against a nearby boulder or stone hut.

"Argus, hunt!" Jon Tayt ordered, and he strode up to Maia, grabbed her arm, and pulled her into the deeper shadows of the grove. The boarhound loped into the woods, snarling viciously.

There was barking and growling and suddenly a man's voice shouted in pain.

Two more soldiers awaited them in the shadows.

"They are yours," the hunter said to the kishion, and he changed course, pulling Maia after him. The kishion needed no greater warning to lower his blades and thrust forward, engaging both men at once. As the hunter led Maia away from the scene, she heard a cough of surprise and grunts of pain as the two men strove against the kishion. Maia nearly twisted her ankle on a rock and tried to correct herself. They dodged through trees, heading toward the murmur of a brook somewhere to the right. The darkness was a shield for them.

A shriek of pain sounded in the night, and moments later, Argus padded up next to them, panting.

"One less hunter for us to face," Jon Tayt said with a grim smile in his voice. "They probably have more than one, bad luck. Always best to have two of something if you can afford it. Argus here can take down a bear. You think I am joking. You will see if we meet one."

They reached the banks of the small brook, and Jon Tayt guided her to some round stones protruding from the waters and ushered her across. The trees swayed as the whipping wind picked up and began to howl, blowing icy tendrils at them. In a moment, the kishion leaped across the small brook and joined them. "Two more were watching the direction we fled, so I dispatched them as well."

The hunter snorted. "There are many trails off this mountain. If we take that one," he said, pointing, "we will be trapped along the lake. I know of a cave farther down the mountain where we can find shelter, and the village of Roc-Adamour is at the base of the mountain. It is the crossroads in this Hundred. It will be difficult for them to track us if we go there first."

"How far?" the kishion asked, searching the trees behind them for signs of pursuers.

"Before next sunset if we hurry. There are some more supplies I would like to obtain if we are going to travel the mountain ways. There is an inn there called the—"

Lightning lit up the night sky with a brilliant fork of energy, blinding them all.

"Not a cloud in the sky, by Cheshu," Jon Tayt said with surprise, squinting. He stared up at the milky swarm of stars as another jagged line split across the mountain valley. The wind began to rush against them, increasing in pressure and ferocity.

The kystrel burned against Maia's skin, and she realized someone had summoned the storm with the power of the Medium. Coldness shot deep into her bones. Lightning struck a tree behind them, blasting it into fire. Argus howled and began barking.

"Hush!" Jon Tayt said, cuffing the dog. Flames leaped up the bark of the pine and the branches were soon blazing. The wind kicked up the flames even higher, causing the ashes to spread and fan out, igniting other trees in the valley.

"Lady Marciana!" shouted a powerful voice in the darkness. She recognized it, having heard it inside her mind at the Leering she had used to summon water. "Surrender to me now, or I will burn this village. I have chased you long enough, and my patience is at an end. You cannot leave this mountain, or all these people will die."

It was Corriveaux.

The wind was so strong she had to clutch her borrowed cloak around her throat to prevent it from flying back into the brook. She felt mewling hisses all around her, sensed invisible shapes. Anger and fear battled within her.

Another explosion of light came, and yellow tongues of fire began to devour another tree.

"I grow impatient!" Corriveaux shouted into the night.

Maia looked into the kishion's eyes. He shook his head subtly no. Anguish filled her heart. How could she abandon the poor villagers? They had done nothing to deserve such a fate. Indeed, they had done naught but show her kindness. She had no doubt that Corriveaux's threat was sincere, and her heart wrenched. Could she really spare her own life at the expense of theirs?

She turned back to the village, intending to fight off the Dochte Mandar who threatened them.

"I think no," Jon Tayt said, gripping her arm to stop her. "Listen to the man's voice. He was already going to murder them. We must flee down the mountain, my lady."

"I can stop him," she said, trying to control her fear. The force of the Medium was building a charge in the air over her.

She turned to face the blazing trees and summoned the power of the kystrel. Clenching her teeth, she unleashed her emotions and flooded the medallion with all of the darkest parts of herself—her rage, humiliation, fear, and despair.

The wind began to shift immediately, drawn to her call, her summons.

"No, Lady Maia!" Jon Tayt warned. "You will draw him down on us!"

She felt the power building inside of her, rising like a tide. Her confidence increased, and she experienced that tickling giddiness that always made her want to laugh. "Stand away from me," she said fiercely.

The winds collided. Her leg muscles began to tremble under the mental weight of the magic she wielded. Another shaft of lightning struck near her, shattering a boulder into blackened fragments. The light did not blind her this time. She retaliated, sending a crackle of energy toward her enemy. With the kystrel burning around her neck, she could sense his presence, could see that he was very near, perched on a solitary rock by the shore of the lake. His eyes glowed silver, as did hers.

I found you.

She could sense his triumph as his thoughts clamped down on hers with the strength of iron bars. Maia wrestled against the compulsion to surrender. She pressed against him, shoving with all her strength. Another mind joined Corriveaux's, latching around her like shackles. Then another mind. There were three of them, three Dochte Mandar.

I have her. Kill her protectors, quickly!

No! Maia shrieked in response, her will bulging against the prison they had created. Her shoulder burned, as if she were supporting a heavy weight over her head. The power drove her to her knees.

"They see us!" Jon Tayt shouted. Soldiers charged at them from the burning mass of trees, heading toward the brook with bared swords.

Maia grunted with exhaustion, and suddenly another shaft of lightning touched ground right in front of the advancing men, scattering them. A few had charred faces as they fell limp to the ground.

You will obey me! Corriveaux's thoughts screamed at her. *Yield to me!*

I will not, Maia replied, her mind turning black with the strain of resisting him. She felt the veins on her face begin to pop and blood dribbled down her cheeks. The power flattened her until she was facedown on the ground. She could not hold them off. She could not disrupt their combined wills.

We have her! We have her! Corriveaux's thoughts blasted at her. An axe whirled and struck an oncoming soldier. Argus howled.

Then a hand struck the back of Maia's neck and she slumped into the dirt and forest debris. Her ears rang with a tinny sound, a high squealing noise that cut through the commotion.

No! No! Corriveaux's thoughts were desperate as her unconsciousness released her from his grip. She was grateful for that at least.

Strong hands picked her up. Then she could remember nothing.

CHAPTER FIVE

Lady Deorwynn

Maia fidgeted with excitement, unable to keep from smoothing the front of her gown as she watched Pent Tower loom ever closer. The carriage wheels clacked and clattered on the rounded cobblestones, and though its progress was slowed by all the activity in the street, a mounted escort bearing the tunics of Comoros helped move things along. It had been almost four years since she had seen the castle, had been home, and her heart churned with excitement. She had mastered the language of the Pry-rians during her stay in Bridgestow and was looking forward to demonstrating her knowledge to her father. She was nearly thirteen and had grown physically as well as mentally during her long absence from her father's court. She understood the workings of a Privy Council. She valued the advice of wise leaders and had listened diligently to their tutoring. Some of her decisions had been controversial, but her father had never countermanded her. She secretly hoped he would be proud of her accomplishments.

The time away from her mother had been difficult. Because women were not permitted to write, Maia had only received verbal messages from her mother or notes dictated to scribes and then read to her, whereas she had received various writs, commands, and notes from her father. Though, by necessity, she pretended she could not read them when others were around, she had kept several of the documents in her chests. When she was alone, she delighted in reading them and tracing the ink scribbles with her finger.

The sun crowned the keep as the carriage rumbled across the vast drawbridge, and she nearly leaped from her seat when it finally came to a halt. In the courtyard, amidst the dismounting knight-mastons who had escorted her, she saw the black cassock and wild hair of Chancellor Walraven, but he was also wearing a fur cloak that was brown and speckled with jewels, as well as the ceremonial stole of his office. He smiled as she waved through the opening of the carriage. A footman from the wall of onlookers briskly carried over a pedestal to help her descend.

"*Prevaylee, pria hospia, cheru Marciana,*" the chancellor greeted her, bowing fully at the waist.

"*Prevaylee, Chancellor,*" Maia replied with a deep curtsy. "If you believe I have forgotten my mother tongue, you need not fear it."

The chancellor beamed at her with pride. "You are old enough to dance around the maypole. Look at you!" She felt her cheeks grow warm at the sight of the affection in his eyes. "You are nearly a woman grown. The reports I have from your sojourn in Pry-Ree do you credit and justice. Your lord father is proud of you, child. You must believe that. He sent me to greet you in person and escort you to him in his solar."

"Thank you, Chancellor," Maia replied. "I have missed seeing you."

He smiled at the compliment and extended his arm. She smoothed her tailored gown again before taking it, and then started across the inner courtyard. As they passed, she noticed the groomsmen emerge from the shadows to take care of the mounts and unharness the carriage. She nodded to them and smiled, winning surprised looks from several of the men. She had learned in Pry-Ree that attending to even the lowliest of servants would win her great esteem and improve the diligence of the servants' work by making them feel acknowledged.

After crossing the threshold of the keep with the chancellor, Maia's eyes began to adjust to the dark. There were a few Leerings posted nearby to offer light, and she admired the ancient carved faces that, though pitted and worn, still showed smiling expressions. The sights and sounds of Comoros satisfied a deep hunger within her, and she longed to touch even the wooden doorposts and wainscoting. The palace was immaculately decorated, for her father was a fastidious man who tolerated nothing unkempt or slovenly. She swallowed her nerves.

"You have returned home during difficult times, Lady Maia," the chancellor whispered to her. He was careful to pitch his voice low to prevent others from eavesdropping. "I am afraid you will soon learn of it, but let me prepare you as best I can."

"What has happened?" Maia asked, her pulse starting to race. Nothing in the summons home that she'd received had alarmed her.

"Things happen by degrees, my lady. Such is the way of the world. Unpleasantness grows like mold on cheese. I fear that the extent of it will be startling to you. Relations between your parents have . . . deteriorated since you left for Bridgestow."

"How so, Chancellor?"

"The castle is used to their arguments now, but it was quite shocking at first, especially when they turned on each other in the great hall. I persuaded them to refrain from arguing in public places, and they try to heed me. Child, their marriage is failing."

Maia stopped in her tracks and stared up at the chancellor with wide eyes as sickness bloomed deep in her stomach. "What?" she whispered hoarsely.

The chancellor patted her arm and urged her to move on. Passersby had taken notice of her reaction, she realized, and the glances of sympathy she received told her they knew she was coming home to disaster.

"Come, Maia. Do not linger."

Somehow she made her legs begin to move again. The swish of her skirts was distracting, even chafing, and she felt emotions bubbling up inside her like a kettle poised over too hot a fire.

"My parents were married by irrevocare sigil," Maia whispered through half-clenched teeth.

"Yes, I am aware of the maston custom," the chancellor said. "It makes this situation more painful, to be sure. Your parents have come to loathe each other. Your mother seeks to mend the rift, but your father will have none of it. He shames her publicly. His tongue is quite acid, I tell you. Steel your heart, child. You must prepare for this meeting. Do you still forswear weeping? Your father has often praised you for not weeping as other children do."

Maia clenched her free hand into a fist, feeling the dark, terrible swirl of emotions settle in her gut. "I never cry in front of others, Chancellor. It is a sign of weakness. What will happen?"

"I have said more than I should. I wanted you to know before seeing your father. He is angry oftentimes. I know you love him.

I know you will probably fear him. Stand firm, Maia. Steel your heart."

"Thank you for warning me, Chancellor," Maia replied, her throat thick. They mounted the steps to the solar together, moving side by side. She would have loved to run her hand over the cool stone edges of the walls; instead she clasped her stomach in an attempt to protect herself from the nausea that threatened to weaken her. Her throat was dry, but she mounted each step as if it did not take an uncommon strength of will. At the top, fragrant floor rushes awaited them, crunching under their boots with sweet scents as they trod over them toward the solar.

There was a woman in the hall ahead, pacing. As they drew closer, the woman's head shot up to look at them. Maia recognized the woman, Lady Deorwynn of Chester Hundred. She had long golden hair, eyes as blue as a cloudless sky, and a charming smile. Maia was not quite as tall as her yet, but she recognized Lady Deorwynn as one of her mother's ladies-in-waiting. She had two daughters who were close to Maia's age. Their names were Murer and Jolecia. Maia's memory had always been exceptional, but she did not see either daughter nearby. Instead, there was a little boy half hidden by his mother's skirts.

"Welcome back to Comoros, Lady Marciana," said Lady Deorwynn sweetly. Something flashed in her eyes, a look so confusing that Maia could not, in her limited experience, interpret it. It was the look of someone who hated her but did so with a sumptuous smile. The woman flicked some of her golden hair over her shoulder and approached them, looking down her nose at Maia. "You have grown taller, I should think. My girls are taller, of course, but you do look handsome. I have always adored your eyes, Marciana. My Hundred, Chester, is so near the sea, and your eyes look like they were fashioned out of seawater. I am quite envious." She reached out and pinched Maia's chin, tilting her head one way and then another. The possessiveness of her touch was humiliating. Maia wanted to shove her hand away, but she felt a palpable threat coming from Lady Deorwynn's eyes.

"Thank you, Lady Deorwynn," Maia said.

"Mama, make her go," said the little boy. He was barely visible from around the woman's skirts, but she could see part of his face and . . . it made her blood run with ice.

"Do not fret, Edmon," she replied, tousling his hair. "This is Lady Marciana returned from Pry-Ree. Our Hundred borders Pry-Ree as well. Is not she pretty?"

The little boy peered at Maia, his eyes wary and distrusting. Her throat caught at the sight of his little face. It was like staring at her father as a young boy. The shape of his nose, the same shade of sandy-brown hair. Even his eyes matched her father's— and her own.

"How . . . old are you, little Edmon?" Maia managed, her voice faltering a little. She struggled to steel herself, willing her eyes to stay dry, her voice to harden.

He scowled at her, refusing to speak.

"The duckling is almost four," Lady Deorwynn said, playing with his hair. Her eyes were filled with an unspoken challenge when they met Maia's, as if she were daring her to speak what was so obvious. When she did not, she leaned over and kissed the boy lightly on the head. "He has a little brother as well," she added like a knife thrust.

"The king is expecting to see his daughter," Chancellor Walraven said disdainfully. "I would not like to keep him waiting."

She gazed at the chancellor, her eyes flashing. "Of course. I would not wish to detain you. Welcome home, Marciana." The words were innocuous, but there was venom on her breath.

Chancellor Walraven escorted her to the door of the solar. The thick oaken door had a multitude of carved squares on it, many of them offset with other squares—the maston symbols. Her heart lurched as she glanced back once at the little boy and his mother, both gazing at her with persecuting eyes.

When she entered the room, Maia saw her father pacing, hands clenched behind his back. She had always thought her father the most handsome man in all the world. He was fit and trim, with the body of a hunter and sportsman. He had the reputation of being an excellent swordsman, diplomat, and ruler. His eyes crinkled at the edges when he saw her, and a genuine smile lit his face, but there were smudges above his cheekbones, shadows that had not been there before, and a subtle fringe of gray lined the edges of his hair. He wore his hair cropped close, in the southern fashion. His smile was so handsome it melted her heart, but she could see that his delight was suffused with discomfort . . . suffering.

"Maia," he breathed, throwing wide his arms.

She wanted to run to him, just as she had as a little girl. She wanted him to sweep her up, to soothe her with kisses and promises and dispel the awful dream that had suddenly plunged her soul into darkness.

The chancellor released her arm and she approached her father, dropping to a formal curtsy in front of him.

"What is this nonsense?" he asked, his eyes suddenly stern. "Maia, you are home! I am grateful to see you. I want your embrace, not formality. Come here!"

She choked down her feelings and came into his arms. There was a smell about him. Not the scent of cinnamon or some contrived odor. Just the smell of his skin, his breath, and she felt a surge of girlish emotions that threatened to ruin her composure.

It almost made her forget her disgraced mother, and little Edmon who shared her father's eyes. Almost.

"That is better," he said, giving her a hearty squeeze. He held her away from him by the shoulders, gazing down at her with obvious pleasure. "You are quite beautiful, Maia, though must not all fathers think that about their daughters? Look at her, Walraven. She is a beauty."

"She is, Your Majesty. And she has fulfilled her charge remarkably well for one so young. You could trust her with any errand. She is loyal."

"I know," he replied, pinching her chin just as Lady Deorwynn had done. The gesture made her flinch. He gazed at her lovingly, but there was that bit of something in his gaze . . . it smelled of guilt and shame. "I commend your tailor. What fetching colors on you. I like the style. Though you have traveled for quite some time, you arrived here neat and clean. I respect that. Tell me, Maia, are you still as sober a child as you once were? The Pry-rians can be a giddy bunch. Their ways do not seem to have changed you. I see no marks of it anyway."

"No, Father," she replied humbly. "I am grateful to be home. Where is Mother? I thought I would find her here with you?"

She had struck a nerve and a blow at the same time, not realizing it until it was too late. Her father flinched noticeably. "Ah yes, well . . . there is all that." He began to pace away from her, gathering his thoughts, sorting through his words as if trying to determine the best ones to use. "Your mother is no longer here."

Maia felt a jab of pain in her ribs. "I see." She swallowed.

He let out a pent-up breath. "It would be best to get this said and done." He turned and looked at her sternly again, his eyes narrowing coldly. "I have banished your mother."

Maia flinched, but said nothing. Her cheeks were flaming.

"Where is she?" she asked in a kitten of a voice. She had to repeat herself even to be heard.

"Muirwood, I think," her father said dismissively. "It is in an out-of-the-way Hundred full of bogs and swamps. I have heard nothing but trouble about the ruins and the slow process of rebuilding. That abbey will never be done, I fear. But that is neither here nor there, Maia. Your mother is banished. I am seeking to have our marriage annulled." He looked at her pointedly. "For that to happen, Maia, I must banish you as well."

Her heart rumbled inside her chest. She stared at her father as if he were a stranger. "Why?" she asked, her voice threatening to betray her. "Have I not pleased you, Father?"

He waved his hand dismissively. "No! It is nothing like that, Maia. No, no, that could not be further from the truth. I care for you, and I always shall. You are precious to me. But you cannot be my heir. I will not allow my kingdom to become a principality to another. There are many wolves prowling for you, Maia. Many would-be suitors who would love to claim your hand and my throne. No! I will not allow it. We are chief among the kingdoms. We have the most ancient noble blood, the strongest Families. But I am not growing any younger, Maia, and your mother could not carry another child to term, no matter how many vigils I kept. Something about your birthing . . . damaged her. I cannot allow a daughter to claim my throne. The Naestors would invade and overrun us if they knew a woman was to inherit." His tone was turning uglier by the moment. His face twisted with rage. "I cannot show them a hint of weakness. Even Chancellor Walraven agrees that a woman cannot inherit Comoros without drawing all of our enemies to our shores. I must have a son. A warrior who can defend us when I am too old."

In her mind, Maia thought of the timid little boy hiding in his mother's skirts.

Maia's tongue finally loosened, the strain of the situation too much to bear in silence. She stared at him in shock and disappointment. "How can you do this, Father?" she said with outrage. "You are a maston! You married Mother by irrevocare sigil. It cannot be broken! You cannot just banish her. She is a noblewoman in her own right, by her own rank. She is of the ruling Family!"

His face twisted with unsuppressed rage, and he strode up to her quickly. "Do not speak to me thus!" he spit at her. "You are my child and you owe me your allegiance and your obedience. You need not fling my oaths in my face. I know what I am doing. It is the only way to preserve our kingdom. You are a child. You cannot understand the ways of men and women."

"I may be young, but this is wrong, Father! Surely you realize that. What offense have we committed to earn such a punishment? Is it just? A wife may be put away for adultery, but surely it is you who have—"

The look of rage on his face brought blind terror into her mind. He struck her across the mouth, a stinging slap that silenced her words and rocked her backward. "You will be *silent!*" he threatened her, his voice wavering with emotion. "You watch your tongue and guard your speech. I will not listen to such talk from my own flesh and blood. Be still!" He loomed over her, and Maia felt the stinging pain on her cheek and the flavor of blood in her mouth. Her knees trembled so hard she was afraid she would crumple onto the floor, but she held firm. She stared up at her father with loathing, her eyes dry.

His eyes were on fire with fury. One of his fingers jabbed at her nose. "Let me be very clear, Daughter. You are henceforth *banished* from my household. You are no longer my natural child. I have forsaken my maston oaths and no longer wear the chaen. I say it clearly so that there can be no misunderstanding between us. I do not believe in the benevolence of the Medium. It is real, I know that. But it is cruel and vicious too." He spread his arms wide, as if daring her to contradict him. "But you will say nothing of this to anyone else. For the preservation of this kingdom, for the sake of the people, I will pretend as though I am faithful to the order. I will not persecute mastons or halt the rebuilding of the abbeys. I will fulfill my duty to complete them and reinstate the full rites. But I *cannot* remain bound to your mother, whom I *hate* with every bit of loathing and rancor you can possibly imagine. I cannot bear to even look at her, which is why I have sent her far away."

Maia's eyes widened with defiance. "Very well, then send me to my mother," she demanded. "If I am to be banished, I would go to her. To Muirwood."

Her father shook his head. "Oh no, I dare not let you go. Even if your eyes continue to accuse me. You are far too valuable a prize for my enemies. Those who pursue your mother's interests will be disinherited, and their lands will be forfeited. But anyone seeking to abduct and control you will be guilty of treason. You will stay here in Comoros." His look was grave and stony. "You are banished here, Maia. To Pent Tower."

"May I see my mother first?" Maia whispered, her throat too tight to speak.

"In time. Perhaps. If you are faithful to me. Now trouble me no more, child, until I call for you. Chancellor—escort her to the tower prepared for her."

This you must always remember. The hunter is patient. The prey is careless. These are wise words from the man who trained me to survive many hardships.

—Lia Demont, Aldermaston of Muirwood Abbey

CHAPTER SIX

The King's Collier

As Maia regained consciousness, she was first aware of a strange new smell—a peculiar scent that clung to her clothes, her hair, even her skin. She struggled to open her eyes, and it was so dark she wondered for a moment if she had been blindfolded. Light stabbed her eyes from slits on her right and she twisted to try and determine the source. The boarhound, Argus, was resting against her back, its coarse fur a source of heat and warmth. The dog lifted its head when she moved and gave an exaggerated yawn, as if scolding her for sleeping so long.

"Awake. Finally."

It was Jon Tayt's voice, gruff in the shadows. She had not seen him there, but her eyes picked him out as they adjusted to the dimness. Her muscles were sluggish to respond when she struggled to move. She would not have felt any more spent had she swum upstream against a river. Still, she was aware enough to discern that she was in a small stone cave, and to hear the wind keening outside. There was no sign of the kishion, and that concerned her.

Maia sat up and grazed her head against the ceiling of the cave. As she did so, she realized she had been sleeping on a strange pallet. Instead of straw, the ground was covered in strange green leaves dusted with fuzz. It was the source of the peculiar smell.

"What is this?" Maia asked, bringing one of the crushed leaves to her nose. It reminded her of mint, but it was different somehow.

"I call it mule's ear," the hunter replied. "See the shape? It grows wild up here on this side of the mountain. Good for bedding down on."

A low growl sounded in Argus's throat.

"Bah, be quiet," the hunter scolded. He sat against the rock wall of the cave, a throwing axe cradled in his lap. "Old dog."

Maia reached down and stroked the hound's neck, gently caressing its pelt. It looked back at her, its tongue lolling from its mouth.

"I do not want you spoiling my hound now, my lady," he said, a wry smile in his voice. "I would cut off the hand of any man besides me who tried to tame him, but since you are not a man, I will leave your hand intact." Jon Tayt's boot edged out to nudge the dog's flank. "He guarded you all night, even when you were thrashing. Bad dreams?"

Maia blinked, awash in the memories. This was the second vivid dream of her childhood she had experienced recently. It felt almost as if the Medium were trying to communicate something to her while she slept. Not only were the dreams vivid, but they were part of the series of events that had led to her quest. Her heart was on fire with the emotions of the past—feelings she struggled to bury. What was she supposed to learn from revisiting her old memories?

"Hmmm? Bad dreams?" she replied evasively. "Some, I suppose. Did I fidget, truly?"

The hunter nodded. "A little frightening to watch. I thought you might be chilled, but you were sweating. Then, when I started to worry it was a fever, you cooled down. You are a riddle, Lady Maia." His voice became very serious. "Why are you traveling with a *kishion*?" The emphasis on the word showed his distaste. "I don't need to ask why the Dochte Mandar are hunting you, the medallion you wear and your silver eyes are answer enough. Ach, what trouble brings you to Dahomey?"

Maia stared at him, wondering how much she should trust him. He was Pry-rian, so he did not share all the political machinations of the Dahomeyjans, whom she knew very well not to trust. He had aided in her escape from Corriveaux's men, and in so doing had probably become an outlaw himself.

"I cannot help you truly," he said, "if you keep secrets from me. Let me start with what I already know . . . what I wheedled out of your protector. If *he* did not think I could be trusted, I doubt I would have woken up, if you get my meaning. He said something about a lost abbey you found in the cursed woods on the other side of the mountains. You were passengers aboard the *Blessing of Burntisland*, which if you ask me, is a strange name for a ship. Your father's escort is dead or, ahem, murdered. The Dochte Mandar have captured your ship, so you will not be sailing back the way you came. What did you come to Dahomey to find?"

Maia continued to stroke the boarhound as the hunter spoke. She realized, of course, that the kishion *would* probably try to kill the hunter. He knew too much. But he had forsaken his quiet trading village in the mountains to help her, and she would do everything in her power to save him from the kishion's blade. She stared at his coppery hair and felt that uneasiness stir inside her again, warning her that she was about to be foolish.

"When my father cast the Dochte Mandar out of our realm," Maia began slowly, continuing to pet the animal, "our people began to suffer from a variety of strange behaviors. A cycle of . . . viciousness. It was not the same as the Blight that pummeled our ancestors. Rather than a revolt of nature, it was a revolt against decency. My father was desperate for answers, so he searched through their tomes—the records of ancient days preserved by the Dochte Mandar."

"I thought our forefathers kept the tomes," Jon Tayt said, wrinkling his nose. "The mastons."

"Yes, the maston records go back to the time of the Scourging, when our forefathers sailed away from these shores. The records of the Dochte Mandar describe what happened to this land *after* the mastons left, when the abbeys had all fallen or been ruined. When the mastons returned and found the Naestors inhabiting the seven kingdoms, they discovered that the Naestors had learned to interpret the tomes of the Dochte Mandar and resurrected some of their beliefs. The Naestors feared the mastons, for their tomes claimed it was they who had summoned the Scourge. These new Dochte Mandar sought a truce with the mastons, allowing them to claim their lost kingdoms. Some of the noble Families were even invited to take up rulership of the various kingdoms, but not of Naess itself. They have guarded their secrets diligently."

"What secrets?" Jon Tayt pressed, leaning forward.

"The secrets of the lost abbey," Maia answered. "Only the bravest of the Dochte Mandar ventured into the lands south of here to find it."

"You mean the ruins of Dochte Abbey?" he asked.

"No," Maia replied, shaking her head. "That abbey is no more. Only its bones remain . . . and it will never be rebuilt. I sensed that as soon as our ship drew near. There is a curse on that island because of the innocents who were murdered there." Maia shuddered as a dark and foreboding feeling settled over her. The evil memories seemed to darken the very air around them. She banished the thoughts from her mind, exerting her will. "Enough of that. I will not speak of it. In the lost abbey, I learned that the answers I seek can be found in Naess. The High Seer of the mastons is there, a woman. I must find her and the records that talk about the Myriad Ones. They are the beings who defeated the mastons a century ago. If I do not hurry, the situation in Comoros will worsen. And my kingdom will not be the only one to fall prey to them."

"By Cheshu," Jon Tayt said, breathing quietly. "You say the High Seer is a woman? The Dochte Mandar forbid women from reading."

"I know," Maia answered. "But that is what I learned. I . . . I can read myself." She looked down at her lap, feeling a subtle blush rise to her cheeks.

"And if that were not enough to bind you to a pole and light you on fire," he said darkly, "the charm you wear around your neck certainly would." He grunted and shifted to one knee before rising. "As I said, it explains why the Dochte Mandar are hunting you so fiercely. Ach, what a kettle of fish." He tapped the haft of the axe against his meaty palm. "Let me tell you something you should know."

Maia nodded and brushed away one of the mule's ears that clung to her sleeve.

"The King of Dahomey, blight the man, is always on the prowl for another war. Rumor has it that he intends to invade Comoros because your father cast out all the Dochte Mandar. He claims his motives are pious, of course, but a wild goose never reared a tame gosling." He sniffed, spat, and continued. "If he got his hands on you, my lady, he would use you to cause a civil war in Comoros. He has not been king for very long. The man has a reputation of being a notorious rake. He is a seasoned warrior and always has an army in the field to test the boundaries of his neighbors. A greedy little seeder with the ambition to rule all the kingdoms. I cannot work for a man like that, and I have refused his offers to do so. His lot are insufferable, and I stopped caring long ago how much he is willing to offer me—some men cannot be bought for coin when the cause is wrong." He wiped his nose. "Not that I throw away coins, mind you, but that man is greedy, ambitious, and dishonest. He's no maston. What I am trying to say, Lady Maia, is you have trouble coming behind you as well as trouble in front of you. Our best hope is to get some supplies in the little town down the mountain and then avoid as many other towns and villages as we can and cross over to Mon." He looked at her and growled stiffly, "Unless they are hunting you there as well?"

She shook her head. "Your plan sounds reasonable, Jon Tayt. How far is the nearest town again?"

"Before dusk if we stop yammering and start walking." Argus lifted his head, ears suddenly pointed straight up, and a growl eased from his throat.

"Ah, your *protector* is back," he quipped. Hunched over, he maneuvered to the edge of the cave and exited into the sunlight. Maia found her sack and quickly slung it around her shoulders and edged her way out as well, the boarhound trotting ahead of her.

The kishion glowered at her as she emerged.

"I slept overlong," she apologized. Some of her strength had returned, and she felt light-headed with hunger.

"Some sleep while others *kill*," he said with a savage frown on his face. Her mood darkened in the face of his wrath. "They have no more hunters following us, you can be assured of that. I got as many of them as I could in the dark, but in the daylight even a blind man could follow our trail. We must go."

"I am sorry," Maia said, gripping the kishion's arm.

He thrust her away. "Why must I keep repeating this lesson," he said with a dangerous tone in his voice. He pitched it lower, but he did not seem to care that Jon Tayt could hear him. "You are tenderhearted and it will get you killed. That man hunting us, he does not care how many innocents perish to achieve his aim. He is not bound by the rules of *your* conscience. Innocent folk will die because they crossed our path. Settle it within yourself, Lady Maia. It is a harsh reality in this world that those in power need no justification and beg no excuses. Even your father is this way."

Maia's heart shriveled with dread at the words. Her heart pounded with fury, and she wanted to force him to deny it. Her father had been a maston. A descendent of the first Family and the ruling houses of Comoros. He would not stoop to murdering his enemies as the rulers of Comoros had done in the days of her ancestors, the days before the mastons fled the realm on ships.

"I do not. I will condone neither the death of innocent villagers nor the purposeful deaths of my enemies," Maia said through what felt like chalk in her throat.

"What would you have me do?" the kishion sneered. "Beg them to stop hunting us? The only reason they stopped hounding our trail was fear. They feared me; they feared the dark. We must use whatever weapons are available to us. At present, we have little but our ability to flee. Two men against twenty is an unfair fight under any circumstances." He turned and gave an earnest look to Jon Tayt. "Lead on, hunter. We must not let them overtake us on the trail."

The burly hunter sheathed the throwing axe in his belt. "Yes, I am not squeamish about leaving corpses behind us to rot in the woods. Or under rocks." Maia watched him bend over near the edge of the cave mouth and scatter mule's ear leaves over a thin, rough cord half hidden by the edge of the stone. She realized he had triggered it to collapse.

***

Maia's feet were aching by the time they reached the end of the mountain trail and arrived at the town of Roc-Adamour. The sun was dipping quickly in the sky, casting a purple shade over the town. Maia stared at the scene before her with wonder and fascination. The town was nothing like she had expected, for it had been built into the side of a craggy cliff face.

Most of the towns and cities in her kingdom were built on flat ground and overlooked beautiful lands. This was rocky country, thick with dense woods and jagged boulders. There was a luxurious manor house on the top of the craggy mountain and she could only imagine how exquisite the view must be. The town was built lower down the mountain face, a series of tall but narrow buildings with highly slanted roof lines that were connected together, though they came in a variety of sizes and shapes. Lower down, along the flatter lands, was another series of buildings. If Maia had to guess, she thought perhaps several hundred people lived in the town, which Jon Tayt had dubbed Roc-Adamour, or in her language, the Rock of the First Fathers. It was an ancient town by the look of it, but the ruins and rubble were at the fringe of the town and the core of interior buildings was new and maintained.

There were no walls to fortify the town, but the terrain provided a natural barrier to conflict. Lanterns and torches were already starting to be lit around the settlement, giving it a peaceful air. None of the lights from the manor house at the top of the crest had been lit. It seemed abandoned.

"Your friends will have trouble finding us here," Jon Tayt said with a broad grin. "There are many inns and travelers here since this is a major crossroads in the Hundred. More than one road comes in and out, so finding our trail will be tedious. It will buy us time. The big house on the top is one of the king's manors. That is where the Dochte Mandar will likely go to solicit help. The other places midway up the cliff," he said, pointing, "those are for the rich traders. We will not be staying there. And over there is a little haunt I know near the edge of the cliffs, hunkered deep down by the woods. Easy to hide, easy to flee. Not many know of it. The people here keep to themselves. Follow me."

Maia craned her neck as they entered the town. The streets were crowded, which brought a sensation of safety she had not experienced for some time. She had worried her accent would betray her if she needed to speak Dahomeyjan in their journey. Traveling with Jon Tayt would lessen the chance of discovery because he was likely known by reputation, which would save them from asking questions of strangers who would remember them. She was grateful to have his help and determined to reward him handsomely in some way.

The kishion did not gawk at the tall, slender structures as she did, and he kept an impassive look on his face as they slipped into the shadows of early nightfall. "Raise your hood," he ordered sharply.

She was tempted to defy him, but she obeyed.

They walked down the main street, ignoring the shopkeepers and traders for the most part, though Jon Tayt did purchase several meat pies to stave off their hunger as they crossed the majority of the town. They finally stopped at a small two-story dwelling, also with a pitched slate roof of heavy stone shingles. It had two wings, and its walls were coated in ivy.

Jon Tayt entered first, stomping his boots on the rush matting as he entered, and the smell of wine and roasting meat made her mouth water instantly. There was a main hearth, full of lively flames, and the room bustled with patrons who joked and bantered with each other, adding to the lively setting. Stag antlers and even a huge bust of a moose hung from the walls. The main room was narrow but deep, and it appeared as though all the rooms were up the narrow stairs that flanked each wall.

Maia was startled by the commotion, but it felt pleasant to be around people again, all of them chattering away in another language that was lilting and beautiful to her ears. She could understand what they were saying, felt confident that she could mimic the cadence of their speech if need be. Jon Tayt scouted for an empty table, but without much luck. Argus's tail wagged vigorously, and he snouted along the ground for fallen bits of food.

The heat from the fires was starting to suffocate Maia, and she edged her cowl back from her face a bit, feeling the warmth and light play on her skin. She was bone weary from the hard journey that day, but she wanted to enjoy and savor the commotion and companionship, even if she did not wish to be noticed.

Her eyes gazed around the room, taking in the details, and she felt a small smile threaten her. She indulged in it for just a moment. On each table were little vats of melted cheese, and patrons were dipping hunks of bread into it on small skewers. The smell of the melting cheese was enthralling.

As she looked from table to table, she noticed one man was sitting alone, his leg propped on another chair in a lanky pose, swirling a goblet near his chin as he watched the patrons of the inn—exactly what she was doing. He was tall and broad with dark hair that went down to his shoulders. When she saw him, her heart took a shiver and a jolt, for he was one of the most handsome men she had ever seen. It was a dangerous kind of handsome, and he had the smug look of self-assurance that said he knew exactly how others regarded him.

His gaze met hers, and the swirling cup stopped. The goblet came down on the table with a thud. A bright smile stretched across his face, a look of delight that sent shivers down to Maia's blistered feet.

"Tayt!" the man shouted across the room, his voice surpassing the drone of everyone else.

Jon Tayt whirled at the salute, his eyes narrowing when he saw the man seated at the table by himself. "Ach," the hunter muttered under his breath. "It had to be him. By Cheshu, why *tonight*?" he murmured with a groan.

"Who is that?" Maia asked cautiously as the man sat upright, waving his arm vigorously for them to join him. Her heart skittered with dread.

"He's the king's collier," Jon Tayt said, defeated. "Not a word. He cannot be trusted."

CHAPTER SEVEN

Roc-Adamour

Maia had a penchant for being disappointed by handsome men. She was not one who instinctively trusted those who could win someone's favor with a charming smile or gallant behavior. Those traits, life had taught her, were often wrapped up in shallow-mindedness and the spoiled stubbornness of people who were used to getting their way. Things often came too easily for men and women like that, perhaps because others deferred to beauty too readily. Though it pained her to admit it, her own father had always allowed beauty to get the better of him.

They approached the man at the table, except for the kishion, who had melted into the crowd without a word. Just she, Argus, and Jon Tayt made their approach, and Maia moved forward warily.

The man scooted his goblet away and scrutinized them. He gave Maia a cursory look, his eyebrows wrinkling slightly as he took in her disheveled appearance, but he greeted the hunter with enthusiasm.

"At the end of another mountain expedition by the looks of you," he drawled, slapping the tabletop good-naturedly. "How many in the party died this time?"

"Only three or four," the hunter said blandly. "A boring trip."

The man reached out to Argus, but the boarhound growled menacingly, and he withdrew his intent. He stood and bowed with a flourish to Maia. "Feint Collier, at your service."

"*Feint*?" Maia asked with surprise.

Jon Tayt let out a short, wicked laugh. "A common mistake, lass. The king's collier fancies himself to be a swordsman. When you trick your opponent by pretending to strike in one place before quickly switching to another, it is called a *feint*. As you may guess, he has a reputation for such trickery."

The man took the teasing good-naturedly. He indeed wore a blade at his hip, inside a rather battered scabbard. His vest tunic was dusty and frayed, though it was made of supple leather. His shirt was open at the collar. Now that she saw him more closely, she realized he was young—probably around her age.

"I have, it is true, a reputation with a double meaning," he said, smiling at Maia with a look of mild annoyance. "*Feint* Collier, if you please. Tayt calls me Collier, and I call him Tayt. I discovered this little inn through my association with him, my lady. He is an expert in all things culinary, as you can tell plainly from the length of his belt."

"It is unfair to tease a man about his appetite," Jon Tayt said waspishly.

"As fair as it is to tease a man about his swordsmanship?" Collier answered, quick as a whip. Both men chuckled. "By Cheshu," he continued with a mocking lilt in his voice, "but you both look hungry.

Share my table. There is room for all, even your skulking friend over there. I was bound for Argus tomorrow anyway to find you, Tayt, so I thank you for sparing me the journey."

"I never refuse to eat at another man's expense," Jon Tayt said and sat down at the table. Argus curled up beneath his chair, wary.

After Maia had seated herself, Collier followed her example and then leaned forward, planting his elbows on the table. "Tayt knows everything about everything. I am sure you have realized this already. The best way to care for a horse. The best way to sharpen an axe. How to construct a sturdy building. How to find water where there is none. No man in Dahomey is as prolific in his knowledge of useless things as our friend here."

"Useless?" the hunter said with a chuckle. "I found the Torvian Gap and saved you thirty leagues of riding. How is that useless?"

"The worst part about him," Collier continued to Maia, ignoring the comment, "is that he cannot hold his tongue. He talks all day long and snores and babbles all night. Even in his sleep he longs to talk. But I do not need to tell that to you. You have clearly endured hardships while roaming the mountains with him, so you must have learned these things for yourself."

Maia did not like being the focus of attention. This man was clearly trying to engage her in conversation, and it made her uncomfortable. But she knew she would need to speak eventually.

"You are the king's collier," Maia said, trying to keep her Dahomeyjan plain. "What is that?"

"He shovels the king's stables," Tayt said wryly. "Not even the king's horses smell like daisies."

"You are insufferable," Collier said to Jon Tayt, shaking his head, his brow wrinkling. It smoothed as soon as he shifted his gaze to Maia, regarding her with interest. "My lady, a collier is Master of Horses—the king's, in my case."

"And is the *Mark* here?" Tayt asked dryly.

"You keep calling him that and he will have your head," Collier said with annoyance. "My master is encamped with the army thirty leagues away." He saw the look of confusion on Maia's face and explained. "Tayt calls the King of Dahomey the *Mark* because he's rather fond of coins and luxuries—"

"And women," the hunter interrupted.

Collier waved him down. "Yes, he does have a reputation for that as well. He once promised to pay Tayt a thousand marks to become his hunter, and Tayt refused. He is totally daft, as you already know. Stubborn as an unripe walnut."

"Ah, but you cannot *purchase* loyalty," the hunter said, winning Maia's respect even more.

Collier waved over a servant, who arrived moments later with a large platter filled, puzzlingly enough, with raw meat and loaves of bread. Once the servant had left the platter on the table, Collier continued. "I am known as the king's collier because when I was a boy, I shoveled his stables. I learned everything I could about horses and keeping them, in order to be useful. I am entrusted on many errands throughout the realm, which suits my personality, for I truly loathe being in one place for very long. Life in the saddle suits my personality."

"And with the Mark riding hither and yon with his army all the time," Jon Tayt said, "he sends Collier to deliver messages and prepare others for his arrival as he goes this way and that. He knows the roads of the kingdom almost as well as I do. The mountain passes . . . passably well. Did you like the play on words?" He chuckled to himself. "He can unshoe or shoe a hoof as well as any blacksmith . . . but not as well as me."

"Of course, there is only one *proper* way to shoe a horse!" He rolled his eyes and belted out a laugh.

"One more thing you should know about him," Jon Tayt said. "He is also called *Collier* because he is a wretched, and they take on the name of their profession. The old king of Dahomey had quite a brood of children. Most of them born on the right side of the sheets. Save one. Which abbey were you abandoned at?"

That news startled Maia, and she saw the crack in Collier's mask of frivolity. A darkness seemed to shadow the man's face. He was staring at her again, his bright blue eyes slightly narrowed, but after a moment of silence, he smiled self-deprecatingly and shrugged. "Lisyeux Abbey. We cannot any of us choose our station in life," he said. "We only choose what we make of it. I have a good life. I do what I most enjoy. And for the most part, I am unmolested as I ride dangerous roads because thieves and villains think twice when they see me coming. They know I do not fight fair." His expression turned more thoughtful. He lightly jabbed a finger at her. "I will not hesitate to stab out an eye or cut off a hand when it suits me. Enough about *my* name and who I am. Who are you, my lady? What Hundred do you hail from?"

Maia was not sure what she wanted to say, but she was certain she could not reveal her true identity to him. She was rocked by the strange contradictions in his life and his demeanor. He was handsome, to be sure, but his agreeableness was clearly not born of rank or station.

"I will also add," Jon Tayt said, interrupting again, "that Collier is a notorious flirt, so do not answer any of his questions. He is a rogue himself, despite his talk of bandits and thieves. Leave the talking to me."

"When can we *not* leave the talking to you?"

"You have done very well for yourself, Collier. Push the tray nearer and I may be more quiet."

"Wait for the broth and cheese, Tayt."

"I am happy eating raw meat right now. But here they come with it." Several of the serving girls arrived, carrying pots and iron stands and small oil lamps. The lamps were positioned beneath the pots in the iron stands so their flames would heat the bottoms. Maia had never seen such a setup before and she watched curiously as the cheese and broth began to seethe again.

Tayt skewered several pieces of meat with thin forks and then dipped them into the pot. He asked the serving girl for a tray of vegetables and pulled out the skewers a moment later. The meat had been cooked in the broth, and Jon Tayt offered a steaming portion of it to her. He himself used the skewers to eat, pulling a strand of meat off with his teeth.

"This little place has the best broth and cheese," Tayt said to Maia. "The recipe is Pry-rian. I taught it to them."

"Naturally, *you* taught it to them," Collier said with an exasperated look.

"The quality of an inn is not determined by how many fleas infest the pallets. It is judged by the food." Tayt grabbed a hunk of bread from the table and dunked it deep into the bubbling cheese.

"Your friend will not join us?" Collier asked in a low voice.

Tayt glanced over his shoulder, and they both saw the kishion standing at the counter with a cup of ale or some other drink, sipping it slowly.

"He is the sullen type and does not enjoy jovial company. Never disturb a man in his humors. Try the cheese," he offered to Maia, ripping off another hunk of bread and dipping it into the molten cheese. It was pale yellow with a brownish powder floating on the top. Maia mimicked his action and dipped some bread in. It was hot enough to burn her tongue, but the flavors made her start with surprise. It was delicious! She was uncomfortable eating with the stranger, who seemed to be watching her very closely.

"Ah, she likes it," Collier said with a grin. "Are you as quiet as your friend at the counter, my lady? What is your—"

"You said the Mark's army is thirty leagues away," Tayt interrupted. A flash of anger came in Collier's eyes. "Is he bound for Roc-Adamour? I noticed the manor house looked dark as we arrived."

Maia was grateful for Jon Tayt foiling the man's attempts to draw her into conversation. She felt assured enough to speak to him without giving away too much, but the less he learned about her, the better.

Collier pursed his lips and shook his head. "No. He is not coming here. As I said, I was planning to ride to Argus to see you. You said you would not work for the Mark even if he paid you ten thousand. What about twenty-five?"

"Twenty-five marks?" Tayt asked incredulously.

"Twenty-five *thousand*," Collier said. "You could almost buy your own Hundred for that. Perhaps you want a title to go with it? The king's sheriff?"

The hunter dabbed the bread with cheese and stuffed the piece in his mouth. He brushed his hands together and wiped crumbs from his tangled beard. "The more he offers me, the less I trust him. I am not *worth* even five hundred marks. No."

Collier nodded in satisfaction. "I told him as much." He turned to Maia again, his voice dropping conspiratorially. "If I ask you about the weather in the mountains, are you permitted to speak? Or will Tayt interrupt me again?"

"It was quite windy," Maia replied, a small smile dimpling her mouth. Despite herself, she was a little flattered by the persistence of his attentions. But she was equally resolved to limit her interactions with him.

"She speaks!" Collier said with a laugh, clapping his hands.

"I will not serve that man," Tayt said, lifting another skewer from the pot of seething broth. He mumbled with delight as the hot meat burned his tongue; he was clearly savoring it. "Tell him no amount of coin will seduce me."

"He is quite determined to remain poor," Collier said to Maia. "Yet I respect him for it. You cannot buy integrity, as the mastons say. No man can hold his virtue too dear, for it is the only thing whose value will ever increase with its cost. Our integrity is never worth so much as when we have parted with our all to keep it." He grinned. "I memorized that one, though I am not a maston myself."

Maia nodded, studying his face, saying nothing. She noticed a little scar on his left cheek, just under his eye, that could only be seen up close. His eyes were so blue, it was like looking into the sky. She squelched the curious feelings this observation aroused, knowing they would soon be on their way and she would never meet this man again. Feint Collier, a wretched of Dahomey. It was a rare thing to abandon a child in her kingdom. If a child were abandoned at an abbey in Comoros, there were any number of families who would step forward and quickly claim it. Her heart went out to him, but she could not allow herself to care. Not when a loose word from her or Jon Tayt could reach the King of Dahomey so quickly.

"Where is the Mark's army going then?" Jon Tayt asked.

Collier chuckled. "If you will not be part of it, then I certainly should not inform you of the Mark's intentions. He is mustering soldiers from all the Hundreds and stationing men at all the passes. Anyone seeking to cross will be forbidden to do so. Anyone crossing from the other kingdoms will be detained and questioned. I thought, at least, I should warn you, my erstwhile friend and expert in all things trivial. Do not cross the mountains, Tayt. Stay to the lowlands for now."

A disgruntled frown came to Jon Tayt's mouth. "That is my *business*, leading others across the mountains!"

A wry smile came in return. "I did offer you a sheriffdom, Tayt. You will remember that. Sometimes integrity comes at a steep cost. Enjoy your meal. I will pay the landlord ere I leave. Coin will be scarce for you in the months to come." His look became serious. "If you change your mind, send word for me at one of the king's camps. The password is 'Comoros.' You saved me two days' ride, which I thank you for. How *is* the village named after your dog? Other than windy?" He nodded deferentially to Maia.

"What?" Jon Tayt asked, looking more and more surly as the news sunk in.

"The village. How is Argus doing? How many live up in the mountains these days?"

Maia's thoughts darkened as she remembered that night—the lightning, the Dochte Mandar, and the fate that had come to the villagers. The taste of the warm cheese turned bitter in her mouth.

"The same as always," the hunter muttered angrily.

"I thought I saw smoke coming from the mountains earlier today. Was there a fire?"

Maia's stomach began to clench with dread. Were these questions innocently asked? Collier was an astute man. He had noticed them and observed them before calling them over to his table. He had commented on the kishion's marked absence from their conversation. Was he a hunter himself?

"Yes, a lightning fire struck last night. Wicked storm blew in over the mountains."

"From the cursed lands," Collier said. "Something foul is always coming from there. The Dochte Mandar are up to something. Do you know anything about it?"

Jon Tayt shrugged. "I do not do work for the Dochte Mandar

either," he said firmly. "Every year or so, one of them wanders into Argus and then crosses the mountains, but they never come back."

Collier frowned, picking from the heel of bread on the tray. "I do not trust the Dochte Mandar," he said simply, his voice very low. "Maybe King Brannon of Comoros was wise to expel them from the realm."

Maia focused on chewing a piece of meat, trying to keep any emotions from showing on her face. Collier was watching her closely, she knew, watching for a reaction. She dipped another piece of bread in the flavorful cheese, though the hunger had shriveled in her stomach.

"Well," Collier said with a breezy voice as he rose. "This inn may have the best supper in Roc-Adamour, but it does not have the best rooms. If they lack space, come to the Vexin Inn up the hill, where I am staying tonight."

"You do not stay at the mansion?" Jon Tayt asked. "The stables there are spacious. You showed them to me once."

"No one stays at the manor unless the king is on the way. Even we lowly servants stay farther down the mountain. It was good to see you, Tayt."

"You as well, Collier, though I have even less reason to favor the Mark now. He just killed my work."

"You have always managed to fall on your feet, Tayt. My regrets to your purse, but heed my warning. Do not try crossing the mountains. I do not think my voice would lessen any punishment if you were caught flouting this one." He looked again to Maia, and his swagger softened. "It was a pleasure meeting you, my lady. I only wish I had learned your name."

"Thank you for your hospitality," she said, nodding to him respectfully. But she did not oblige him.

The Naestors are a cunning people, as I have warned you. Let me paint in your mind something of the visions I have seen of the future. The whispers from the Medium speak softly. The land of the Naestors is a place of dark pools, sheathed in ice and shadows. They are not builders; they are conquerors. When they claimed our lands, they did not understand how to build castles and abbeys out of stone. They did not comprehend the workings of pulleys and levers. They inhabited our coasts first, then our cities. When the first mastons returned, the Naestors organized a council of the wisest Dochte Mandar. In your day, great-granddaughter, the Dochte Mandar advise political rulers. They also proselytize a different doctrine than the mastons'. Some manipulate themselves into positions of great responsibility. This council was the start of all that.

Some of the Dochte Mandar advocated war with the mastons. Others advocated abandoning their spoils completely and retreating to the north. The wisest one prevailed. He was also the most cunning of the Dochte Mandar. His name was Victus. He advised that the mastons be greeted as the true rulers of the lands. Each kingdom was given a Family to rule over it. They sought to learn from us, to discover our secrets of the reading and engraving of tomes, the building of structures, and the carving of Leerings. They would watch us and learn from us. And when they had seen the completion of the first abbey, when they had gleaned the knowledge they craved, they would rise up and seek to destroy us. Not through their own force. But by turning our Families against each other. The Dochte Mandar would be the puppetmasters.

—*Lia Demont, Aldermaston of Muirwood Abbey*

CHAPTER EIGHT

Escape

There was a soft tap on the door, breaking Maia's reverie. She had been sitting at the open gabled window of the inn, staring into the night sky and watching the flickering light from lamps and torches throughout the town. Trees crowded the inn, and some of the branches came near enough that they almost touched the walls. She sat with her elbow on the sill, chin resting on her palm.

The knock startled her, and it was only then she realized she was fondling the kystrel, which hung loose over her dress. She quickly plunged the medallion back into her bodice and adjusted it to hide the whorl of shadows painted across her chest. The fabric of the burgundy gown Jon Tayt had given her was warm and comforting. She had stripped away the tattered servant's gown and washed it in the lukewarm tub of bathwater following her own bath. Her hair was still damp, but it felt so much better to be clean.

Rising from the window, she walked to the door and raised the latch. The kishion stared at her for a moment, one eyebrow lifting as if he hardly recognized her, and then Jon Tayt followed him inside, Argus trailing after. The boarhound sniffed at her, and she dropped to one knee to caress his muzzle and head.

Jon Tayt shut the door and latched it firmly. The room was too small for so many, but the hunter had said he and Argus would be sleeping in the common room that night. The kishion would keep watch over her as she slept.

"You look a different woman, by Cheshu," Jon Tayt said, scratching his throat. "I have some healing paste for the scratches and bruises. It will help."

"Thank you," Maia replied. She walked back to the window and shut it, resting against the sill. "I am grateful for the bath. It was overdue."

He glanced at the edge of the tub, where her wet dress was folded. "Ah, and you washed the other dress. Let it hang by the brazier to dry in the night. You will need it again when we try to cross the mountains. Always have layers. In the morning, I will fetch the supplies we need early so we can be on our way. The king's army may be thirty leagues away, but that is closer than I would like."

"What do you make of what Collier told us tonight?" Maia asked him, but she included the kishion in her look, seeking his input as well.

"Part threat, part warning," the hunter said. He sniffed and shrugged. "These mountains are vast, my lady. And I know a few trails that the king knows not. Some are more dangerous than others. I was warning your friend—"

The kishion interrupted. "He knows a pass into Mon that no one takes or guards. There is a grey rank there, he says."

"My lady, a grey rank is worse than a bear. In Pry-Ree, they are called the Fear Liath. They prey on the mind as well as the flesh. It is possible to cross the pass if you start at sunrise and make it through while there is daylight. The risk is being caught on the other side after dusk. These things move with wicked speed."

"We know," Maia said, her heart cringing with the memories.

He stared at her, slack-jawed.

"We faced one already," Maia said. "It sounds like the best route to avoid the sentries, so we must take it."

"Lady Maia," Jon Tayt said, stepping near her. His eyes were earnest. "I have faced nearly every beast or creature that roams the woods. I fear very little, not storms or shadows or even hulking bears. But I do dread the Fear Liath, and I cannot protect you from one. Neither can he."

"It is as you said, we will travel during the day and cross the mountains before dusk."

"It is a hard journey, my lady."

"I am used to hard journeys. That is our road. We must avoid Dahomey's army."

An amused smile came over Jon Tayt's mouth. "Of course. But when I ready for a trip, I plan for the worst. The worst is the Fear Liath, but there are other dangers. In mountains such as these, there are flash storms. It can be sunny and cheerful one moment and then, with no warning, a storm can come in from the other side, dropping a mountain of snow in short order. Or the wind can be especially fierce. Crossing that pass is not the same every day. Any of these hindrances may delay us enough . . ."

"We must take the risk," Maia said, frowning with determination. She pushed strands of dark damp hair over her ear and folded her arms.

His forehead wrinkled in concern. "If we get caught in the mountains at night, this thing will hunt us and kill us. I would advise that we choose another little-used pass. We may need to fight past sentries, but I would prefer that to the risk of facing a Fear Liath."

Maia glanced at the kishion. His eyes were wary, but he nodded at her. Strangely, she knew what he was thinking.

"The Fear Liath will not delay us," Maia said. "I can send it away."

Jon Tayt sighed. "I advise that we are taking unnecessary risks. But I am only your guide. You pick the trail."

"Thank you. There may be no need to use my magic at all. We may cross the mountain in daylight and be done with it. We leave in the morning."

"Very well. Come, Argus." He clapped his leg and the boarhound rose from Maia's feet and trotted to his side.

After they left the room, Maia listened to the heavy sound of the hunter's boot steps move down the hall and then clomp down the steps. As the sounds started to fade, she folded her arms and stared at the kishion.

"Do not harm him when this is done," she said.

A twitch of a smile came and faded. "I knew you would insist on that," he replied gruffly, shaking his head. "You trust men too easily."

She looked him level in the eye. "No, not really. I do not trust that you will not harm him unless you promise me that you will not. Promise me."

"I make no such promises," the kishion replied, anger reaching his eyes. "I would kill the dog first. He is the more dangerous of the two."

She gritted her teeth. "He has been a help to us."

"I do not argue that. But he knows who you are. He knows much he is *not* saying."

"Do not harm him, kishion," she warned.

He took a step closer to her, his face hardening. "I will do what is in your best interest, my lady. Whether or not you see it thus." His eyes narrowed coldly. "While we are threatening and warning each other, I will add my own. Say nothing to him about me. He made his own choices. I made mine when I agreed to protect you. Now get some rest while you have a bed. We will be sleeping on the ground tomorrow."

Her heart burned with anger, but she decided not to argue. She did not truly believe she could dismiss him from service. Her father had hired him, and she had the suspicion he would not abandon her willingly. That meant she would have to help Jon Tayt survive the kishion's blade. She nodded stubbornly and went to the bed. It was small and narrow, like the room, but it had been over a fortnight since she had set sail from Comoros. Sleeping here would be a luxury. Turning away from the kishion, she stared at the window and watched the branches outside sway with the wind. There were so many conflicting priorities in her heart, the mass of them burdened her. Her people were being destroyed by a power they could not see—the Myriad Ones. The King of Dahomey preyed on weaker countries and was obviously preparing to invade her father's realm. Her protector wanted to kill everyone who was useful to her. The Dochte Mandar hunted her.

Sleep did not come quickly. She worried about all the things she could not control in her life—so much so, her mind felt like bursting. To calm herself, she began to think and remember some of the sayings she had learned from Chancellor Walraven's tome.

The greatest deception men suffer is from their own opinions. Why does the eye see a thing more clearly in dreams than the imagination does when awake? As every divided kingdom falls, so every mind divided between many studies confounds and saps itself. As a well-spent day brings happy sleep, so a life well spent brings happy death.

The last saying brought a chill to her heart, along with a memory from when she and the kishion had landed on the beach of the cursed shores. *You will all die in this place. This is the place where death was born.*

Why did it feel, in the darkness of the inn, that she had gained an acquaintance with death? That it stalked her, as well as everyone who followed her? They would all die, she suddenly realized. Even the kishion. Because of her.

And then there were the last words from Walraven's tome. The words that had haunted her since reading them, for they were the last words her friend had written before his death. In her mind's eye, she could see him sitting in the tower, wearing wooden clogs, his hair disheveled, and his eyes weary and mournful.

While I thought that I was learning how to live, I have been learning how to die.

***

A pebble clacked against the window, waking her.

The room was dark, but the sky was just starting to grow pale. The noise roused the kishion as well.

"The window," he said warningly. "Lie still."

He moved from his position in front of the door on cat's feet and soundlessly slinked to the edge of the window.

Another pebble tapped against the glass.

"Who is it?" Maia whispered. "Can you see?"

The kishion reached out and opened the window, keeping himself in the shadows. The open window brought in a rush of birdsong that whirled and whistled through the morning sky in exuberant noise and variation.

A figure blotted the frame of the window and Feint Collier dismounted the sill and came inside. As soon as he was on his feet, he held both of his hands out and up, showing he was unarmed.

"I know you are behind me, sir," he said, "with a knife ready to plunge into my back. I swear I climbed that tree not to seduce this woman, but to warn you both that the Dochte Mandar are on their way here and will be barging into the common room before long." He turned his head slightly, glancing back at the kishion. "Are we friends then? I came to help you, so I would rather not get cut open."

Maia hurried off the bed. "Thank you for the warning. We will go."

"I would advise you not to leave from the ground floor. The inn will be surrounded, and while I do not mind tweaking the nose of a man like Corriveaux, he has at least fifty men with him, a solid description of you all, and he seems rather determined. I would advise the window and the roof."

"Why do you aid us?" the kishion asked curtly.

"Oh, a man has any number of motives."

The sound of marching steps came from the hallway downstairs.

"What about Jon Tayt?" Maia said. "One of us must warn him."

"Already done, my lady. I met him as he was leaving the inn to get supplies. I told him where to meet us. Shall we?" He extended his hand to her. There was a mischievous smile on his face, and Maia's heart hammered in warning. Rather than take his hand, she hurried and stuffed her tattered gown in her pack and quickly grabbed a cluster of grapes from the nearby tray. She felt rested, strengthened, and—once again—panicked.

Once she nodded her readiness, Collier stepped onto the sill and climbed out the window onto the gabled roof. Maia poked her head out into the morning sky. The sun was rising quickly, dispelling the shadows of night. She saw some men holding torches down on the street below. They were spread out across the grounds.

A hand came down from the gables and Collier seized her wrist and helped pull her up to the roof. The kishion followed, moving soundlessly as they scaled the stone shingles of the gables.

"Quietly," Collier whispered, finger to his mouth. The slope of the roof was steep, but he managed it with grace, then reached down and helped her up the roof as well. His hand was warm in hers, and he gave her a smile.

She did not smile back. She felt like retching. They had been harried from one place to the next. The Dochte Mandar were desperate in their hunt.

"The shingles are made out of stone," Collier confided in a whisper, "because when part of the mountain crumbles off, it rains stone as well as water. The villagers have made use of what resources they have. Over that way. See how the roof meets the wall of the mountain on that end? We're going up to the next tier of the town. Then up again to the manor house. That is where Tayt will meet us."

She stared at him. "The manor house is still empty?"

"Of course, save for us. There are horses in the stables. I saddled three for you already, and they are waiting to go."

She stared at him in surprise. "You did?"

He grinned, pleased by her expression. "Yes, I did. A trail leads out of Roc-Adamour from the manor house, one that will not be guarded by the Dochte Mandar. They are idiots—they do not know this town very well. It will take some time before they realize where you have gone."

They reached the edge of the roof, and Maia craned her neck to peer up the crumbling cliff that stretched high above. "How will we climb it?" she asked.

He squatted at the edge of the roof. "You will see when it is lighter. We cannot climb it in the dark without a lantern, and it would be impossible for us to use a lantern without attracting attention. Patience."

The kishion came up behind them, and for a moment, she sensed he was ready to shove Collier off the roof to his death. She shuddered at the thought and deliberately edged closer to Collier, putting herself in the way.

The sky side of the hill was purple with the dawn, the colors reminding her of plums and velvet. Some of the houses were just starting to sputter awake, and lazy plumes of smoke from the first fires rose like mist off the rooflines.

"A moment longer," Collier said. He seemed almost giddy with excitement. His long arm pointed. "Do you see it yet?"

Her eyes were still adjusting to the dawn light, but she did see the small sliver of stone jutting up from the roofline. There were ridges in the cliff that formed a makeshift ladder.

"It is not far to the next level. If there were a rope, it would be easier, but the ledges are wide enough. Just follow me, and we will be up there in a moment, before the sun can reveal us. I will go first to show the way. Come."

He rose, brushed his hands together, and then pressed his chest against the wall of the cliff and stepped onto the first jutting stone. He beckoned for Maia to follow. Her heart was hammering loudly in her ears, but she had faced more terrible challenges than this, so she joined him in his ascent. The kishion glanced back along the roof and then followed them.

She hugged the rock as she shuffled sideways up. Collier pointed out a series of higher ridges, leading ever upward. Cautiously, she proceeded to the next ledge, and then the next. Her boot slipped once, causing a spasm of shock, but Collier's hand pressed against her back, steadying her. "Easy, lass," he whispered.

There was a hanging ledge just above them and Collier planted his foot in the gap and clambered onto it. He leaned down to pull her up after him and then clawed through some brush that was growing in the gaps of the stone. They had made it; they had entered the second tier of the town. Maia breathed heavily, grateful for the reprieve, and moments later the kishion joined them, his eyes wary and watchful.

"Follow me," Collier said confidently, and they walked down the main road that wound its way around the darkened houses. The sounds of their boots mingled with the birdsong, and Maia felt her panic tapering off.

"Thank you for helping us, Master Collier," Maia said, keeping pace with his broad stride. He was tall and strong, reminding her of a sturdy warhorse.

"You are welcome. There is a secret way up to the manor house over there. Do you see that tall building? That is the inn where I stayed last night. Corriveaux arrived during the night with soldiers, and word spread quickly. A servant thought I should know. I paid him well for the news. The king would surely want to know fugitives are being hunted in his land." He gave her a sidelong look, his expression indicating he knew she was the fugitive but did not care. "Have you seen any?"

She quelled a smile at his banter, but she knew she still could not trust him. With the King of Dahomey in league with the Dochte Mandar, both were dangerous to her. Whatever reasons Collier had for helping her probably had little to do with gallantry.

With the sun rising, the purple shade turned to orange. The air smelled fresh and clean, and she felt her muscles invigorated by the walk. She brushed her hair behind her ear and craned her neck, looking up at the vast manor sprawling along the top of the hillside.

Collier's voice was urgent yet hushed. "People are coming. Quick, move into that gap between the buildings."

The three of them found shelter in the gap, which brought them to the edge of the cliff face again, this part of it even steeper than the last. After following Collier through some twisting passageways, they reached a thick grove of trees, split by a narrow shelf of steep stone stairs leading up arduously between a series of clefts and boulders.

"The climb is rugged, but it is the fastest way to the stables."

The kishion stared at Collier, his eyes suspicious.

"I know you do not trust me," Collier said, returning the look. "But bear in mind that I am risking a great deal to help you. That should count for something. If you were to tell anyone that the king's collier aided you, it would not go well for me. I trust we have mutual reasons to remain quiet on this. Do you agree, my lady?"

Maia nodded.

"Well enough. Up the steps then."

It was not long before Maia's legs were burning with the effort of climbing the stone steps. They were crooked and too steep, but Collier seemed to mount them easily with his long legs. She grimaced as she pushed herself, but the cool morning air helped her make it to the top of the final cliff. The trees on the lower level provided the travelers with cover from any prying eyes.

The manor house occupied the expanse of the hilltop. The three-story behemoth had a sloping roof and a single parapet on one end, topped with a cupola and an iron spike. A huge oak tree stood in the midst of a small terraced garden with neat, trimmed hedges. Some small arches of stone built into the rocky cliff helped extend the lawns and grounds slightly. Several gray doves flew overhead, cooing as they went.

There was no smoke from any of the chimneys of the manor. No signs of life at all.

"The stables are in the rear," Collier said, directing them around the tall parapet to some stone sheds where they could hear the nickering of horses. So far, he had been true to his word. "This way."

They reached the tall wooden doors, and Maia prepared herself to be betrayed. Why would this man have helped them escape the Dochte Mandar? What motive could he possibly have to betray his king or his king's interests? She glanced at the kishion and saw the blatant distrust she felt, mirrored in his eyes. She would use the kystrel if she must.

Collier reached for the massive door handles and pulled one of the stable doors open. Inside stood four saddled horses with bulging sacks fastened to their harnesses—provisions for their trip. Without pausing to look back at Maia and the kishion, he strode inside, kicking up dust and straw as he approached the first, a beautiful cream-colored stallion, and greeted the animal warmly by running his hand over its hide. Then he went to the other three, whispering to them in coaxing tones and patting their flanks. His talent with the beasts was unmistakable.

"The brooding mare the color of soot is named Revenge. He is yours, my brooding friend," he said, turning toward the kishion. "This brown is yours, my lady. Her name is Preslee. She is fast, so do not give her head unless the need is dire." He stroked her long nose and then clapped her flanks warmly. "She can run. That may be useful to you." He moved on to a shorter horse, a pony. "Chacewater is for Tayt when he arrives. He is small but sturdy, as are Tayt's legs. Anything larger and he would need a bucket to stand on to even mount her. He may not be able to keep up like the other two, but he is tough. These mounts should suit you all."

Collier went over to his cream stallion and swung up into the saddle in a fluid, practiced motion. The sword dangled from his hip. "I will ride back through town as if going to Argus, since that was my original destination. The road behind the stables will bring you east, away from Corriveaux and the Dochte Mandar, to the town of Briec. If you would, leave the horses there with the innkeeper. The man's name is Clem Pryke. It is the largest inn, so it will not be difficult to find. I will come back in two days to pick them up and bring them back here, no one the wiser."

He leaned down in his saddle, looking at Maia with an expression she could not interpret. "So I must leave you."

"How can I repay you for your help?" Maia said, still struggling with the relief she felt finding all had been arranged as he had said. The stable was clean and orderly, with tack and harnesses hanging from pegs on the walls. Barrels of provisions were stored beneath them. It was well kept.

"Will you give me your name?" he asked.

She stared up at him, at this handsome, mysterious man. He was a wretched, yet he had overcome the disadvantages of that class. She longed to know how. Her banishment had made her feel as she imagined a wretched would. Except she knew her Family.

She had believed for many years that no one would ever want a princess who had been banished. Her father had made it very clear she would never marry.

She shook her head no, not daring to trust him further, or even to trust herself.

"Someday, my lady," he said, his piercing blue eyes drawing her in. He smiled broadly. "Someday you will trust me."

CHAPTER NINE

Whitsunday

M aia, the fire is burning low. Attend to it." Lady Deorwynn's voice caught Maia midstride as she was heading to the cupboard for porcelain cups. She quickly finished that duty and then went over to the hearth to tend to the dying fire.

As Maia knelt on the flagstones, the pain in her stomach grew. It was almost unbearable, and it took all her will not to moan. She closed her eyes, feeling beads of sweat on her brow, and clutched her abdomen. She tried to breathe through the pain, hoping the air would not whistle from her mouth and draw unwelcome attention.

"Please, Maia, you are so lazy. I told you to tend the fire, yet you do nothing but sit there and stare at it. Is it stubbornness, I wonder? You think I will fetch a servant instead? Really, child. So lazy."

Maia clenched her teeth and reached for a poker hanging from a nearby peg. She stabbed the chalk-gray coals, mixing them around before stirring up the winking embers. Half hidden in the soot, the Leering glowered at her from the stone wall deep inside the hearth. It was a small one with a wicked grin full of torture; it seemed to be smiling because it enjoyed her pain. It was a hideous Leering.

She stared into its eyes as she set a log from the pile beside the fire into the nest of coals. Bending close, she started to blow on the embers, creating puffs of ash. The sounds of sizzles and crackles popped in her ears and the log started to smoke. As she worked, her loathing of Lady Deorwynn seethed inside of her, a force so strong she dared label it hatred. The woman had usurped her mother's place in her father's heart . . . leaving no room for any others. While her daughters were pampered and spoiled as princesses of the realm, Maia's position continued to worsen.

The Leering's eyes started to glow.

Maia stared at the eyes in amazement. Twin pinpricks of red-hot heat stared at her from the soot. The Leering was responding to her emotions. Though Maia had learned long ago to act calm when she was feeling anything but, she knew that the Leering had somehow sensed her buried feelings, that it had awoken because of them.

She stared at the half smile, half grimace on the Leering's mouth and leaned back from the hearth.

Burn.

The thought flittered through her mind. Had it even come from her? Fire roared from the hearth instantly, sending out billowing white tongues of flame. She scuttled back in fear and also a gust of excitement. The entire mouth of the hearth was ablaze.

"For certes, Maia, I told you to revive the fire, not burn down the castle! How many logs did you feed into it?" Lady Deorwynn's voice was outraged. Maia stood, staring with wonder at her creation, startled by the immensity of the flames. She had caused that. She had used a Leering with no more effort than it would take to blow a feather.

Maia rubbed her arms, ignoring the plain coarse wool. It was not quite a peasant's dress, but it was certainly nothing like the gowns she had worn all her life. Servants were never to outshine their betters.

As if summoned by her thoughts, the door burst open, and Lady Deorwynn's daughters rushed inside. Murer and Jolecia—the banes of Maia's heart. Murer's gown was the finer of the two, of course, decorated with elegant colors slashing through the sleeves and trim and a fancy pattern, and she was literally dripping with necklaces and jewels. Her hair was blond, like her mother's, only curlier, and pinned up with gems and the like. She had a beautiful smile that was full of teasing, and a razor tongue that could leave someone's feelings in shreds. Her sister, Jolecia, had straight hair, also blond, and she mimicked everything her sister did, though with less success, and was constantly jealous and petulant as a result.

"Mother!" Murer said with relish, "The Earl of Forshee just arrived! I am so grateful my new papa decided to visit Billerbeck for Whitsunday. The Earl of Forshee! He has several sons, and they are quite striking."

The flames from the hearth had died down. Lady Deorwynn sat on a cushioned seat and picked up her needlework. "They may be handsome, but they despise my Family. They will not suit you, dearest."

Murer approached her mother quickly. "But what if one of them fell in love with me? Might that not *tame* their Family's hostility against us?"

"There are five brothers," Jolecia said. "We can each have one."

Lady Deorwynn clucked her tongue. "No, do not be simple. The Forshees have been loyal to Papa's enemy."

Maia bit her tongue. That was the word Lady Deorwynn used to describe Maia's mother. With the fire now in full bloom, she went back to the porcelain cups and began serving the girls' favorite drink, apple cider.

"I should not be ashamed to love a Forshee," Murer said. "They are handsome, Mother. But I think you have someone else in mind for me?"

"Do you have a match for me as well?" Jolecia said, a slight whine in her voice.

Lady Deorwynn worked at the stitches studiously.

"Mother?" Murer pressed after a little silence, her voice eager.

"Why should you confine your aspirations to an earl, my daughter, when there are members of the Family abroad who are kings?" She said it in almost a playful way, but Maia could hear the deep ambition behind the words, like an echo in a well. "The King of Dahomey has two sons who are legitimate. The eldest is nearly your age, Murer."

There was silence as daughter stared at mother, dumbstruck. "To be . . . Queen . . . of Dahomey? The cursed kingdom?"

Maia felt a prick of apprehension and envy, remembering that, at one time, *she* had been betrothed to the heir of Dahomey. She had always thought of the cursed shores with a degree of curiosity, and if things had turned out differently, she would have reigned over them one day. She stifled her resentful feelings.

"I would not wish *that*," Jolecia said. "I should be frightened to live in Dahomey. Their Leerings are cursed!"

"They do have strange customs there, do they not?" Murer said. "You once lived there, Mother, and always ridiculed them. And the Family who was chosen to rule . . ." There was a pronounced note of distaste in her voice. "We all know about *that* heritage, do we not? I should think one of the Earl of Forshee's sons would be infinitely preferable. I have been curling my hair for Whitsunday, as you can see."

"She will not let me curl mine," Jolecia murmured.

"I have heard the Forshees fancy that," Murer went on. "But Dahomey . . . truly, Mother?"

Lady Deorwynn continued stitching, saying nothing.

Murer went to the tray where Maia had finished pouring the cups. "Thank you," she said. Then her expression changed, as if she had only then recognized it was Maia who had served her and not one of the other girls. The look turned to disdain.

Holding the cup elegantly, she took a dainty sip and walked behind the couch. "Today is Whitsunday, Mother. Even the servants are allowed to dance around the maypole with their betters. Is Maia going to dance?"

A blush of hot shame shot through Maia's cheeks at being drawn into the girl's devious web. She cursed Murer under her breath.

"Even the wretcheds are allowed," Lady Deorwynn said musingly. "I suppose we cannot forbid it." The needlework flashed like silver knives. "But really, who do you think will ask *her* to dance around the maypole? Even the local villagers here at Billerbeck Hundred know who she is." She looked up from her work, flashing a malicious glance at Maia.

"I am not feeling well," Maia said in a low voice. "I did not plan to attend."

"Oh, but you *must*," Lady Deorwynn said, setting down the needlework. "Why do you think Papa chose Billerbeck to celebrate Whitsunday? Why make such a long journey for the occasion?"

Maia used to know her father's thinking. In the past, she would have been able to answer the question accurately. Now she did not understand her father.

"I do not know," Maia said softly. "Likely it is the *farthest* abbey from Muirwood."

Lady Deorwynn rose, her eyes flashing with anger. "You have a wicked tongue."

Maia stared at her coldly, saying nothing.

"You must learn humility, child. That is the way of the Medium, is it not? So proud in your heart still. Well, only through suffering do we learn, as the Aldermastons *and* the Dochte Mandar teach us. You have *much* to learn." It sounded like a threat.

"If she does not wish to attend the maypole dance, Mother, we should not force her," Murer said. "Whether she dances or not, there will be shame enough."

"Papa wishes her to be seen by the Forshees," Lady Deorwynn explained patiently. "To show them that she is well, that she is treated with kindness and compassion. She is not a prisoner in Pent Tower, as the rumors say. So you see, Maia, even if you are unwell, you must attend. No one will dance with you anyway. You are a thing to be pitied."

"I will attend if Father wishes it," Maia said dispassionately. She never called him *Papa*.

Her heart ached, but she did not let it show on her face. As the sisters began talking about gowns and garlands, she silently left the solar. She pressed one hand to her abdomen, trying to push down the pain and ill humor. Since her banishment, her strength had flagged and she had been sick quite often. She suffered from ulcers in her stomach, according to the healers, which they treated with herbs and tinctures. Nothing worked. She had even sent for the Aldermaston of Claredon for a Gift of healing. Any maston could call upon the Medium for a Gifting to aid another person. The Aldermaston had tried unsuccessfully. Sadly, he had explained it was the Medium's will that she suffer from her ailments.

Maia passed through the common room, which was crowded with servants preparing for the Whitsunday feast that would be held prior to the festival. She was grateful for the commotion, for it would help prevent others from noticing her. Even though Maia could no longer wear elegant gowns, even though she was forced to wear the gowns of the servants, she still earned sympathetic glances from visitors. From their pained looks, she knew that while they silently disagreed with her father's decision to banish his wife, they would not speak up for her if it meant defying him.

This was her first Whitsunday since coming of age. For many years, she had imagined what it would be like. This was the one day when there were no longer any divisions by rank. Even the lowliest were permitted to attend the feast. Boys and girls were allowed to dance around the maypole together, holding hands as they spun around the tall pole festooned with flowers and ribbons. A princess could dance with a lowly shepherd boy. When a girl and boy turned fourteen, they were finally allowed to participate. It was a custom that had been passed down through the centuries. As Whitsunday approached, the girls would fret constantly about who would ask them to dance. The boys, on the other hand, would steel their courage and ask for dances they would otherwise never dare request. There was powerful symbolism in the ritual, she realized, and she had attended the festivals throughout her childhood. At her request, her father had taught her the dance when she was six. She had even seen her parents dance around the maypole together, and the memories were like clutching knives to her bosom. The pain in her stomach worsened, as it always did when she thought about the time before, and she knew she had to quiet her mind.

But how could she not remember? She had not seen her mother in years. This Whitsunday, her mother was in Muirwood Abbey, moored in some swamp-infested land full of gnats and bogs that no one cared enough to visit because it was still being erected. It was the most ancient abbey of the realm, yet other abbeys had been completed sooner. Why was that? Perhaps because the destruction had been more severe. It was said that only the Aldermaston's kitchen had survived intact.

Maia imagined her mother in that kitchen. Alone. Grief stricken. Ailing. Maia had heard that her mother's health was in jeopardy. Her father had sent the finest healers to treat her, for he did not want the suspicion of murder to tarnish his reputation further. What pained her more than anything about this Whitsunday was that she had begged Father to send her to Muirwood for the occasion. She had asked him to send half of his army, if necessary, to ensure she returned. Her father had laughed in her face and said that he could not trust half his army because they might be sympathetic enough to her mother's plight to rise up in rebellion against him.

"Lady Maia!"

She whirled at the sound of the voice. She was just about to leave the common room for the stairwell when she spied Chancellor Walraven waving to her.

She brightened and approached him.

"I was going to the library," he said. "Would you care to join me?"

"I would. I thought I might not see you until the festival this evening. How long have you been in Billerbeck Hundred?"

"A fortnight already," Walraven said, smiling at her. He led the way up the stairs to the upper floor of another part of the castle and entered the library. The floor rushes smelled of mint. Everything had been freshly changed in anticipation of the king's arrival.

It was midafternoon, but the light from the windows was still bright. Maia went to the glass and stared outside. She could see all the way to the village green, where the maypole stood proudly erect. A small crowd had gathered around it already. Another pang went through Maia's stomach, and she clutched it with one hand.

"Your bowels still ail you?" the chancellor asked at her shoulder.

She nodded, seeing his reflection in the glass, his wild gray hair askew.

"I personally think it is because they make you wear those drab gray gowns," he said with a hint of teasing. "It is the color of storm clouds. Not light puffy ones, but the dark thunderheads. They say it might rain this evening. The weather can be unpredictable in this Hundred."

"Why did Father choose Billerbeck for the Whitsunday celebration?" She pressed her fingers against the glass, feeling the subtle ripples on its surface.

"You are a wise girl," he replied meekly. "Why do you think?"

"I do not know him anymore," she replied flatly, bitterly.

"You know him better than you are willing to admit. He is no longer the man you have fond memories of, child, though part of his old self still exists. I see it now and then. Let me teach you to tease out the answers you desire. That is the way of queens." He folded his arms. "What does your father desire the most?"

"A divorce from my mother."

"He married her according to the maston customs, though."

"Yes, he did, by irrevocare sigil," Maia said, staring at the billowing ribbons hanging off the maypole. Someone had tied or tacked the ends to the wood, yet still the ribbons twitched as if they longed to fly free.

"According to the maston rites, the irrevocare sigil is permanent. However, it is only in force if both husband and wife honor the oath. The maston tomes list certain special situations that would give rise for the dissolution of the irrevocare sigil."

"If one of the spouses is unfaithful." Her heart was black with dark thoughts. *As you were, Father.*

"Yes. Unfaithfulness is grounds for dissolution. Your father knew this and has given your mother the opportunity to break the marriage. But she has not. She refuses."

"So, instead, he divorced her according to the customs of the Dochte Mandar," Maia said. "There are multiple grounds for divorce in your creed."

"There are. It is a much more . . . *flexible* . . . state in our culture. The trouble is that the king was not married according to the customs of the Dochte Mandar. His marriage to Lady Deorwynn is lawful in the eyes of some and unlawful in the eyes of others. It is a tangled web, to be sure. Much like that maypole yonder."

"A web he has inflicted on himself," Maia said with a throb in her voice. She swallowed.

"Why, then, are we at Billerbeck Abbey?"

Maia thought long and hard. "Lady Deorwynn says it is to show people that I am still alive."

"She is a fool. If your father were to harm you, the kingdom would revolt. Many see you as his only legitimate heir."

"My mother will not start a rebellion," Maia said. "Neither will I. Nothing but destruction and war can follow when a kingdom fights itself. Our history is full of it. War always draws out the Myriad Ones. Is that not what the tomes say?"

"Yes. A tragic tale, to be sure. I have read the tomes. Your father sent me here to discuss the divorce with the Aldermaston of Billerbeck. To seek his input and his wisdom. To learn if there is anything in the tomes, in *any* tome, to justify a man putting away his wife, except for adultery."

Maia turned and looked at him in surprise.

"What did you find?" she asked, her eyes gleaming.

"There was one reference," the chancellor said, staring out the window. "But it does not help your father's case. I knew it would not, but alas, we must obey our king's wishes."

Maia turned to look at him, feeling alarmed and concerned. "I thought the bond could only legitimately be broken for one reason. I have read the tomes, as you know. You taught me to read them. There is another?"

He nodded, saying nothing.

"Please, Chancellor. Tell me."

He shrugged. "It does not pertain to this case, as I said."

"But what is it? What is the reference?"

He looked down at her, smiling compassionately. "I do not mean to cause worry, Lady Maia. You would have no cause to know about it because it is not written in the maston tomes . . . only in those kept by the Aldermastons. The provision is mentioned in the tomes of the Dochte Mandar, however, so I knew of it. It is part of the maston lore that is limited to those who have passed the maston test. Which, sadly, may never happen in your case because your father intends for you never to study at an abbey *or* to marry. If you had any children, you see, they would be rivals to his heirs by Lady Deorwynn. He will not allow it. I am hesitant to say more on this subject because you will likely not be given the chance to learn it through the natural course."

Maia swallowed. "Please, Chancellor. I wish to prepare myself. I do intend to take the maston test someday and will try to persuade Father. I started a fire Leering just now. All by myself, with hardly a thought."

"You did?" he said, impressed. His smile was beaming. "I can only do that with my kystrel!"

"I did it on my own," Maia said, flushing with warmth at his praise.

"Well, that is certainly an accomplishment. I do not believe you will have any trouble passing the maston test, to be sure. Women are not allowed to read, of course, but as your ancestors discovered, one from the proper Family does not need to be able to *read* in order to pass the maston test or tame a Leering. So you desire it still?"

"Yes," Maia said fiercely. "My mother is one. My father . . ." she swallowed. "What is the reference you mentioned? I will learn it eventually. You must tell me, Chancellor."

He smoothed his hand over her scalp tenderly, as if he were an Aldermaston himself, about to bestow a Gifting on her.

"Well, I do not see the harm. The Medium responds to our strongest thoughts and emotions, so if you feel strongly about it, you *will* become a maston someday, lass. I do not doubt it, particularly given your talent. Even if you had to sneak away from Pent Tower and visit Claredon Abbey!" He glanced at the door and around the chamber, making sure they were alone. He dropped his voice lower. "As I said, there is knowledge in the Aldermastons' tomes that is limited to those who have passed the maston test. That is the proper place to learn it. What I will tell you comes from the tomes of the Dochte Mandar. It is scribed in my own tome, in fact. As you know, the irrevocare sigil binds a man and woman together through the power of the Medium. The bond is so permanent that the marriage will last beyond the pale of death. A man—or a woman—may divorce his spouse on grounds of adultery. You already know this. There is another cause. A man may discover that his wife is a *hetaera*. That is grounds as well."

The word sent a shiver through Maia, though she knew not why. "What is *that*, Chancellor?" She could not even say the word, for she feared it would burn her tongue.

Walraven shook his head. "That you must learn for yourself when you face the maston test. Hetaera are powerful with the Medium because they use kystrels. They brought the Scourge upon the world, which is why the Dochte Mandar have banned women from using the medallions. But I assure you, child. The argument is useless in this case. There have been no hetaera for ages."

Emotions are the most ungovernable of human frailties. How I have learned this to be true! In the tome of Aldermaston Aquinar, he scribed a saying to give himself strength to manage his heart. He wrote, "Give me a waking heart, that no curious thought can withdraw me from the Medium. Let it be so strong that no unworthy affection can draw me backward, so stable that no tribulation can break it, and so free that no election by violence can make any challenge to it." That is what I have always desired—a waking heart. One that can never be lulled into complacency.

—Lia Demont, Aldermaston of Muirwood Abbey

CHAPTER TEN

Nightmares

L ady Maia! Wake up! Wake up!"
   She awoke to the sensation of hands gripping her shoulders, shaking her roughly, and a burning feeling against her chest. The emotions of the dream were so vivid that when her eyes flew open in sudden terror, she could not remember where she was, or even her age. The kystrel seared against her skin, and she felt the power of the Medium flood through her, urgent and panting and swelling like the tide.

It was Jon Tayt who had grabbed her shoulders, she realized. His face was pressed but a few inches from hers.

"Stop the magic!" he begged her.

She saw the kishion kneeling nearby, hand on his dagger hilt—looking for a moment as if he would slit her throat if she did not stop.

The power and fury of the Medium roared in her ears, irrepressible. She felt the vastness of the world at her fingertips, as if in that moment, she could encircle the entire land, all of the king-doms, in her arms, as a lavender gathers a heap of laundry.

"Please!" Jon Tayt's eyes were desperate. He had a look of awe as well as fear, and in the mirrors of his eyes, she could see that her own eyes were glowing silver.

For a moment, she could not relinquish the magic, though she tried. The wind howled, blasting her hair and cloak. This squall she had created was as powerful as a sea storm, and it hurled against them violently.

Enough, Maia thought with a twinge of fear, but a force of command. *Be still.*

The kystrel began to cool against her neck. With it, the winds died down. She stared at her surroundings, confused. Three horses were tethered to a fallen log, and they were all rearing and bucking, whinnying in terror.

Jon Tayt sighed with relief, releasing her shoulders, and then rushed to calm the mounts. Three horses. Three names—Revenge, Chacewater, and Preslee. Not horses from her stables when she was a child, but horses loaned to them by Feint Collier. She blinked rapidly, trying to dispel the turbulent emotions her dream had left with her.

"They are getting worse," the kishion said in a low voice.

"What do you mean?" Maia asked him, drawing her cloak around her bodice. She knew this latest surge of magic would only have enlarged the tattoo. How much longer did she have before she could no longer conceal it?

"The nightmares."

Rather than look at him, she fussed with the edge of her bur-gundy gown and flicked away bits of debris from the fabric.

"Tell me."

She finally met his eyes. "I am not confessing my dreams to you, kishion."

He brooded and shook his head. "My lady, this last one brought a storm down on us so severe it frightened away game in all directions. The horses nearly killed themselves trying to flee from you."

"I am sorry," she said through clenched teeth. "But I cannot *control* my dreams. None of us can. See? The magic is tamed now. Jon Tayt is soothing the horses. All will be well in a moment."

The kishion shook his head. "They are getting worse, though."

She struggled to keep her composure. She wanted to yell and scream at him, to unleash the childish emotions awakened by the dream. But she had to keep her feelings under control. She pressed her fingers against her mouth, as if that would stop her from blurting out anything she did not want to reveal.

All her life, she had bottled up her emotions. That was the way of the mastons, after all. And the Dochte Mandar too. She knew what became of a person who lost control of their wants, emotions, and desires—she needed only to look as far as her father. It was one fate she would not allow herself to suffer. So she could be poked, but she would not flinch. She could be teased, but she would not retaliate. Deep down, though, a well of anger and indignation had built up inside her, and it threatened to break loose. She dared not allow it.

Maia closed her eyes, burying her turbulent feelings. A shaky breath came from her, followed by another, calmer one. Chancellor Walraven's warnings were still fresh in her mind. She knew the dangers of her own power. For if she could make rats and mice fling themselves from a tower window, she could also drive a man to kill himself. Such pure power needed to be safeguarded behind iron self-control.

"I will be all right, kishion," she said more softly. She looked him in the eye, showing him her calm exterior.

"What if they continue to grow worse?" he asked her pointedly.

"Then wake me as Jon Tayt did," she replied. "They are just bad dreams from my childhood."

He snorted dismissively. "You are *still* a child."

"I am eighteen," she reminded him. "Some of my cousins were married when they were thirteen or fourteen. Most were plight trothed, as I was, as babes. I am not married, but I am *not* a child."

"But are you an innocent?" he said with a strange look on his face. "I will wake you next time. Perhaps a pan of cold water will do."

She shook her head and stifled a cough. He was about to rise and leave, but she caught his arm. He stopped and gave her a curious look.

"The nightmares are from the past," she whispered. "I do not understand why I am being forced to relive my most painful memories at night, but the Medium must have a reason. I wish I could dream about the years before I was nine. Those are all pleasant memories."

He nodded. "Before your father sent you away."

"To be honest," she said, looking around, "I do not even recall falling asleep last night. Where are we?"

"It was after sunset when we found these ruins," the kishion said, standing.

She looked around and saw, through the haze of dawn, the skeletal remains of an abbey around her. Columns of broken stone sat crouchbacked and ominous nearby. The lawns were overgrown, and she thought she spied the charred stump of a maypole fastened in the midst of the green.

"You were practically asleep in the saddle," he said, reaching down and grabbing her by the wrist to help her stand. "You just curled up on the turf and bedded down in your cloak. Jon Tayt and I feasted like kings. We saved you a plate, though it grew cold."

She shook her head, smiling wistfully. "I do not remember. I was weary from the pace we set yesterday." Her stomach growled, startling them both, and Maia laughed. "My appetite bears witness to the truth of your story."

A faint smile tugged at his mouth. "I searched the grounds this morning for an orchard with fruit. Remember the one we found at the lost abbey? The garden?"

A mixture of memories flooded her mind. Her time with the kishion had always been fraught with tension. "The maston garden," she said, brooking a smile. "The fruit was still fresh. Did you find any?"

He shook his head. "There were some barren trees. All wild, with nothing to eat."

"The Leerings have all been stripped away," Maia said, walking up to one of the towering stone buttresses. She could not sense a single one amidst the rubble as she ran her hand along the rough surface. "The Naestors harvested the Leerings. See the gashes up there? They were chiseled away."

"Why would they do that?" he asked.

Maia stared up at the pocked surface. "They learned to control them after finding so many of these," she said, patting the kystrel beneath her bodice. "But they lacked the maston lore to build their own Leerings or forge their own medallions. They tried. They carved faces into stones. They mimicked the designs perfectly." She dropped her hand away and started walking toward Jon Tayt, who was beginning to saddle their mounts. She looked back at the kishion. "They could copy a Leering, but they lacked a maston's authority to give it power."

He walked with her toward the horses. "You are not a maston yourself, are you?"

She shook her head. "No. I was never permitted to learn. I know I would have passed. I can work a Leering without a kystrel, which most people cannot do, but I can only use the Medium's stronger powers with it. Strength in the Medium comes from your Family, and all my ancestors were famous mastons. I would like to become one too . . . someday."

Jon Tayt yanked hard on one of the girth straps. "Ach," he said with a huff, catching her last words, "just slip away to Tintern Abbey in Pry-Ree and the Aldermaston will grant your request. If you were a maston, you would have no need to trifle with such jewelry." He gave her a sidelong look. "Now that these beasts have calmed down a bit, there is a right way to saddle a horse and a wrong way. Collier knew the right way, but if you adjust the harness like so," he grunted, moving the straps, "it makes it easier on the mount to carry you. We rode them hard yesterday. So we will give them a bit of a rest and walk them this morning, then ride hard later on."

Maia walked up to Preslee and stroked her flanks, murmuring softly as she did so. "Did you check the hooves for pebbles?" she asked.

"I always do that first," he said with a tight nod. "No sense saddling a lame horse. The hooves are hale and sound. The stables had a dozen other beasts in addition to these. The king likes to have fresh horses for hunting."

Maia fetched a bag of provender from the saddle and started to feed her horse, grabbing a hunk of bread for herself. Preslee nuzzled the bag and began nickering with delight. Maia wished she had an apple to give her as well.

"I can do that, my lady," Jon Tayt said, giving her a confused smile.

"I miss having my own horses," Maia explained, shaking her head. "I always cared for my own. I know the right way to saddle them as well, Master Tayt."

"Ah, but do you know the right way to throw an axe, my lady?"

She looked over her shoulder at the hunter, her lips pursed.

"I see you do not." He gave a deep laugh. "You were taught languages, dancing, horsemanship, hawking, diplomacy, and either the lute or the virginal."

"The lute, virginal, *and* the regal," Maia corrected. "I was also taught Paeizian fencing."

Jon Tayt snorted. "You and Collier share that in common then. He is a strong advocate for Paeizian fencing—hence the nickname. However, I can kill *any* Paeizian fencer with an axe from thirty paces away. Shameful they taught you to play the *virginal* and not how to throw an axe!" He grinned and then bellowed with laughter.

"You have convinced me that my education is incomplete," Maia answered, enjoying the look on his face. "You must teach me."

He clapped Chacewater on the flanks and started to give him a brisk rubdown. "Let me finish saddling the horses first. Always best to be prepared to ride and ride quickly. Take a brace of axes to that maypole stump and I will show you there. Hup, easy boy."

Maia fetched two axes lying next to his rucksack and she carried them across the green to the charred maypole stump. She noticed the kishion scouting the grounds, looking as sullen and surly as usual. But her feelings about his sternness and solitary ways had evolved considerably over the past weeks. While he was not affable like Jon Tayt, she had found herself admiring his determination, survival instincts, and even his constant closeness. She was grateful to have both men as her protectors.

Argus trotted up to her as she reached the maypole, and she crouched to greet him. He was guarded with her, not as playful as he was normally, and she realized that the magic of the kystrel had frightened him away.

"It is well, Argus," she said coaxingly. "I will not harm you."

The boarhound sniffed at the grass near her before shifting his attention to her face. She stroked him, remembering her own spaniels and puppies as a child. She used to have a livery, men who wore her badge and colors—blue and forest green—horses and maidservants and advisors and cooks and hawks and longbows and Pry-rian fletched arrows. Everything she could have desired had been hers, and in abundance. All that had been stripped away when she was banished. And she had not even been banished to a distant castle or sent off to an abbey where she might have become a maston. She had been forced to watch as every luxury that had been taken from her was bestowed on Lady Deorwynn's daughters.

Argus's tongue lolled out of his mouth as he panted. She stroked his coat, jealous of the simplicity of Jon Tayt's life.

"You are spoiling my hound," he muttered as he approached. "You should kick him almost as often as you pet him."

"*You* do not do that," Maia commented wryly, standing.

There was a smile in his voice. "Of course not, lass. He has saved my life. More than once, truth be told. You do not kick a dog who has saved your life. I want you to kick him so that he stops fawning over you all the time. He seeks to please you. Yes, Argus—do not deny it! I can see it. Shameful." He tossed the hound a bit of dried meat, and Argus loped away to start gnawing at it.

"I am more suited for a dog's company than a person's," Jon

Tayt admitted, drawing one of the axes from his belt. He flipped it and caught it by the handle. "I like to talk and Argus likes to listen."

"A fitting pair you two make," Maia agreed.

He smiled at her. "I like you, Lady Maia. Nary a whine or a whimper from you since we left the village named after my dog. Only when you sleep." He took a step forward and hurled the axe, which spun lethally end over end until it buried itself in the center of the burnt maypole with an ominous *thuck.*

"You step forward with the opposite leg as you release. You want to be at least five paces away from your target at first. Work on accuracy at short distances. Then go farther and farther back. You want to cluster them if you can." He threw the second axe and it bit into the wood right next to the first. He smiled at himself and walked up to the post to yank them both free.

"The blade should spin twice before striking the post. If you are too close, you will hit with the haft. That could crack a man's nose, true, but I would prefer to split his head open."

He walked back to where she stood. "Let me show you again. Hold the haft here," he said, gesturing with one of the weapons. "Feel the weight of it. I sharpen these blades every other day so they will stick when they hit. No use carrying a dull axe. They can even deflect a sword, like so." He demonstrated a parry with one of the axes and then swept the other toward her neck, slowing the blow as it came near her. "Always carry three or four. It does not take long to yank one loose from a dead man and throw it again."

"You are dangerous," Maia said. Though his choice of words made her wince, his abilities were impressive.

"There is a right way to throw an axe. Some people think it is like throwing a dagger. Very different. The kishion can show you that skill. My expertise is with the bow and the axe. I would rather drop a man at thirty paces. He cannot cut you with his sword if he is already dead, you see."

"Truly," Maia agreed.

"Hold it so, as I showed you." He stood behind her, rotating her so that she took a solid stance facing the maypole stump. In Maia's mind, she imagined children dancing around the maypole, the ribbons slowly twisting and sheathing the dark wood with an interplay of color. There was dancing and fun, laughter and clapping. She could almost hear the music from her first maypole dance at fourteen, the sound of the lutes and pipes. Round and round they had danced—the noble Family dressed in bright colors fringed with fur, the servants and lower classes dressed in plainer garb, but sharing equally in the enjoyment of the occasion.

All except her. In her mind's eye, she could see herself . . . her fourteen-year-old self . . . standing to the side, hungry to participate. Begging the Medium with her thoughts for one young man of the bunch, even a lowly butcher boy, to muster the courage to ask her to dance. The music swelled in her mind, the clapping growing louder. Laughter and cheers filled the night sky, bright with torch fire and the honeyed smell of treats.

Lady Deorwynn had been right, though. No one had dared anger the king by asking Maia to dance. Not one offer had been made.

Maia hefted the axe and hurled it at the maypole. It stuck on the first attempt.

"Humph," Jon Tayt said gruffly. "A few more. You certainly do not lack the strength."

CHAPTER ELEVEN

The Earl of Dieyre

They sheltered at midday in a grove of aspen near a clear brook to rest and water their mounts and eat from the provisions in the saddlebags. The kishion had left them so he could scout the area for safety. As Maia pulled out a wrapped loaf of bread, a bit of color caught her eye in the bottom of the saddlebag. There, nestled amidst a cluster of three pears, she discovered a flower. She reached inside the bag and withdrew a small white lily. It was tiny but beautiful, and it had been left—quite deliberately—in her saddlebag.

A slight flush rose in her cheeks as she cupped it in her hand and stared at the six elegant petals. Feint Collier had left her this flower. It was a trifle, really—just a small gesture, and yet it touched her deeply. She sighed and then hid the flower again. She stood for a moment, trying to understand the mixed feelings that were stirring in her heart. She did not trust them. She did not trust *him*. Still, it was a thoughtful gesture and a small spot of brightness in a path drenched in shadows.

"Do you hear that?" Jon Tayt said, rising suddenly from the crouched position he had affected to drink from the brook. He wiped his mouth and beard and walked to the edge of the grove. After a few moments, Maia heard it as well. She had no doubt the kishion would have already heard the sounds. A rider.

Judging by the sound, the horse was at a full gallop, and sure enough, they could soon see a lathered mount plunging down the road. It came from the direction they were headed, riding hard and fast for Roc-Adamour. Maia stayed hidden in the fringe of trees, but she saw the colors of the rider's tunic and his black felt hat. It was a royal horseman. Not Collier—the rider was too short, and she had not seen him wearing anyone's livery the previous night.

The rider passed their position and was gone in moments, leaving a trail of settling dust.

"Not a royal scout," Jon Tayt said, scratching his throat below his pointed beard. "A messenger. He could break his neck and the horse's legs riding that fast. A pity for the horse. What an idiot."

"He wore the king's colors," Maia pointed out.

"I noticed that. Collier said the army was north. We're heading east. Maybe the rider is trying to catch up with Collier. Whatever the reason, we should get these steeds to Briec and be gone. From there, it is two days' journey to the pass we need to take to cross into Mon."

"The sooner we are out of Dahomey, the better," Maia said determinedly.

"Was it the poisonous serpents, the flesh-eating ticks, or the endless gnats that most charmed you about this fair kingdom?" Jon Tayt said with a crooked smile. "Ach, I do miss Pry-Ree at times."

She felt a whisper in her mind, a dark warning. *You will all die because of this place. This is the land where death was born.*

"Your face clouded over just now," Jon Tayt said, his expression changing to one of concern. "What is it?"

She could not tell him about the whispers from the Medium. It had been a few days since she had last heard one. They seemed to come to her more frequently when danger was near. They warned her of it in advance, which was one of the reasons she had come to trust them. She had learned from studying the chancellor's tome that the whisperings were often subtle and disguised as her own thoughts. Experience had taught her it was true.

"Just a memory," she lied, patting his meaty shoulder fondly. "I was almost the queen of this realm, you know."

He looked at her, surprised. "How so?"

"I was very young when the Mark was born, and my father negotiated a marriage alliance between our kingdoms. I started learning Dahomeyjan when I was two. I have always loved learning different languages. The marriage alliance was rejected long before I was banished. But I have never forgotten that my first husband was going to be the Mark."

"You know the history of the Mark's Family, do you not?" Jon Tayt said.

Maia smiled and walked back to Preslee, stroking her soft neck and wishing, against all hope, that somehow she could keep her. It was a foolish thought. The whim of the spoiled princess she had once been.

"It is a famous story, Jon Tayt. Yes, I know it."

The kishion walked up. "I do not. Tell me."

Maia was not surprised. The kishion were trained in fighting and murder, not history. She wiped the hair from her eyes and faced him, gripping the saddle pommel and preparing to mount.

"When the mastons left these shores before the Scourge, one of my ancestors, Lia Demont, made a prophecy of sorts about the Earl of Dieyre. She cursed him to survive the Scourge. She said that he would be the last man left in this land, and that he would live to see her words fulfilled. He was a noble from Comoros who fought in the civil wars that followed the Scourge, but he was also invested with a rank in Dahomey. He eventually married, though he always searched for Lia's sister-in-law, Marciana Price, the one woman he truly loved. She had fled the shores with the mastons. Dieyre ultimately married a noblewoman from Dahomey, the Queen Dowager's younger sister, thus inheriting even more lands in Dahomey. Because of his prowess on the battlefield, he continued to gain rank in both realms and eventually overthrew the King of Dahomey. Then he overthrew Comoros. One by one, the kingdoms fell, and Dieyre proclaimed himself emperor of all seven kingdoms."

They both stared at her, listening to her words. As she spoke, she could almost hear the clash of blades. There were screams far distant, as if the very ground had gorged itself on too much blood. Maia shuddered, feeling sick.

"Say on," Jon Tayt asked, his voice thick.

"The Scourge was raging by then, destroying the people with a terrible plague. Yet still Dieyre fought. He was driven from his throne three times, and three times he returned with an army to reclaim it. It is believed that the final battle happened in Dahomey; it is said there was a mass slaughter that only he survived. He was nearly disfigured with scars and fainted from the loss of blood. Yet he survived, the last man, just as Lia had predicted he would. He wandered the kingdoms, searching in vain for another living soul. There were none. All had either perished by the sword or by the Scourge."

A feeling of blackness swelled in her heart. It was a terrible story. One that had always afflicted her. What would it have been like, she had wondered, to be the last man on earth? To see the fulfillment of a maston prophecy that had proved unavoidable? She cringed at the memory, feeling sympathy for the lonely creature he must have been.

Maia swung up into the saddle, feeling the black history taint her mood. She stared down at the kishion and Jon Tayt. Both looked back at her with grave expressions, clearly wondering if there was more. There was.

"You see, Emperor Dieyre—as he called himself—was the last man . . . until the Naestors came. They first discovered the ruins of Comoros and Pry-Ree. They sent ship after ship, investigating the ruined kingdoms. These were longboats, not the large sailing ships that the mastons left on. Eventually, they found Dieyre, ruling in the ruins of a desolate castle in Hautland. He was old by then. He lived among them for only nine months before he died. It was he who taught them to read the tomes they plundered. Some were maston tomes that had been secreted away. Some were tomes from the Dochte Mandar. In a way, the Naestors blended the two, learning how to control the Medium in proper ways through use of the kystrels. The Dochte Mandar among us now are not the same as the ones who lived during the days of the Scourging, though they kept the name."

"By Cheshu," Jon Tayt said in a small voice. "That is quite a tale, is it not? How much of it is true, I wonder?"

"Even the mastons believe it is true, Jon Tayt. When they returned, they found the Naestors inhabiting their lands. Many could speak the ancient languages, or at least well enough to communicate." Maia stroked Preslee's mane. "But Dieyre had left a prophecy of his own before he died. He told the Naestors that a woman with a child of his seed had gone with the mastons. He named that child's posterity as his heir, the heirs of his empire."

"By the Blood," the kishion swore softly. "The greedy Mark is his kin?"

Maia nodded. "Do you understand why I must flee Dahomey as quickly as I can? If the Mark captures me, he will claim my birthright as the king's daughter to win another kingdom for himself. The Mark wishes to rule *all* the kingdoms, as Dieyre once did. I have just told you what happened when one man tried to do that."

"Everyone perished," Jon Tayt said flatly.

***

They reached the town of Briec well before sunset, having ridden hard for the remainder of the day. The town was fenced in by a low, crumbled wall that would not have repulsed an army of any size. Jon Tayt explained how the towns farther north were all heavily fortified and had seen battles throughout the years as the various kingdoms plundered one another.

The town was not large enough to have its own abbey or castle, but the main inn served as the largest and most distinctive structure in town. There were at least six gabled roofs in the same style she had seen in Roc-Adamour, except the main building looked like six of the long, narrow Roc-Adamour buildings smashed together into one. Each gabled roof had a different style and size, and several jutted out at odd angles. A large central chimney rose above all the roofs and vented a cloud of smoke. The stables were adjoined to the inn, and they found a stable boy ready to take their mounts from them.

The interior of the inn had an enormous common room with trestle tables and a single fire. It was full of travelers with packs, staves, and heavy boots, who had stopped to share drinks and rest from their various journeys. The room was warm and lively, and a set of musicians were tuning their instruments near a small stage at the far side of the room. Maia stared longingly at the troupe, eager to hear them play. Several of the inn patrons waved at her and her fellow travelers, acknowledging them cheerily. Some glanced more than once at Maia, and she regretted not raising her cowl before entering.

"How long should we stay?" she asked Jon Tayt.

"I will walk about the village a bit to gather news," he replied, nodding at a fellow who seemed to recognize him. "With the Mark's army so near, it may not be wise to stay the night. Get some food and drink for supper. I will be back soon. Try not to draw attention to yourself."

Maia nodded and headed toward an uninhabited table in the shadows, trailed by the kishion. A server brought over a tray of meat and bread and oil with herbs to start, collected a few coins from them, and then returned later with a cruse of oil and a pot of bubbling cheese and another filled with steaming broth. Maia was now familiar with the custom and began to skewer pieces of meat and set them in the pots to cook. The kishion was not one for conversation, so they silently dunked the bread into the cheese and ate.

The musicians began to strike up some music, an airy tune. Some of the younger patrons began clearing away the trestle tables to form a space to dance. It seemed like this was the place that many of the young in town came to enjoy themselves. They began some of the popular dances that Maia had learned as a child, and soon the floor was thrumming with reverberations from their shoes and boots, and the music filling the hall was joined by ardent clapping. The feeling was lively and fresh, and it reminded her of some of the court parties her father was famous for. He was a lively dancer himself, and Maia had always enjoyed it.

The kishion snorted, brooding over a cup of wine.

Hoping to glean some information, Maia asked one of the serving girls if she could see the innkeeper, whom Collier had identified as Clem Pryke. The girl nodded and left to fetch her master. Moments later a man came up to the table, furiously wiping a tankard with a rag. "Welcome to the Gables," he said. "We do not have any rooms free, but you are welcome to enjoy a meal and dance with us, lass."

"You have no rooms available?" Maia asked curiously, surprised they were already so full.

"The king's army is nearby, and I have been asked to hold rooms in case. I am sorry, my lady."

"And what if the king's men do not come?" asked a familiar voice.

Maia had not seen him approach, but she instantly recognized Feint Collier's voice, and it startled her. He put his arm around the innkeeper's shoulder, emphasizing the difference in their heights.

"You know as well as I do, Master Collier, that I am paid for the rooms whether they are used or no. Had a sack of coins left with me earlier this day, in fact. Was not expecting you for several days. You are early."

"A change in my plans," he replied with a broad smile that seemed to be directed at Maia. "If the rooms are to sit empty unless the king's men arrive, may not she be loaned one? Let her have a room, Clem. She can have mine. I would just as soon sleep in the stables. You know that."

Maia felt a flush of pleasure, which she stifled immediately, and shook her head. "We will not be staying. I was only asking out of curiosity. The Gables is a lovely inn, Master Pryke."

Feint Collier clapped the innkeeper on the back. "When my lady commands, I must obey. You have a good stable lad, Clem. He knows how to treat a horse. Here is an extra crown for him. Who are the musicians? Where do they hail from?"

"From Pinnowe," the innkeeper said. "Good music always draws in a crowd. Best to you all." He gave them a warm smile and a nod, then left.

As soon as the innkeeper faded into the crowd, Feint Collier's expression changed, turning deadly serious. "The village in the mountains was massacred," he whispered through clenched teeth.

Maia felt a jolt of queasiness. "It was Corriveaux," she whispered. "He was traveling with soldiers who wore the king's uniform."

Raw fury flooded his gaze. "When the king hears of this . . ." he said. "I swear they have gone too far. Many souls escaped in the dark and fled to Roc-Adamour. They said it was the Dochte Mandar who did it. Like in olden times. They came from across the mountains, from the cursed lands. They were chasing someone." He looked at her pointedly.

"This you already know," Maia said. Her stomach felt like a hive of ants. "Why are you here?"

"Maybe I wanted to see you again," he answered quietly, "before you disappear forever."

Maia swallowed, her insides buzzing. "I *must* disappear," she whispered. "No one who is near me will be safe. We must go." The kishion scooted his chair back and rose, his eyes full of malice as he gazed at the intruder at the table.

Collier shook his head. "I have thrown them off your trail," he said. "They are searching Roc-Adamour still, looking from house to house and stopping every person attempting to leave. They believe you are still *there*." He gave her a coaxing smile. "I bought you time, my lady. No need to flee."

"Thank you," she replied. "But we are not safe *here* either."

"Sit," Collier said, swinging his head to the kishion. "Finish your meal at the least. You can have my room. It is as I said, I will sleep in the stables or here in the common room on the floor."

Maia shook her head. "You have already done too much," she said. "We returned the horses as promised, but you cannot help us without endangering yourself. Even now, you are taking a great risk."

"I know," he answered with a smile. "I cannot help it, I was born to wager the odds. I *want* to help you."

Maia wished Jon Tayt would return quickly. She wanted to leave. She wanted to bed down in the forest, away from the music and the cheese and the warmth—away from this handsome man who had left a flower in her saddlebag. Collier made her wistful for something she knew that she could never have. At least not while her father governed her life.

"You must not," she said, shaking her head.

He scowled, frustrated by her refusal. "Very well. Then give me one boon at least."

She sighed. "I will not tell you my name," she answered stubbornly.

He shook his head, his expression serious, his tone intimate. "Not that, lass. Just give me one thing."

She felt conflicted and anguished. Where was Jon Tayt? A prickle of uneasiness sent her body into a panic. "And what is that?"

"A dance," he said, extending his hand to her. "If you must go tonight, then give me this memory to take with me. Please, my lady. Dance with me."

In my day, the Dochte Mandar had a saying, which I believe has survived centuries in their tomes: Be extremely subtle, even to the point of formlessness. Be extremely mysterious, even to the point of soundlessness. Thereby you can be the director of your opponent's fate. The supreme art of war is to subdue the enemy without fighting.

—Lia Demont, Aldermaston of Muirwood Abbey

CHAPTER TWELVE

Surrounded

It was not the maypole dance, for there was not a maypole in the common room. It was a ring dance, like the ones they did at court, and the mix of sounds from the lute, flutes, coronets, and box bells sent a giddiness through the air that only added to Maia's nerves. His hand was warm and calloused and full of strength.

Maia was much shorter than Feint Collier, and she had to look up to see his face. His smile told her that he was pleased with himself for having finally claimed her. She steeled herself against that smile, wanting the tune to be over with so she could escape into the night. There was a dreadful apprehension in her stomach, but it was mingled with the flutterings of dancing for the first time since she had come of age.

"You have me to yourself at last," Maia said to Collier as they twirled around the slow-moving circle. "What do you have to say?"

"I was hoping to enjoy the moment a bit longer before ruining it with words."

"Are you such a poor speaker then?"

He shook his head. "I love conversation. It is only that with you, certain topics are clearly forbidden. Such as your name."

"Yes," she said.

"So is your origin. Your Dahomeyjan is flawless, but you are not from this land. You certainly have a *gift* with languages."

She cocked her head at him. "A curious word to use, Master Collier."

"I used it deliberately."

"You said you are not a maston," she said to him, dropping her voice lower. "Yet you use such words and even quote from the tomes."

"I am not a maston. Are you?"

Maia felt the probing nature of the question. She shook her head.

"I thought not," he said with a subtle nod. "My father was, yet he sired a wretched and would not claim me. I do not think well of mastons."

They separated and went down the line, exchanging partners three times before meeting up again. The time they spent apart passed in a blur. His hand grazed hers. So warm. His deep blue eyes were inquisitive.

"I have another question for you, my lady," he said, gazing down at her with a half smile.

"I will answer it if I can."

They twisted and went the other way as the circle reversed its order. Her feet felt light and easy—the dance was slow enough that it was not difficult to keep up with the changes.

"You are traveling with a kishion. Is he a threat to you, or a protector?"

A shiver of cold shot through Maia's stomach. "Why do you ask that?"

"Come, my lady. He has a dark look. I sense you are in danger with him. Even now, he is watching us too keenly. Will he try to kill you if you leave with me?"

Maia looked at him in surprise. "I am not leaving with you."

"That came out wrong. Let me try again. It is difficult talking with a murderer staring at you so intently."

"Staring at me?"

"No, at me! I know you do not trust me, but you trusted me enough for this dance. Thank you. What I want to know is if you can dismiss him. Did *you* hire him for protection or did another?"

Maia swallowed, needing to choose her words carefully. "I am with him by choice, Master Collier. If you tried to take me from here by force, he would hurt you . . . not me."

A proud little smile twitched on his mouth. "He could try. How good can such a man be to have earned so *many* scars?"

Maia looked at him in concern. "Do not provoke him, I beg you. He has seen twice as many winters as you or I."

"I do not intend to, my lady. I fear more for your safety than my own."

"Very generous. But we must depart this evening. When Jon Tayt returns, we will go. Thank you for the horses."

"It is my pleasure to help you," he said, dipping his head graciously. "Where are you bound?"

She smiled and shook her head.

"Another forbidden question. Let me try again. Do you play any instruments? You keep staring longingly at the minstrels."

"I love music."

"Ah, I would love to hear you play!" He nearly crowed with delight.

"Another time perhaps," Maia said, shaking her head.

"Then you concede there is a chance we may meet again?" he quipped. "That restores my faith."

"That is not what I meant," she said, trying not to quash his feelings.

"You injure me again, my lady," he said with a sigh. "You will not say where you are from. You will not tell me where you are bound. How will I find you to hear you play?"

She bit her lip, enjoying his teasing banter—probably too much. She needed to keep her thoughts clear. He was trying to trick her into revealing too much.

"If the Medium wills it, it will happen," she said softly.

He frowned at that.

The song came to an end, and she dropped in a curtsy as he delivered a stiff bow. There was no sign of Jon Tayt and she cursed the hunter's name under her breath.

"One more dance," Feint Collier said. "Your guide has not returned. Favor me with one more dance."

She looked at him, at the strange mixture of emotions on his face. He seemed almost alarmed, his blue eyes brooding with unsaid words. "Please. Just one more."

A strong surge of warring emotions threatened to topple her control. She had enjoyed dancing and felt slightly light-headed at the thrill of it. Here was a handsome man giving her attention in such an obvious and flattering way. But she was conflicted by the strong feelings of unease brought on by the belief—nay, the knowledge—that his intentions were not as honorable as he proclaimed. He had purposely separated her from her companions more than once. Yet she was completely lost in this situation, having never been the pointed focus of a man's attentions.

She looked around the room, feeling it spin slightly around her. Where was Jon Tayt? They needed to leave, but he was nowhere to be seen.

"Just one more," she said, feeling a sensation of guilt even as she said it. The prickle of apprehension she felt about accepting his offer was reason enough to rebuff him, yet there was a swelling sense of rebellion inside her as well. She had been denied even the simplest of pleasures since coming of age. Her father had allowed her to attend his court for a time, but while she had been outwardly included in the royal social circle, no one had ever dared ask her to dance. Most of the time, men were afraid to even speak with her.

"The newest dance at court is called the Volta," he said. "Do you know it?"

Maia looked at him and shook her head no. "I do not know the latest court dances."

"Then I will teach you," he said with a bow. He turned to the musicians and spoke loudly. "Play a galliard, but at twice the usual tempo." He began clapping his hands sharply. "That will work." The music twitched in the air, bringing with it a lively feel. The other dancers cleared away, which brought Maia and Collier to the attention of everyone in the room. The scrutiny made her wince inwardly, but it was too late to excuse herself without attracting even more notice.

Collier did not give her a chance to escape the situation.

"Side by side," he said, taking her hands and bringing her next to him. "Gather around." This last was addressed to the others. "Watch first, and then copy us. The Volta." He began a series of intricate steps, similar to a Pry-rian expression she had seen before but never learned. It took her several tries, but then she discovered the complexity and unraveled it.

"Well done," he praised, bringing her forward and then backward, repeating the movements. "Now a broader circle." He took her left hand in his and placed his right on the small of her back, guiding her around in a larger circle. Some of the other young dancers joined them, their faces beaming with the pleasure of learning a new court dance. Some were still struggling to do the footwork from the earlier part, but others were catching on.

"You are a wonderful dancer, Master Collier," she said.

"Such things are necessary at court, but it helps to have an accomplished partner," he replied, deflecting the praise. "This is not your first galliard, I think. Now for the twirl. Legs straight and push off my shoulders." Suddenly his hands seized her by the waist and he lifted her high in front of him. She pressed her hands against his shoulders and pushed as he twirled her around before setting her back down lightly. "Two more . . . ready and lift!"

She flew through the air again, her stomach gliding in her throat as he twirled her about a second time. It was exhilarating. And she heard several of the girls gasping with delight as their partners lifted them too.

"Now for the third one," Collier said, beaming at her as he raised her into the air again, causing her hair to fan out around her. She was too breathless to speak when he set her down.

"Last part," he said slyly, bringing up his elbow. He gestured for her to do the same and struck hers opposite with his. "Then back around again, the other way." She mirrored his movements, their forearms blocking each other as they turned and danced. Then his arm was around her waist and he led her to finish the circle.

She was flushed and giddy with pleasure by the end of it.

"Again!" he shouted, clapping fiercely, sending a feeling of pure pleasure shooting through her.

"My lady," came a warning voice at her ear. It was Jon Tayt. She turned and saw the look in his eyes, a smoldering brew of anger and panic. Argus growled next to him, pale fur glistening in the torchlight. "The king's men rode into town just now."

Her heart lurched. "We must go," she said.

"I thought the same," he said through clenched teeth. "Then I found you dancing. We must make haste!"

She did a half curtsy to Feint Collier. "Thank you, sir."

He stared at her intently, as if he could read through her if only he tried hard enough. "What concerns you? The soldiers? They will not care who is dancing."

"I must go," she insisted. The kishion had joined them now, his face a mask of anger and menace.

"The king's camp is leagues away, if not more," Collier replied, brushing it off. "There is no need to worry."

"We left the king's horses in the stables as you advised," Jon Tayt replied. "Someone will recognize the brand. We must go. Now!"

"Take the south road then," Collier said. "The riders come from the north. You remember the password in either case. Go." He stared hard at Maia and then bowed. "Thank you, my lady. I will treasure the memory."

"Thank you, Master Collier," she replied. The kishion handed her a pack and she slung it over her shoulder. They walked briskly to the rear doors of the inn, and the hunter opened them. She glanced back into the common room and saw Feint Collier standing there, arms folded, watching her leave. He had a hard look on his face. He nodded to her once.

She nodded in farewell and stepped into the night.

When the door shut behind her, Jon Tayt's words were sharp and angry. "My lady Maia, you have been amazingly foolish. Ach," he half growled, "another moment and we would have been trapped in there. At least twenty men rode into town wearing the king's livery, swords, and hauberks. Soldiers, my lady. The army is nearer than Collier reckons."

She swallowed her words and followed them into the night, but she soon noticed they were going east, not south.

"He said the south road—"

"Aye, and because *he* said it, I will not take it. I warned you from the first *not* to trust him."

"He has helped us so far, Jon Tayt." She felt herself bristling with defensiveness.

"He is the king's man," replied the hunter. "The Mark does not suffer traitors, and would not even make an exception for his half brother. I was picking up supplies and keeping an ear open for news when I learned he was here, which alarmed me. He clearly followed us. He is marking our trail to make it easier for the king's hunters to capture us. Take the south road. By Cheshu!"

She did not tell him about the flower in her saddlebag. She suspected Feint Collier was offering his assistance for another reason altogether, and it flattered her. But Jon Tayt was wise to be so distrusting. She respected him even more for it.

"I was only waiting for you to return," she answered, trying to keep the peevishness from her voice. "I knew we needed to leave."

He snorted and spat. "I had taken you for a sensible woman. A rare thing to find, I can tell you that. But I presume you lost your head when the music started, as most women do." He grumbled to himself. "By Cheshu, dancing with the king's collier."

Still, Maia did not regret it. Could not regret it, even if he were right about the nature of Collier's attentions. The panic she had felt began to subside as the stars twinkled into view in the dark sky above them. In truth, she wished she could have stayed back at the inn, enjoying the cheese and broth. She would have danced all night had she been allowed. All of the years she had practiced and learned the steps were not wasted. She would remember this night, this taste of a life that had been taken from her.

Take the north road.

The whisper in her mind startled her. A sliver of silver moon emerged from the tips of the pine trees at the edge of the town. As she stared at it, her heart burned with emotion from the dance at the inn. She wanted to see Collier again, but that would be foolish. Suddenly, a throb of warning touched her mind and the kystrel started to burn. She stopped walking and clutched her chest, feeling the heat emanating from the amulet.

"What is it?" the kishion asked, noticing her hesitation immediately.

She stared at him, not sure what to say.

"Lady Maia?" Jon Tayt asked with concern.

She grimaced, feeling again the pulse of warmth and warning in her heart. "We must take the north road," she announced.

Jon Tayt stared at her in stupefaction.

"That puts us on the path to the king's army," the kishion said.

"I know," she said, shaking her head. "I . . . I cannot explain it. I feel that we need to go that way. Urgently."

Jon Tayt scratched his neck and winced. "That does not sound right, my lady."

"I know it does not. It goes against common sense. We were walking and I—" She sighed. "The north road."

Jon Tayt looked at the kishion and then back at her. "It is the last place they would look or suspect we would go."

The kishion frowned. "You have not directed us like this since the Leerings. It is the Medium?"

Maia nodded.

Jon Tayt threw up his hands. "It goes against all wisdom and common sense. Why not? What do you say, Argus?"

The boarhound barked once.

Maia knelt in front of him and stroked his fur.

"We will be surrounded by the king's army in moments," Jon Tayt said. "I want to state that now in case you decide after we are captured that it was a bad idea."

She straightened and looked him in the eye. "Trusting these feelings, as rarely as they come, has kept us alive so far. I do not know what lies ahead. But I trust it."

***

They had not traveled far down the north road before they were surrounded by riders.

CHAPTER THIRTEEN

Treason

The sunlight came slanting through the windows of the chancellor's tower and glimmered off the polished aurichalcum of the tome on Maia's lap. She loved tomes—loved the meticulous engravings so gently and delicately inscribed. Not only was a tome a thing of polished beauty, but it revealed the beauty of the writer's mind. Each tome was filled with the wisdom of the ages, scrawled by hand and etched into the metal pages to be preserved for centuries. You could learn about a man from his thoughts, from what he found important. Some learners chose to fill their tomes with extensive translations of one man's thoughts . . . an Aldermaston's, perhaps, or one of the founders of the Dochte Mandar. The tome in her hand was a mixture of both, for Chancellor Walraven always strived to stretch the boundaries of what he knew.

She looked up from the sheaf of aurichalcum, pressing her warm hand against its cool metal. She was sick with worry, her insides clenching and twisting with the dread of anticipated news. Her entire future hinged on the outcome of the trial, as did that of her father's kingdom.

To help ease the agonizing wait, she had sought refuge in the chancellor's tower and tried to calm her nerves by reading his tranquil words.

The chancellor had explained the situation to her in great detail before leaving for Muirwood Abbey. When Maia had learned he was bound for that abbey, she had begged him to bring word to her mother. Though he was, as always, sympathetic to her cause, he had refused, as he could not accommodate her without compromising his relationship with her father. It had been obvious from his distraught and haggard visage that the immensity of the problem weighed on him like stones. She had asked him in a whisper to explain the situation fully, to trust her to be discreet and never betray him.

"But what if not betraying me requires you to betray your lord father?" he had asked her wistfully, his eyes settling on her with compassion. "I would not ask you to do that, child. Your first allegiance must be to your Family."

Then he had told her what he could of the complicated situation. As she knew, her parents had been married by irrevocare sigil. Only Maia's mother had grounds to dissolve the marriage, but if she were to relinquish her claims as the king's wife and queen, Maia would be disinherited formally and forever. Her banishment would become permanent, as fixed as an irrevocare sigil itself. The queen would not do that.

So the king was trying to dissolve the union politically and divorce her according to the laws of the Dochte Mandar. That would mean bringing Comoros under the power of the Chief Scribe of Naess, and the maston Families of the realm were against such an extreme measure, for it would give the Dochte Mandar unprecedented authority in the realm.

So a trial had been ordered to take place in Comoros to legally disavow the marriage. Only there was one problem. The queen refused to attend. She had claimed the right of sanctuary at Muirwood Abbey, and as a maston herself, she could not be forced to leave the grounds, no matter how much her husband blustered or threatened her.

Maia rubbed her shoulders, trying to suppress the shivering. Her soul was full of blackness and evil thoughts. She was proud of her mother, proud of her strength and her convictions. But Maia herself had no ability to claim the rights of sanctuary. She was a political pawn. Her mother had asked repeatedly for Maia to be sent to Muirwood to visit her, but each request was refused.

The king had threatened to march an army to Muirwood to take her by force, thereby breaking another maston oath, but the noble Families of the realm refused to acquiesce or obey the summons should he choose to make good on his threat. More and more of the ancient Families withdrew from court and stayed in their own Hundreds. In their place, a web of courtiers had emerged to insinuate themselves into her father's good graces and sow discord in his ears. Lady Deorwynn's Family were chief among these.

So it had been arranged for the trial to take place at Muirwood itself, where the Aldermaston of Muirwood would preside over it. Maia would have given anything to attend. The bitter feelings between her parents were creating a rift in the kingdom. It was doing the same thing to her heart.

She stared out the windows, enormous dread weighing down on her, and watched as a single rider entered the castle bailey down below. Her heart shuddered with the premonition of the news, and she set down the tome and began to pace the tower, wringing her hands and feeling sick enough to vomit.

There was a commotion on the stairs below, and she heard the clud of many boots ascending the tower. Were these soldiers coming to arrest her? She felt herself go pale with fear, and she tugged at her sleeve nervously. Before she had the chance to act, the door opened. She saw the felt hats of the soldiers first, followed by the maston swords belted to their waists. They were knights! She stared at them in surprise, and some of them gave her puzzled looks in return.

"What are you doing here, Lady Maia?" one of them asked.

"Who is it?" came a voice from lower down the stairwell.

"The king's daughter."

Maia swallowed as a middle-aged man reached the top of the steps. He wore a fine fur cloak, a green satin doublet, and—most importantly—the gold chain of the office of chancellor around his neck. Her eyes widened. What had become of her friend?

"Greetings, Lady Maia," the newcomer said, bowing quickly. "Ah, here to welcome me to my chamber."

"My lord, forgive me," she stuttered, her mind whirling end over end. "I was anticipating—"

"Walraven's return, no doubt. Yes, you were close to him, I daresay. He was fond of you as well, to be sure. Well, this creates an awkward moment, but we will survive it. Your father has named me as lord chancellor of the realm."

She stared at him in blank shock.

He smiled benignly at her look. "We have not met, Lady Maia, but let me remedy that. I am Tomas Morton."

"I know you by reputation, my lord," Maia said, surprised. "You are a lawyer in the city and famous for your writings on ancient maston customs. You wrote a treatise on the reign of Lia

Demont and the unified kingdom she ruled when the mastons fled these shores."

He smiled at the tribute and bowed again. "No doubt your highness has not read the book yourself, as women are forbidden to read, but I have sympathy for you there, for Lia Demont was not allowed to read until she was older."

"It was read to me," Maia said sheepishly. It was a half lie. She *had* read the book herself too.

"Well, perhaps we can discuss it someday. But greetings aside, I did not expect to find you up here upon my return from the trial at Muirwood."

"You were there?" Maia pressed.

"Of course. That is where the king appointed me his new chancellor. I am sorry to bring evil tidings to you, Lady Maia. Your father has ordered the expulsion of the Dochte Mandar from Comoros. Immediately. Irrevocably. Illegally, I might add, but such it is."

Maia sat down on the window seat she had so often occupied in her childhood, unable to summon the presence of mind to speak.

"You are amazed, to be sure," Chancellor Morton said.

"I am," Maia whispered. She looked up at him and then swept her gaze over the knight-mastons who had gathered around them.

"Let me explain, as best I can, my lady." Before continuing, he wiped his mouth and adjusted his own felt hat, as if he were loath to relive the experience. "The trial did not go as your father had hoped," he finally said. "Queen Catrin, your mother, refused to accept the authority of the court or its legal mandate to disinherit her. She was defiant, but very humble, and she begged her husband to reconsider his rash desires." He tapped his lips, growing silent. "I tell you, my lady, she was very convincing. She spoke with poise and passion, warning all that a great calamity would befall the kingdoms if your father's breach of the maston decrees continued unchecked. On her knees, she begged your father's pardon and committed herself to overlook his transgressions and mend the marriage." His voice grew quiet. "My lady, the Medium was there so powerfully, we all felt it. We sensed the danger brooding in the room. She said we have fallen away from the maston rites, that we have forgotten our duty to rebuild the abbeys. She said we have been blinded by the machinations of the Dochte Mandar, who pit the kingdoms against one another and seek to destroy unity through intrigue."

Maia felt her heart bursting with pride for her mother. Tears pricked her eyes, but she would not let them fall. A timid flame of hope kindled inside her.

"What then, my lord?" Maia said in a hushed whisper.

"The king was silent. He was fearfully silent. The noble Families of the realm had all sent emissaries to try and persuade him to reconcile with your mother. She knelt in front of him, tears streaming down her cheeks. Everyone was moved. The king demanded proof of her accusation against the Dochte Mandar, proof that they were plotting against the realm." He walked to the edge of the chancellor's desk and picked up an ink-stained quill. "The chancellor's own hand condemned him. The queen said they needed to look no farther than the chancellor's own satchel bag for evidence of treachery. There they would find a letter addressed to the chief scribe of the Dochte Mandar plotting against the realm, planning for a time when the Dochte Mandar might take full authority of Comoros. You can imagine the uproar, my lady. Only the Medium could have told her what was in the bag. The king ordered for the chancellor's kystrel to be ripped from his neck and melted by a blacksmith, but he was not wearing one when he was apprehended. Even now, I have orders to expel every Dochte Mandar from the kingdom, save for Walraven."

Maia's eyes widened. "Why? My lord, is he to be punished?"

"He is under guard, my lady. He will not be permitted to leave Comoros. Not even his bones. He knows too much."

Maia stood and rubbed her arms, her heart pounding fast. She had trusted Chancellor Walraven. She had trusted him implicitly. Had he been using her all along? Was she one of his pawns in this terrible web of intrigue? Her heart was breaking at the mere thought of it.

"What of my mother?" Maia pleaded.

Chancellor Morton stared at her with sympathy. He sighed. "Catrin is still banished from court. Your father refuses to reconcile with her."

Maia felt as if she had been struck a second physical blow.

"His Majesty the King has told me that you are forbidden to see or speak with her. There will be no messages delivered. That is his will."

She stared at him in horror. "Lord Chancellor, this is unjust!"

"I agree, Lady Maia. The King is very wroth. He did not get his way, and he learned that Walraven betrayed him. You can be sure, he is quite angry still and lashes out as a man in pain is wont to do, injuring the very people who are trying to heal him. I am but a humble lawyer, Lady Maia, but I am also a maston. I will speak the truth in plainness and wisdom, as the Medium sees fit to bestow on me. We will purge the realm of the Dochte Mandar. Then I will seek to reconcile you to your father. Until then, be patient, my lady."

Maia nodded gravely, her heart blistering with heat, and descended the steps of the tower. As she left, she heard the chancellor say, "Search the entire castle. We must round up every last one."

The main hall was engulfed in activity, and as the news spread, people jostled past each other unseeing. Maia was quickly lost in the crowd. She bumped into the edges of the wall, nearly tripping on the scattered floor rushes. The noise of the common room became deafening, and she longed for the solitude of the chancellor's tower. She knew she would not be permitted refuge there again.

"Lady Maia."

She barely heard the words through the fog in her mind. Someone touched her shoulder.

Maia turned, confused, to see a page. He was about her own age and dressed in the king's livery.

"He bid me give you this," the boy murmured softly, holding out a small package of folded paper with a wax seal. The seal was affixed with the king's ring—the ring that the chancellor wore.

She looked at the boy, who glanced nervously around, thrust the package in her hand, and then vanished into the crowd.

Maia hastily retreated to the gardens behind the castle grounds, crushing the small packet in her hand. Her heart pounded with anxiety. The packet was heavy, as if it carried coins. But she suspected—nay, she *knew*—what was in it. The wax of the seal rubbed against her palm. She fought down her emotions, struggling to breathe, and found a quiet stone bench amidst the tall hedges. She glanced around furtively, making certain she was alone and had not been followed, then sank onto the bench and broke the seal.

She opened the stiff paper and saw the first words of blotchy ink. Chancellor Walraven's handwriting. The edges of the kystrel peeked out beneath the next fold in the paper. Her heart thrummed with fear and excitement as she set the medallion on her lap. Then, smoothing the paper out, she started to read.

Lady Maia,

I did what I did for you. Your father is determined to abandon your mother and you, his rightful heir. All his thoughts are bent on it, and as you know, the Medium responds to our deepest thoughts and emotions. I fear the curse he is bringing on his kingdom as a result. To delay this collapse, your mother and I made an alliance at Muirwood. I will fall so that you may rise. You are the rightful and lawful heir to the throne of Comoros. There are no grounds for your father to forsake his marriage. I have done my best to shield you, but it is not enough. He will punish you for his failure to rid himself of his wife. In so doing, he will punish the land.

The Dochte Mandar will be expelled. When we are gone, you will soon discover that our presence held at bay a malevolent force. You will feel the presence of unseen beings who will wish to do you harm. I can no longer protect you from them, but I leave this kystrel for you.

I may never see you again, Lady Maia. I had hoped to serve under you when you became queen. I fear I may not live to see that day. My only regret is that I never sought to become a maston myself. Had I served the Medium with but half the zeal as I served your father, then it would not have left me naked to mine enemies. Until we meet again, in Idumea.

Your servant.

Maia felt the tears slip from her lashes and drip onto the folded paper, smudging some of the words. She struggled to rein in her feelings, but she could not, and hung her head, weeping softly in the gardens.

Chancellor Walraven had sacrificed his position, his eminence, and his future to preserve her right to inherit the throne. To stall the decline her father's debauchery had caused in court and throughout the kingdom. Weeping was an unfamiliar act. She did not like the way it made her tremble and shake, her nose drip, the wildness it threatened to unleash inside her. She wiped her nose on her sleeve, trying to calm herself. What a strange mixture of emotions. Gratitude and sadness, hope and desolation. She would not be able to see her mother. She would not be able to see her friend, her mentor—the man who had taught her to read even though it was forbidden by his own people. She would remember that. She would always remember *him*. She sighed, struggling to tame her tears until she finally succeeded. She wiped her mouth and read the letter twice more.

Once she had it memorized, she turned her attention to the kystrel. Cupping it in her hand, she felt the hard edges of its woven, whorl-like pattern. It did not represent any specific creature. It was just a ring of interwoven leaves that were neither uniform nor precise. A kystrel—named after the falcon. A small bronze chain was affixed to it.

Maia stared at it, remembering that long-ago day when she had watched the chancellor use his kystrel to summon mice and rats to the tower. At the time, he had said she was too young to use one. He had warned that her years as an adolescent would be full of turbulent emotions—a storm of feelings she would have to learn to control before using a kystrel. He had promised to give her one when she became an adult. The fact that he had done so now meant that he did not expect to live to see that day. The thought grieved her.

Maia straightened the chain and slung it around her neck. She waited, pensive, trying to see if she would feel any different. But she felt the same as she always did. Nothing had changed.

She tucked the kystrel into her bodice so that its cool metal was pressed against her skin, then folded the paper tightly and hid it in her girdle. She wondered if she would see Walraven again.

He will be dead in a fortnight.

Maia stopped, eyes wide. She had heard the whisper in her thoughts as loudly as if someone had spoken them. It made gooseflesh spread across her arms and neck and a shiver go down her spine.

A fortnight later, when news arrived of Walraven's death, she learned to trust the voice of the Medium.

The Naestors fear us greatly because the Dochte Mandar have taught them to. They have witnessed the evidence of the Medium's destruction when a people violates laws of justice, honor, and compassion. Thoughts bring good or ill, depending on the prevailing temperaments. More than anything else, the Naestors fear the annihilation they witnessed after coming to our shores and the mastons who, despite the fervor of their faith in the Medium, could not prevent it. You will learn, great-granddaughter, that the Dochte Mandar took upon themselves the duty to control the feelings of the population. They seek to prevent another Blight. What happens to the flood when the levees are stripped away?

—Lia Demont, Aldermaston of Muirwood Abbey

CHAPTER FOURTEEN

Myriad Ones

Y ou say the watchword is 'Comoros'?"

Maia stared up at the captain, high on his saddle. He was a big man with a blond turf of stubble on the dome of his head and a trimmed goatee. He had an easy smile, but his eyes bored into hers and stared up and down her body. A twitch at the corner of his mouth flashed and was gone.

All around these men, Maia could feel the sniffling, snuffling reek of the Myriad Ones. Oily blackness gripped her heart. There was a mewling sound, inaudible to the ear, that felt like the whine of a bow driven over a lute string at an awkward angle. It made her teeth hurt and her stomach shrivel.

Jon Tayt hefted an axe in his hand, and the hound Argus growled threateningly.

There were twelve men in all—each on horseback, dressed in the king's colors, and carrying weapons. Three had crossbows.

"Let us pass," Maia said, her voice sounding hollow even to her.

The captain of the riders looked at her. His eyes burned with desire. "Kill the dog and the hunter. Bring her to my tent."

Jon Tayt planted his foot and hurled the axe at the nearest man holding a crossbow. The blade snapped the taut crossbeam, and the mechanism shattered in his hands. Argus snarled and barked furiously, yapping at the horses' legs as he darted in and out between them, causing the steeds to snort and buck at the commotion.

Jon Tayt drew another axe and sent it winging into the chest of a second crossbowman, toppling him from the saddle.

The kishion struck from the shadows of the road. He had skulked into the darkness the moment they heard the riders' approach, and now he emerged, digging his dagger into the captain's leg, making him howl with pain.

Someone grabbed a fistful of Maia's hair and yanked, dragging her backward. She tripped as her attacker's horse jostled her and pain shot across her scalp. Reaching back, she grabbed the man's gloved wrist and tried to pull him off his horse, but all she managed to do was collide with the beast.

"I have her!"

Ignoring the pain, Maia twisted to get a better look at her attacker, only stopping when she saw a dagger dangling from a sheath on the man's belt. She let go of the wrist and grabbed the hilt, pulling it free.

Another horse boxed her in on the other side, and two arms reached down to pull her up by the armpits. The motion threw her off balance, but at least her hair was free. She struggled against his grip, but he easily turned her over, stomach down, and gave the horse a sharp kick to get it moving. In a series of quick movements, Maia stabbed his thigh with the dagger, drew it out, and stabbed him a second time in the hip. Grunting with pain, he dropped the reins and grabbed her wrist to prevent a third strike. He swore at her, the words laced with anger and pain.

Something yanked on her boot and pulled her off the horse. She landed sharply on the road, the impact knocking the wind out of her. Argus crouched over her, defensively snapping and barking with savage fury.

"By the Blood, kill them all!" the captain roared.

Maia struggled to kneel, trying to breathe through the fiery pain shooting through her lungs. There were so many soldiers. Hooves trampled dangerously near to her, one nearly crushing her hand. She choked for breath, feeling a surging panic.

Dust clotted in her eyes, stinging them. She hunkered down, becoming as small as she could, but a horse still knocked her over. She was going to be trampled. Argus yipped with pain.

Maia could feel the Myriad Ones swarming her, drawn to her terrified emotions, feasting on them. There were hundreds of them—no, perhaps a thousand or more. She could feel their effect on the crazed horses and the lust-filled soldiers, in every blade of grass that surrounded them. The immensity of the feeling swept over her, like the stars glittering in the sky above and the crescent-shaped moon. She felt them probing against her clothes, rooting into her skin—hungry to be part of her, to claim her, to squirm their way inside her. Her heart wrinkled with dread, and she felt a burning sensation in her skin.

Maia lifted her head, drawing on the power of the kystrel.

She blasted the Myriad Ones away from her, sending them scattering about like leaves before a hurricane. She conquered the ache in her stomach enough to struggle to her feet. Clamping an arm around her middle, she lifted her head and stared at the wounded captain, who gazed back at her with terror. Her eyes were glowing silver, she knew that well enough, so he clearly knew she was using a kystrel.

She snuffed out his lust like a candle doused in a bucket. His courage, his fierceness, his bravado—she wrapped these up in the tangled veins of the kystrel and stripped him of everything that made him a man. His horse bucked with horror, and he slipped off the back, crashing to the road in a heap of gibbering fear.

The soldiers saw her and knew her for what she was.

"By the Blood!" someone screamed.

"Kill her! Kill her!"

One crossbowman still lived. He lifted the stock of his weapon and aimed for her heart. Maia sent out a blast of fear, throwing it in every direction like a shattered bottle of glass. The jagged bits flung into everyone. The crossbowman blinked, threw down his weapon, and spurred his horse to flee. Maia whipped the horses with her mind, making them believe they were being hunted by lions. Rather than respond to bit or bridle, they charged recklessly and quickly as far as they could.

Maia stood there like a beacon of fire, her shoulders drawn in, her cloak whipping about her as the crackle and pop of thunder rippled overhead. The winds were drawn to her, and she no longer felt any sign of the Myriad Ones. They were all cowering and skulking away from her.

Argus whined and cowered from her, so she let go of the kystrel's power, feeling it drain from her slowly. Then came exhaustion, as it always did. There were a few twitching soldiers on the ground, and the kishion went to them one by one, snuffing out their lives.

Jon Tayt collected his axes, his expression dark. He glanced at her without speaking as he finished his dark task, then walked over to where the captain lay sniveling with fear. Jon Tayt was not a tall man, but he towered over the fallen captain.

"Never threaten a man's hound," he said in a flat, unemotional voice. Maia turned away as the captain was killed.

***

When they finally rested that night in the woods, Maia dreamed about her past again. She awoke, the dream still fresh in her mind, her emotions as vivid and real as if she had only just been informed of Chancellor Walraven's death. All these years later, she could still remember every word of the note he had written to her.

Had I served the Medium with but half the zeal as I served your father, then it would not have left me naked to mine enemies. Until we meet again, in Idumea.

It was the custom of kings and queens to choose the wisest and most able counselors in the realm to advise them. The practice of consulting with a Privy Council was centuries old, dating back to before the mastons fled the kingdoms. The chancellor always led the Privy Council's discussions, and while Walraven's influence and power had not always been appreciated, it had always been felt. He had been the most powerful Dochte Mandar in the realm . . . moreover, he had been her staunchest advocate and friend.

The memories brought a painful ache.

She opened her eyes to ground herself in reality. She was tucked into the shade of a fallen tree whose exposed roots twisted like a tangle of vines. The kishion sat nestled in the cover of ferns with her, his eyes closed, his breathing shallow. A small creek murmured next to them.

It was midmorning, but Maia still felt exhausted. They had walked through the night to put distance between themselves and the scene of slaughtered soldiers. Several times during the night they had listened as hunting horns blasted in the trees. There was no doubt the king's army was hunting them now. After finding a suitable shelter in the ferns beneath the fallen tree, Jon Tayt had gone back to cover their trail and make false ones. He still had not returned.

Maia rubbed her eyes, careful not to rouse the kishion from his nap. Argus lay near her, she noticed, head resting on his paws. She reached out and stroked his fur, apologizing in her own way for frightening him the previous night.

Birds chirped in the tree heights, and the drone of insects offered the illusion of tranquility. The woods were full of the king's men, she realized. But the woods were vast. It would not be easy for the others to find them if they held very still.

As she stroked Argus, she thought about Walraven again, remembering him with fondness as well as sadness. His actions—his sacrifice—had resulted in the Dochte Mandar being expelled from the realm. And he had known, prophetically, that things would go horribly wrong.

The news of evil had begun with his death. Her father had summoned Walraven to Comoros to stand trial for treason. Everyone knew that he would be condemned and executed, for his own hand had betrayed him. But Walraven took ill on the journey and died of a fever and chills before reaching the city. His body was interred in an ossuary in a mausoleum. There were whispers that he had been poisoned, but the coroners found no evidence of that. Because he had died a traitor, his lands and wealth were forfeited to the Crown. The Dochte Mandar were all given a fortnight to vacate the realm or risk execution.

When they left, the devastation began.

Word came next of a pack of wild boars roaming the hinterlands, besetting villages and killing children. The hunters sent to destroy the pack had failed. Wolves began marauding through the woods as well. Without the Dochte Mandar, the many Leerings in the kingdom were useless, forcing people to carry water or harvest fuel for fire. There were mastons, of course, who could and did use them, but their number was small compared with the Dochte Mandar. The extra work angered the people—a feeling that began to fester.

Soon riots broke out across the kingdom, but that was not the worst of it—tales started to pour in from around the realm, each more horrid than the last. A man with a scythe had gone on a rampage in his village, killing innocent villagers. A mother had drowned her three children in a well. A young man had set fire to a barn full of his village's grain right before winter. It seemed that every fortnight, another tale of woe would arrive, and the court would gossip and statutes would be passed forbidding this or that. But while a deadly spring that poisoned all who drank from it could be cleansed, this madness kept no pattern. No, it was mercurial and erratic, which meant no one knew when or where the next tragedy would strike. The only commonality was that such things had never occurred under the gaze of the Dochte Mandar. Expelling them from the realm had fundamentally altered Comoros. The people began to fear it was another Blight.

Maia brushed her hair back from her ear, listening to the clicking noise of a series of insects speaking to each other across the vastness of the woods.

Suddenly Argus's head lifted and his ears shot up. His pale fur twitched. A low growl rumbled in his throat.

Maia reached over and touched the kishion's knee.

His eyes opened immediately.

"I am sorry—"

She pressed her fingers against her own mouth, signaling for him to be silent.

He rubbed his eyes and shifted forward onto one knee, cocking his head. Then, motioning for her to stay put, he stepped into the soft mud of the creek. The water did not even go up to his knees, but it muffled his footsteps as he ducked under the fallen tree and disappeared from sight. Maia felt a rumble in Argus's throat and she patted him to quiet him. His ears quivered and his tail had stopped wagging.

The kishion returned shortly thereafter and motioned for her to join him in the water. She grabbed her pack and followed, plunging into the cold water, mud churning beneath her boots. She ducked under the bridge of the fallen tree, trying to keep her cloak from being soaked along with her skirts, and came through into sunlight and solid land on the other side. A bird fluttered past, trilling a song.

The kishion awaited her just past the tree.

"I hear voices coming this way," he whispered in her ear. "Keep low and follow."

Maia obeyed, hunching down and following him as he trailed along the creek, staying inside the lapping waters. The ferns offered some cover, but she knew it was not much. Her heart thrummed with anxiety. Argus, who trailed behind her, wagged his tail and stared into the woods.

A few moments later, she could make out Jon Tayt's voice.

"I tell you, I have not seen a soul these last three days except for you lads. If I had, I would tell you. I am just a humble woodsman who fells trees for a living. Do you think the king would hire me? I can split wood faster than any man—"

"Be silent!" barked another voice. "Can you not stop talking?"

"If that pleases you, my lord. I was just saying that an army needs wood for fires, does it not? I can cut a cord of wood faster than you can put on your boots."

Maia smiled in spite of herself. She recognized that Jon Tayt had been captured and was trying to warn her by talking loudly.

"Be still, man!" said another, cuffing him.

Argus growled.

Maia tried to grab at the dog's ruff, but Argus broke through the brush of ferns and ran to his master.

"A boarhound!" someone shouted.

The kishion uttered a low curse.

Twigs snapped behind them. The kishion whirled, dagger in his hand, but something whistled and struck his head, knocking him down. He did not move. Maia dropped down beside him and turned him over. She feared an arrow had pierced him, but there was no mark on his body. He was quite unconscious.

Maia heard the whistling noise again and something hard struck her temple.

Her eyes filled with blackness and she slumped into the bed of ferns, joining him in oblivion.

CHAPTER FIFTEEN

The Mark of Dahomey

It was the throbbing of Maia's temple that woke her. As she struggled to open her eyes, she felt herself bounced and jostled so much she quickly lost the sense of up and down. Her wrists were bound together, her arms were bound to her sides—her ankles were secured as well. She struggled for a moment against the bonds and tried to calm the swelling panic that speared her heart.

Her movement had a sway and bounce to it, and after a few moments of startled awareness, she realized that she was being carried. Not on horseback, but on a litter of some kind, two long branches or poles with a blanket or cloak slung between them to cushion her. One man marched in front of her, another behind her. The sky was draining of color as she blinked, the woods filling with purple shadows. She could sense the Myriad Ones everywhere, thronging to the procession as it moved through the trees.

She tried to quiet her heart and focus her thoughts. It was not too late—she could still summon her magic. She could—

It was then Maia realized that the kystrel was gone.

She was defenseless against the Myriad Ones, and she now understood why they were flocking so thickly to her. They were drawn to her helplessness. She could sense their greedy thoughts as they whirled beside her in the twilight, waiting for full dark to attack her, to feed on her fears, to worm their way inside her skin, to steal her will and supplant it with their own. She began to wrestle against the bonds, her terror mounting with every hammerstroke in her chest.

"She is rousing," one of the soldiers muttered.

"Do not speak, lass," another warned. "Or we have orders to gag you."

She twisted against the litter, trying to count the men. She could see a dozen or more, all wearing the tunics of Dahomey. Trailing after her litter, she could see the kishion and Jon Tayt stumbling forward, hands bound in front of them with chains, pulled along by a rope secured to their bindings. Blood smeared across half of the kishion's face. His hooded eyes stared at her, searching her face. He said nothing. His expression was hard as stone, implacable. She knew he was plotting how to escape.

Jon Tayt was dejected, his chin lowered in shame as he walked. She could not see any weapons on him. She was surprised, and startled, to see that his boarhound had been spared. Argus padded beside him, jaws muzzled with leather straps, tail bent low between his legs. Her heart sang with relief at the sight of him, but while her friends were alive now, their futures were unsure.

The Myriad Ones hummed around her gleefully, reveling in her capture, her defenselessness.

"You found her?" came a voice from ahead. She strained to see, but her position forbade it. The jostling walk came to a halt.

"Aye, Captain. The hunt has ended. We ran her to ground."

"We found her before Corriveaux did. Is she alive?"

"Aye, Captain. As His Majesty ordered. A little bruised, but unharmed. What do we do with the two traitors?" He snorted and spat.

"They will stretch by a rope come dawn. They butchered the watch, remember? Take them away. No food. Keep them under heavy guard. If they try to flee, kill them. Do you have her medallion?"

"It is right here, Captain."

Maia heard the whisper of metal from the kystrel's chain as it was placed in the captain's hand. The Myriad Ones were gleeful, and she felt them pressing closer, snuffling against the taut fabric of the litter. It made her stomach sour.

"Set her down."

The men carrying her litter lowered her into the brush. One of them slit the ropes at her ankles with a dagger. Two others hoisted her up onto wobbling legs. Someone steadied her. The captain carried a torch, revealing a face with a blond goatee and crooked teeth. He raised the torch and stared at her, eyeing her with animosity. The chain from her kystrel gleamed brightly in his hand.

"The king wishes to see her?" one of the soldiers asked curiously.

"Aye," the captain said with a trace of smugness. "He's with Feint Collier right now. Collier has seen her before, and the king wants him to identify her. She is as described." He looked her up and down, his eyes narrowing. "Wine-colored dress. Dark hair. A beauty. The eyes are not glowing, though." He smiled shrewdly.

"I think we have the girl. If you will, lass, follow me to the king's pavilion."

A band of ten soldiers walked with her, flanking her from behind. Maia's eyes were pinned to the chain dangling from the captain's hand. Her muscles were bunched and sore, and her head still throbbed. She looked back and watched as Jon Tayt and the kishion were led a different way with Argus. It pained her to see them marched to their deaths. She grieved for them, but she was determined to plead with the king for their lives. Not that he would listen to her.

Myriad Ones were everywhere in the king's camp. They hung over it like the smoke from the dozens of cooking fires. The men were bedding down for the night—some of the fires had spits roasting meat across them, and she could both hear the clank of cups and smell the wine within them. Everything and everyone was filthy, and she wrinkled her nose at the stench. Some of the soldiers leered at her as she passed them, others butted each other and pointed at her. She drew the eyes of everyone in the camp. Her stomach quailed with fear, but she put on a brave face. Somehow, she had to get the kystrel back. With it, she knew she could scatter the army and send them running. Without it, she was powerless.

In the center of the camp was a cluster of huge pavilions. Some were still being assembled, but the main one—the king's— was already erect with a pennant fluttering from a pole at the center. Guards were stationed at the entrance, and she could see the lanterns illuminating the interior. The air was muggy and hot and she felt a bead of sweat trickle down her cheek. She mustered her courage, preparing to face the man she had been promised to marry as an infant.

The captain showed the kystrel to the guards stationed outside the tent. She looked away, unable to bear the sight of it in his hand, and saw several horses tethered nearby—one of them Feint Collier's cream-colored stallion. She dreaded seeing him again under these circumstances, but maybe he could help her escape? The thought of being near him again so soon after their dance made her stomach flutter. Jon Tayt had said Collier could not be trusted, but she secretly hoped the hunter was mistaken. She would have to be careful of what she said in front of the king. She did not want to incriminate Collier if she could avoid it.

The guards parted the curtain and the captain walked in first, ducking beneath the heavy folds of fabric before turning and ushering her between the poles supporting the entryway. To Maia's surprise, there was a Leering with a lantern hanging from its jaws on each side. She could sense their power as she passed them. Once she was inside the tent, the feeling of the Myriad Ones faded.

The ground was carpeted with bearskins. A small brazier filled with sizzling coals sat at the center of the room. The top of the pavilion was open, allowing the smoke to escape outside. The fabric of the pavilion was pale, decorated with purple trim and a design of strange flowers and runes.

There were several people inside the pavilion, but the first person she noticed was Feint Collier. He did not look like a man about to be decapitated for treason. He stood beside a man to whom he bore a pronounced familial resemblance—they were almost of a height, though the king was shorter, and they were both handsome with dark hair and broad shoulders. The main difference was that the king looked slightly younger, wore a colorful doublet, and glittered with jewels, from the earring in his right lobe to the rings glittering on his fingers and the jeweled saber at his side. Even his belt was studded with gems.

Maia dropped to one knee and bowed her head in respect. Her stomach churned with conflicting emotions. She knew the protocols of the Dahomeyjan court and wondered how long she would be able to preserve her secret without telling an outright lie to the king.

"My lord," the captain said, "I bring your captive as you commanded. The killers who accompanied her have been confined and await your orders. We found a tree of suitable height."

"Thank you, Captain."

Maia was startled at how much the king's voice resembled Collier's. Even in this they were alike.

"As you asked, we stripped her of this before bringing her to your lordship."

She heard the sound of the kystrel chain unraveling. Glancing up, she could see it dangling from the captain's gloved fingers. If her arms were not bound, her wrists wreathed in ropes, she would have leaped for it. The woven strands of the kystrel sang to her, called to her. It was *her* magic. It was also her only hope of escape.

The king walked forward, looking at the kystrel as if it were a dangerous serpent. He gingerly took it from the captain, barely touching it with his own gloved hand, and then walked over to a small camp table and set it down by a jewelry box. It gleamed and Maia hungered for it. She kept her eyes downcast.

"Leave us," the king ordered.

"My lord?" the captain asked warily, his goatee twitching with nervousness.

"She is bound with ropes, Captain, and my collier will run her through if she tries anything foolish. Depart."

"As you wish, Your Majesty," the captain said, and he did as ordered, leading his men out of the pavilion. The evening shadows had deepened, but there was sufficient light in the pavilion. The interior did not smell of the filth of the camp, and she noticed some incense sticks poking from the lip of the brazier. The two men stared at her as she waited on her throbbing knee.

"Well, Your Majesty," the king said with a snort. "I shall leave the two of you alone to talk."

Maia's head jerked up with startled surprise. The king stroked his chin, winked at Feint Collier, and then walked to the opposite side of the pavilion, parted a secret fold, and disappeared.

Maia stared in disbelief.

Collier scratched the corner of his eye, looking a little abashed, and then walked over to help her to her feet.

"You?" Maia whispered, her breath tremulous. She was bewildered.

"I am whoever I want to be," Collier replied. "It is one of the many privileges of being a king. For you, I am Feint Collier. To many, I am called the Mark of Dahomey, though I resent the nickname. People believe whatever they want to believe anyway." He unsheathed a hunting dirk from his belt and walked behind her. She felt a prickle of apprehension and fear before the ropes binding her arms were severed and fell away. Her wrists were still secured together, but the gesture gave her a sliver of hope.

"Welcome to Dahomey, Princess Marciana," he said, touching a lock of hair by her neck. "Or do you truly prefer *Maia*, as I have been informed?"

She shivered at the familiarity of his touch and whirled, backing away from him. "You deceived me."

He smiled proudly. "Thank you."

"You knew who I was all along?" Maia pressed.

"Your beauty is renowned, my lady. It took more than blisters, scabs, and dirt to conceal it. And be fair, I did try to tell you."

"How so?" Maia asked, her mind racing.

"The flower I left in your saddlebag. A lily of Dahomey. The royal flower. I wanted you to know that I knew who you were, so I gave you a hint. You have been under close guard and I could not speak freely, lest the kishion slit your throat or mine."

"He was sent to protect—"

"He is a hired killer." He walked over to a small tray and grabbed a few salted nuts and began munching them. "Your father likely paid him to keep you from falling into my hands. How very rude of him to treat his future son-in-law that way."

Maia stared at him in shock.

"Yes, I deceived you most shamefully," Collier said with a mock bow. "Did you not enjoy it, though? I certainly did. I will always remember that dance in Briec. There was such a wicked innocence to it. You did not know who I was. I pretended not to know who you were." The self-satisfied smile on his mouth made her want to slap him hard across the face. "Rarely am I so entertained." He finished the nuts and brushed his hands together smoothly. "So, for the rest! Now that I have captured you, my lady, I am not going to hold you for ransom. No, nothing like that. I will not execute you, nor will I allow the Dochte Mandar to do so. I will set you free this very evening and you may go on your way to do whatever mischief you were sent here to accomplish. All I ask, my lady—and it really is a small request—is that we marry immediately."

"You are mad," Maia gasped in wonderment.

"Hardly. Cunning, wise, treacherous, and—to many a lady— charming. Let me put it this way," he continued, sitting on the edge of the small sturdy table. "I seek to fulfill the plight troth of our infanthood, solemnizing our union under the auspices of the Dochte Mandar—for I am *not* a maston and neither are you!" He grinned with triumph. "As my wife, you will provide me with the lawful grounds to invade your kingdom and claim it on your behalf, deposing your feckless, ruthless, and quite possibly *insane* father, giving us the thrones of Comoros and Dahomey. My ambitions, naturally, do not end there, as with our combined strength, we will topple the other kingdoms and then invade the homeland of the Naestors." He rubbed his chin thoughtfully and winked. "We can accomplish all this by Whitsunday. What do you think?"

Maia stared at him. She blinked, trying to rally her wits. Was he serious? Was he toying with her? She was still reeling from all the double-dealing and deceit.

"You are too quiet," he murmured, shaking his head. "That surprises me. Perhaps you prefer a little more nuance in your trickery. I, myself, tend to take few things in a serious vein. But I am quite serious, Lady Marciana, about all that I have suggested." He approached and she backed away. "My tone may be jovial, but I speak in earnest. If you are squeamish about murdering your father, we can confine him to Pent Tower for the rest of his old age. He has confined *you* for quite long enough." She saw a certain heat radiating in his eyes, an anger that belied his teasing. "You are the rightful heir of Comoros. What he has done to you . . ." His voice trailed off and she could see him mastering himself.

"What he has done, he has done," Maia said, trying to find some strength in her voice. "I am here because he bid me to save my people. When the Dochte Mandar were expelled from the realm, it unleashed a threat."

"Of course it did," Collier said arrogantly. "The Myriad Ones have always been among us, in my kingdom most of all. This is where they have glutted themselves to excess," he said in an offhanded way. He went to the table where her kystrel rested and took a goblet of wine, drinking a swallow from it. "Men are too weak to resist their baser instincts. They must be ruled, and I intend to be the one who rules them, as my ancestor Dieyre once did."

Maia stared at him and shook her head. "He ruled over their demise."

He frowned and shook his head at her. "He failed because he could not claim that which he desired most. The love of a certain woman." He tipped his cup toward her. "A woman named Marciana. Is this not rich in irony? I wish to be your husband. I wish you to rule by my side. But do not expect love from me, and do not expect me to fall victim to you. I will never consummate our marriage vows with a kiss. I have read the tomes, and I know *what* you are. I told you I was not a maston, but I faced the maston test. I failed it, though I learned much in the process. I know why your father sent you to the lost abbey, and it has nothing to do with vanquishing the Myriad Ones or any such nonsense." He set the goblet down on the table and lifted the kystrel, dangling it by its chain.

"You want this back," he murmured softly, his voice like bubbling cheese.

Maia stared at it, aching at the sight of it so close. Her wrists chafed at their bonds.

"I can feel your thoughts *writhing* for it. As I said, I seek an alliance with you—one that will start with our immediate marriage. This very evening under this very moon. I have been candid regarding my intentions. With your help, I can seize and conquer all the kingdoms, which we will rule together." He swung the medallion back and forth, teasing her. "The lost abbey is where the hetaera's Leering was taken when Dochte Abbey fell. The Leering is carved like a serpent. A serpent in a circle. Its mark is branded on your shoulder. Come, Maia," he insisted, his voice husky and soft. "No deceptions between us. I will give this back to you. I know you must have already used it against me, for I dream of you at night. You can use me and twist me as you will as long as you give me the power I seek. I will give you your freedom. Marry me—tonight—and it is yours."

I have been to the hetaera's lair and faced their test. It was the Medium's will that I leave a curse on their Leering, a curse bound by irrevocare sigil. A curse to last for all time. I faced the Queen of the Unborn, Ereshkigal, who sought to turn me into her slave. She threatened me and my posterity with revenge. The Leering was too powerful to destroy, but it was moved from Dochte Abbey, hidden away by the Dochte Mandar. You must understand that it still holds great power, and its brand—two entwining serpents— can still be burned into a shoulder. It is usually the left shoulder. That is how you can tell a woman is a hetaera. In my day the hetaera seduced kings and sheriffs and secretly plotted to have all the mastons murdered. My own mother was killed by a hetaera. In your day, many mastons are weaker in the Medium than the Dochte Mandar who use kystrels to amplify their power. But a hetaera would be even stronger—she would have the power to destroy their civilization. I must warn you that the curse I placed on that Leering is still in force. A hetaera's kiss will bring a plague. The Naestors fear this above all else, and they will murder any girl who wears a kystrel or has the mark on her shoulder. Eventually, they will kill any girl who even learns how to read.

—Lia Demont, Aldermaston of Muirwood Abbey

CHAPTER SIXTEEN

Fate

Maia was so startled, so amazed, so frightened by Collier's words that she could only stare at him, dumbfounded. She closed her eyes, trying to untangle the conflicting thoughts, convulsing feelings, and tremors of dread that threatened to mute her permanently. She had been to the lost abbey. That much was true. She had ventured into the area that contained a dark pool, a place the Dochte Mandar had used to commune with the dead. She had beheld the Leering of which he spoke, had felt its raw power. But she had not touched it. She had been too afraid.

But she could also appreciate that to this man, her sudden presence in his kingdom could be misinterpreted in a thousand different ways. She wore a kystrel around her neck. Surely that would persuade him of his own accuracy, if nothing else did!

Though Collier was wrong about her, his accusation sent thoughts dashing around in her mind, colliding and sparking and crumbling to dust. Why had her father sent her to the cursed shores of Dahomey? What were his true motives? She could only guess, but had not Chancellor Walraven said that one of the ways to dissolve a marriage by irrevocare sigil was if the wife was found to be a hetaera? She had read about the hetaera in the tomes of the Dochte Mandar. She knew the legends of their deadly kiss. Had her father sent her to *become* one?

That thought sent a searing shard of wrath through her soul.

She opened her eyes and stared at the Mark of Dahomey. He still dangled her kystrel in front of her, as if she were some fish that would succumb to a hook if only the correct bait were presented.

"You misunderstand a great many things, Your Majesty."

"Please. Call me *Collier*, and I will call you *Maia*. Our pet names for each other."

She clenched her jaw, feeling the swell of fury rise up inside her. She squeezed her fingers into fists, wishing she were strong enough to shred the ropes that bound her wrists.

"I am *not* a hetaera," she said tightly. "You have misunderstood me entirely, and in so doing, you have deceived yourself most of all."

He chuckled softly, shaking his head. "Anger is an excellent way to conceal a lie. It is so easy to feign outrage."

"I am not dissembling," Maia said, stepping forward. "I am not what you think, but I can understand why it must look that way to you. You also already know that the Dochte Mandar are hunting me and seek to murder me, but—"

He waved his hand. "I will not let them harm you," he interrupted. "Of course they seek your death. Let me shield you from them. They fear you because they know you are more powerful. More powerful than them. And more powerful than the mastons."

She shook her head. "I am not what you think I am." The thought was repulsive.

"Well, there is a very simple test to prove your innocence," Collier said languidly. "Open your bodice."

Maia flushed with shame and rage. "I bear the kystrel's taint."

"Of course you do. Let me see your shoulders. Long ago the hetaera would cover the marks on their bosoms with paints or tattoos, but nothing could cover the brand. It was always the *left* shoulder, I believe, though I do not know if it makes a difference. How about we start there?" He smiled mischievously.

Maia felt heat and awkwardness battle inside of her. She was not a hetaera! But she was also not about to disrobe in front of this man to satisfy his vulgar curiosities.

"No," Maia said, shaking her head.

He sighed and then sat on a camp chair, the kystrel still dangling from his fingers. He rubbed his eyes. "I should have seized you in Roc-Adamour," he grumbled. "I nearly did, but I enjoyed the hunt too much. And dancing the Volta with you . . . I meant what I said. It is a memory I will cherish forever. The look on your face!" He rubbed his chin thoughtfully. "This is not about treachery and murder, Maia. I wish to speak plainly, for I see you as my equal."

"Your equal?" Maia interrupted, holding up her wrists and showing him her bonds.

He waved her implication aside. "In rank and station," he said. "We were plight trothed when we were infants! Did you not, for many years, consider yourself to be training for the day when you would be Queen of Dahomey? You speak the language remarkably well. You are a little shy about our customs, but truly you are a charming girl. You are beautiful, which I had not fully appreciated until we met. You are caught in a spider's web, spun up in silk, and your blood is being sipped by creatures in your father's court. I have known this, Lady Maia. My spies are well paid. I desire to invade your father's kingdom, but not just to accumulate power. I have pitied you many years."

"So now *I* am the wretched and not you?" she replied evenly. "My father did not send me here for the purpose you suggest."

"Then why did he send you? I will humor you for a moment by listening to your lies."

She wanted to box him on the side of his head. It took all of her self-control to salvage her dignity and pride and stare him down. "When my father expelled the Dochte Mandar from the realm, we were immediately afflicted by the Myriad Ones."

"Naturally," he said with a shrug. "Why do you think I keep two Leerings posted at the entrance to my tent? You can hardly sleep in a rough camp like this one without drawing thousands of them. Why do you think we scavenge the broken abbeys for them?"

She gave him an angry stare.

"I interrupted you. Forgive me." He fell quiet, though he seemed to be chafing with impatience. He swung the kystrel back and forth, back and forth.

"As soon as the Dochte Mandar left, the Myriad Ones invaded our realm. We have mastons, but they were not strong enough— or plentiful enough—to withstand the tide. Our kingdom is fracturing from within."

He looked about to say something, but he clenched his jaw tight and did not.

"I was sent by my father to seek the lost abbey to learn from the rites of the dark pool how we could overcome the dangers we face and keep the kingdom united. I visited the hetaera's Leering. It was hidden away behind a stone door. There were dead Dochte Mandar all around it. Skeletons. None of them were allowed to leave."

Collier leaned forward, listening intently.

"I learned that the answers I seek—the solution for saving my people—can be found in Naess. There are records that were taken there, and only the High Seer—a woman—can show me where they are. That is where my fate binds me. I must go to Naess."

"You thought *I* was mad," he muttered under his breath. "You . . . are going *there*, my pretty dove?"

"I must," she said softly. "I will likely not survive the journey. But I must try. My people are murdering each other."

He leaned back in the chair, the leather creaking as he shifted. He sniffed once and then shook his head in disbelief. "You are very good, Maia," he said at last. "Your sincerity rings so true, I almost believe you. You are Gifted with lying. Well done."

She bristled with fury. "I speak the truth!"

"What is truth?" he countered flippantly. "I think your father sent you to the lost abbey to brand you a hetaera. If he can prove you are one, he will be able to claim your mother is as well. Then even the mastons will sanction his divorce, giving him what he has desired all along. A corrupt kingdom where he can practice his depredations without interference."

"Is that not what you desire?" she said angrily. It made her blister with fury to consider her father may have sent her to Dahomey for an entirely selfish purpose. But no matter what his motives were, she had to do this thing. She had to save her people.

Collier looked amused and batted away her comment as if it were a tiresome fly. "The Dochte Mandar. The mastons. They are all the same in my mind. I know a group of heretics in the hinterlands who believe that trees can speak in women's voices. It is all a game of power, my dear. I excel at it. My ancestor managed to unite all the kingdoms under one ruler through the force of his will. I seek to do the same."

"He ruled over a kingdom of bones," Maia said with disgust. "I saw them south of here. He ruled an ossuary."

Collier's look darkened. "At least he ruled something," he said softly. The chair creaked again as he rose. He started to pace. Then he turned to her. "Let me see your shoulder."

"No," she said, shaking her head.

"If you wish, we can be man and wife first," he teased. "Despite your stubbornness and ill humor, I do wish to honor the plight troth. Let me be blunt, lass. I am imprisoning you until you relent."

She screwed up her courage. "Until the Dochte Mandar find me."

"I will move you from one manor to another. From one hide-away to the next. You are too precious for me to let you slip from my fingers again. Perhaps you go to Naess to destroy the seat of the Dochte Mandar yourself. Maybe you will kiss the High Seer and kill her with your lips." He narrowed his eyes. "I am not sure I even believe the legend, myself. For you, I would almost risk it. But just in case the mastons have been telling the truth all along, I do not think I will." He took a deliberate step toward her. "I would not stand in the way of your journey, if you are intent on making it, but you are to be mine." His eyes narrowed with satisfaction. "I will make your father suffer for his ill treatment of you, Maia."

There was a part of her that desired to relent. To throw down her pride, succumb to her shame, and abandon her duty. But to do so would mean marrying a man who believed her a hetaera— a man who was willing to destroy the world so long as he could rule it. And though she knew her father intended for her never to marry, she longed for it. Her heart's wish was to be a maston, married by irrevocare sigil to another maston. She believed in the bond, though her father did not.

Still, her father was the one who had brought the kingdom to this precipice, and if he had truly sent her to the lost abbey with the hope that she would become a hetaera. . . . What a twisted dilemma she faced. But could she depose her own father? Could she commit treason? If only she knew her father's true mind, his true intentions for her. She hardly knew her own heart.

"I do not wish my father harm," she finally said.

"Done."

She looked at him curiously.

"This is a marriage negotiation. Name your terms, Maia. A political match. Here are my terms. I will not love you. I will not consummate this marriage. I will vow it on the Medium or whatever oath you would have me take. Now name yours."

"Release me," she said, holding up her bonds.

"Done." He drew the dirk again and slit the bonds. The ropes fell away, and she felt a jolt of relief. She rubbed her sore wrists, staring at Collier as she would a mountain lion.

"Your terms are too easy, my lady. I do not ask for a dowry in coins or land. Comoros itself will be sufficient. But though I will claim it on your behalf, you will be queen in your own right."

"I am not going to marry you," Maia said, shaking her head. "You will release me and help me on my quest."

He stared at her for a moment, then shook his head. "No, I will only help you with your quest after we marry." He held up the kystrel again, dangling it dangerously close to her.

"It is my understanding of the hetaera lore," he said slyly, "that if a man wears her kystrel, he shares her power. They are bound together. Like . . . wedding bands, you might say. What would happen if I wore *yours*, I wonder? Would my eyes glow silver? Would your tattoo transfer to my flesh? It would give you *more* power, would it not?"

Maia's mouth went dry. That was written in the tomes of the Dochte Mandar, a warning to any man who wore a kystrel, that the hetaera who had forged it must already be dead.

"Ah, by the look on your face, I see I have struck near the mark! What would happen to us both, Maia? We would be inseparable. Would I do your bidding, or would you do mine? Whose will is stronger?"

"Do not," Maia warned as he lifted it higher.

"You are so subtle," he said, flashing her a handsome grin. "You bid me to do the very opposite of that which you wish me to do. Oh, how I am enjoying this game! I almost put it on right away to force you, but it is so much more pleasurable to dance around the threat. Marry me willingly, and I will give it back to you. If you do not, I will wear it and infest you with my thoughts and ambitions . . . or perhaps it will be the other way around. Our minds will begin to entwine, will they not? This is delicious!" He stepped closer to her, his piercing blue eyes cutting into hers. "I do not fear you, Maia, but I may be rash and this may be foolish. Willingly marry me. That would be my preference."

A voice came from beyond the tent flap. "My lord?"

He scowled with displeasure. "What is it?" he barked.

"The gallows are ready. The hunter's dog is whining. Should we spear it, or do you wish to keep it in your kennels?"

He cocked his head at Maia. "Do you wish to keep Argus or not? It is your choice. I have plenty of dogs. Another wedding gift?"

"Do not hang those men," Maia said desperately. Her stomach clenched with dread. In her surprise and panic, she had forgotten the threat to her companions.

"Hanging, beheading . . . makes little difference to me. The kishion deserves to dangle from a noose. Jon Tayt rejected my proposal and defied my invitation. He would not serve me for any amount of coin, which makes him useless to me. I will execute them both."

Maia grabbed his wrist. "Do not harm them!"

His eyebrow crinkled with surprise. "They *must* die, Maia. I do not believe you are squeamish. This is another trick. You are so very good at deception. I applaud you, truly."

She dug her fingers into his wrist. "They are my loyal servants. They obeyed me. If anyone is to be murdered tonight, it should be me."

"That would defeat the purpose of my alliance," he said, clucking his tongue. "Though plenty have been murdered since you entered my realm. The village on the top of the mountain. The guards on the north road. I deliberately told you to take the *south* road, did I not? And yet you rushed into the teeth of my men in an act of defiance."

"You know we were attacked by the Dochte Mandar in the village," Maia said, feeling more desperate with each moment. "Corriveaux and the Dahomeyjan soldiers are to blame for that. Not I."

"And the watch on the north road? Hmmm?"

Maia's face turned hot. "Your captain ordered his men to kill my protectors and bring me to his tent!"

Collier's eyebrows lifted. "Truly?"

She wanted to pound on his chest with her fists. "Everything I have told you this evening *is* the truth!"

"Then show me your shoulder and *prove* it."

"I am a king's daughter," she murmured.

"I am a king's son," he replied.

She knew that if she showed him her shoulder, he would discover she was not a hetaera.

An idea came to her. She wished she had the kystrel to advise her, but she did not.

She looked into Collier's eyes. They were so blue she could drown in them. She saw the little scar on his cheek and wondered how he had gotten it.

"You are so interesting," he murmured softly, reaching out and brushing aside some of her hair. "Why do you resist what is clearly in both our interests? You are not like I thought you would be."

"My lord?" reminded the voice from outside.

He paused, hand still touching her hair. He raised his eyebrows questioningly.

Her voice broke, almost unwillingly. "Release them. Set them free. Promise to let them go and not to harm them or injure them in any way. Pardon their treason in writing and with your seal." She swallowed. "Then I will marry you."

He stared at her, his eyes glimmering with delight. "Done."

CHAPTER SEVENTEEN

Headsman's Noose

She walked alongside Collier through the smoke-filled camp. He had changed from his rider's tunic to an elegant doublet, black velvet and trimmed with gold sigils of the Dahomeyjan lily. He wore ceremonial chains around his neck and a signet ring on the little finger of his right hand. The same sword was belted to his waist, but his countenance and stride completely transformed him from his former persona. He had the bearing of a ruler as he walked through the camp with firm deliberation, stopping in front of an enormous tree with two long ropes dangling from it. Two stools stood by it, and kneeling before them were the kishion and Jon Tayt. Maia's heart raced.

She heard Argus barking and saw a man wrestling with the boarhound, who had been fitted with a collar and a leather leash.

"Let them go," Maia pleaded, wringing her hands.

Jon Tayt's head whipped around, his eyes bulging with fear until he saw her. He smiled, though his expression looked more like a grimace. Then he looked at Collier, his eyes showing first confusion and then sudden understanding.

"Ach," he muttered. "Now *that* is a surprise."

Maia started to approach, but Collier grabbed her arm, preventing her. "Not too close," he urged her. "Give the order."

"Release them," Maia said in a voice of command. "Set them free."

The guards stared at her in surprise, then glanced at Collier for his orders.

"You heard my lady," he said with a curt nod.

Jon Tayt's eyes glowered. A dark look came over his face as several soldiers approached and loosened his bonds.

"Bring his dog," Maia said, motioning to the soldier who still struggled with Argus.

As Jon Tayt struggled to his feet, the boarhound charged him and began licking him with a frenzy. The hunter whistled for Argus to heel and stared at Maia in shock. "By Cheshu, what have you done, lass?" he asked in Pry-rian.

Maia felt her heart aching, but she could not reveal her plan. Not in front of everyone. She answered in Pry-rian, "I release you from my service. May we meet again someday in Pry-Ree, in the mountains where men fear to tread."

Collier gave her an angry look. "No more chat," he said waspishly. "That is enough."

"I released him from my service," Maia replied, her expression equally dark. "He is Pry-rian, so I did it—"

"Yes, yes, be done with it. Take this letter," he said, handing it to the hunter. "It bears my seal. You have a fortnight to quit the realm, Tayt. Return to Pry-Ree or Paeiz or wherever you choose. But if you set foot in my domain again, you will hang. As for you." He turned his angry gaze to the kishion. "All my instincts tell me that you will be nothing but a problem for me later, and I should end your life tonight. I will not have you roaming my kingdom freely. Captain, take him to Calis and put him on a boat. I do not care where. Make sure he is not unbound until after you have deposited him on a ship and it has weighed anchor and left. If he attempts to flee, stab him in the ribs and spill his guts." He clenched his teeth. "If you come near my lady again, I will kill you myself."

The kishion's eyes were hard and violent. He nodded once and said nothing, but his scarred cheek twitched.

"Send him away. Tayt—have some ale before you depart if you wish. But you must leave my camp before midnight. My lady wishes to spare you the noose, and so I obey her will."

"Maia," Jon Tayt said, his voice low and purposeful and full of warning.

"All is well, Jon Tayt," she said, looking at him fiercely. "Do as I bid you this one last time."

Argus seemed to sense something. He padded up to her and she lowered to caress his fur, getting a wet lick on her cheek for her efforts. It made her smile, and her throat closed with emotion. "Keep him safe," she whispered to the boarhound.

Jon Tayt stood there, perplexed and obviously uncomfortable. "Well, Your Grace, thank you for not executing me, but I will not linger. Argus, come."

The boarhound nuzzled Maia one last time and then trotted to catch up with Jon Tayt as he started to walk away. The hunter paused and turned, thought better of what he was about to say, and then disappeared into the smoke. The Myriad Ones mewled with frustration at having lost their kill for the evening.

Maia watched as the captain who had brought her to the tent arranged for the kishion's banishment. His arms were still bound, his wrists tied behind his back, and she watched as he was helped onto a horse. His head hung low in defeat as someone took the reins for him, but she could see the defiance in his posture. He glanced back at her once, his eyes full of enmity. He then looked back and rode into the dark with the riders.

Maia felt a jolt of relief that she had managed to save both of her protectors, but she felt the loss of the kishion especially, since she was unlikely to see him again. They had been through so much together, and without him, she would have never survived this long. Better for him to be exiled than slain, but she would miss his companionship. Now she needed to buy some time and delay Collier's plan. She hoped Jon Tayt was wise enough to realize that she had been telling him where to meet her again. The mountain pass guarded by the Fear Liath—the one they had planned to use for their escape. If she could get her kystrel back, she would leave for the pass immediately.

Maia and Collier returned to the pavilion, walking side by side. As they moved through the camp, she took note of details she had missed on her first whirlwind tour. The clank of pans and smell of sizzling meat filled the air. Fires crackled and the smoke shifted with the winds. She saw nobles dressed in finery mixing together, their garb more like their king's. The common soldiers had stacked their breastplates and helmets near their fires, where the armor glimmered in the light. Stands of pikes stood at various positions throughout the camp.

Maia looked at the Leerings as she passed them, studying the design. They looked as if they had been taken from the ruins of an abbey, which cohered with what Collier had told her. The interior of the tent smelled soothing, and Maia suddenly realized she was starving. In their absence, trays of meat and vessels of melted cheese and broth had been arranged around one of the fur rugs.

"Are you hungry?" Collier asked her.

"Very," she replied. With the haze over the camp, she could not make out the stars through the open roof.

He settled down on the rug and motioned for her to join him. It was by the brazier, so it was plenty warm. She knelt and smoothed the fabric of her skirt.

"What questions do you have for me?" he asked, skewering some meat and placing it in the broth. He did several, including some for her.

"You said you faced the maston test," Maia said. "At what abbey? How old were you?"

"How old do you think I am now?" he asked, arching his eyebrows. "Do you remember?"

She nodded. "I was a little child when our parents arranged the marriage. You are two years younger than me," she said. "I remember that."

"I have always preferred the idea of marrying someone closer to my own age than a rich heiress who would only desire me for my youth and handsomeness." He winked at her. "I took the maston test a year ago. I knew I would fail it and I wanted to be done with abbey life. My ancestor Dieyre was restless also. You know most of the history, do you not? Of my Family?"

She dipped bread into the bubbling cheese and savored it. "Dieyre sired a son through a wretched from Muirwood before the Scourging. That child was not a wretched, for the mother, a lavender named Reome, acknowledged the parentage. He was adopted into a Family, thus removing the taint of illegitimacy."

Collier nodded. "Would you care for some wine or cider?"

"Water, if you please."

"I will not poison you, Maia," he said with a chuckle. "Or twist your thoughts with drink. As I said, I prefer a willing partner."

"Water, please."

He nodded and went to a table and poured some water from a pitcher into a fancy carved goblet. After delivering it to her, he served himself a glass of wine and sat back down on the rug.

"So when our ancestors returned from the distant shores to reclaim the lands, they learned that Dieyre had been the last man alive in the kingdoms. Most of my Family were strong in the Medium. My father was particularly devout as a maston. But I lost my faith, you might say, in Paeiz."

Maia looked at him in curiosity. She smelled the cup first, tasted it, and made sure it was just water.

"As you know, all the various kingdoms continue to fight and wage war on each other. There was a land dispute between Dahomey and Paeiz. With so much of my kingdom still cursed, arable land is precious. What began as a border skirmish turned into a full-out war. My father summoned the army and went north and clashed with the Paeizian forces. It was a humiliating defeat, Maia. You know of it?"

"Yes, I learned of it when I was settling land disputes with Pry-Ree. War is wasteful."

"We may agree to disagree on that point. My father was captured and humiliated by the Paeizians. In order to secure his release, he had to give them his two sons as hostages. My brother, whom you met earlier this evening pretending to be me, and I were sent to live at an abbey in Paeiz and receive our maston training there. To be honest, I spent more time finding ways to slip away from the abbey than I did learning to read and engrave. I was always discovered and fetched back, mind you, but I learned a few things that cannot be taught in tomes." He removed the steaming meat skewers from the pot and set them down on a tray shared between them. She studied his hands, the small nicks and scars showed he was used to work and had been in many fights. It made her wonder how his hands had been so abused, especially since she now knew he had never been a wretched.

"Thank you," she said, taking one of the skewers and eating the meat from it.

He waved her off as if it did not matter at all. "I met the king's collier in Paeiz, who was often sent to the abbey to report on my brother and me."

"What abbey?" she pressed.

"Antimo," he answered, smiling. "Full of vineyards and orchards. It is a beautiful place. The king's collier would come and go as he pleased. He was excellent at Paeizian fencing and started to train me when I was but ten."

"You have studied for many years then," Maia said, impressed.

"Yes, I was more disposed to weapons than tomes. And wine. I have very discriminating tastes, you will learn. I know that cider is a popular drink in Comoros. I like it, but apples are not the best fruit." He took a bite from a meaty skewer and paused to savor it. "So my brother and I spent our formative years away from my father's court. I was envious of my mentor's freedom and wished that I could escape the drudgery of the abbey as he did, riding across the kingdom delivering messages and reports to and from his king. Before I even became king, I created the idea of Feint Collier. When I finally returned home, I would steal away from my lessons at the castle and ride long and hard and visit every corner of my father's realm. That is how I met men like Jon Tayt and many others, who know me by my disguise rather than my true rank." He tipped his wine goblet toward her. "So you see, that is another reason I pitied you, Maia. My imprisonment was the result of defeat. My father had no choice but to use his sons as hostages. He did all he could to raise the ransom to secure our release, and it took many years. Your father, on the other hand, imprisoned you himself. Did you not ever think of escaping?"

Maia sighed. The comfortable warmth of the fur rug and the savory food was distracting her from her objective. She was still angry at him for his blatant deception, but she could now see that trickery was part of his personality, part of his heritage even. She wanted to learn more about him, for it was impossible to tell how much of his reputation as the Mark was true, and how much had been his own invention. And she could not deny the little wriggling fish of jealousy in the pit of her stomach. He dared to do things she would never dream of doing. Loyalty was her duty. Not just to her father, but to her people.

"We are very different," she said after taking a quick sip from her drink. "You always sought to escape Antimo Abbey. You wanted to be free. What I desired above all else was to be *sent* to an abbey. I want to learn from the tomes."

"Done," he said, winking at her. "In my realm, it will not be forbidden."

"You would defy the Dochte Mandar?" she asked challengingly.

"I defy everyone, including you." He sat up and brushed his hands together. "I hunger to humble Paeiz. Dahomey is too weak to do it, but with Comoros, I will prevail. I think Pry-Ree will be wise enough to submit to us without an invasion. They are the smallest kingdom, and we do owe them something for saving us all. One by one, chit by chit, mark by mark, crown by crown. I am deeply ambitious, Maia."

"I can see that," she agreed. "What you ask me to do is called treason, though, in my kingdom. My father declared me illegitimate."

"And I will make him repent his words and actions," Collier answered. "Just as my father was humiliated by the King of Paeiz,

I will humble your father. I am gathering my strength to invade Comoros, Maia. One of the terms of surrender I was willing to accept was you. You are his heir, whether he admits it or not."

She shook her head. "How can I betray my own people?"

"How can you stand by a father who tossed aside his lawful marriage and banished his wife and his daughter?" He leaned forward eagerly. "What else do you wish to know of your husband to be?"

She stared into his eyes. "How can I trust anything you have told me?" she asked, sighing. "Nearly every word you have spoken to me has been a lie."

"Lies are the spices that garnish a dish. They do not change a fowl into a fish. They only season them."

She shook her head, not convinced. "A pretty saying, my lord, but it does little to ease my apprehension."

"What do you fear?" he pressed.

"You said if I married you, you would let me go. Why would you do that? You said you would not consummate the marriage because you believe I am a hetaera. What if I am not? Besides, your plan gives me plenty to fear—such an act would be considered treason in any kingdom."

He snorted. "You are trying to *save* your kingdom. Or at least, that is what you pretend. Your father sent you to my kingdom to find a cure for the Myriad Ones. The only cure is to allow the Dochte Mandar back into the realm. He is too stubborn to realize that. But truly, Maia, does this not all hinge on whether or not you are lying to *me*? I want to believe your stories, but they do not align with common sense. You have admitted going to the lost abbey. Prove you are not a hetaera. Or I will force you to reveal yourself by wearing your kystrel. As I have said, I would prefer for you to be willing. But you will wed me before the sun rises. Dieyre waited too long for his Marciana. I will not make the same mistake."

Maia tried to settle her breathing. Involuntarily, she started to tremble.

"Are you cold?" he asked.

She was not. She was terrified. She hoped enough time had passed to give the kishion an opportunity to escape and for Jon Tayt to put some distance between himself and the camp. "So you seek to marry me regardless? Even if I am not a hetaera?"

"Truly, I do," he said. "The political advantage exists regardless. Surely you realize that."

"Yes," she said. Why could she not stop trembling? She was suddenly so very tired. Weariness and exhaustion plundered her strength. She had been in flight for so long; her muscles ached with fatigue. The supper in her stomach was pleasant.

"Are you all right?" he asked, looking concerned.

"I am weary, that is all," she said.

"I know I have said it before, but you are not what I expected," he said, giving her a probing look. "Not at all. I had truly expected you would be more . . . willing. It almost seems as if you have a conscience."

She stared at him and smiled sadly. "I do."

He took another gulp from his cup. "Very well. Time to lay aside the games. Prove your words through actions. I spared your servants, though little they deserved it."

Maia nodded. "Let me prove my innocence." A horrible, guilty feeling swelled inside her breast, though she little understood it. *The Medium will guide you*, she assured herself. It had led her to the north road. It had led her to this man's tent. She had to trust it. She had to trust the path she was on.

Maia began to unfasten the lacings on her bodice, loosening

them enough to expose her shoulders. It mortified her, for the first few strings exposed the curving tattoos that had climbed up her chest—a mark she normally went to great lengths to hide. Her fingers shook and she struggled to compose herself, for she was blushing furiously, embarrassed for his guarded eyes to stare at her so fixedly.

"The kystrel leaves a taint on the skin, as I said," she explained as she worked loose the weave. "Even the Dochte Mandar have it. It is a consequence of using the magic."

"I know," he said, his eyes still studying her.

Maia felt her breath quickening. He was staring at her hungrily now. Her mouth was suddenly dry, and she knew she should hurry and finish the deed so she could cover herself again. Clumsily, she undid a few more lacings, just enough—and then pulled the fabric away from her shoulder.

His eyes widened.

The feeling in the pavilion changed palpably. It was a dark feeling. She felt something stir inside her blood, radiating like a furnace of power. Maia felt a whisper through the shadows.

She jerked the fabric back up, covering her bare shoulder. Inexpressible horror jolted through her. She had seen it as clearly as he had.

The brand on her shoulder.

The two serpents.

Why do children fear the night? Just as dark is the absence of light, and despair is the absence of hope, so these symbols exist between day and night. I have seen in my life that the manifestations of the Medium are strongest when the souls of mankind are awake, their thoughts aroused and vigilant. When darkness comes, so come the Unborn. A friend from my early days at Muirwood liked to quote The Hodoeporicon, *"Retire to thy bed early, that ye may not be weary; arise early, that your bodies and minds may be invigorated."*

—Lia Demont, Aldermaston of Muirwood Abbey

CHAPTER EIGHTEEN

Privy Council

As the voices began to rise, sizzling with heat, Maia looked up from the parchment map, her ears instinctively drawn to her father's words. She loved being in her father's solar, for here she had access to maps, globes, quills, ink, and even little books, which she was forbidden to peruse outside his presence. That Lady Deorwynn was arguing with the king in front of several members of his Privy Council, seated at a nearby table, surprised her. She was normally more circumspect. And the uncomfortable looks on their faces showed they wished they were anywhere else at the moment. The chancellor's mouth was actually gaping open with shock.

"I do not want her at court any longer," Lady Deorwynn said scathingly. "My daughters should not have to befriend and comfort someone who has been banished. You may as well isolate us all in Pent Tower!"

"If my lady would like me to accommodate that request," her father said, his voice hot enough to sear, "it can be arranged!"

"Send Marciana away!"

"And where would you have me send *my* daughter?"

Maia's stomach roiled with disquiet at the argument, which sent tendrils of nausea through her. Her ulcers had only grown worse after trouble had broken out across the kingdom, and the physicians could do nothing for her.

"Kenningford," Lady Deorwynn snapped. "I can think of a dozen other suitable places. Send her away from court, my lord. I beg you. She is given far too many privileges for one of her station."

Maia noticed the Earl of Forshee scowling, but it was hard for her to tear her eyes from the main players in the argument.

"Privileges?" her father snorted. "You amuse me. I learned that you forbade the servants from lighting her brazier in the mornings. She was suffering from chills."

"Why should a servant trudge all the way to the tower for *her*?" Lady Deorwynn countered. "A little hard work would warm her up!"

"I will not send her away, madame. I am deaf to the idea."

Maia glanced at Lady Deorwynn's daughters. They were quietly sewing in the far corner of the room, their postures perfect, and their expressions indifferent to the storm raging around them. But Maia knew they were listening to every word, and she had no doubt the words would be used as barbs to torment her later.

Lady Deorwynn knelt by the high-back chair, her hands touching the king's jeweled surcoat. "I beg you! I cannot tolerate her. The looks she gives me. They would curdle milk, I tell you. She is insolent, lazy, and stubborn."

"Say no more."

"I must! You shame me by allowing her to stay at court. I am mocked because of her presence. The sneers and quips are intolerable! I beg you, my lord. Send her away!"

Maia swallowed, setting down the map she had been studying of the various kingdoms. She had been tracing the borders of Dahomey with her finger when the argument became loud enough for all to hear. She had only visited Pry-Ree, and though she knew it was unlikely to happen, she longed to see all the realms. She took any chance she could to speak with ambassadors from the other kingdoms, to learn little bits about their ways and manners. Being sent to a distant manor house far from her father and mother, where she would be isolated from everything that interested her and everyone who cared for her, would be a terrible fate. She had long wished to join her mother's exile at Muirwood, but that was impossible. Her father's heart was flint.

He stared down at Lady Deorwynn coldly. "Mayhap if you treated Maia more civilly, there would be less gossip and fewer sneers! She is my daughter, and I will not exile her from court. She has been obedient to my orders, patiently suffering her disinheritance and *your* mistreatment of her. By the Blood, woman, if you treated her with a bit of compassion, there would be none of this rancor in my house!"

Lady Deorwynn came to her feet with startled fury. Her eyes blazed with rage; her jaw quivered with emotion. "How dare you!" she said through clenched teeth.

"How dare I? She is my daughter, not yours. If you treated her with a morsel of dignity . . . but I see that is beyond you. You care only for your own flesh and blood."

Lady Deorwynn trembled with rage. "I treat her," she said venomously, "with all the dignity she deserves considering her *rank*, which you, my lord, gave to her. What shall I hear next, that you plan to marry her to the Prince of Hautland? A banished daughter? You mock me, my lord, you mock me!"

"I have problems enough to vex me," the king said curtly. "Why do you add to my griefs? Out! Out!" He flung his arm wide, nearly hitting her. "Give me peace, woman."

Lady Deorwynn retreated, subtly, beyond his reach. She gave a deep curtsy, but her face was full of anger and anguish. "As you bid me, my lord," she snarled. Then, sweeping up her skirts, she turned and stalked away from the solar chamber, snapping her fingers twice as she went. Her daughters bowed their heads, sighed, swept up their needlework, and followed in her wake.

Maia felt a throb of triumph at how her father had defended her in front of Lady Deorwynn. But Maia knew the woman's games, knew that she would make her father suffer for the humiliation. Though they bickered often, their fights never lasted long, and words shared on a pillow seemed to tamp the flames of anger that often blazed between them.

Her father knuckled his eyes, his head stooped and downcast. Seated quietly near him, mute, were several members of his Privy Council. They watched him wrestle with his emotions, wisely saying nothing.

He rubbed his beard and exhaled deeply from his nose, staring off into the distance. He fidgeted one of his ruby rings with his lips, toying with it, smoldering. In the past, Chancellor Walraven had always been there to dispel his more violent emotions. She felt the kystrel beneath her bodice grow warm in response to her thoughts, so she chased them away. Many members of the Privy Council were mastons. What would they think of the king's banished daughter if her eyes suddenly started glowing silver?

Her father had always been an emotional man, easily swayed by his feelings. He could be all sunlight and warmth one moment, with easy smiles and a teasing tongue; and in the next, he could be as hard and violent as a whip, his words lashing out with stinging barbs. The Dochte Mandar had helped regulate his mercurial sways. But now that Walraven was dead and the other Dochte Mandar had been exiled from the realm, her father had more trouble than ever achieving equanimity.

His head turned and he looked at her, startling her.

A grieved smile twisted his mouth, and he beckoned for her to approach him. His summons surprised her, but she promptly obeyed, setting aside the map to come to his side. Her coarse woolen skirt rustled as she knelt by his chair. He cupped her cheek with his palm.

"I would have you near me, Maia," he said softly. "You . . . comfort me."

Her heart skidded with pleasure and she gave him a rare smile in return, saying nothing. He motioned to a chair from the table. "Sit by me. We discuss grievous matters." There were flecks of gold in his hair still, but she was surprised, being so near him, by how much silver was already there.

She pulled the chair up next to him and sat down, resting her hand against his. The rings on his fingers were jagged and rough, but the skin beneath hers was warm.

Chancellor Morton was frowning at her, not certain how to proceed after the embarrassment of the interruption.

"Say on, Morton," her father commanded. "Ignore the trifling arguments between my lady and myself. I daresay if I eavesdropped in your household, I would find cobwebs in the corners of your manor house as well."

"Few spiders, my lord. Mostly ants. We cannot seem to rid ourselves of the menaces. Would there were a Leering that would banish them." He seemed to realize the blunder of his poor choice of words. "My apologies, we were discussing the sanctuary privileges of Muirwood Abbey."

"Yes, we were, Chancellor Morton. You are a scholar of no small reputation, and you have said that I cannot compel a maston to leave the sanctuary by force."

"Yes, that is what I was expressing. The charters of the abbey clearly—"

"The charters were granted by a king. Why, then, cannot they be revoked by one? Hmmm? I know the charters. I know the *tradition*. But I am King of Comoros. My word is law in this land."

"To a point, Your Grace," Morton said delicately. "Were you not anointed king at Muirwood as a child? Who put the anointing oil on you as king? Was it not an Aldermaston? If you were given your authority under the auspices of Muirwood, you cannot then revoke a privilege given by the very hand that ordained you." He leaned forward, gesturing to emphasize the absurdity of the idea.

"What if I had been anointed king at Augustin Abbey?" her father said angrily. "Is it because the deed was done at Muirwood?"

"It could have even been Billerbeck," Morton replied. "All the abbeys in Comoros pay homage to Muirwood and Muirwood pays homage to Tintern where the High Seer sits."

"Pry-Ree," the king said with a sneer in his voice. "We used to rule that kingdom . . . long ago. It sickens me that they are the least of the kingdoms, yet they have authority over their betters. That the High Seer can block my divorce based on maston custom."

"You agreed to that custom when you chose to marry the queen—"

"She is not my queen!" her father thundered, pounding his fist on the table. "You must watch your tongue, Chancellor!" His eyes burned with fury, and Maia saw the chancellor's expression tighten like a walnut shell. He took the brunt of it quietly. Her father's anger continued to fester. "I am no more her husband than that iron poker by the fire is my wife. I would that she were dead." Maia's heart shriveled with blackness upon hearing the words. She sat as still as a mouse, not daring to remove her hand from his. His words were like shards of glass crunching under boots. "Yet it begins with a thought," he said in low, strangled words. "I will have this divorce, Chancellor. You must find a way."

His face paled. "My lord—" he paused, swallowing. "There is no *legal* way to compel it."

"I am not faithful to our marriage vows," her father snapped. "By all that is right and just, she should divorce me." He slapped the table, less violently this time, and grumbled under his breath. "Find a way, Morton. Put all your thought into this. I would not have my authority undermined by an Aldermaston in a sniveling kingdom less than half the size of our own, full of giant trees and . . . and . . . spoiled grapes. Tintern has authority over Muirwood. I think not. Oh, I think not. It should be Muirwood that compels the others."

"As Your Majesty knows, the Aldermastons of Tintern have always been those chosen as the High Seer since the return of the mastons. They are the strongest in the Medium."

"I care not for the history lesson, tutor," her father said with a sting. "I do not wish my realm to be governed by the whims of Tintern Abbey. I am a king-maston by law, yet I cannot command those who live in the abbeys, who are said to be outside of the king's tax. Well, the cost of rebuilding abbeys *chokes* my income.

How many people live under the shadow of an abbey to avoid paying taxes? Hmmm? Look at Augustin. To see its decadence and splendor, you would think the abbey had hardly been damaged before the Scourging. It was pride that felled our kingdoms. It was the love of treasure within the abbeys themselves."

Maia shrank from her father at those words and hid her hands in her lap, trying not to tremble.

One of the other men from the table stood, planting his palms down on the table. "If Your Majesty seeks an example of pride, then look no farther than your own mirror."

Maia stared at the grizzled man. He was older than her father, much older. His dark hair was well silvered and his angry, brooding look surprised her. She had rarely heard him speak since coming to court. He was the Earl of Forshee, an earldom that was as far from the throne of Comoros as one could get.

Maia saw the tendons on her father's hand harden like cords.

"I wondered when you would first find your voice, Forshee," her father said angrily.

He was a powerful lord of the realm and he had five sons. Two of whom were already married by irrevocare sigil, leaving three as valuable prizes. Maia knew Murer had been vigilantly pressuring her mother to marry one of them.

"I came to court at your command, Your Majesty," Forshee said darkly. "I did not seek a seat on your Privy Council. I will accept nothing for my service to you. In return, I give you my most candid advice, and it is up to you whether to accept it or not. You speak like a spoiled child who does not get his way. You are *not* the highest law of this land, Your Grace. The Medium is. Do you even wear the chaen, my lord? I see you have stripped away the other vestiges of your beliefs. Your selfish thoughts will ruin this kingdom."

Everyone was silent, staring at the ancient earl with shock and, Maia could see, a touch of relief. Someone was risking himself enough to speak up to her father. Maia knew the earl had a bold reputation for being fearless and strict. But always fair. He was a descendent of the Price Family, a cousin to hers.

"Well," her father said icily. "You have said quite enough, have you not, my lord Forshee."

"There is more," he replied sternly, "but you are not man enough to hear it."

"Do not hold back," her father said, his eyes narrowing coldly. "By all means, vent your spleen if it helps."

"As you wish. I fought alongside your lord father," Forshee said with dignity. "I fought alongside him during the Dark Wars. He was a man of integrity. A man of prowess. A maston." His voice fell lower. "He would be ashamed if he had lived to see you now."

Maia's throat constricted. She stared at the earl, then at her father, watching his neck muscles bulge. His shoulders jittered with repressed anger. "Is . . . that . . . all, Forshee?"

The earl nodded and seated himself at the table, looking at the king as if he were no more significant than a moth.

Her father pushed against the armrests of his chair and rose, bringing himself to his full height. Even his legs trembled with rage. "I had sought to make an alliance between our Families, Forshee. I know my stepdaughter Murer fancies one of your sons. But I cannot bear the thought of enduring your sanctimoniousness during holidays and such occasions. I brought you to my Privy Council because I value your wisdom, your excellence as a soldier and warrior, and the strength your Family brings to this realm. Your service has been undisputedly a value to the throne." He clenched his fists and planted them on the table. "I know that you do not approve of me, Forshee. I could see it in your eyes before you said a word, and it disgusts me. You have five strapping lads. And you leave them five farthings apiece for your insolence and your treasonous tongue. I would not let any of the daughters of my realm marry into such proud and conceited stock as yours. Away from my sight! You displease me, my lord earl. And you will suffer for it."

The Earl of Forshee rose again, his expression calm and untroubled. He dipped his head in salute and walked purpose-fully to the doors of the solar and left. Maia stared at her father, at the dangerous glint in his eyes.

He turned to Chancellor Morton. "Draw up orders to arrest Forshee before he leaves the castle. He will be bedding down in Pent Tower tonight."

"My lord?" Morton said, aghast.

"His five sons will also pay the price for his insolence," her father continued. "Summon them all to court. If any defy the summons, arrest them. I want to gather them together for a lit-tle reunion. Maybe a few dark days in a dungeon will lance the boils that afflict their spleens. Now, Morton. Now! Draw up the papers now."

"Y-yes, my lord," the chancellor said, his face pale.

Maia saw her father's jaw trembling. He began to pace near his chair. "When you have finished the arrest order, I wish you to decree all efforts to rebuild the abbeys to cease forthwith. No more stone to be quarried. No more oxen to carry them. No more roads to be repaired. We will halt the work for a season and show traitors like Forshee there is a price to be paid." He paused, realizing the play on words. "A Price. Yes, there will be a Price to be paid."

He chuckled to himself and then turned to face his Privy Council, his knuckles pressing against the tabletop. "Does anyone else wish to speak?"

The shocked silence thrummed in the room.

"Good," her father said contemptuously. He turned to Maia's chair, the passion already beginning to cool in his eyes. "My dear, would you like a chance to visit Muirwood before the roads are closed?"

CHAPTER NINETEEN

Vow

Yes."

It was Maia's own voice, her own mouth that said it. The sensation was like coming awake from a vivid dream, one that blurred like fog and syrup. Somehow she had fallen asleep in the king's tent. Her memories were muddled and thick, and though in her mind's eye she was staring at her father and answering his question, she realized ponderously that her memory was distorted. Her father had never asked her if she wished to go to Muirwood. He had never given her that option. The image of her father crumbled away, and she discovered another man standing before her, wearing the black cassock of the Dochte Mandar. He faced her direction, but his gaze shifted to someone next to her.

"Most illustrious prince," the man said, his voice formal and speaking Dahomeyjan, "is it your will to fulfill the treaty of marriage concluded by your late father and the King of Comoros?

And, as the Dochte Mandar has sanctioned this marriage, do you take Princess Marciana, who is here present, for your lawful wife?"

"Yes, I will," said Collier.

The threads from her dream still billowed about her mind. She realized in the back of her mind that in front of her sat a wooden altar piece—a small one set near the brazier in the king's tent. A stone Leering rested atop it, the face chipped and chiseled and blunted by hammer strokes, but still visible. Power emanated from it, and she realized she was kneeling in front of the altar, her arms resting on it. Collier's arms were next to hers. Slowly, so slowly it felt as if she were turning a huge boulder by herself, she twisted her neck and saw Collier's profile, his deep blue eyes gazing intently at the Dochte Mandar.

"You have declared your consent before me. May the Medium strengthen your consent and fill you both with pleasing Gifts. What we have joined hither, men must not divide."

"Until death us depart," Collier said, bowing his head.

"Even so," said the Dochte Mandar amiably. "It is the tradition amongst the Dochte Mandar for the husband to kiss his wife after the vow, Your Majesty."

Collier smirked. "Thank you for the recommendation, Trevor. Not at the present however." He rose to his feet and then gripped Maia's hand to pull her up. Her knees were shaking, and she steadied herself on the edge of the wooden altar.

"My lord brother, thank you for being witness. Thank you as well, Earl of Lachaulx. Are those birds? Is it dawn already?"

Maia's mind whirled like a child's top, and she felt as if she would kneel and retch. The tent spun faster and faster.

"Your wife is pale, brother."

"Here, my lady, let me help you to a chair." Collier took her arm and led her to his camp chair, the one she had seen him in before. What had happened to the night? It felt as if she had dozed for but a moment or two, not slept away the entire evening. Why could she not remember? It was like a great wind had kicked up a storm of dry leaves in her mind, veiling all her memories. She had hoped to forestall the marriage by pledging to marry him later, once her quest was complete.

"My liege, I will take my leave of you. Some of the men are rousing and preparing to ride."

"Thank you, my lord earl. I will join you later. I would appreciate a moment alone with my wife."

A few guffaws of laughter sounded, and Maia's heart jolted with a spasm of dread. She cast her eyes around the pavilion as the other men departed from the tent flap in front. It spoke of her disorientation that she had not noticed them until they were leaving. The place looked different in the pale dawn—starker and less magical. The brazier only had a few licks of coals left inside, and the nearby tray of food had been reduced to crumbs.

Why could she not remember? In her last recollection, she was sitting with him on a bearskin rug. He had insisted on seeing . . . what? Her shoulder. He wanted to see her shoulder, to see if she had the hetaera's brand. The pieces of memory clashed in her mind.

An image flashed in her memory. The brand of the double serpent.

She remembered.

Horror exploded in her heart. What, by Idumea's hand, had she just done? She bore the mark of the hetaera on her shoulder. How had she not seen it before? It was obvious, yet she had no memory of how it had gotten there. Desperate for answers, she replayed her trip step by step. Nothing stood out, except . . .

Since leaving the lost abbey, her dreams had been particularly vivid. She had thought it was the Medium's will for her to relive parts of her past when she fell asleep at night, that the memories were being sent to assist her in some way. Suddenly it seemed as if the answer were altogether different. For days now, she had not been her true self at night.

Oh no, she thought miserably. *What have I done!*

Had her experience in the lost abbey enabled one of the Myriad Ones to take possession of her body as she slept? Had she returned to the hetaera's Leering later, unwittingly, and received the brand? After visiting the dark pool within the lost abbey, she had lost consciousness for a time. It could have happened.

"I am sorry I do not have a ring to give you yet," Collier said. "But in fairness, you did already receive one from my father. Do you recall it?"

Maia's thoughts scattered, collected, and then scattered again. She trembled in the chair as if she had been struck by a fever. She hoped she would not vomit. "It was a silver ring," she whispered, trying to quell the panic. "With a large diamond."

He smiled. "The very one. Too small for your finger now. Maybe your smallest one." He reached out and took her hand, caressing her smallest finger with his thumb. "I was not there, of course, being nothing but a babe myself. But there were two emissaries present—Chancellor Walraven and Aldermaston Bonnivet—as well as both of our fathers. When Bonnivet gave you the ring, or so he told me later, you said to him, 'Are you the Prince of Dahomey? If you are, I wish to kiss you.' I find that sentiment deliciously ironic now."

Maia stared into his eyes, feeling lost and abandoned. Her last memory was exposing the brand on her shoulder. Something had smothered her mind in that moment, a presence thick as oil, making her black out. She obviously had not passed out. What had she agreed to beyond the marriage?

"What is it?" he asked her, dropping to one knee by her chair.

"My thoughts are a bit wild at the moment," she answered truthfully. "Forgive me if I am unwell."

He patted her arm and then rose. "Wine would only make you sick. Some water then?" She nodded briskly, and he went to fill her cup again. She had married him. In front of witnesses as well. What could she say to repudiate her actions? If she revealed that she was a hetaera, she would be murdered for certain. Was there a way she could be freed from the curse? There had to be! The maston lore spoke of the hetaera. She needed to find an Aldermaston. Muirwood.

She shivered violently at the thought and gratefully accepted the cup brimming with water and gulped it down.

"Easy, lass. Do not drown yourself in it," he teased.

The enormity of her situation spread a cloak of shadows across her mind. Had she been corrupted by Walraven as a child? Had his guidance and care been a means to an end? But how could that be? Her father was the one who had sent her to Dahomey. Walraven fell in disgrace, losing his title and his lands before his untimely death. But he had given her his kystrel, wrapped in a note. At the time, she had taken it as a sign of his unshakable faith in her, but could there have been a darker purpose? Was the kystrel's magic irrevocably linked with the hetaera's power? Where could truth be found amidst so many shadows?

Truth is knowledge. You must seek the High Seer. She knows the truth.

Maia shuddered in response to the whispers that would send her still to Naess. Was it even the Medium that spoke to her? How could she know whether to trust that inner voice? After all, it had sent her here. It had sent her on the north road. She pressed her fingers to her lips, stifling a sudden compulsion to weep. No, she could not! She did not cry like other girls. She did not surrender her will to her emotions. Maia pulled her feelings tight, wrestling against them. A small hiccup bubbled up. Her lips. She felt their shape against her fingertips.

Her lips could kill a man.

Help me, she thought desperately. *Mother, help me! I am lost.*

She had to make it to an abbey. The closest she could find. Only an Aldermaston's power could save her now.

She looked up at Collier. His expression was so enigmatic. He was studying her closely, watching the whirl and shift of emotions in her eyes. He said nothing, only stared.

"What is wrong, Maia?" he whispered, putting his hand on her shoulder. "Your countenance has changed . . . again. Do you seek your . . . your mother?"

"My lord!" shouted a voice from outside the tent. "Riders! It is the Dochte Mandar from Roc-Adamour!"

A grim look played on Collier's face. He stood and began pacing. "Delay them."

"My lord, they are on my heels!"

Maia heard pounding hooves, the snort of several horses frothing with foamy spittle. She heard a sharp voice and the thump of boots hitting the dirt. She recognized the voice.

"Is His Majesty within?" Corriveaux barked. Her heart spasmed with dread.

"You must give my lord leave!" said a strangled guard. Maia felt the Medium ripple in the air and then the tent flap whipped apart and six Dochte Mandar stormed inside, Corriveaux leading the way.

He looked no different from how he had appeared in her mind. His trimmed beard was immaculate, but his skin was flushed and dripping with sweat. He wore his kystrel proudly on his chest, its metal gleaming against the black velvet fabric. He was a thin, lanky man, and his eyes were sharp as daggers. He saw her crumpled in the chair, and a look of blazing triumph coalesced in his eyes.

"She is *here,*" Corriveaux whispered savagely. "My lord, has she touched you? Has she . . . kissed you?" His eyes were sick with dread and a little excitement.

Collier stood with easy confidence. "I am not a patient man under most circumstances. But truly, Corriveaux, this is deplorable timing. You cannot barge into your king's tent uninvited. Be gone." He waved a hand in lazy dismissal.

"Your Majesty, this is a matter of grave urgency. Your very life is in peril. Come here. Step closer to me." He gestured slowly, as if Maia were a snake coiled to strike.

"Do you think she is going to stab me? I have been with the princess all evening, sir. We have enjoyed each other's company in a most pleasant way, but *not* in the way you are supposing. I believe I ordered you to leave."

"Your Majesty," Corriveaux said, his distress growing more visible. "You must hearken to what I have to tell you. She is indeed the banished Princess of Comoros, but she is more than that."

"You say truly," Collier said, chuckling. *She is my wife.*

Maia stared at him in surprise. She had heard the thought as surely as if it had been whispered aloud.

"This is not a moment for jesting, my lord," Corriveaux snapped. "If her mouth has touched you in any way, you are a dead man. It is my duty to your highness to offer you protection and advice. This creature is a spawn of darkness. She may already have corrupted you. We tracked her from the dark pool of the lost abbey. She is hetaera! There is no denying it."

"How do you know this?" Collier said with open contempt.

"You ride here like lions seeking prey, but must I remind you that *I* am the master of the realm? You have much to answer for, Corriveaux. Like traveling with soldiers impersonating the king's men. Like the village of Argus. If you were part of that massacre—"

"—My lord, if you will indulge me a *moment* longer," Corriveaux said, his fists clenching. He had finally found her after hunting her for days. He was not ready to let her go. Maia could see his desperation, especially at the mention of the mountain village.

"I have indulged your intrusion with remarkable patience. No, I have not kissed or been kissed by this woman. She is not a camp follower, Corriveaux. Not a harlot. She is the Princess of Comoros."

"She is the *banished* princess," Corriveaux corrected. "My lord, our spies in Comoros became aware of the plot. Her father sent her to the lost abbey to reawaken the hetaera order and begin the killing of mastons. She has the potential to destroy not just an insignificant village but every person living in Dahomey and beyond our borders. Not only does this allow King Brannon to divorce his wife, but it gives him the power to remove all those who oppose him. We have a spy very close to the throne, my liege. We learned about the vessel, *her* vessel—the *Blessing of Burntisland*. We found it moored off the cursed shores and captured its crew. They revealed her presence in your kingdom, my lord. We sent word for you by courier, but Your Majesty is difficult to find these days. She is a danger to Comoros, to Dahomey, to all the kingdoms. My lord, she *must* be taken to Naess and interrogated and executed. She is an abomination! The empire fell due to the plague the hetaera unleashed on these shores. Surrender her to me, my lord. I have enough men to contain her."

Maia was terrified. She was trapped like a mouse, unable to flee. Even if she had her kystrel, which she did not feel around her neck, she could not have repulsed so many.

"I will give due consideration to all you have told me," Collier said after a long pause. "Now depart, Corriveaux. Before I call my guard."

Corriveaux looked down at the ground, his brow wrinkled with frustration. Maia felt a whisper of dread go through her, followed by a feeling of immense fear. When Corriveaux raised his head, his eyes were glowing silver.

"I fear you are under her sway, Your Majesty," he said softly. "Your will is not your own."

In a flash of speed, Collier's blade came out of its sheath and he was suddenly right in front of Corriveaux, the tip aimed at his heart.

"You *dare* use the Medium against me?" Collier threatened. "Stop or I will run you through. I see your eyes, Corriveaux. Look into mine."

Maia felt a surge of power rise up in the pavilion. It came from Collier, but she felt it, as surely as if it had been drawn from her muscles and bones. *He has my kystrel*, she realized. *He wears it!*

Corriveaux's eyes widened with shock. He held his hand up in a placating gesture. "Oh, my lord king, what have you done?" He backed away slowly, trying to put some distance between the tip of the blade and his chest.

"I do not believe in your superstitions," Collier said. "You use the kystrels to control our hearts and minds. I am protected from you. Remember that. Now, I have several nooses that were not put to use last night. You can all share them between you if need be."

"That will not be necessary," Corriveaux said, retreating to the tent flap. "You clearly have the situation well under control. I should not have doubted your wisdom."

Collier barked a laugh. "You will answer for this, Corriveaux. Report to my Privy Council and await my judgment."

"Yes, my liege. As you command." Corriveaux bowed deeply. As he lifted, he shot Maia a murderous look, his lips twisted with rage.

The King of Dahomey had her kystrel. He wore it around his neck. She could see the thin chain against his skin. They were bound together now, and not just as husband and wife. The other five Dochte Mandar who traveled with Corriveaux sulked out of the tent after him.

Maia thought she heard a bird chirping. How she heard it past the wild hammering of her heart, she did not know. She rose from the chair, feeling her legs strengthen beneath her.

Collier sheathed his blade and turned, brushing his hands. "I told you I would protect you, Maia. I do not think they will be fool enough to defy me." He gave her a charming smile. "I am going to summon my armies to invade Comoros. It is time to depose your father. Shall we?" He offered her his hand.

"You wear my kystrel," Maia said hollowly.

"You *gave* it to me," he said with a laugh.

"I am sorry." She swallowed.

"For what?"

Sleep, she commanded in her mind, shoving her thought at him.

He collapsed in a heap on the ground.

Maia knelt carefully by his crumpled form. He breathed deeply, his chest rising and falling. So easy it would be. So easy to kill him. A small kiss on his cheek was all it would take. The thought in her mind horrified her, and she realized with a jolt that it was not her own.

Maia reached for the chain of the kystrel around Collier's neck. As her fingers drew near, she felt her left shoulder begin to smolder with pain. Her muscles seized up and locked. She could not stretch her arm any farther, try as she might. Pain and nausea swept through her.

She felt . . . disapproval.

Maia huddled next to him and stared down into his sleeping face. The face of her husband. This was not the royal wedding she had dreamed of as a child. There had been no pageantry. No Aldermastons with gray cassocks and wise airs. It had not been a maston wedding, performed in an abbey by irrevocare sigil.

She was grateful for that much.

She pulled her arm back and found that she could move it again. The being trapped inside her—the Myriad One whose name she did not know—would not allow her certain actions against its interests. She breathed deeply, trying to steel her heart. She reached down and squeezed her husband's rough hand.

"I am truly sorry, Feint Collier," she whispered. "But I cannot let you use me to destroy my father." She gave the hand another squeeze. "Do not try to find me, for I will run from you for the rest of my life."

She rose and looked down at him one last time. There was her pack near the mouth of the tent. She grabbed it. Spying one of his cloaks rumpled on a chest, she swung it over her shoulders, raised the cowl, and slipped out the back of the tent into the dawn air.

There was once a wise Aldermaston who said, "Gold tests with fire, woman with gold, man with woman."

—Lia Demont, Aldermaston of Muirwood Abbey

CHAPTER TWENTY

Peliyey Mountains

The morning sky was hazy with camp smoke as the soldiers awoke and began stirring the ashes from the previous night. Some bent low and breathed on the cakes of ash, coaxing them to life again. Others carried piles of sticks, ready to feed the flames. Maia passed them as a shadow, swathed in Collier's big coat.

"We could use more wine in our rations," a big man muttered as she passed. "My head is aching."

"Because you drank too much wine last night."

Maia walked past them with a firm stride, wanting to hurry without appearing to do so.

She heard the crunch of boots behind her, coming on her left, so she switched directions, going around another campfire. The sounds of pursuit persisted. A lump of fear settled into her stomach. She did not want to use the kystrel's magic to flee, but she wondered if she would even have a choice. Though it no longer hung around her neck, its power was as accessible to her as ever—more so.

"Keep walking," the kishion said at her elbow as he passed her. "Follow me."

She startled as he walked past her. He wore a tunic with the king's colors, the fabric stained and blotchy. There was a slit in the back, peeking just above his belt, and it was dark red from blood. He marched on ahead of her and she kept pace, the two of them weaving through camp like wraiths. One man had pierced a hunk of bread with his dagger, she saw, and was ripping pieces from it with his teeth.

The first streamers of sunlight bit her eyes. The light coming into the smoke came like fingers through silk. It was dawn, a new day. A terrible day. She felt as if she had tripped and tumbled down a steep hill, bouncing off rocks and colliding with trees on the way down. She could hardly tell which way was up.

She stared at the kishion's back, wondering if he was just as confused as she was or whether he was involved in her mission in a way she did not yet understand.

There was much she did not know, but she did know something. She could not continue with her quest until she visited an abbey. She needed to find an Aldermaston who could rid her of the Myriad One who was nesting inside her—the one who emerged at night, forcing her to dream. Maia was grateful it was dawn. She could not allow herself to fall asleep again, not before she rid herself of the evil being inside her. She would push herself to stay awake, to walk for days if need be. There were abbeys under construction throughout all the kingdoms. Which one was nearest?

The kishion stepped into a grove of trees and Maia followed him, slipping through slender branches that caught at her cloak and tried to snare her. The bark was smooth and glossy. They meandered their way through the copse, which became thicker the farther they went. Twigs and brush snapped as they made their noisy way, but the sounds of the camp fell farther behind.

They had been walking for quite some time when something crashed through the undergrowth, and Argus bounded into view. Maia's heart leaped and she knelt amidst some ferns as the boarhound rushed up to her and started licking her face. She seized him by the ruff and hugged him, dangerously close to tears.

"Is Tayt with you, Argus?" she crooned. "Is he nearby?"

The kishion snorted. "We did not abandon you, Lady Maia."

She stroked Argus's ears and rose, staring at him gratefully. "Thank you." She had traveled with the kishion for days now, even slept near him in the wilderness, but she did not know if she could trust him. She doubted herself. She doubted everything except the hound's loyalty.

As they followed the direction Argus had come from, Maia began to hear the nicker of horses. There were three, she discovered, tethered to the spindly tree branches, and Jon Tayt was grooming them. As they approached, he finished brushing one down and dropped to inspect its hooves.

He looked up at her and smiled through his pointed beard. "Ah, we all survived the night, by Cheshu. I, for one, am grateful. Thank you for interceding for us last night, my lady. My friend here says we were not in any real danger, but I was not feeling so calm at the moment. A fine kettle of fish we were in. Sorry I did not heed your hint about meeting you at the mountain. We were not willing to let you try to escape all on your own."

"How did you escape?" Maia asked the kishion.

He looked at her and smiled darkly. "There is another kishion in the king's camp," he said. "He gave me a sign so that I might know him. Loosened my bonds and slipped me some weapons for the ride. I killed the escort not far from here, took the horses and a uniform, and was watching the tent when the Dochte Mandar arrived. I saw you slip out."

"Does the king know about the kishion in his camp?" Maia asked, her eyebrows lifting.

"Of course not," he replied blandly. "If I had been hired to kill the king, I would have had help getting into his tent."

Maia noticed that Jon Tayt was staring at the kishion with brooding eyes. He said nothing. "How far are we from Mon?" she asked.

Jon Tayt shifted his gaze to hers. "We are near the mountains that separate us. The mountains are called the Peliyey. I believe what Collier—ach, I mean the king! He said the passes are guarded. If he is truly planning to invade Comoros, then he does not want his own kingdom sacked while he is gone."

Maia took a deep breath, conflicted. No, her priority was to find an abbey. She lowered the cowl and swept loose her hair.

"Where is the nearest abbey?" she asked Jon Tayt.

"What?"

"The nearest abbey. Where is it?"

He looked at her, confused, his brow wrinkling. What could she say? They did not know the truth about her yet. She had to keep it secret until she could meet with an Aldermaston.

He scratched the whiskers along his neck. "There is Rivaulx to the north, but it's on the border with Paeiz. There is Lisyeux in Dahomey, but it would be foolish for us to go there." He squinted. "There is Cruix Abbey, though. It is in the top of the Peliyey, where three kingdoms are divided by three rivers. It is a hard climb, my lady."

Maia remembered it now from the map she had studied in her father's solar. Cruix Abbey.

"Aye, it is on the border of Dahomey, Paeiz, and Mon. Take me there."

"Why?" Jon Tayt asked.

She shook her head. "I learned something in the king's tent last night. That is all I can tell you right now. I need to visit this abbey. The sooner we leave Dahomey, the better. Get us across the mountains."

***

They rode hard through the woods and gave the horses their heads when they reached the lowlands, which stretched out to the foot of the mountains. Gradually, Maia became aware of the power of the Medium all around her. It was in the blades of grass, the puffy clouds chasing across the sky. She felt the Medium in the rocks and boulders, in the flowers and seedlings. It was even in the wind. Her awareness of it had expanded, so much so it felt as if she were seeing the world as it really was for the first time. It was right in her skin, in her very pores. She could feel her blood thrumming in her veins, her heartbeat rhythmic and constant, a drum of power. She sensed the lives of birds and squirrels, of tiny insects too small to see. She could command them, she realized. They were aware of her as well, and she could sense their small minds brushing against hers, drawn to her like moths to a flame. The new powers frightened her.

She remembered again the way Walraven had summoned all those mice and rats. *She* could do that, she realized, and with little effort. As they rode, she sensed hawks floating overhead. As soon as she became aware of them, her mind seemed to reach out to them of its own accord, and suddenly she could see the panorama of the landscape from their perspective, including the three riders galloping in the fields below. It was jarring, watching herself from the hawk's eyes. She saw her hair streaming behind her, the horses' hooves churning relentlessly as they brought them toward the mountains.

The plains were lush with groves of evergreens. The Peliyey rose suddenly and sharply from the verdant valley floor, a colossal hunch of rugged stone that was wreathed in white from high mountain snows. Beyond the first battering rams was a grouping of even taller mountains, totally white with snow. The range dipped and stretched for leagues both north and south. Through the hawk's eyes, Maia could see tiny hamlets nestled in the foothills of the giant range, but none within the range itself. There were towering waterfalls dotted around the mountains where the snow ran off and melted. It was enormous, breathtaking, and Maia's heart filled with giddiness at the strange sensation of seeing it from both the hawk's current perspective and its memories.

There was a rift in the mountains, a trail leading up to a lower pass. Their destination.

Maia?

The voice in her mind startled her and sent her slamming back into her body. It had been hours since they had left the king's camp, and she could feel the grogginess in Collier's thoughts.

Maia, where are you?

As he awoke, she could sense his surroundings. He was still in the tent, jostled awake by one of his guards, who had grown alarmed by his long silence. Through the kystrel around his neck, she could feel his growing fear, which he quickly mastered. She had guessed as much earlier, but here was the proof. The magic had bonded them together. He took a cup offered by his brother and drank it quickly. He gave some curt orders, for the men were restless.

"Where is Lady Marciana?" someone asked him.

It was so strange, feeling like she was still in the tent with him when she was hours away. He was sick with worry, wondering if linking himself to her had been a terrible mistake. She saw him as he was inside, saw the mixture of human feelings that he carefully guarded and concealed from others, but could not hide from her. She could strip his soul bare. It would be so easy. There was nothing he could do to protect himself. Yes, the kystrel gave him power—the ability to summon the Medium and command it to perform. But in return, it gave her absolute power over his mind, his thoughts, his feelings. His everything. She could bend him, twist him, make him into anyone she wanted him to be. She could . . .

Maia was horrified at the deliciousness of the feelings surging up inside her. At the welling hunger.

Maia?

His thoughts were timid. She could feel him reaching out to her, and it would be so easy to respond. It did not matter how many leagues separated them.

Their very souls were entwined because of the kystrel. When it had been wrenched from her neck, she had felt empty and anxious without it. But because *he* was wearing it, her powers were only magnified. The stain of the tattoo would grow on his chest now while hers started to fade. She could sense it vividly now, the mixing of their minds, the drawing together.

I sense you, he thought. *Why will you not answer me? You are mounted and riding fast. It makes me a little . . . ill. How strange this feels. You can hear me? I sense that you can. Answer me.*

He gave another curt order to someone and stormed out of the tent. She could feel his anger starting to throb, frustration mingling with it. He inspected his stallion's saddle and then scolded the boy who had prepared it for doing it wrong. He touched his heart, covering the kystrel with his palm.

Maia, answer me! I sense you . . . east. You are riding to the mountains. One of the passes is very dangerous. You must not go there. There is a creature in the mountains. No one can kill it.

She wanted to get his thoughts out of her mind. She pulled her awareness away from his, feeling the jolt and shudder of the horse as it charged beneath her.

Maia stared at the mountain range. The air was crisp and lovely, the scent heavy with the smell of grass and earth. She stamped at the horse's flanks, riding harder, faster, trying to escape the thoughts flitting through her mind. She had always loved horses and was an accomplished rider. A horse meant freedom, which is why her father had given all of hers away.

She would not answer Collier. Though that sick yearning inside her said otherwise, she did not want the ability to control him or root around inside his mind. He had been so reckless, not willing to recognize the danger of his actions. What would happen when she fell asleep? What would the Myriad One do to him through her?

No, she could not fall asleep—not just to save herself, but to protect him.

Behind her, she could hear Jon Tayt calling out, but his words did not fully reach her. Her cloak whipped about her shoulders, fanning out behind her like a banner. Tears stung her eyes from the wind beating against her face. Faster, she wanted to ride faster!

She had studied a Dochte Mandar's tome about the hetaera. She had learned about them, been warned about them, but really . . . so little was commonly known about them, only tidbits chronicled by Dieyre before his death. She knew about the brand on the shoulder. She knew that once a hetaera gave her kystrel to a man, her powers increased. She had also learned that hetaera always betrayed those who held their kystrels. Betrayal was their favorite tool.

Maia, please! Answer me. What would you have me do? You said last night you would guide me. Do you want me to invade Comoros? Do you want me to topple your father?

Maia gritted her teeth, anguished by her feelings. She could use her powers to stop him. But using them would only increase the Myriad One's sway over her.

She tried to shut him out of her mind. She tried to bury his thoughts away where she could not hear him. Maia kept her gaze fixed on the approaching mountains, the hulking snow-capped peaks and rugged edges. It was beautiful, yet she was filled with nothing but dread.

She knew that no matter how hard she rode, she could not escape Collier's voice in her head. She would not be able to escape until she found an Aldermaston who could banish the Myriad One from her body.

Cruix Abbey. The thought burned in her mind like a seething coal from a fire pit. She had to reach the abbey without sleeping.

Yet why did that thought also bring with it a small throb of glee?

CHAPTER TWENTY-ONE

Fear Liath

The air in the mountains sliced like knives with each frozen breath. Maia was grateful now that Jon Tayt had insisted she bring both gowns, for she had needed them for the arduous journey rising into the Peliyey Mountains. While the view from the valley below was majestic in its splendor, it had been a difficult climb, taxing both her strength and her determination.

Jon Tayt had warned that because they were entering the mountains so late in the day, it would be hard to cross the Fear Liath's lair before dark. Maia did not feel she had a choice. She could not linger in the valley to wait out the night, not when falling asleep could be disastrous. She could feel the awareness of the Myriad One inside her. Now that she knew it was there, her own thoughts so intermingled with its that she was not sure which were truly her own.

They had left the horses down on the valley floor, for the ground was too treacherous and steep for them to make the climb.

Mules would have been better companions for such a journey. Maia had wrapped herself in both of her gowns and Collier's cloak, and even with her rucksack against her back, she still felt the mountain's chill. Her legs throbbed with the punishing climb, but she was determined to make it through the pass in time.

Not only did she have a Myriad One trapped inside her head, but she also had to deal with Feint Collier. It took some concentration and focus to block out the thoughts of where he was and who he was with, but after a persistent effort, he fell silent.

As she walked, she pondered why she had not told him the truth about her predicament. In those first moments after awakening, she had been too disoriented, confused, and frightened to think straight. But why not tell him now? He believed she was a hetaera. The mark on her shoulder could not be explained away. Yet she had not willingly accepted any hetaera vows, and she could not remember how it had even happened. She might not be able to control what she did when she lost consciousness or when the being inside her took control, but she could at least explain the situation to Collier. Certainly he could choose not to believe her, but was that truly a reason to remain silent? She struggled with indecision.

The mountains rose steeply, and she paused to drink from her flask of water. Jon Tayt did not look winded at all, and he stopped to wait for her, hooking his thumb in his broad belt. Argus sniffed at the dirt and stone of the trail thoroughly. She looked back and saw the kishion, his eyes fixed on her, as they always were. She wondered again what, specifically, her father had hired him to do. Would he be honest if she asked him?

She fixed the flask to her pack again and nodded for the hunter to continue. The path was narrow and rugged, meandering through broken rocks and sparse vegetation. There were no trees at this height, and the rock fragments were so sharp they could slice through skin. She smelled mule's ear on the wind, just the essence of it, but she could not find any of the plant with her eyes.

As they continued their journey, she began to tease out the root of the reason she had not told Collier the truth. She did not *trust* the King of Dahomey. He was her husband, legally, but he had used artifice to win her. He did not have a history of being a trustworthy man, and if she were going to bare her soul to someone and confess her shame and her troubles, there needed to be some degree of mutual trust. Perhaps she would tell him, but not until he had proved himself a faithful confidant. But then, why would she want a husband who had deliberately sought to marry a hetaera?

The sun began to set before they had even crossed the top of the pass. Their boots crunched in snow and ice, against which they stood out in stark contrast—an easy target. Her nose was cold and pink, and she felt the air growing thinner, making each step a trial of energy. There was no denying that her physical strength was ebbing.

"How much farther?" she asked Jon Tayt after catching up with him.

He glanced down at her, his eyes dark. "I warned you before we started that we were fools to cross the mountain so late in the day." She saw the nervousness in his eyes. The normal jovial smile was gone.

"I can keep going," she said. "We are not discovered yet."

"We have no choice but to keep going, Lady Maia. If that thing catches us in the mountains, we are all dead unless you can banish it."

"Have we crossed into Mon yet? Or are we still in Dahomey?"

"Dahomey," he replied. He wiped his dripping nose on the edge of his gloved hand. "These mountains are vast, running north to south. Mon is still a way to the east, over a few more ranges. Cruix farther north. We will join a mountain trail that runs along the ridges. It is the one we were warned not to take. All the lower passes will be guarded on Dahomey's side of the mountain."

He focused on the ground ahead and fell silent. Maia struggled to match his relentless pace, but she managed it.

"Why are we seeking an Aldermaston?" he asked her softly. "Why this one?"

She did not like his question.

"I have my reasons, Jon Tayt."

"I know. You said you wished to be taken to the land of the Naestors. Now we are going to an abbey."

"Trust me that I have said all I can say," she replied.

He sighed and then asked her no more questions.

***

The moon was silver in the sky, fringed with hoarfrost and gleaming like a cold jewel. The temperature had fallen rapidly, and each breath brought a fog of mist from their mouths as they huffed their way down the far slope of the pass. They had crossed it at midnight, knee-deep in snow. Her feet ached with cold, her toes feeling more like stones than flesh. She hugged herself and plunged on. The stars twinkled in the sky—mysterious and fraught with meaning.

"Ach," Jon Tayt swore, coming to a halt and holding out his arm to keep her from stumbling.

"What is it?" the kishion asked.

Tayt pointed down the trail where a thick bank of fog had appeared, drowning out the moonlight.

The hackles rose on Argus's neck, and a low growl sounded in his throat.

"We are above the clouds," the kishion said. "That is all."

Jon Tayt shook his head. "No, I have not seen the like of this before in these mountains. The clouds do not settle midmountain like this. Only the ones high enough to cross can make it over, and they usually dump snow. This is unnatural."

Argus barked sharply and Tayt cuffed him. "*Chut!* Quiet, dog!"

Maia could feel tendrils of fear creep into her bones, wilting her courage. "It was not behind us after all," she said dully, feeling a fool. She had thought they would be safe after crossing the pass.

"Aye," Jon Tayt said, drawing one of his axes. He sniffed. "Well, if a Fear Liath wants to pick at my bones, it will have to murder me first. No sense going back up the mountain. These mists can move quickly, I have heard, when the beasts are hunting prey."

"We fight it?" the kishion asked.

"No," Maia said. "I brought this danger upon us. I will see us past it. The creature will let us pass."

"I have heard it said that only mastons can tame these ilk," Jon Tayt said gruffly. "Let us hope your amulet fares as well."

Maia ignored the comment and began walking ahead of them. When Jon Tayt tried to pass her, she waved him back. As she walked, she summoned the kystrel's power. It responded immediately, hungrily, and she felt it wash over her in cinnamon waves of pleasure.

There was Collier in her mind instantly. *Maia—are you in trouble? Where are you? I feel cold and fear.*

She ignored his intruding whispers and summoned power and strength from the amulet. The wind began to pick up and tousle her clothes. She knew her eyes glowed silver, and she hoped the sight of her coming would be enough to discourage the beast in the mist.

From the wall of fog, a barking chuffing noise sounded. Argus whined with fear. Maia felt the tendrils of terror weaving around her own heart, but she banished the feelings with her power. It was like shedding a mantle and leaving it by the wayside. The fear could not seed within her. The mist loomed as she approached, the fog churning with anger as she neared it, unafraid.

"By Cheshu," Jon Tayt said, his voice thick with emotion. She could sense his terror and awe, and she used her power to strip it away, emboldening him. The kishion had stopped in the snow, his hands trembling as they drew his daggers. Even he was afraid. She sipped the fear from his soul with her kystrel.

Maia halted, seeing a shadow in the fog cloud. It was a massive hulking shape and she heard the thick crunch of snow as it padded forward. At the shoulder it was at least eight spans high, wider and thicker than a monstrous boulder. Plumes of frost came from its snout as it chuffed again. Argus quivered with restlessness.

"Stand aside," Maia ordered. As if it were not frightening enough on its own, it emitted a force that instilled fear. She shielded her companions from it, taking the brunt of it on herself. Her heart was hard as flint. She stared down at the beast, feeling the winds coming more forcefully at her back, making her cloak billow.

The beast snorted, fixed as an obelisk. She could feel the defiance in its bearing. She was challenging it in its own lair.

It had only an animal intelligence, but it was keen and cunning and terribly vicious. It came forward, rippling with muscle and sinew and shadow.

Maia held her ground, immune to its power, but she realized the only weapon she had against it was the kystrel's magic.

Stand aside or I will destroy you, she thought, sending the words at it like shards of glass from her mind.

Give me meat. One man's fear to savor. The other may pass.

The thoughts were half formed and facile, but she could immediately read its intent. The Fear Liath intended to claim a sacrifice for passing the mountain. A life. It hungered for fear. It fed on despair. It did not care whether she gave it Tayt or the kishion. But it would have one of them.

No, Maia challenged, her thoughts churning with anger. *I will destroy you instead.*

The beast's thoughts seemed to chuckle. *I will have my meat. I devour fear. I will take it!*

It started to come at her, bounding forward on its front paws. She should never have tried to best it in its own lair, let alone at night, when its power was strongest. The chuffing noise turned into an earsplitting roar, and she saw only the slaver, the fangs, the claws. She would have quailed without the kystrel.

"Maia!" Jon Tayt shrieked in despair. He stepped in front of her, throwing his first axe at the beast's head. The axe went true and struck the monster, but to no effect, deflecting into the snow. The second axe followed the first, whistling as it spun, and it also bounced off the monster's snout.

Maia could sense triumph in the being's primitive mind. She struck out with the magic, blasting it with every emotion and feeling she possessed. It wanted a feast, she would give it one, by Cheshu! The wind howled through the canyon, sending her hair flapping in front of her face, her cloak whipping wildly. The beast tried to claw her, knocking Jon Tayt aside, but the kishion lunged and shoved her down, taking the next blow himself. The claws raked through his cloak, his shirt, and she could see steam rising from the gash on his arm. The kishion jutted the dagger into the beast's neck, but the blade would not penetrate.

The ice bit into Maia's forearms, and she struggled back to her feet, sending a hot blast of fear into the beast's chest, just as she had done to the one that guarded the bones of the fallen soldiers near the lost abbey. The memory brought with it a realization. That other beast had fled after snatching some of the soldiers. She had not defeated it at all. It had let them go after taking its tithe— its meal of fear to digest.

The creature's jaws snapped at the kishion, and she heard him call out in pain as its teeth bit into his side and lifted him off the ground.

"No!" Maia screamed, holding out her hands and welling up more power. She had to conquer the beast. But how? The wind screamed and howled, mirroring her anger and frustration as the Fear Liath began dragging the kishion away, his blood smearing and steaming the snow.

Argus snagged at the kishion's boot, snarling and tugging, trying to keep the man from being dragged away. The beast did not slow its pace.

Maia screamed in rage, watching as her protector was ripped away from her. Her mind went black with murder, and thunder crackled in the clear sky above. Still, the Fear Liath slumped off into the fog, dragging the kishion's body with it. Argus could not master the beast's strength and had to release the boot cuff.

Maia sagged to her knees, her eyes burning. From the fog darted silver-furred beasts, timber wolves, who rushed at the Fear Liath and began snapping at it savagely. The howling she was hearing was not only from the wind. It was the sound of wolves. The pack surrounded the gargantuan creature, challenging it for its prey with snarls and snaps. The commotion was deafening, and Maia watched in surprise as the wolves attacked the Fear Liath. She felt the Myriad Ones all around her, snuffling and sniffing at her, drawn to the spilled blood. The sky was suddenly full of bats, fluttering from the trees and sky like an arrow cloud.

The wolves tormented the Fear Liath until it whirled and struck, bringing its savage claws around and impaling one wolf after another. Its teeth tore into their ranks, but their numbers were astonishing—whenever one fell, another filled the gap, howling and barking and snarling.

Maia could not believe the sight unfolding before her, but there was Argus, dragging the kishion through the snow, away from the fray and toward them. Jon Tayt huffed forward and hefted the man over his shoulder as if the kishion were a wounded stag, then barreled away from the scene like a man intent on preserving his life. Maia rose from the crushed snow and ran after them, witness to the ferocity of the battle between the creatures of the forest and the Fear Liath. As she ran down the trail, trying not to stumble, she saw another pack coming in to reinforce the first, then another. The howling filled the night sky, and she realized that she had summoned them to her aid with the kystrel's magic.

She remembered Walraven's study again—the avalanche of mice and rats. The ability to bend another creature to your will—even unto death—was a terrible power. It was an awesome power. The wolves and bats had known no thought other than to do her bidding.

A huge roar sounded behind her. It was the roar of a predator whose prey had escaped it.

When Colvin first taught me about kystrels, he admitted he would have ripped one from my neck had he discovered it to be the source of my power. I still remember the fear in his voice as he described their powers to me. When a hetaera has given hers to a man to use, she becomes even more deadly. There is power unleashed when the emotions of a man and a woman mingle as one. Her influence can continue to grow undetected. I give you this as a sign that the hetaera have returned. The abbeys will begin to burn. So it was in my day.

—Lia Demont, Aldermaston of Muirwood Abbey

CHAPTER
TWENTY-TWO

Cruix Abbey

Maia knelt on the hard flat rock and slit part of her cloak with a dagger. Jon Tayt worked feverishly to dress the kishion's wounds, blood staining his thick fingers. The kishion writhed and groaned, but he did not struggle against the ministrations, not even when the hunter produced a stubby needle to puncture his skin. He was given an arrow to clamp between his teeth, which he did, grunting with agony as the wound in his ribs was knit closed. Maia felt her cheeks drain of blood, but she could not take her eyes off the man. How she admired him for enduring the hardship of pain with such courage.

"Ach, it is deep," Jon Tayt muttered darkly. "A few more stitches. Maia, hold his legs down!"

They were still in the mountains, but they had not stopped their flight until they were far from the Fear Liath's lair. The scene in front of Maia was such a strange contrast—the sun shone brightly in the morning sky and birds flitted around harmlessly; the view from the rocky bluff where the kishion lay thrashing was dazzling. Jon Tayt worked with brutal efficiency, knowing how to apply pressure to ease the bleeding and how to suture the wounds with gut and needle.

Maia held down the kishion's legs at his knees, but he fell still. She glanced up at his face, fearing he was dead, and saw that he had only lost consciousness. His chest rose and fell fitfully.

"Thank Idumea," Jon Tayt growled. "Oblivion is the best remedy for pain. Did you see how deep the creature's teeth gashed him? *Ach*." He leaned back on his ankles, wiping his dripping nose on his forearm. "What he needs is a healer, Maia. This wound will infect, I have no doubt it will."

"But will he live?" she asked, coming around and pushing two fingers against the throbbing at his throat.

"Who can say? Death comes for us all. Took a nasty gash on his arm. Let me try some woad on that to help stop the bleeding. Grab some from my pack. It's in a leather pouch the size of my hand, stained blue at the mouth."

Jon Tayt continued to work on closing and bandaging the wound in the kishion's side while Maia hunted through the pack until she found the woad. It had already been ground into powder, and she dipped her fingers into the bag and began smearing it on the claw wounds across his skin. The fabric around the cuts was stained with blood.

"Should we bathe the wounds first?" Maia asked.

"If we had a pond, yes. But he will die if we do not get him to a healer soon. He may die regardless." He sighed deeply. "I have seen worse, by Cheshu, but not many. I once saw a lad who tripped and sliced his leg open to the bone. Lay the woad on thick, lass. There you go. Do not be stingy."

Maia worked quickly, covering the wounds on the kishion's shoulder. In short order, the makeshift bandages were applied to keep the tender areas away from the elements. She was exhausted and drained, but grateful that Jon Tayt had been there with her. His knowledge had been invaluable.

"How far to Cruix Abbey?" she asked him.

"Two more days at a slower pace. If he could walk, we might get there faster. But even if he does, it will hobble the journey. We have left a trail a blind man could see, so we best hope the bloody Dochte Mandar still think you are with the king. The abbey is the fastest way to find a healer. I know a prince in Mon who would help us, but his castle is farther north."

"How do we carry him?" Maia asked, brushing her stained hands on her cloak.

The hunter snorted. "We?" He hefted the kishion up on his shoulder. "Argus!" he clicked his tongue and the dog padded up next to him.

***

A small fire crackled, warming Maia's hands. She fed it with small chips of wood. Jon Tayt had built it in the hollow of some stones to help prevent the light from revealing them. Argus was huddled next to her, pressing against her leg, muzzle buried in his paws. He stared dolefully at the flames. Jon Tayt leaned against a nearby tree, his beard drooping against his chest, the low rumble of snores coming from him regularly. She heard the woodland insects of the night clicking and clacking in the dark, lulling her to sleep, but she struggled against their call. They all needed to rest, but Maia could not let herself fall asleep. *Only two more days,* she repeated again and again in her mind.

After a while, another noise joined the chorus of the night—the chattering of the kishion's teeth. Her own cloak had joined his, both of them tucked up to his neck, and he was so near the fire it threatened to singe him. She stared at the kishion's sweat-drenched skin, feeling a terrible premonition that he was battling his own death in his sleep. It was strange to watch him sleep. She wondered how many times he had watched her. As if he had been roused by her thoughts, his eyes suddenly opened and he struggled against the clutch of the cloaks.

"Be still," she murmured, placing her hand on his chest.

He squinted and glanced wildly around the darkness before returning his gaze to her, his expression softening into relief.

"Good," he mumbled, blinking fast now. "I dreamed I was buried in an ossuary. Still alive." He shuddered again. "Nightfall?"

"Yes," she replied, gazing down at his face. He had walked part of the way that day, but his legs were weak, and the pain from his wounds was so intense it had made him black out again.

"It does not hurt," he mumbled. "I can go on."

"Let Tayt sleep a moment longer," she said, patting him. "Rest a bit. I will keep watch."

He looked her sternly in the eye. "You look weary."

She gave him a shallow smile. "You look injured."

He grimaced at the comment and adjusted his bulk slightly. Convulsions rocked through him again.

"You should leave me," he whispered hoarsely. "I am slowing your escape."

She smirked. "I think you know me well enough by now," she said, "to know that I will not do that."

"You should, though," he said simply. "If you have ever longed to escape me, now is your chance. I am helpless."

"I do not repay loyalty with dross," she answered.

A look crossed his face. It was as inscrutable as most of his expressions were, but it was almost as if he were surprised by her words. He chuckled darkly, causing an agonizing coughing fit. His body shuddered with his injuries. "Never make me laugh, lass," he said in a half-strangled voice. "It is a torture. I am *not* loyal to you. I was paid well."

She brought up her knees and rested her forearms on them, then rested her head on her arms and looked at him. "We are well past the obligations of duty, kishion. I saved your life last night. Just as you have saved mine countless times."

"If you were wise," he said with a stifled groan, "you would abandon me right here. Right now. I do not deserve pity. Yours especially."

"Perhaps not, but I give it to you anyway. I am grateful we have a moment to talk. There are questions I must ask you."

His chest heaved and sagged, but his icy gray-blue eyes did not shy from hers. He said nothing, though she could tell he dreaded her questions.

"Will you be truthful?" she asked him softly.

He continued to gaze at her, then nodded once. It was the best she was going to get from him.

"Did my father . . . did he hire you to kill me?" She needed to know.

His eyes were hard stones. His jaw quivered with the chills and suppressed emotion. "Yes."

Maia closed her eyes, feeling weariness and pain. "I thought so."

"Only if you were caught. If you were abducted by the Dahomeyjans or the Dochte Mandar, I was ordered to kill you lest you fall into their hands and be used against him."

She opened her eyes again, feeling the sweet temptation of sleep. She rubbed her forearms with her chin. "Thank you for answering truthfully."

"I have told you before, Maia. I do not deserve your pity. I still have no qualms about killing you if the need arises."

"I imagine one cannot *be* a kishion if one has too many qualms," she said. She looked him firmly in the eye. "There may come a day when you are called upon to fulfill your duty." She paused. "Perhaps I will even be the one who asks you to do it."

He looked at her with confusion.

She stared down into the fire and began stroking Argus's head. "Something happened to me at the lost abbey. Something I had not expected. Do you remember when I came out of the tunnels? You were fighting off the wolves."

"I remember," he said.

"One of the soldiers tried to strangle me and I unloosed the magic of the kystrel. I fell unconscious. I do not know how long it lasted, but I fear it was quite a while. When I awoke, you were watching over me and had already tended your wounds." She stared at the fire. "When I am asleep . . . I am not myself. Am I?"

The fire crackled and snapped, sending off a plume of fiery sparks.

He was quiet for several moments, though he still shivered fitfully. Finally, his words came out as a whisper. "It is at night when I fear you the most."

"Why is that?" she asked, continuing to stroke the boarhound.

He was cautious in his answer. "I have seen you rise in your sleep. Your eyes are open, but you do not respond to anyone. At first I thought you were sleepwalking, but it is different. You mumble in your sleep in many languages. Mostly gibberish to me. You walk the camp, gazing around as if everything is strange to you. Even your walk is different. You examine your arms as if they are not yours. You stare at the sky and smile . . . in a dangerous way. The Dochte Mandar teach that we, each of us, is reborn from a past life. Seems to be some color of truth in that when I see the changes that come over you at night. In truth, you frighten me more than the Fear Liath."

The sleepiness fled from Maia's eyes. She knew about the Dochte Mandar's preoccupation with past lives. She had read about it in their tomes. They believed souls were endlessly born and reborn. A king in the past could become a peasant in the future. But more interesting, at least to her, was the fact that their doctrine was a corruption of the legends of the Myriad Ones— spirit creatures who so longed for a body, they would take any form they could get, even an animal's. She rested her cheek against her arm again and said nothing more to the man her father had sent to kill her.

***

The mountains were vast and endless. Had Maia not been so utterly exhausted, she would have relished the climbing and descents. Jon Tayt had pointed out to her the vast variety of plant life and vegetation that existed on the high mountain trail. There were occasional majestic waterfalls that poured never-ending cascades down jagged bluffs. The trees were dark green and towering, but they could not overtake the size and stone of the peaks.

Maia and Jon Tayt helped the kishion walk, each of them taking one of his arms around their necks to bolster him up. When he grew too weary or sick to walk, they dragged him. His skin was flushed with fever, the wounds oozed putrid smells, and ghastly coloring showed how much his body was ravaged by his injuries.

When Maia finally saw the abbey, she was surprised at how small it was compared to the steep cliffs it was nestled amidst. The abbey had been built into the side of a cliff, only this cliff was infinitely taller and broader than the one supporting Roc-Adamour. A huge swath of evergreen trees nestled up against the lower reaches of the abbey, offering a colorful contrast to the steel-colored stone. Only a few scattered firs clung to the crags and seams of the mountain. The abbey was built along the bend of a ridge, and behind it, Maia could make out four other ridges. The mountain trail led beyond even that, and her mind filled with wonder at the distant sight. The abbey was four levels high, made of pale stone with gently sloping roofs and walls of varying heights. It was not a grand abbey like those she had seen in Comoros, but it was impressive—if only because the workers had needed to hammer rock so high up in the mountains to build it.

Unfortunately, they had to hike down to hike up. At the floor of the canyon rested a tiny village set beside the river, impossible to avoid for any who traveled to the abbey. There were small outer buildings, one with a waterwheel that dipped into the river gorge. The locals spoke a blend of three languages, though mostly the tongue of Mon. Maia did not know that language, but she was able to communicate as though they were Dahomeyjan travelers, and the locals did not understand whether her dialect was true or not. They seemed surprised to have visitors from Dahomey, but not enough to probe into the circumstances.

There was a healer in the village named Dom Silas, a wizened man with graying hair that had once been black, and he set to work on the kishion at once, clucking his tongue and chattering on in his native tongue. The hamlet was small, with only twenty or so structures. Dom Silas indicated that the kishion's injuries were severe and that he would need time to know whether he could be cured. Jon Tayt had passable knowledge of his language.

"I will stay with him," Jon Tayt said. "Go to the Aldermaston and perform your errand." He took another look at her. "You can barely stand, lass. Do you want to rest here first?"

"I dare not," Maia replied thickly, gripping his meaty shoulder before leaving the healer's chamber.

She started up the thin mountain trail leading to the abbey, excited and nervous simultaneously. What would she tell the Aldermaston? How much would she reveal about herself? Should she reveal her true identity as the daughter of the King of Comoros? Should she show him the taint of the tattoo shadows at the base of her neck? Should she show him her shoulder? She knew from her experience that the grounds of an abbey were a political entity unto themselves. A maston could seek the right of sanctuary there, but she was no maston, so that privilege was not hers to take. She hoped the Aldermaston would know her language, but she was prepared to communicate with him any way she could.

As she climbed the mountain, her feet sore from the constant abuse, her stomach twisted with worry and dread. Most of all, she feared what this Aldermaston would say or do when he learned the truth about her. Would he be compassionate to her plight, or would he judge her? She was ashamed of what she had become, but she had not voluntarily chosen it. Her thoughts were so muddled from lack of sleep, she could barely arrange them. She staggered on the trail, trying to keep her boots from sliding off. Craning her neck up, she breathed deeply of the pine and the clean air.

Her stomach coiled with queasiness.

It was nearing dusk when she reached the abbey doors. She had not slept in three days, but despite all her fear and doubt, a sprig of hope lingered in her bosom. The Aldermaston would be able to help her. He could at least cast out the Myriad One. She wanted to sob with pent-up relief, her throat constricting. She pounded on the door before seeing the rope nearby and pulling it. Maia covered her mouth when an iron bell rang out in the dusk, feeling awkward and nervous and unsure of what to say.

A pair of boots approached the door and jangled the keys in the lock.

"*Abrontay! Cenama majorni?*" The man who opened the door had dark whiskers and snowy hair and looked like a porter. He was speaking a language she did not know, which she assumed was Mon.

"Aldermaston," Maia said, seeing the man did not wear the cassock of the order.

"*Cenama, mirabeau. Constalio ostig majorni. Vray. Vray!*" His hand flitted at her dismissively.

"Please," Maia said, switching to Dahomeyjan. "I must see the Aldermaston!"

The porter looked at her, confused. "Dahomish? I see. Are you maston? No? Only mastons can come at night. Show me a sign."

She stared at him in confusion for a moment, but he did not want to wait for her to respond. "Go back to the village, little girl. I said that wrong. Young woman. Go along. Go!" He waved her away again, his eyebrows wrinkling with disdain.

He shut the gate door in her face, and she heard the locks click back into place.

CHAPTER
TWENTY-THREE

Shame

Maia rested her forehead against the heavy wooden door. It was already almost twilight. She knew she would not make it back down to the village with her remaining strength. Nor could she wait outside the abbey all night without falling asleep. She slapped the door repeatedly with the flat palm of her hand. Receiving no answer, she rang the bell again. It clanged loudly, the sound vibrating under her skin and shooting down her spine. There was no answer on the other side.

Not knowing what to do, she knelt against the foot of the door, pressing her cheek to the wood. She was so tired. She slammed her hand against the door, then listened for sounds on the other side. There were obscure noises, the tramping of feet or boots, but no one came near the door. The sunlight melted away, bringing shadows. Smoke shapes snuffled at her in the emerging darkness, and she shuddered at their presence, enduring the discomfort. She blinked rapidly, trying to keep her mind clear of the fog of sleep. Beyond her lids, she sensed a primal power, like the waves of the sea, churning against her, threatening to sweep her away with its might.

Maia rose and yanked the bell again, sending the noise clanging into the night. She was so tired and filthy.

Please, Aldermaston. Please come.

After some time passed, she heard boots come to the door, and the porter opened it again. He looked at her peevishly. "Away, brat! The Aldermaston will not see you until morning. Go!" He gestured at her in annoyance.

She shook her head. "I cannot go. I must see him tonight."

He scowled at her. "I can give you a lantern." He drew one out from behind his back and offered it to her to take.

She folded her arms, refusing it. "I do not need light, I need the Aldermaston!"

He snorted, shrugged, and slammed the door in her face.

"Please!" Maia begged, pounding on the door again. If only she had thought to take one of Jon Tayt's throwing axes, she could have started hacking away at the hinges. Again she knelt at the door, feeling the tide of power rise inside her, threatening to wilt her resolve. She bit her lower lip, desperately hoping the pain would distract her from her dark thoughts. Her knees ached from the position, but she was determined not to drift asleep.

Time passed slowly, the night's chill seeping into the stones and wooden door. She could see her breath in the moonlight. Struggling to her feet, though the pain felt like knives shooting down her legs, she tugged on the rope again, clanging the bell.

Please come. Please. I need help.

She saw a glimmer of light under the crack of the door just before it opened. There was the porter again, frowning and holding a lantern. He stared at her, his expression stern as an owl, and then motioned with a jerk of his chin for her to follow him into the courtyard.

Her relief was wary, but she obeyed and followed. The inner courtyard was small, and they passed a gate of iron, which he closed and locked behind them. Each iron pole was topped with an ornate spike. The courtyard was paved in stone with small stone flower boxes along each side, overflowing with hardy mountain wildflowers. Leerings were set into each of the boxes, emanating a soft glow. She could hear the pattering of a fountain, and when she peered farther into the courtyard, she found the source: eight light Leerings encircled a water Leering that spewed a tall fountain onto the tiles beneath. The water drained from grates at the edges. Across the small courtyard, several dark-haired and olive-skinned learners watched her, but they kept to the shadows and spoke amongst themselves. She could not hear their comments over the splashing of the fountain.

The porter swayed the lantern and brought her to a small stone building built into the cliff side adjacent to the abbey. She craned her neck as she followed him, taking in the sight of the anvil-shaped mountain that towered overhead, making her feel insignificant.

She passed another Leering and felt it glaring at her as well. The eyes accused her. She did not feel that she belonged here.

The porter approached the door and rapped on it firmly. It was opened by an older man with silver hair, a prominent nose, and a stooped back—another servant, judging by his appearance. He waved for Maia to follow him inside, but before she did, she gripped the porter's arm.

"Thank you," she said humbly.

He snorted again and ambled back toward the gates. Maia followed the crow-beaked man into what she assumed to be the

Aldermaston's residence. Her stomach churned with uneasiness and shame. Even though she was frigid with cold, she felt a bead of perspiration trickle down her cheek. She wiped it away. Her mouth was dry.

The old man said something to her in the language of Mon, which she did not understand.

"Dahomeyjan?" she asked him.

He shook his head and then stopped at a door that was already open. Within, Maia saw a short, stubby man with a full beard and slight stubble on his head dressed in the gray cassock of the Aldermaston order. He was standing, gesticulating to two other men while speaking vehemently in a language she did not understand. The men nodded and departed the room. The Aldermaston, who still looked agitated, beckoned for Maia to enter.

He had dark eyes and a snapping temper. He spoke in Dahomeyjan. "I am told you are rude and disobedient. Also that you do not speak our tongue. You are from Dahomey then?"

Maia swallowed, feeling even more ill at ease now that she was here in the Aldermaston's house. This was not the beginning she had hoped for. "Forgive me for arriving at such a late hour, Aldermaston."

He scowled and observed her more closely, his brows furrowing. "You are not from Dahomey," he said upon reflection. "Though you speak the language well. What other tongues do you speak?"

She stared at him, wondering how much she should reveal. "May we speak privately, Aldermaston?" She nodded toward the still-open door.

"I do not intend for this to be a long conversation," he replied curtly. "I had a learner break his arm climbing one of the walls today, and the healer says it needs to be set, which will be excruciating. My stomach is growling for the supper I have not yet eaten. There are scrolls to read, tomes to engrave, and punishments to dole out this evening, my dear. I do not have much time to spare. But you were persistent. Is it money you need?"

Maia shook her head no.

"You are not a maston, though. You did not give the porter a sign."

She shook her head no again.

He walked around the edge of the desk and pulled at the strands of his beard. "My porter believed you were obdurately seeking alms. I typically make such visitors wait a day before speaking with them. I have learned in my six years as Aldermaston that delaying a day will make the majority of your problems fly away." He grimaced and then clasped his hands in front of his portly belly. "What do you seek? You are not even twenty by the look of you."

"I am not," Maia confessed.

"Where are you from?"

She sucked in her breath. "I am from Comoros."

His brows needled like daggers. "Comoros?" He coughed, looking at her as if she had said she had somehow dropped down from the moon.

"I am Princess Marciana. Please call me Maia."

"The bastard?" he asked curtly, coughing again.

She bowed her head and nodded.

"This is not at all what I suspected. Indeed!" He shook his head incredulously and scratched his bearded throat. His fingers were fidgety. He grabbed one of the scrolls off the desk before setting it back down just as abruptly. He looked down, then back at her again, sharply. "Can you prove your claim? Do you have a signet ring or some other way I can identify you?"

"No," she said, shaking her head. "Please, Aldermaston." Her insides churned with dread and shame. She should flee. She should leave. How could she reveal herself to a man so distracted and contemptible? She tried to master her unpleasant emotions. "I need your help."

He shrugged, obviously perplexed. "With what, may I ask?"

She stepped closer to him, dropping her voice lower. "Help me," she whispered. "I . . . I . . . am . . ." She could not say it. Her tongue was too thick in her mouth.

"What?" he asked, crinkling his brows. "Speak up!"

She tried to make the sounds, but her throat locked up. She was miserable with shame. "I am not a maston. I wish to be one, as my parents both were, but my father has denied me. Aldermaston, I am a hetaera. Please . . . you must help me. I am so very tired . . . so very weary. When I fall asleep, I am not myself. It . . . takes over. Help me!"

His eyes and mouth widened as if she had sloshed a pan of boiling water on his face. He walked around her swiftly, went to the open door and slammed it shut. He turned, staring at her in unbridled fear now. "*What* did you say you were?"

"I have become one . . . undeliberately. I was not trained in an abbey. I have been banished for many years. My father sent me to Dahomey, to a forgotten abbey where I found the hetaera's Leering—"

"Stop!" he said, holding up his hand. He bit his forefinger, muttering to himself in another language. It was a long moment before he looked at her again. "And you came here? To Cruix Abbey? Why? Why here?"

"I do not want this *thing* inside me," she moaned, wincing, clutching her breast. "It takes an Aldermaston to cast away a Myriad One." She wrung her hands together miserably. "I was hunted by the Dochte Mandar in Dahomey and fled across the mountains. I have not slept in three days trying to reach this abbey."

"Sit down," he ordered.

She looked at him in confusion.

"You are ready to collapse. Please, sit down."

Maia nodded and gratefully seated herself in one of the many wooden chairs. Her shoulders slumped. He walked up behind her.

"Close your eyes. You cannot see the maston sign. I will Gift you."

Relieved, she obeyed and bowed her head, allowing him to press his thick hand against her head. This was a Gifting. She began to shiver. Her stomach twisted into knots, and she felt the terrible urge to retch.

"Lady Marciana," he said in broken Dahomeyjan. "Ah . . . I place upon you a . . . a . . . Gift. Yes, a Gift. By Idumea's hand, I . . . sense in you . . . the presence of one . . . the . . . presence of a . . . Myriad One." She heard his breath begin to pant, and she felt the churn of power swelling up inside her. *Not here!* she pleaded in her mind. *Help me!*

"By Idumea's . . . hand . . . I bestow . . . a . . . Gift. Of Knowledge." His breath came in short gasps, as if he were racing up a stairwell. "You must . . . seek . . . the High Seer. She . . . is . . . she . . . calls . . . all the new . . . Aldermastons. She anoints them. Only one . . . with the Gift . . . of Seering . . . can name . . . *ungh* . . . name . . . the Myriad One . . . vested . . . inside . . . you. Seek her . . . in . . . Naess."

The Aldermaston jerked his hand away from her head and continued to breathe in huge gulps. Maia whirled and saw his hand was covered in blisters, as if he had grabbed a burning kettle by the handle. He gripped his wrist with his other hand, sweat streaking down his face. He stared at Maia with fear. He was trembling and quite pale.

"Not . . . my . . . abbey," he groaned. "Please! Not mine!" His look was not angry, only desperate. "Go! You must go! Now!"

Maia rose from the chair. "I did not seek to bring evil here," she said, staring at his blistered palm.

"I know it," he muttered. "I saw into your heart. But you *are* a hetaera. You are bound to a Myriad One. You must learn its true name in order to send it away. Only someone with the Gift of Seeing can know that."

"But I thought all Aldermastons—"

He shook his head violently. "No! But three days ago, the whispers of the Medium bade me to hold vigil. Not just to go without sleep for three days, but also to go without food and drink. I did not understand why. It weighed on me. I was so busy and tired. If I had held vigil, I *may* have been strong enough in the Medium to help you tonight. I cannot send this one away. It is too strong. *You* are too strong in the Medium. Stronger than me. Your lineage . . . child . . . it is powerful."

"Aldermaston!" she begged, seeing his face blanch.

She felt a familiar heaviness wash over her. She remembered the powerful force of the waves as they crashed against the hull of the *Blessing of Burntisland*. No matter how strong the sails or taut the ropes, the ship had been thrashed about unwillingly. It was as if those waves were buffeting *her*. She tried to walk against the current pulling at her, but it felt as if her clothes and skin were too heavy for her to resist.

He raised a trembling arm, his face beaded with sweat. "I . . . rebuke . . . you . . ."

The tidewaters of power swelled inside her, sweeping her under the crest. She heard a voice. Her own voice, but it was not her speaking.

"You know too much now, Aldermaston."

"Depart!" he croaked hoarsely.

Maia heard herself laugh. "You cannot banish one who is already banished. No man can tame *me*, Aldermaston."

"The High Seer is a *woman*," the Aldermaston said angrily. "The Dochte Mandar will bring you to Naess."

There was another silver laugh. "I know. I intend them to. Foolish man. You thought a little gate and door could keep me out? We are many. We are one." She began to chant the dirge from the tome. *"Och monde elles brir. Och cor shan arbir. Och aether undes pune. Dekem millia orior sidune."*

"No," the Aldermaston groaned. "Please, no!"

"Och monde elles brir. Och cor shan arbir. Och aether undes pune. Dekem millia orior sidune."

"No! I beg you, no!"

"Och monde elles brir. Och cor shan arbir. Och aether undes pune. Dekem millia orior sidune!"

Maia felt the waves of power crest inside her, a sensation that set her fingers tingling. She was still conscious, though her awareness had been shoved into a corner of her own mind. She struggled to regain control of her body, but it was like shoving one of those sea waves. There was nothing to push against.

Boots pounded down the corridor, and the door of the Aldermaston's chamber flew open. He had sagged to his knees, one hand resting on the table, the other quivering as he tried to hold up the maston sign with his hand.

"Aldermaston!" someone shrieked. "The abbey! The abbey is burning!"

There has never been a time in which mastons have not been persecuted. There is a never-ending war, you see, between the mastons and the hetaera. The hetaera, whose order has prevailed and survived for many thousands of years, received a mortal wound in my generation, of which the monster must finally die. Yet so strong is her constitution, great-granddaughter, she may endure for centuries before she expires.

—Lia Demont, Aldermaston of Muirwood Abbey

CHAPTER
TWENTY-FOUR

Princess of Comoros

There was a soft tap on her bedchamber door. Maia looked up from the window seat from which she had been watching the commotion in the bailey below. She rose and walked to the door and opened it. There was her chamberlain, Nicholas Creed, crushing his velvet cap in his hands. He looked miserable.

"What is it, Nicholas?" she asked with concern. "Is your wife well? Is it one of your children?"

"Lady Maia," he said dejectedly. "I bring ill tidings."

Maia's face blanched. "Is my mother dead?"

"No! No, by the Blood, no!"

Maia sighed in relief.

She heard the sound of boot steps ascending the stairwell. "What is it, then, Nicholas?"

"I must let them take you away, Lady Maia. You are to be removed from the palace."

Her heart started to wail in protest. "Where?" She seized his arm. "Am I being sent to Pent Tower?"

"It is not as bad as that."

"You look so grave, Nicholas. There is more news you have not told me."

He bit his bottom lip. "They will be here shortly to take you. I cannot spare the blow. Forgive me, Lady Maia, but this is none of my doing. Your lord father, the king, is sending you to be a lady-in-waiting to your stepsister, Lady Murer." He cringed when he said this.

Maia stared at him in disbelief. "What do you say? Nicholas, I do not understand."

He swallowed, scrunching the velvet cap even more. "Your father has signed an act naming Lady Deorwynn's children as his legal and lawful heirs. He has declared Lady Murer Princess of Comoros. You are now . . ." He started to choke on the words. "You are now to be known as Lady Maia, the king's daughter."

"My father signed this?" she said in astonishment. "I am now considered his . . . his bastard?"

Nicholas Creed nodded miserably. "I am on assignment from His Majesty's chamberlain. While you have been forbidden to wear your state gowns and such, you will now surrender *all* of your clothes, your badges, your dishes, your treasure. They will be given to Lady Murer. You will wait upon her at Hadfeld Manor."

Maia's legs trembled beneath her. "Hadfeld is the manor of Lady Deorwynn's mother and father!"

"Yes. They are your masters now. You are forthwith forbidden to use the title of princess in any correspondence or to insinuate that title in any form, per your father's command. Ladies Murer and Jolecia are acknowledged as the true princesses of the realm and their brothers as princes."

She watched as the men reached the top of the stairs and began marching down the hall toward her.

"Who are these men?" Maia demanded.

"They are here to take your gowns and clothes, to prevent you from despoiling any. Including the one you are wearing."

"But what am I to wear?" she asked in horror.

"A servant's livery," Nicholas said with sadness. "I am sorry, Lady Maia. I will not be your chamberlain any longer. You are to report to Hadfeld immediately to assume your new station."

Her eyes burned. "Did you see my father's orders? Did you see them yourself, Nicholas? Or was Lady Deorwynn the one who issued the command?"

"I heard it spoken by the king himself," he said, nodding, and stepped away as the men began to push into her room. Some carried crates and wooden boxes. Her dwelling was small, so it did not take them long. She stood there stunned, watching as the men stuffed away her clothing and packed all of her limited possessions. It was like watching the theft of her memories. She covered her mouth, horror-struck, as her chamber was ransacked.

How could her father treat her in such a way? She had not seen him lately, due to his travels and hunting trips, but what had persuaded him to finally disavow her as his trueborn daughter? Her stomach cramped painfully and she worried she would be sick on the floor rushes.

Crates and chests were strapped shut and hefted out of the chamber. The pillows and tasseled blankets were stripped away. Soon she was staring at an empty room. One thought dominated all others: She had to see her father. She had to know if this was truly his will and not Lady Deorwynn's manipulation. Had his heart been shut to her?

"Nicholas, you must help me," she whispered.

"My lady, what can I do?" he said with anguish. "I am the king's servant."

"Yes, but can you deliver a message to him? Please, Nicholas!"

He shrugged helplessly. "It will not do any good, my lady."

"Just tell him that I wish to see him. That I wish to plead my case to him."

He fidgeted. "I will try. That is all that I can promise you. I am sorry, my lady. You deserve . . ." His voice trailed off. He did not trust himself to finish the sentiment.

A rough man walked up to her. "The gown too, lass. We were told to take it all."

She stared at him. Though Nicholas had warned her, she was galled by this man's effrontery. "You will take it from me by force?"

"If I must, lass. My orders are from the Lady Shilton. You are to appear before her in a servant's smock. Off with the gown then."

"No," Maia countered. "I am the Princess of Comoros."

Nicholas flinched. "My lady, that is in defiance of the king's command."

"You are the king's *bastard*," the man said with a smirk. "If you won't give it over, then—"

He reached for her and she stepped hastily back. "Let me change, you villain! Unhand me!"

The kystrel grew warm against her skin as her heart simmered with fury. She had to calm herself. She fought against the surge of power billowing inside of her. If her eyes went silver, everyone would know. If they stripped the dress from her, they would see the kystrel around her neck, the small shadowstain on her chest beneath the chemise. If they saw that, she would be executed.

"Whatever your pleasure," the man said dryly.

"Give her a moment of privacy!" Nicholas implored. "Please, can we be civil? Is someone fetching a servant's gown? Ah, there it is. Bring it forward, man. Come on, hand it forth." He clutched the fabric. It was gray with a hint of green. The collar and the sleeve edge had a design on it. That was the only finery to it. She stared at it, at the lack of color and fashion. Lady Deorwynn sought to complete her humiliation. Maia clenched her teeth and took the garment.

"Let me change," she said stiffly. They relented and shut the door. Maia leaned back against it, battling the wrenching sensation in her stomach. She wanted to cry. Instead, she squeezed the fabric to her face, willing herself to be calm and steady. The gown smelled as stale and dusty as it looked.

Knowing these were not patient men, Maia quickly discarded her gown. Her mirror had been carried away already, so she could not even use it to change. She closed her eyes, struggling to master herself. There was a firm knock on the door.

"We have orders to present you straightaway!" came the rough man's voice.

Maia pulled on the servant's dress. It was too short, exposing too much of her ankles and wrists. It was tight across her chest. There were lacings in the back that she could not reach. But it covered the medallion and the shadowstain. She opened the door.

"Nicholas, can you help me?" she pleaded.

The rough man snatched her fallen gown from the floor with a grunt and stuffed it under his arm.

Nicholas frowned and nodded, and he helped tie up the lacings in the back with clumsy fingers. Maia felt humiliated and angry, but she kept control of her expression. When he was done, she thanked him.

She stared at her room one last time, missing it already and feeling strange and uncomfortable in her new dress. Nicholas escorted her down the stairs to the bailey, where the men had assembled to escort her to Hadfeld. She recognized one of them as the new Earl of Forshee—Kord Schuyler. The previous one had been stripped of his title and sent to Pent Tower with all of his sons, save one. He had been given the title for one simple reason. He fawned over her father and did whatever he was asked to do. She would get no sympathy from him.

The new Earl of Forshee was a large man with a hooked nose and iron-gray hair. As he stooped from the saddle and looked at her without compassion, he smiled. "Are you ready to pay your respects to Princess Murer, Lady Maia?" he asked condescendingly, his mouth twitching with a smile.

She stared up at him, her eyes like daggers. "I know of no other princess in Comoros except for myself. The daughters of Lady Deorwynn have no claim on such title."

He looked delighted. "Well, we shall see how long your stubbornness lasts, lass. We shall see."

***

Maia's life at Hadfeld was intolerable.

Though her title was a lady-in-waiting, she was given the most horrible room in the manor house, a dormer room in the attic with a cracked window that let in the cold and no brazier for warmth. Lady Shilton refused to give her a gown that fit her better, so her wardrobe was limited to the one ill-fitting garment that had been tossed to her in her old bedroom. She discovered immediately that Lady Shilton had been ordered by her daughter, Lady Deorwynn, to humiliate Maia routinely. Her illegitimate station was rubbed in her face at every meal, at every encounter. She watched with resentment as Murer had Maia's clothes altered and enhanced, having gems and jewels sewn into the bodice and trimming. The new princess treated Maia with disdain and ordered her about the manor, forcing her to do arduous chores meant to demean her.

The cold, chafing environment crushed Maia's spirits, and she found herself frequently ill, with a persistent cough nagging in her throat. She knew no one at the manor cared for her. The other servants stayed away from her for fear of having their own work increased if they were caught assisting her or associating with her in any way.

Maia wondered if even the wretcheds at the abbeys were treated with more dignity. Her treatment during mealtimes was so horrible that she took to eating as much as she could during breakfast. Later, she would claim she was too ill to eat, and ask for bread and milk to be brought to her in the attic. This happened for several weeks until Lady Deorwynn heard of it. Thereafter she was forced to take all her meals in the hall, where her tormenters could continue to rail against her.

Maia refused to acknowledge her new station, however. She realized that her situation was an attempt to force her mother, who was still at Muirwood, to divorce her father. She was a game piece now in their rivalry, and no matter how much her father may have cared about her, she knew he would use her to achieve his ends. That he would stoop so low wounded her.

However, Maia did not use her title out loud, for when she did, Lady Shilton would immediately strike her face. Several stinging slaps had proved the point, so Maia refused to speak of it, but she also refused to deny her station, despite the others' constant wheedling.

Part of Maia recognized that she was dreaming, that she had already lived through those miserable days in Lady Shilton's manor. But she could not wake up. It felt as if she were on a small boat on a lazy river, being carried along its current. The dream was like a prison, forcing her to stay unconscious no matter how she tried to rouse herself, sucking her back into the nightmare of her time with the vicious Lady Deorwynn and her children.

The river of her dream seemed to speed up, and Maia recognized the moment it was leading to: her father's visit to Hadfeld. After learning of it, she had wandered the manor with giddy excitement. If her father could only see her suffering, she knew his heart would soften, and he would summon her back to court. Her servant's dress was torn and soot stained. They would not offer her a replacement or even a second gown, so she was forced to huddle beneath a blanket in only a shift after she washed it and it hung drying. She would do that at night, after the other servants had gone to bed, so she could use a fire Leering to dry it more quickly. If only her father could see her, he would end the cruel punishment aimed at his true wife, Maia's mother.

When the horses arrived at Hadfeld, Maia found a window and watched, her excitement exploding inside her chest. But she was quickly snatched away by a groomsman and swept up to her room in the attic. The door was locked to keep her inside. She had pounded on the wood until her hands were bloody, furious that she would not be able to see her father during his visit. She paced the room, ears straining for footfalls on the steps. Surely he would summon her. Why else would he have come to Hadfeld?

The afternoon waned, and she was about to give up hope when she heard boots marching up to the attic. Her heart began to pound with excitement. She waited at one side of the room as the door was unlocked. Two men entered, but she only recognized one

261

of them. One of her visitors was handsome and wore a soldier's uniform with her father's crest and a sword belted to his waist. One of her father's knights—Carew. The other wore a nobleman's finery and the stole of the chancellor's office around his neck.

She curtsied formally, despite her ragged dress.

"Ah, Lady Marciana," the chancellor said. "This is Captain Carew. I am Crabwell. Do you know of me?"

"You are the king's new chancellor?" she asked.

He nodded discreetly. "I served under Chancellor Walraven as a scribe. He always spoke highly of you. He said you had great intelligence. A natural gift for languages." He switched his tongue to Dahomeyjan. "Is that still true?"

"It is, my lord," she responded in kind, changing her inflection.

"Wonderful," he said flatly. His eyes were dark and brooding. He looked nothing like Walraven, save for silver in his hair. He was broad around the shoulders, though not very tall. He tugged at one of his gloves. "I understand from Lady Shilton that you stubbornly cling to your past title as princess, refusing to acknowledge the Act of Inheritance."

Maia stared at him, feeling her hope turn to ash. She sighed wearily, feeling her shoulder slope. "Lord Chancellor, who gave you your title?"

"The king. Your lord father," he answered crisply.

"And if my father wishes it, could he remove the chancellorship from you as he has with your predecessors?"

"Naturally," he responded. "He is the king. Which is why, by the Act of Inheritance—"

She cut him off. "My title was not given to me by the king," she said firmly. "It is not a title that can be stripped away by an act. I am the Princess of Comoros because my mother is the Queen of Comoros and my father is the King of Comoros. They were anointed such by an Aldermaston." She shook her head gravely. "How can I submit to an act unless it comes from that same authority?"

The guardsman smirked at Maia's little speech and gave her an approving nod.

The chancellor eyed her shrewdly. "So what you are saying, Lady Maia, *the king's daughter*, is that you will renounce your title if an Aldermaston proclaims it so?" His smile was mocking. "I think that can be arranged. Very well, I bid you good day. Captain Carew, let us depart with the king's retinue."

"Please!" Maia said, grabbing his sleeve. He looked down at her unwashed hand with disgust. "May I see my father and kiss his hand? I will not even speak to him. I wish only to see him."

Chancellor Crabwell shook off her grip. "Lady Maia, the king's daughter, that is entirely under *your* control. Should you wish to be reinstated to court immediately—today—all you must do is renounce your title. It is only your extreme stubbornness that prevents this."

"Did my lord father say this?" she asked him with a hard edge in her voice.

"Indeed he did. Good day, Lady Maia, the king's daughter."

He nodded to Captain Carew and they both turned and left. The door was locked behind them. Maia stared at the peeling paint, her heart heavy and weary. As she listened to the boots thudding down the steps from the attic, she realized that her father would soon depart without even attempting to see her. She bit her lip, determination burning in her heart. He would see how far his daughter had been reduced. It was unthinkable for him to leave without at least acknowledging what he had done to her. She hurried to the window and thrust it open. A fragment of glass wobbled out and fell.

Maia climbed out of the dormer window and carefully pulled herself onto the roof. Doves hooted and fluttered away from her as she carefully trod up to the spine of the roof and came down the other side, toward another gabled window. She could hear the nickering of horses and carriages from the host assembled in the courtyard below. Flags and pennants whipped in the wind, and she felt her hair streaming across her face. She had not been outside for months, as the Shiltons would not allow her to walk the gardens or enter the streets for any reason. She had been starving for sunlight.

As she reached the far end of the roof, she caught sight of a small terraced ledge just below her that connected to the master bedroom. The terrace overlooked the courtyard. She crouched on the edge of the roof, feeling several loose shingles beneath her feet, and scooted to the edge. There was her father, striding across the courtyard with Crabwell and Carew in tow, deep in discussions with them both. Maia almost lost her courage, but she did not quail. She jumped off the edge of the roof onto the terrace edge just below. Her legs jolted with the impact and the sound attracted attention.

"On the roof!"

"Look, someone jumped!"

"My lord, be careful!"

Maia made it to her feet and went to the edge of the terrace, staring down. "Father!" she cried out.

He stared up at her, wearing ostentatious robes and finery, his hat plumed with several enormous feathers. He stared up at the terrace, and she saw his look of shock at seeing her up there, her dress threadbare and torn, her hair disheveled and filthy.

Maia sank to her knees, bowing her head and clenching her fingers together in a mute appeal.

There were gasps of shock and surprise. Her eyes bored into his.

"Please, Father," she whispered. "Please do not let me stay here. It is killing me."

He looked up at her, his expression twisting with sorrow. He bowed to her once, touching his velvet feathered cap. Then he mounted his stallion and rode away, not looking back.

CHAPTER TWENTY-FIVE

Wayfarer

Maia awoke from the deep slumber slowly, feeling the warmth of sunlight on the crook of her back and hearing the warbling of birds. It was an effort to open her eyes, and when she did, her surroundings were unfamiliar. There was another sound she heard, a soft scraping noise, like a bird scratching a trunk with its beak. Her head throbbed dully as she pushed herself up, twigs and brush poking her breast.

"Ah, she awakens. It is noon and she revives. *Sangrion.*"

Maia started, for the voice came from behind her and she did not recognize it. She looked over her shoulder and found a man sitting cross-legged in the brush, his back against a large pine. He wore a dirty cloak over a dirty frayed tunic and worn leather sandals. His hair was thick and dark with spikes of white through it. He had intense dark eyes that were regarding her with an inscrutable look.

"Good noon, sister," he said, his accent heavy and thick.

Maia blinked at him, feeling a sudden jolt of fear. She did not know him, yet he knew her . . . or at least something about her. The fringe of silver at his throat—a chaen shirt—marked him as a maston, and a tome lay open on his lap. He bore a stylus in his left hand, and she could see from the aurichalcum shavings that he had been engraving. That was the scratching noise she had heard.

"Who are you?" she asked hoarsely. Her throat was so thick she could hardly speak.

He chuckled and wiped the shavings away from the tome. "I am a wayfarer. A wanderer. I travel the kingdoms writing the history of the people. This is Mon. It is *my* country."

Maia's uneasiness clotted inside her like blood. "You are a maston."

"Aye, sister." He looked down at the tome and touched the stylus to continue writing. The little scratching noise sounded again.

Maia could feel a threat bubbling inside her. Anger seethed like a stewpot, though she did not know why. She sat up and looked around. Her rucksack was nearby. The small movement revealed the stiffness and soreness of her muscles.

"And you, sister, are a hetaera," he said, still scriving, without looking up.

She stared at him in dread and fear. She felt the power of the kystrel begin to hiss in her heart. She did not want to hurt him. "I must go," Maia said worriedly.

"Stay," he said curtly. "I have not delivered my message."

"Message?" Maia asked. Something told her to be afraid of this man. That he would harm her if she stayed. She did not trust the impulse, but she wanted to bolt into the trees as fast as she could.

"I am not a *pethet*, sister. I will not harm you. It is noon. The Unborn are weakest in the daylight. The power grows inside you, though, even now. You must be rid of it soon, before it claims you fully. Then others will join it, and you will be lost." He smiled viciously. "It *wrestles* for you. Will you let it win? Hmmm?"

Maia looked at him pleadingly. "Can you make them go away?" she asked with breathless hope.

He shook his head and clucked his tongue. "I cannot. I am a wayfarer, sister. I write the stories. I do not make them."

A violent spasm of rage made her want to strike out at the man, but she folded her arms and dug her hands into her ribs to regain control of herself. She started to rock back and forth.

"What are you writing in your tome?" she asked, her teeth starting to chatter.

He smoothed his hand across the gleaming page. "The truth, sister. Only that."

She licked her lips. "And what is the truth that you write now?"

His wizened eyes locked on to hers, and she felt shame splash color on her cheeks. She looked away, unable to hold his penetrating gaze.

"I wrote that a hetaera from Comoros, *the king's daughter*, burned Cruix Abbey to the ground. It was *my* abbey, sister." His face was solemn, not accusing. "I do not hate you for what you did. Who am I to judge the king's daughter? The truth is your father is a *pethet*. He does not deserve the title 'father.' However, there are many *pethets* who wear that title, though it fits them poorly. When *pethets* rule, the people mourn. I do not judge you, sister. I have written your sad story for many years."

Maia felt tears burning in her eyes. "Are they . . . are they all dead at the abbey?" she gasped. In part of her mind, she could see the cliffs burning with fire as the abbey went up in flames. That sick foreign part of her reveled at the sight, thrilled by the scorching flames.

The man's voice was firm and void of emotion. "The Alder-maston only and not yet. He could not flee." He sighed. "You kissed his forehead, sister. Your lips bring a curse. They bring death." His voice dropped low. "A betrayer's kiss. It has always been so, even on Idumea."

Tears trickled down Maia's cheeks—a foreign sensation since she so rarely cried. The tears were hot and wet and they seared her skin as they fell from her lashes. "I am sorry," she gasped. Maia gazed up at the tops of the trees, her heart dying with regret. She buried her face in her hands and wept. She should fling herself off a cliff. She had to save the world from what she had become. Death was the only way to end the madness in her life. If she could not control her actions, if she could not stop the Myriad One inside of her, she could at least do no more harm.

"Do you think that would help, sister?" the stranger said softly, his voice slightly mocking. "Your thoughts are tangled with *her* thoughts. Do you realize that? If you jumped, she would cause the Medium to blow you back up to the top. And then *another* of your choices would bind you to her."

Maia stared at him, her eyes wet. "You can hear my thoughts?"

"It is one of my Gifts," he replied sternly. "What a burden!" Then he chuckled softly to himself. "You can imagine the joy of hearing what everyone you meet thinks of you. *Pethet recolo!* There is fat, smelly Maderos! His breath reeks. His ankles are too skinny and his middle too ripe. He is crooked. He is ugly. Bah!" He waved his hand in the air. "How quickly we judge each other. How quickly our thoughts condemn us. The Medium looks on the heart, sister. Not the face. You are judged by the choices *you* make. Not the choices of others."

She looked at him pleadingly. "How can I rid myself of this . . . this creature inside of me?"

"Bah, you already know! Seek the High Seer."

Maia struggled with her doubts. "That is what the Aldermaston of Cruix told me. But the Myriad One also seems to be sending me to Naess. How do I know what the Medium's will is?"

He scratched the corner of his mouth with the butt of the stylus. "I told you that your thoughts are tangled. You are deep in the enemy's power. But your *lineage* is strong in the Medium." His voice hushed. "Very strong, sister. You must learn to discern between the voice in your head and the voice in your *heart*." He then tapped the stylus against his temple. "Aldermaston Josephus said, 'Truth I will tell you in *your mind* and in *your heart*, by the Medium, which will come upon you and dwell in your heart.'" He sniffed. "Aldermaston Pol said, 'The peace of the Medium, which passeth all understanding, will keep your hearts *and* minds.' You must study at an abbey, sister. There is much wisdom in the Aldermastons' tomes. More wisdom and truth than you have found in the tomes of the Dochte Mandar."

She frowned. "I have always wanted to study at an abbey, Maderos. My father forbids it."

He pursed his lips. "I know, sister. As I have told you, I have written your life. I have a keen interest in your Family. Now, for my message."

She looked at him in surprise, drying her eyes. Somehow, their conversation had made her feel better. A feeling of peace and quiet had settled on her as he quoted from the words of the Aldermastons. It felt as if the ancients' wisdom had tamped down the darkness inside her. "I thought you already had—"

He clucked his tongue. "No, sister. I gave you morsels of counsel from an old man who has seen much of this vile world. I was sent with a message to give you." He opened a large leather knapsack and rummaged through the contents. "Ah, *blessit vestiglio!*"

He pulled out a folded paper with a wax seal. "I saw her melt the wax to fix the seal," he said. "It has not been opened or changed by anyone since leaving her hand."

Maia stared at him in surprise. "Who?" Her heart began to burn inside her.

He did not reply, only handed her the letter.

Maia snapped the seal and unfolded the paper, which trembled in her hand. The first word made her heart seize with joyful pain and the tears flow afresh.

Daughter.

It was written in ink, in a tremulous hand. It was from her mother. She had never seen her mother write anything in her life. Always she dictated to secretaries or scribes who wrote her letters for her, as women were not permitted to read or engrave. The hand was elegant, and Maia could see a hesitance in her choice of wording, as if it were not a natural thing for her to write. She mopped her tears on her sleeve and read impatiently.

Daughter,

I have heard tidings today that I perceive (if they are true) that the time is very near when the Medium will prove and test you. I am glad of it. The Medium will not suffer you to perish if you beware offending it. I pray you, good daughter, to offer yourself to the Medium. I have heard that you suffer much under Lady Shilton. If she brings you orders from the king, I am sure you will be commanded what you should do. Listen to my counsel, Daughter. Answer with few words, obeying the king, your father, in everything save only that you will not offend the Medium and lose your own soul. Go no further in learning the ways of the Dochte Mandar. And wheresoever, and in whatsoever, company you shall come, observe the king's commandments that are right.

One thing I especially desire for you, for the love that you do owe unto me. Keep your heart and mind chaste, and your body free from all ill and wanton company. Do not desire any husband save he be a maston. I dare to hope that you shall see a very good end and better than you can now hope for. We never come to Idumea but by our troubles. More than any earthly Gift, I desire above all to see you again, before death separates us.

Your loving mother,
Catrin the Queen

Maia wiped her nose, watching as the tear splotches on the paper stained the ink. She looked down at her lap, feeling as if a warm blanket had been draped around her shoulders. Just those few words, written in her mother's own hand, gave her more comfort than she had ever known.

What a wreck Maia had made of her life. She knew, though, deep inside, that despite her wrongs, her mother would forgive her and still accept her. She so longed to see her.

"Is my mother still at Muirwood?" Maia whispered thickly.

"Aye, sister. But your destiny bids you north."

She sighed, then looked painfully at Maderos. *Will I ever see her again?*

Maderos gave her a lopsided smile. "All things are possible to the Medium," he answered.

Maia rose and hefted her rucksack onto her shoulder. She bit her lip. "I will not venture near any abbeys on my journey," she said. "I did not know . . . what would happen. I am sorry."

He stuffed his tome in his leather bag and grabbed a gnarled walking staff, using it to rise. The staff was misshapen with a knobby end. It looked like the twisting root of a hulking tree.

"As I told you, sister. You are condemned for your choices. Just as the Myriad Ones were condemned for theirs."

"How far am I from Naess?" she asked. "It is noon, so I cannot determine which way is north."

He lifted his crooked staff and pointed toward a tall, craggy mountain wreathed in snow. "Across the Watzholt, you will find the kingdom of Hautland. You must cross it to reach the port cities, like Rostick. There you can find a ship. Be wary, sister. The Hautlanders help lead the Dochte Mandar's hunt against women who break their laws. They are the closest kingdom to Naess, so they are the most influenced by them. And beware the Victus. They hunt you still."

"Who are they?"

He smiled knowingly. "You will see, little sister. You will see."

"Will you walk with me, Maderos?" she asked. "I feel safe with you. I do not have any companions now." She thought tenderly on the wounded kishion, knowing he would need to rest before moving. But Jon Tayt and Argus might follow her, and though she desperately wanted to see them, she could not risk their lives with the evil inside her.

A crinkled smile. "No, sister. I delivered the message as I promised. We cannot control the storms or the rain. We cannot prevent the wind from howling. But you can choose to whistle, eh sister?" He began to whistle, and started off to the east. She watched him go, amazed at the speed of his stride. Soon he vanished into the woods, leaving her alone.

***

Maia reached the base of the Watzholt before nightfall. She knew it would be too treacherous to attempt the crossing by moonlight, so she made a small camp for herself in the trees. After living off the land for as long as she had, she knew which herbs were edible, so though she was hungry, she was not starving. A small creek trickled past, providing icy waters to refresh her thirst. Though she was heavyhearted, she did not despair.

Maderos's words repeated over and over in her mind. She had felt such peace when he recited the words from the Aldermastons' tomes, as if those words held the power of the Medium. Was that why learners spent so much time reading and engraving? Could the words themselves be instruments of power? It was an idea she had never considered.

A frosty wind from the Watzholt came rushing down the mountain and ruffled the trees, making her shiver. It would be a difficult climb, she knew, but she had endured many hardships on her journey. She pulled her fraying cloak tighter around her shoulders, huddling in the small shelter she had created. She dared not build a fire for risk of being seen. She did not want anyone to find her, for fear of hurting them at night.

As night fell, she stayed awake, watching the pale moon rising. Although she still feared sleep, she knew she was safer when she was far from some bastion of civilization. She wondered what sort of people the Hautlanders were and when they would learn about the burning of Cruix Abbey. Otherwise she might be recognized by description. If she moved quickly enough, she hoped she could make it to the port city and slip away without being discovered.

Perhaps it was too much to hope for.

Maia heard something.

She lowered her cowl and heard grunts and heavy breathing. A prickle of fear filled her heart. Was some bear or wolf pack hunting her scent? It was coming fast, snuffling through the brush.

She grabbed the strap of her rucksack and was preparing to flee when she heard a distinctive howl and bark. Then Argus barreled into her makeshift camp, licking her face with wild joy.

"You found me," she said, feeling guilt and pleasure simultaneously. "You found me, Argus." She hugged him fiercely, burying her face into his fur. She heard the clomping of boots following the boarhound.

I have learned, mostly through painful experience, never to be dismissive of a friend's accusation, even if it seems unreasonable. More often than not, it is well-meant, the truth, and something I have needed to hear but did not want to. It is an easy thing to be offended. It is difficult to learn something new about ourselves.

—Lia Demont, Aldermaston of Muirwood Abbey

CHAPTER TWENTY-SIX

Hunted

J on Tayt sat in the shadows of the tree, but his eyes gleamed in the moonlight as he stroked Argus's flanks. He had confirmed what she already knew—there were enemies on their trail. Corriveaux had discovered she was not with the king and had crossed into Mon with a retinue of Dochte Mandar, arriving at Cruix Abbey the morning after it burned.

Maia stared at the sky, sickened by the knowledge of what she had done.

"Did they harm the kishion?" she asked him worriedly.

He shook his head. "The healer dressed the wound, but he was burning with fever when I left. I hid him in the mountains."

"You must go there yourself, Jon Tayt," she implored. "Go and guide travelers through the peaks again. It is not safe to be near me." She sighed and tugged her cloak more tightly about her shoulders. "I could not bear it if you or Argus were harmed because of me."

He snorted. "I fear not the Dochte Mandar," he said in a low voice. "They have hunters to be sure, but I am better. We can slip away if we are wary and quick."

"No," Maia said, a little too forcefully. She wrestled with her emotions. "It is not safe to be near *me*. There is good reason the Dochte Mandar hunt me. I am a danger to everyone. Even you."

She heard him scratch the whiskers at his neck. "You felled the abbey."

"Yes," Maia confessed.

"Why? Did they threaten you?"

"No, they were innocent." She felt her throat catch and coughed to clear it.

"Then why, Lady Maia? Why did you do it?"

She stared miserably into her lap. "I was not in control of myself. At night, I have strange visions of the past. They are so vivid and real. When I sleep, I lose control of myself and . . . am taken over by another force. It is like a sickness. I thought the Aldermaston could cure me. Instead, I harmed him."

Jon Tayt sniffed, but he did not look accusing. "Best to keep you away from abbeys then, my lady."

She looked up at him. "I urge you to abandon me. I am hunted by the Dochte Mandar. Now I will be hunted by the Aldermastons. The Naestors, whom I seek, will slay me when they find out what and who I am. I cannot—*will not*—ask anything further of you."

"You've said your piece. Let me say mine." He was silent a moment, the only sounds the rustling of the wind through the trees and Argus's panting. "It gives me some comfort that you did not destroy the abbey deliberately. I have suspected for some time that you suffer from a fever or delirium at night. We have tried to keep watch over you—the kishion and I. The two of us had a truce, so to speak. But you should have *told* me, Lady Maia.

I have an herb, valerianum, that can cause drowsiness and deep slumber when mixed with a tea. It is worth trying, at any rate. Or I can bind and gag you at night . . . truss you up like a slaughter-bound boar and tie you to a tree. If you had told me, I could have helped ere it came to this." He grunted. "You were foolish and you were proud. But you are not guilty. I have seen your heart, and you are fair and just, even to those who do not deserve it. You stopped Feint Collier from hanging us. You have always tried to save innocents, even at great cost to yourself. So I will say this one thing and then we are done, by Cheshu." He scooted forward a bit, staring her full in the face, his eyes boring into hers with an almost feverish intensity. "You cannot dismiss me. I am not your servant to be banished. I am your friend. If Argus trusts you, and he nary trusts *anyone* but me, then you are fit companionship. A friend does not abandon a friend during troubled times. That is when the friendship is needed most."

Maia's eyes pricked with tears. Something had come loose inside of her during Jon Tayt's speech. She was grateful beyond words and felt a soothing balm of relief as tears slipped from her moist lashes.

"I do not deserve your friendship," she said, swallowing her tears. "But thank you."

"Bah, do not weep, lass. You do not shed tears on a trifle, which is one of the things I admire most about you. There are only two good reasons to weep, by Cheshu. The death of your mother or the death of your hound. Everything else is a trifle to be endured."

Maia laughed softly at the sentiment. "Well, my mother is still alive. Still banished at Muirwood Abbey, so it seems." She thought of the letter Maderos had given her. "I may not be fit to be called her daughter, but I hope to change that. And Argus . . ." She reached over and pet him. "He has not forsaken me either."

"Get your *own* hound," Jon Tayt said teasingly. "Every lass deserves a good hound. When Argus sires some pups, one shall be yours."

Maia sat quietly for a while, massaging her shoulders in the gloom. "So you left the kishion burning with a fever. Will he survive?" she asked finally, almost dreading the answer.

"He is a hardy man," Jon Tayt said. He sniffed. "I gave him some feverfew. He was very low and may not survive the day. But if he does recover, I would not be offended."

Maia smiled sadly and shook her head. Part of her was relieved, but she would miss the kishion. He had come to feel like a friend.

Argus's head snapped up, his ears taut.

"*That* would be a sign," Jon Tayt whispered, "that we should be on our way up the mountain."

***

The storm struck the Watzholt as they reached the other side of the ridge. Fluffy feathers of snow blasted into them, propelled by a howling wind that made each step a struggle. Maia's fingers and toes felt like ice, and the scarf over her mouth made it difficult to breathe. The drifts were up to their waist and getting deeper.

The Watzholt range rose up like a ridge of sharp teeth, and while they were only seeking to pass between the crevices, it was still high and the air thin.

"I know these mountains!" Jon Tayt shouted over the wind. "There is a village on the other side, but it is far. We may freeze to death before we get there!"

Maia shivered with the cold, wishing there were a Leering she could use to summon heat.

"Do we go back?" she shouted at him.

He shook his head, his coppery beard white with snow, like a grandfather's. He looked excited, as if the storm pleased him.

"What do we do then?" she yelled.

"Build a cave," he shouted. "Over there, in that drift! Come on!"

He slogged over to a lumpy portion of the snow and sank down to his knees. He withdrew one of his throwing axes, using the handle and blade like a shovel to dig away the snow. He waved her over and handed another one to her. Maia knelt beside him and began digging too, wondering what madness Jon Tayt was attempting. At least digging was easier than walking in the blizzard, and the work had her heart beating fast.

"Why do you look as if you are enjoying this?" Maia said through chattering teeth.

The hunter grinned. "This storm is covering all of our tracks. Even with a hound it would be difficult for them to track us now. Dig!"

It took hours of shoveling through the packed snowdrift, but they dug a cave into the mountainous pile and then a little chamber higher up. It was not tall enough to stand in, but the walls of snow provided protection from the shearing wind and ice, and Maia's shivering began to subside.

Argus whimpered from the cold and Maia pitied the beast, though she wished she had a coat of fur instead of two soggy gowns sticking to her. Her breath was a mist as she let it out, and everything around them was a uniform white. The wind moaned from the tunnel.

After he had finished packing the snow on the floor, Jon Tayt brought out his pack and fished through it for some food to eat. He looked positively cheery.

Maia clutched her stomach and dug her hands into her armpits to try and warm them. Her hair was damp, and clumps of ice clung to the tresses. It was still daylight, but it felt like twilight in the cave.

"Here," Jon Tayt said, offering her some dried beef wedged in a crust.

She ate it ravenously, her hunger increased by the effort of digging their shelter. "At least we have enough water," she said, her teeth chattering.

He shook his head. "Never eat snow. It will kill you with cold. You are shaking, lass. Here, lay your head against Argus. Keep close to him for warmth." He brushed his gloved hands together, looking around the shelter with an appraising eye. "Not bad at all. This will do."

She chewed through the stiff bread, drank sparingly from her waterskin, and nestled against Argus's flank as she continued to eat. The bread was a bit hard, and the meat tough and spicy. Jon Tayt munched on a fistful of nuts, then offered some to her. She refused, feeling the fatigue from their efforts settle in on her.

"Stay awake as long as you can," he warned, nudging her. "It is dangerous to fall asleep in the snow anyway, but perhaps more so for you. I will keep watch and wake you if you start to act strangely. Hopefully the storm will pass soon."

She blinked at him and nodded, pulling her cloak tightly over her and Argus like a blanket. Before long she dozed.

Maia.

The voice whispered inside her mind. Her eyes snapped open.

She was aware, subtly, of a presence deep in her mind. It made her cringe. It was her husband. Her mother's warning stung her conscience.

Maia?

She could sense him. He was warm, fed, and comfortable. How she envied him that. He was in his pavilion again, a warm brazier offering heat. She longed to be there, to feel a fur blanket beneath her and eat warm food.

Are you cold? You seem like ice. Where are you?

She could almost smell him. No, she *could* smell him. She could even smell the wine on his breath. Somehow, her thoughts were entwining with his and she was sharing his sensations.

I am cold, she thought to him, almost in spite of herself.

Where are you, Maia?

She did not want to commune with him, but the warmth was so inviting she could not resist it. He took another swallow of spiced wine and it felt as if it went down her throat instead. It warmed her from the inside.

Hautland, she found herself thinking. *We were caught in a blizzard crossing the Watzholt.*

So we are talking now? I sensed you before, but you did not respond. I can feel *the cold. Are you in danger?*

She could feel his warmth and he could feel her chill. It was a strange intimacy, their minds weaving together like this through the Medium. She was grateful for it. Her body stopped trembling.

She stared at the wall of the snow cave, but in her mind, she saw the interior of his pavilion, looking much as it had the night they had spent together. She flushed with embarrassment.

I am hunted, she thought back to him. *What do you know about the Victus?*

It is a secret order within the Dochte Mandar. They are the ones hunting you. Corriveaux is one of them. My spies watch for them, but they are subtle. What do you know about them, Maia?

She breathed out slowly. *Nothing. I heard they were strong in Hautland.*

Their origin is Naess, but Hautland seems to serve their interests the most. I have heard they torture people for information. Or bend them to their will. Be careful.

I will. Thank you, Collier.

Do you need help? She could feel the urgency in his mind, his desire to aid her. *I could send a ship for you. Let me help you.*

She realized she would need a ship to reach Naess. There was no way to route by land. She had assumed she would hire passage on a cargo ship bound to the northernmost kingdom. Part of her resisted letting Collier help. Another part of her wanted to confide everything to him and beg his help.

Please. Let me help you.

She wriggled under her cloak, uncertainty wrestling inside her. *Maybe one thing.*

Yes! Tell me.

I need a ship to carry us to Naess. I may not . . . return. They may kill me.

I will not let them, Maia. Trust in that. You need a ship. You will get a ship. I will send the Argiver *to Hautland. The captain's name is Stavanger. He can be in the port city of Rostick in two days. Is that soon enough?*

Maia felt a flush of warmth, of appreciation. *Yes. It will take several days for us to cross Hautland. Thank you, Collier.*

She felt his thoughts warm with delight. *I wish I could do more. You are very cold. I do not like that.* She could feel anger in his thoughts.

It is just a storm, Collier. I will be all right.

It reminds me of what I heard about how Lady Shilton treated you. She locked you in a room without a fire. She felt his thoughts begin to blister with heat. *I could kill her for all she did to you.*

Maia blinked, surprised. *You knew?*

Of course I knew. I have spies in your father's court. Deorwynn was very vocal in her hatred of you. She gave her mother strict orders to break your will. Yet you did not succumb, not even when they stripped everything from you. Every person who ever mattered to you. Every gown. She could feel the bubbling hate inside him. *When you are crowned my queen, you will never wear rags again.*

Maia felt strange, almost giddy. *You were watching over me?*

Much good that did, he returned blackly. *Remember, Maia, that it was your father who broke the plight troth between us. You and I were promised as infants. I have always thought of you as my future wife. Together, we will rule all the kingdoms. Believe it. You and I.*

She could feel the ambition in his heart as well. His thoughts were burning with it.

Thank you for helping me, Collier. I will look for the Argiver *in Rostick.* She wondered if he might abandon his army to try and join her, but she doubted it. The desire to conquer other lands ran thick in his blood. *I learned there is another kishion in your camp. I do not know who it is, but I thought you should know.*

That is truly helpful, thank you. Let me return the favor. You have been traveling awhile now, Maia. You may not have heard the latest news from your father's court.

Maia was concerned. *What news?*

His thoughts were sardonic and contemptuous. *Your father passed a new act. The Act of Submission. Every man, woman, and child must recognize him as the sovereign ruler of Comoros, independent of every other power, including the High Seer. The Aldermaston of Augustin has already sworn it. Do you remember the previous chancellor, Tomas Morton? The one before Crabwell. He was a maston and refused. Well, he was just beheaded in Pent Tower. Your country is in an uproar over it.*

Maia's heart crushed inside her chest. Her father was breaking every vow. Every covenant.

No, she thought with dread.

The Dochte Mandar will unite against him. I tell you, Maia, Comoros will be invaded. If I do not do it, someone else will claim it. Let me claim it for you. You are the rightful queen.

She squeezed her eyes shut, miserable at the news. *No, Collier. No, do not hurt my father.* Even now, after everything he had done, she could not bear the thought of losing him or seeing him usurped. As long as he lived, she would hold on to the hope he could change.

Still, she could not silence the thought that her father might have finally gone mad.

CHAPTER
TWENTY-SEVEN

Hautland

They were trapped in a cocoon of cold. Maia shivered, snuggled her head against Argus's damp pelt, and tucked in her legs. She could not feel her toes—any of them. Drips of water from the ice plopped in the small pan that Jon Tayt had set out to collect drinking water. She could not remember ever being so miserable and cold, even in the attic room of Lady Shilton's manor. Her hair was stiff with ice and it crackled as she moved.

Jon Tayt snored softly, sitting up against the curved wall of the snow cave, his gloved hands resting on his belly. His nose was ruddy, but he had a contented look on his face. His cap was askew on his head, revealing his balding pate through the loose curls of his coppery hair. She stared at him, feeling a mixture of tenderness and humor. He was so unflappable and surly. Without his help, she would not have made it to the mountains bordering Hautland. She suddenly wanted to laugh. All her life she had wanted to travel and visit the other kingdoms, but she had expected to visit them as a princess, not a fugitive.

An especially loud snore came from his mouth and he startled himself awake. His gray-green eyes blinked open and searched the pure whiteness. Maia tried to hide her smile, but he caught her.

"Glad to see I amuse you, my lady," he said gruffly. He shifted in the cave, twisting his shoulders around to loosen them, then flexed his arms and fingers. "Was I snoring?"

Maia's smile broadened. "A little."

He was abashed. "I fell asleep without watching your rest. At least we did not endanger anyone else. Did you have another dream?"

She shook her head. "It was too cold to sleep." During the night, she had not felt the awareness of the Myriad One inside her. Perhaps it did not relish experiencing the human penchant for suffering the elements.

Jon Tayt bent forward and examined the hole he had carved to get them inside. "It snowed shut. We need more air," he grumbled. After withdrawing an arrowhead, he jammed it into the snowpack above their heads and knifed it viciously upward a few times. Slush sprinkled down on them and Argus whined, but Jon shushed him. A few more pokes and they both heard the gush of air from above. Jon Tayt stowed the arrow away, then craned his neck at the hole and gazed up.

"Sky is blue. The storm is over."

"Thank Idumea," Maia said, brushing her arms. She lifted the pan of water and took a small sip. The water was frigid, but it helped soothe her thirst. She offered it to the hunter and then the boarhound, who finished it. Jon Tayt stowed his gear, hefted one axe and handed her another, and they both began chopping their way out of the snow cave.

As they emerged, Maia gazed in wonder at the crystalline expanse of the snow-clad range before her. It was impressive beyond words, the hulking crags of rock decorated with fresh snow. The air had a bite to it that stung her nose when she breathed, and she gently blew on her hands to try and warm them with her breath.

"Look there," Jon Tayt muttered gravely.

She gazed around the destruction of their cave, but he was directing her gaze elsewhere. While she had been giving the majestic peaks her attention and admiration, Jon Tayt had been examining the ground. Now she could see, plain as day, the trampled ruts of boots. They were everywhere along the pass, cutting a swath from the way they had come and continued down the slope into Hautland.

"Persistent badgers," Jon Tayt groused. "They nearly trampled over our camp as well. They were right on top of us without knowing it." He chuckled darkly. "If one had wandered over here, he would have come crashing through." He sniffed and pointed. "They are ahead of us now, lass."

"Is that a problem or a blessing?" Maia asked.

"Both. It will be easier to hide our trail by walking over theirs. However, if we keep following their trail, it will lead us to no safe place." He scouted the area, examining the size of the prints. She watched and waited as he worked to divine the signs. "Ach, at least thirty men. Mayhap forty." He wiped his nose. "I do not like the odds of that."

"At least they are not coming from behind us."

He shook his head. "Cannot judge that either, lass. If I were hunting us, and granted not many men are as clever, I would not bring everyone in a mass. I would send a group behind to follow the trail." He dipped his fingers into a snowy boot print.

"These tracks are fresh. They may well double back and catch us in between them."

"So going back would be equally dangerous as going forward."

"Danger no matter what we do."

Maia sighed. "We need to get to the port city of Rostick in two days. There will be a ship waiting for us."

"A ship? And how did you conjure that, my lady?" He looked at her skeptically.

She did not want to explain the nature of her connection with Feint Collier and so she did not. She moved some of her frozen hair out of her face. "Which way do we go?"

He pointed with the axe down the mountain.

***

Huge pine and cedar trees crept up from the lower slope of the Watzholt, and the trail disappeared into it. The trees were blanketed in fresh snow and the branches drooped, but lower down the storm had only brought rain, and the trees were vibrant green and lush.

"I like not the look of that," Jon Tayt muttered, standing at the edge of a rock looking down the trail into the maw of the woods. "Good place for a trap. They could see us coming down, but we would not see them until it was too late." He scratched his neck and gazed at the trail from different vantage points.

"The woods will provide cover for us as well," Maia suggested. She wanted a fire to warm her hands and feet. She was still shivering in spite of her many layers. But she had to agree with Jon Tayt—the trees would be an excellent place for their enemies to conceal themselves.

Jon Tayt shook his head and clucked his tongue. "Best to double back and take another pass down." They started back up the slope, climbing away from the thinning snow. Maia despaired ever being warm again. They had not gone far when Argus began to growl and whine, sniffing and roaming around their trail. His ears went up as he stared up the trail.

"Black luck," the hunter said. "Trap is closing." He sniffed the air. "Must be more men following our trail. Better run for the woods then. We must forge our own trail rather than taking this one. It will be easier to hide in the woods. Caught on this slope, we are dead."

Maia's heart began to warm. "All right."

They started back down the trail again and diverted from the already plowed path, heading into fresh snow. The way was steep, but the depth of the bank made it easy to sink their boots into it and slog down. Little bricks of ice came loose from their steps and tumbled down the fleecy slope. Argus followed in their wake, a low threatening growl in his throat.

The sound of a hunting horn filled the air from higher up. Maia looked back and saw men in the gap. The horn blasted again and the noise was joined by the sound of a horn from the woods below.

"Keep going!" Jon Tayt barked, crashing through the snow to carve a trail. The men were still a way up the mountain behind them, but they were running down the trail they had made, closing the distance quickly.

"How many!" he asked her.

Maia looked over her shoulder and saw at least a dozen. She could not see a uniform or insignia. Each was heavily bundled in a fur cloak and hat.

"Too many," Maia answered frantically. "Keep running!"

The snow bucked and heaved as they went down. From the line of trees lower down, she could see men emerging as well. Yet another horn blared, answering the other calls. Dark shapes flitted through the snow farther down, snapping and barking, tethered by leashes. Hunting dogs!

"Ach," Jon Tayt swore. He cut a steep path, trying to close the distance to the woods, but Maia could see they were not going to make it. Their pursuers from behind were covering ground faster than she and Tayt could make it, because the snow was already trampled, providing easier footing. Voices could be heard above and below, mixed with the barks of the dogs. Argus growled and began snapping in return, but he was only one and they were many. Horsemen appeared from the trees below them, streaming into the drift to close off their escape. The woods were teeming with men!

"A fine kettle of fish!" Jon Tayt shouted, wiping his face. His voice was rising nervously. He looked back and hissed his breath. He sheathed his throwing axe and brought his bow out, already strung, and adjusted the quiver bag so it was within easy reach.

Maia stared up at the mountain, watching crumbles of ice and snow come barreling down as the soldiers from above raced downward at them. Small clods of snow tumbled against her legs. She turned her gaze to the soldiers below. It was like a hunting party, complete with hounds, and they were the prey.

She reached down and took a hunk of snow in her frozen palm. She stared at it, taking in the way the sunlight winked off the crystal edges. The approaching soldiers were speaking in a guttural language, full of coughing sounds and unfamiliar inflections. She had never learned the Hautlander tongue, though she recognized its rough speech. The snow crystals in her hand triggered a realization. Snow melted. Snow became water. Water was from storms. Storms were under the control of her power. She was the master of storms.

She felt the kystrel's magic flare. Even though it was not touching her skin, her chest burned with heat. Her mind went black with implacable power and vengeful triumph. She would not be hunted. Not *her*, not by these petulant mongrels. The look of fear in Jon Tayt's eyes told her that her own eyes were glowing silver.

"No, Maia! No! Fight it off!"

He grabbed her arm to pull her after him, but the power flamed to life inside her like a thousand candles, burning away the chill and the frost. She was warm again. She was fire itself. She could feel Jon Tayt's panic bubbling inside him like a kettle, so she snatched away his fear, crushing it like a tinder flame.

Already she could feel the web of the Dochte Mandar. They were responding to her use of the magic and they were rushing at her to tamp and bind her. When they got close enough, they would knit their wills together to forge a cage to block her access to the Medium's power. Maia smiled deliciously. She turned back to the mountain and raised her arms to the sky, her fingers hooked and quivering with strain. Then she brought her elbows in, pumped her fists down and hunched over.

A rippling shock shook the mountain.

The jolt sent everyone except for her crashing to the ground. There was a sound, a sloughing sound, a breath puffed from a giant's mouth. And then the snow began to tumble from the mountain, breaking loose in huge boulders of ice and slush. It came as a wave, a massive slide of tumbling snow that barreled down at them.

She and Jon Tayt and Argus started down the mountainside at a run.

Cries of terror sounded from the men below as well as the men above. The rumble of the avalanche was deafening. Her gray skirts were thick with snow and wet and heavy around her legs, but power and strength flooded her, banishing her weariness. She was plowing the way now, and Jon Tayt and the dog were following in her path. Strange—the snow was parting for her. Fissures of ice crackled and split, shearing away and carving a path down the mountain. They were rushing as fast as they could, a monstrous wave of ice coming hard behind them. The soldiers in pursuit from above were trampled by it, buried alive by the crushing weight of snow.

Down below, the horses were going wild with terror and the soldiers fled into the cover of the trees to escape the coming devastation.

Maia struggled to reclaim her mind. She had lost control of it with a single action, and she struggled to wrench it back. She was still aware, still seeing the scene unfold, but it was as if she were tagging along beside herself. Detached, similar to how she'd felt in the Aldermaston's chamber. She dreaded harming anyone else.

"Too far!" Jon Tayt warned, one hand gripping Argus's leather collar.

The snow roared behind them. The trees were just ahead and men cowered behind the trunks, some trying desperately to climb the laden branches to get to higher ground. It was hopeless. The avalanche billowed like a storm cloud forming over the sea as it came down. It rose higher and higher until it towered over the trees and over all the specks of rock and men.

The sound as it rushed up behind her was monstrous, more terrible than the Fear Liath. They were almost to the trees when the plume of white death caught up to them. Jon Tayt grabbed for her arm, but he was pulled away from her, snatched up by the icy flood. The massive cloud picked her up too, smothering her with thick flakes of snow. It carried her down into the trees, where the wall of white blanketed the entire woods.

Maia was shrouded in snow, facedown. Everything was white. That dark part of her gloried in her power, in the unstoppable force of destruction she had unleashed against the men who sought to tame her. The weight of the snow over her was comfortable, like a blanket. She was perfectly calm and experienced an unnatural serenity. The quelling of noise was absolute.

She did not know how long she had lain there, still as a corpse, when the crunch of hooves broke the quiet.

Then there was a voice, a guttural voice, calling out. She heard the slump of a body landing in the snow and the noise of approaching boots. Her hand was sticking out of the snow. A gloved hand grasped it and she felt her body being tugged loose of the womb of snow.

"Gottsveld! Ich naida strumpf! Gotts! Gottsveld!"

Maia lifted her head, the snow dropping from her face in clumps. A man stood above her, gripping her hand and arm and pulling her up. He was short, his hair a brownish gray that belied his age, which was perhaps thirty. His eyes were blue. He wore a fur cloak, but she could see a prince's tunic beneath it, embroidered with gems and golden thread. His boots were high and rimmed with fur. A hunting horn and a sword dangled from his thick belt.

His eyes were serious as he looked down at her and he seemed anxious to help. But then he saw her face, saw that she was a woman, saw that she was their prey. She read his thoughts as splotches of blood staining the snow, clear and distinct and dirty.

He had not realized who he was saving from the avalanche until that moment. He was alone, his comrades helping to rescue the others.

Maia tightened her grip on his hand, her eyes burning into his. She felt his fear. It was syrupy and delicious. His mouth widened in shock, his pupils enlarging.

She flooded his heart with love and pity. Every hope, every longing, every desire in his heart she blew on like tender coals and ignited. His will shriveled before the heat of hers. And though Maia did not know the Hautlander tongue, the Myriad One did. It flowed from her lips with savage sweetness.

"Och denor, mien frenz. Vala Rostick. Vala Rostick."

You saved my life, dear friend. Take me to Rostick.

Take me to Rostick.

As you have seen, there is a portion of my tome that has a binding sigil on it. I have bound this information so that it may not be spoken of or revealed before it is time. To do so early will thwart the Covenant of Muirwood. But there will be a sign to indicate when the binding sigil may be opened. If it is opened too early, the maston order will be destroyed and the world with it. Cruix Abbey will burn. This is the sign that the hetaera have returned. The Queen of Comoros will be poisoned. This is the sign that the Covenant may fail. Be watchful.

—Lia Demont, Aldermaston of Muirwood Abbey

CHAPTER
TWENTY-EIGHT

Poisoned

A firm pounding thudded on the attic room door. Maia's temples throbbed with pain and the incessant noise made her ears and jaw ache. Her body felt swollen and shards of pain shot through her bowels. She tried to sit up on the bed, but fell weakly back down.

The door handle jiggled and Lady Shilton entered, her face flushed with fury. She had gray streaks through her hair, which had only increased in number in the eighteen months Maia had been living in her accursed manor. She had been beautiful once, but her beauty was distorted by the angry crinkles around her eyes, which she constantly attempted to smooth and hide with powders and ointments.

"Still abed," Lady Shilton uttered with loathing. "You will not eat your meals here, Maia. We fought this battle before and I will not give quarter. You heard the bell ringing. Come downstairs at once!"

"I am ill," Maia said miserably, gripping her stomach. "I do not want anything to eat."

"This is just another one of your provocations," the lady sneered. "You will come downstairs. Now!"

Maia shook her head. "Please. Just let me rest. I am unwell."

"You were well enough last night. The bell rang. You will come!"

"No," Maia said weakly, shaking her head. "I cannot." Her stomach doubled with sharp cramps. All night, she had felt them coming on.

"And I say that you will!" Lady Shilton marched into the tiny attic room and seized hold of Maia's arm. Her fingers dug deeply into the skin, her nails biting hard. Maia winced and struggled to pull away.

"Please, Lady Shilton!" Maia begged. "Not like this."

"The problem with you is that you were spoiled too much as a child. You are obstinate, headstrong, and defiant. You defy your lord father and he is the King of Comoros!" Her voice rose shrilly. "You defy my daughter when she has done nothing but—"

"She does nothing without the intent of humiliating and torturing me," Maia said angrily, fighting against the grip on her arm. "I have not seen my mother in over six years, madame. Have you even gone a day without seeing your daughter?"

It earned her a slap, a stinging one, but the pain was nothing compared to that of her ravaging insides.

"Let me go," Maia moaned, jerking her arm, but Lady Shilton was strong enough to muscle her up from the bed.

"I say you will come and you will come! You will obey me, you rude, thoughtless child! Why should I endure this? You are proud and vindictive. Now come! If I must drag you screeching all the way down the steps, by Idumea's hand, I will!"

Maia slumped to the floor, feeling nausea sweep over her. She hung her head, tears pricking her eyes, but she would not let them fall. She bottled up her hate and her rage, comforted by the knowledge that she could use the power of the kystrel to flay Lady Shilton's emotions like a fishmonger with a blade. But she dared not. Owing to the violence of her emotions, she would not be able to maintain control if she attempted such a thing. And she knew what the cost of revealing herself might be.

"Please," Maia begged, gripping Lady Shilton's sleeve. "Please just let me rest."

"Why must you be so obstinate?" Lady Shilton shouted.

Maia succumbed to her mortification. Despite the pain gnawing in her middle, she rose from the floor. She was nearly as tall as Lady Shilton now, though much more fragile and frail since she had been forbidden to exercise and was still not allowed to walk the grounds. The window of her room had been nailed shut since her last escape, though the crooked piece of broken glass had not been mended.

"Because I have but one gown," Maia said, defeated and ashamed. With Lady Shilton still clinging to her arm, Maia turned her body and showed the back of her skirt, which was black and stained with blood from her flux. "It came on during the night. I was going to wash it after the servants were abed. Please, Lady Shilton." She stared hard into her eyes. "Do not make me come downstairs."

Lady Shilton seemed to see her for the first time. The quivering rage in her lip slowly stilled. The exasperation and violence in her eyes cooled. She was a wicked woman, hurtful and cruel, but she was still a mother deep in her heart. A grandmother too.

"So . . . so often you feign illness," Lady Shilton muttered, the heat gone from her voice.

"I know," Maia said softly. "Would you not if you wore rags and lived up here?"

"It is no more than you *deserve*," Lady Shilton said, her voice betraying her with a hint of compassion. "You are a bastard."

Maia stood up as straight as she could. "I am a *princess*."

A feeling swept into the room. It was powerful, so powerful that it made Maia's voice tremble as she uttered the words. It was a truth spoken. Not the defiant tantrum of a disavowed daughter. It was pure, soul-searing truth.

Lady Shilton quailed in front of the young woman in the tattered bloody dress and released her grip. She took an involuntary step backward. A curious feeling coursed through Maia's veins then. It was a form of power. The truth was a form of power. Was it the Medium? It felt like it.

Maia smoothed her skirts. She had grown a little since being given the servant's gown, and now the hem did not even reach her ankles. Many of the seams had split and torn and she had been forced to beg for thread and needles to stitch them herself. The split at her elbow had not been fixed yet and Lady Shilton's tugging at her arm had ripped it even more. The fabric was threadbare in places. Maia felt self-conscious, but she stood erect and proud, a king's daughter in her heart, though no longer in title.

"I . . . I will not . . . make you come down," Lady Shilton said, retreating toward the door. "Your flux came on last night?"

Maia nodded and rubbed her temples, which throbbed painfully with her pulse. "I am not hungry. Truly."

Lady Shilton slipped out the door and shut it behind her. Maia sat on the edge of the bed, weariness sapping her, but she had won something. It was a small victory, but she treasured those the most. Exhausted, she lay back down on the bed and stared at the hole in the window, watching the gray sky and hearing the wind whistle across the eaves.

Maia awoke to the sound of someone mounting the attic steps. She turned her neck and was surprised when Lady Shilton entered again, more solemnly than she had earlier in the day. She was carrying several things—a tray with a washing basin and a half loaf of dark bread, dripping with melted butter. It made Maia's mouth water just to look at it. Beneath the tray was a bundle of gray-green cloth.

"I have some rags as well," Lady Shilton said. "I thought you might want to wash." Maia noticed the small kettle on the tray as Lady Shilton set it down. "The water is still warm."

Maia stared at her in shock. The woman had never, not once, shown her a kindness. She could hardly believe it.

"Thank you," Maia said, a tremor in her voice.

Lady Shilton lifted the tray and then unfolded the bundle of fabric. It was a servant's gown, one from Lady Shilton's own household. It was what her ladies-in-waiting wore. Maia had fancied the roping on the sleeves and the back of the gown, which cinched the fabric tight. It had always looked elegant and simple. It was a servant's garb, not a lady's, but anything was better than the rags she had worn.

"I thought you might want to . . . borrow . . . a gown while the other one . . ." Her voice trailed off. Her lips pursed sourly, her cheek muscle twitching. "Just give me . . . yours." She swallowed. "I will burn it." She sniffed and waved her hand impatiently. "Come, child. Off with it. I will burn it."

Maia was not sure she could trust her. She was afraid of trusting anyone. That she should find a little sympathy from this hard, stern woman—it truly surprised her. Besides, she dared not remove her gown and expose the kystrel or the shadowstain

302

on her breast. "I would rather keep it, Lady Shilton," Maia said demurely. "For washing days."

"It is no matter to me what you do with it." She sniffed again, handing over the bundle. "I called for my apothecary, Mikael Healer. He is a good man, trained in Billerbeck Abbey, and he will bring you some remedies."

Again, Maia was astonished. "Thank you."

Lady Shilton looked at her with something resembling sympathy, then fled the attic again without another word. Maia took hold of the crust and ate ravenously. It was Lady Shilton's bread, not servant's fare. There were little black seeds in the dough and Maia tasted a hint of lemon and spice. It was wonderful. She devoured it.

After washing herself with the rags and warm water, she held out the new gown and stared at it adoringly. She had always loved her wardrobe and could not believe how majestic the simple gown looked to her now. Being forced to watch Murer strut around in her royal gowns had made Maia sick with envy at first, but that feeling had faded since her imprisonment in Lady Shilton's manor, replaced with desperation for something *else* to wear except for the one ragged dress.

Maia put on the gown and wished, for once, that her small room could spare a mirror. The sleeves were smooth and warm and the gown stretched all the way down and covered her frayed felt slippers. With a brush, she knew she could almost pass for a normal person and not the household drudge.

There was a little flush of warmth in her heart as she smoothed the gown over her body, feeling the cut of it, the shape of it. It felt . . . good.

More steps.

Having eaten every last crumb of bread, Maia quickly drank some water to parch her thirst. She heard voices in the stairwell, a man's voice intertwined with Lady Shilton's, and then the door opened.

". . . come sooner, but some ruffian smashed into me on the street, knocking my cap off, and I dropped everything. The rudeness! I am grateful my leather bag is so sturdy, Lady Shilton. All the vials and stoppers are safe. If he had cracked my pestle, I would have asked the guard to hang the man!"

"It is well enough, Mikael. There she is. This is the king's *daughter*, Lady Maia. This is Mikael, Healer from Billerbeck."

He was a big-boned man in his early forties with a wide girth and balding reddish-brown hair. "Very well to meet you, Lady Maia," he said, squinting down at her.

She bowed her head respectfully and curtsied, wondering if Lady Shilton had given her the dress so this man would not know how poorly she was treated. It was a cynical thought and she squashed it.

He set down the bag and rubbed his hands together. "Chilly being up so high. How do you stand it? Let me see, I can mix a tincture that always is useful in such occasions."

He hummed to himself and fetched his leather bag. Maia sat on the edge of the bed and watched as he lifted out certain ingredients, squinted at some of them, then added them to the basin of his mortar, which he'd settled on the small table near her bed. Lady Shilton stood nearby, fidgeting.

"Some warm water, madame," the apothecary said over his shoulder to Lady Shilton.

She nodded and descended back down the steps. The apothecary looked at a small vial and added a few drops to the mixture, still humming as he went. "Rude man, I tell you," he started to murmur, though it was clear he expected no response. "Walking into him was like walking into a brick wall. I am no small cub myself and he knocked me on my arse. Had a vicious look in his eyes, but he did stop and help me up and make sure nothing was broken. Will have a bruise on my backside, I fear." He rubbed himself gingerly.

Lady Shilton returned and the apothecary smiled and took the cup she offered him. He dumped the powder from his mortar bowl into the water, then mixed it with a cut of ginger root from his bag. "A little treacle is often a good additive," he said with a grin. "But this will do in a trice. Drink it down, Lady Maia. It will help calm your innards."

Maia took the tea and drank it. It was bitter and burned her throat a little, but she had expected the flavor to be revolting and it was not. She had drunk half the cup when another round of cramps started.

She hurriedly set the cup down, wincing.

"Feeling another pang?" the apothecary asked. "You just drank it. It takes some time for the fluid to run through your bowels. I will stay until it works."

Lady Shilton smoothed the back of her hand against Maia's forehead.

The cramping in her bowels became more violent and severe.

"I do not feel well," Maia said, moaning. Her stomach started to heave.

"You look paler," the apothecary said, his expression wrinkling with concern. "Have you eaten anything today?"

"Just some bread," Maia said, holding her arms against her stomach. She was going to be sick.

"The basin!" the apothecary shouted, sweeping up the half-full bowl that Maia had used to wash herself. He got it to her just as her stomach emptied. She clutched the bowl and vomited noisily into it, her stomach wrenching with knife-sharp spasms.

Maia saw spots dancing in front of her eyes. Her temples throbbed and a strange chalk taste coated the back of her throat. She gagged again, hunched over, and retched a second time. The pain in her stomach twisted and wrenched, as if two sailors were playing tug-of-war with it.

"Mikael? What is wrong with her?" Lady Shilton demanded.

"I know not," he said, flummoxed. "This has never happened before."

"What did you give her?"

"A remedy I have used countless times. It usually takes a little while to start providing relief, but I have never seen this result before."

Maia's ears were ringing and their voices became muffled. The bread had entirely left her stomach, but she was not hungry for anything. The queasiness was worse than if she were being tossed about on a ship during a storm. Maia moaned with the pain, clutching the bowl even though it was nearly full of her own bile.

"Celena! Celena!" Lady Shilton screamed down the steps, summoning a cavalcade up the stairs. Maia felt the room spin around her. Her mouth itched. It was hard to breathe.

"What did you give her, Mikael? What did you give her?"

"Everything I gave her is to tame. To quell a stomach, not to upset one!"

"My lady, I am here," a woman's voice said. "What is wrong? Ugh, is Maia sick?"

"Fetch another basin. Quickly! A large one! Go, Celena. Mikael, what is happening?"

"I know not! I have never seen this! I have no cure for what I do not know!"

The commotion in the room grew hysterical. There was stomping and yelling. Noises coming in and out of focus as Maia's mind turned to mush. She was sick several more times, expelling noisily but producing little more than bile and spittle. The muscles in her stomach were tender from the ravaging spasms. The ringing in her ears blended with the shouts and jostling.

Maia lay on the bed, gasping through the ordeal. In time, the jabs of pain subsided and the quivering stilled. When she next became aware, she was drenched in sweat and covered in several blankets. She opened her eyes and they felt stiff and pasty.

Slowly, she became aware of the murmuring voices around her. There was a new voice, one she did not recognize.

"Thank you, Healer. That will be all. Bootwain and valerianum. Yes, thank you. You may go now. I will report to Chancellor Crabwell."

"Doctor Willem, I swear what I told you is true," said Mikael Healer in a nasally whine. "I gave her nothing that I would not dose my own daughters with."

"Thank you, Healer. That is all. You may go."

"Do you think it was poison?" murmured Mikael as he backed away. "I did not poison her! I swear it on my own soul! Lady Shilton, you *know* I would not do such a thing!"

"Of course not, Master Mikael," Lady Shilton said. "I will defend you. You have served my family for years. Do you think it was poison, Doctor Willem?"

"I shall make my report to the chancellor," the doctor replied gravely. "You may go. Both of you."

"She is stirring. Maia? Are you awake?" It was Lady Shilton's voice.

She murmured in assent and rubbed her eyes to open them.

"You will tell the doctor, Maia. Tell him that I—"

"Enough, madame!" the doctor bellowed. "Out!"

The apothecary and Lady Shilton retreated down the attic steps, muttering bleakly as they left.

The doctor was a big, barrel-chested man with a fringe of white hair around the sides of his head and a waxy bald top that glistened with sweat. He sat on a small stool next to her bed, which had been brought up since she did not have a stool. His meaty hands folded and his voice was deep and grave when he spoke.

"How are you feeling?"

"Better," she answered. "I started my flux last night."

"Lady Shilton told me. I saw the bloodstain on the gown . . . if you can *call* it a gown . . . over there." He chuffed. "Living up in the attic of a drafty house. No heat. No brazier. No wonder you are sick and pale. My name is Willem Bend. I am going to recommend to your lord father that you be allowed to exercise. I think rowing on the river would increase your stamina and strength more than doing chores. Archery as well, for your muscles. You are young and need to spend more time out of doors. You are too pale. That should help a great deal."

"That would be wonderful," Maia said gratefully.

He smoothed a lock of hair from her face. "I also plan to tell the chancellor *and* your father that you were poisoned."

Maia swallowed, remembering the chalky taste in her mouth—the sudden and unstoppable nausea. Her thoughts starting to spin wildly.

"I do not believe it was Lady Shilton or her bumbling apothecary." His voice was quiet, raspy. "But you must be on your guard, Lady Maia. If any food tastes strange to you, you should not eat of it. Drink only water. I think the lord chancellor will start an investigation. If someone wanted you dead, they may try again when they learned they have failed."

He leaned forward and then rose, his brow wrinkling. "This concerns me deeply. I must speak to the king about this matter. Do you have a message for him?"

Maia stared at him, her eyes wide. It was a rare opportunity. "Tell him that I love him. I wish he would let me see my mother."

He frowned, his eyes stern and severe. "I will," he agreed with a thick voice. "But I do not believe he will agree."

CHAPTER
TWENTY-NINE

Armada

M aia awoke in a bed. She blinked and looked around, finding herself in a strange place with no recollection of how she had come to be there. Even though this had happened to her regularly since leaving the lost abbey, it was still a jarring sensation. The sheets smelled faintly of purple mint. The bed had four large posts draped with creamy linen veils. Panic thrummed inside her heart and she quickly sat up. She was lying atop the sheets and comforter, still clothed—thank Idumea—but she noticed she was now dressed only in the burgundy gown that Jon Tayt had given her. The tattered gown she had worn underneath was gone. She was baffled at how kindly she seemed to have been treated. It would not have surprised her to have awoken in chains.

Quickly, she scooted off the edge of the bed and nearly stumbled when she hit the floor as the bedstead was much higher than she had anticipated. The room was small and paneled in dark wood wainscoting. There was a single window on the far wall across from the bed, and though thick velvet curtains covered most of it, she could see a faint dawn light. She hurried to the window and pulled the curtain aside.

It was just before dawn. How much time had passed? She had no idea. The window opened onto a rear alley, very narrow. Maia brushed hair from her eyes, trying to quell the feeling of panic. She gazed down at the alley and realized she was on an upper floor. The buildings on either side of hers were quite narrow and two levels high, each with steep shingled roofs. The windows were roughly the same size and shape and all the ones on the upper floors, hers included, had planter boxes just outside growing an assortment of wildflowers. Gutters and sluices lined each rooftop with spouts to pour water down into the gullies below. Farther down the street the road bent, revealing another row of houses with steep roofs and gabled windows. Behind one of these, she saw another house, perhaps four stories high, with a triangular roof. She craned her neck to see beyond the large house and caught sight of a huge scaffolding and a tower under construction. There were no workers on the scaffolding.

"Where am I?" she whispered, touching the glass. The buildings on her side of the street were made of brick. On the other side, the walls were daubed with white plaster and supported by stained wooden beams. The streets below were immaculately clean—the cobblestones looked as if they had been brushed the night before—which was odd for an alley. A few lazy streams of smoke came from some of the chimneys.

Maia pushed away from the window and examined the room. Other than the tall four-post bed, there was a small couch where she found her other dress, her pack, and her boots. There was a corner table on the other side with two small wooden chairs. On the table was the leftover tray from the previous night's meal—cold chicken bones, sprigs of asparagus, and a few crushed lime rinds. She rubbed her stomach and did not feel hunger. There were two goblets at the table. Two sets of dishes.

She stared at the remains of the meal she did not remember eating, her insides twisting with worry, her mind full of fog. She struggled to remember. There had been a snowstorm. A snow cave. She and Jon Tayt had fled across the mountains into Hautland in search of Rostick, where she was to meet with one of her . . . her *husband*'s trading ships. They had been hunted and trapped in the mountains and she had caused an avalanche. She remembered a man pulling her out of the snow. His face was a blur in her mind, but she could easily envision his royal tunic and furred cloak. He spoke Hautlander. Then blackness consumed her world. The Myriad One had taken control again. As she wrung her hands, she wondered how long it had lasted, how many days she had been unconscious, and what had befallen Jon Tayt and Argus. They had not borne the brunt of the avalanche, but even though she respected her friends' survival abilities, she worried about their safety.

Desperate to escape, she whirled and ran to the door. It was locked. She wrested it, but despite her best efforts, it would only jiggle.

She had been locked inside a room? She searched for other signs that would help her understand where she was. Could this place be Rostick? She remembered asking the man to take her there, though of course it had been the *other* who had spoken the question.

The morning light slowly flooded the room through the parted curtain. What should she do? Wait in the chamber for the man to come back?

But why would he have *locked* her in?

She was already feeling uneasy and now dread flooded in. Perhaps he had come to his senses after she had fallen asleep and could no longer manipulate his feelings. Could he have fled to summon the Dochte Mandar?

That decided her. She had to leave.

Maia tried the door handle again. The door itself was sturdy and she lacked the strength to force it open. What other options did she have? Her eyes went back to the window and she remembered how she had climbed out of the garret window in Lady Shilton's house to see her father. She went to it and it opened freely, without even the hint of a squeal. The scent of the flowers in the planter box filled the room. Maia stared down and judged that the street below was too far to jump. She rushed over to the bed and pulled down the long veils and began tying them together. Then she added some of the bed sheets and fastened one end to one of the sturdy posts.

Her stomach churned with worry as her ears detected the sound of movement on the lower floor. Boot falls thudded and tromped. Voices murmured. Maia hurriedly stuffed her spare gown into her pack and flung it closed. She swung it around her shoulders and then took the makeshift rope to the window and tossed it down. After testing the strength of the knots, she climbed up onto the window sill and quickly climbed down to the street below.

The air was chill—the alley still full of shade. She started down the cobbled road toward the place where she had seen the scaffolding. As the highest structure in the vicinity, it would give her a good view of the city. She pulled her cloak hood over her head and folded her arms, walking briskly. The alley was empty.

She realized she had more than one problem. She could not speak Hautlander, and she did not know where she was. Opening her mouth to others would quickly reveal her as a foreigner. She knew that all the kingdoms were perpetually at war with each other, and if her identity was discovered, she would be a ransom target. If they discovered her brand, she would be dead.

At the end of the street, she turned and walked through several more twisting alleys before she reached the scaffolding. There was something familiar about the place. She had never been to Hautland before, but it felt as if she had dreamed of it. The scaffolding surrounded the construction of an abbey, that was plain enough. Maia stared up at the progress, the stone blocks seated on top of each other. There were large wooden cranes and ropes and pulleys, and huge barrels and crates were strapped down nearby. She could hear the lowing of oxen, but they were fixed in pens nearby and all the manure had been swept and brushed away. What a clean city.

The abbey was long and very skinny and tall, jutting up above the houses like a giant spike. Maia walked around the grounds, amazed at the construction. Even though it was not finished, she could see the finished abbey in her mind's eye, with a huge spike-like steeple that was high enough to pierce the clouds. It was a different design than she had seen in any of the other kingdoms she had visited. It was bold and sharp, like a sword thrusting up through the heart of the city.

Maia thought it would help get her bearings if she had a better view, so she walked over to the nearest portion of scaffolding and started to climb. She ascended platform after platform, rising up until she was higher than the lowest rooftops. Then she went higher still, climbing up above the larger mansions. The wind teased the edges of her cloak, but the movement helped keep her warm. From above, it was a strange and interesting city; with so many steep-roofed buildings crammed together she could hardly see the streets. The roofs were so steep in pitch, she could only see the edges like blades of grass.

Turning around and gripping the scaffolding poles, she opened her mouth in wonder as she continued to survey the city beneath her. Three more abbeys were under construction, each one with the same spike-like steeple. She quickly got her bearings and, by turning around, realized that she was on an island, surrounded by a river. It was roughly a circle, though lopsided, and every part of it was covered and paved. The ground was relatively flat, not at all like the island abbey of Dochte. But she could tell that the Hautlanders were hastily building a city to rival that of the ancient Dahomeyjan abbey. Towering walls surrounded the island, and huge wedge-shaped battlements had been built on the other side of the river, with an enormous jagged moat carved into the ground. The city was protected by two channels of water, she realized—the river, meandering north among green hills spotted with trees and, not too far distant, the sea. She was on the northern coast of Hautland. It amazed her.

Rostick.

She stared at the intricate design of the fortifications, the newness of the construction. It seemed as if the entire kingdom had gathered together in this one bend of the river to raise an edifice that would fulfill a defensive purpose while also serving as an outpost for trade. There were the docks! Though the walls separated the docks from the city, she could see the masts of ships down below. And beyond the bridges and battlements, manors and halls, she could see at least seven towers and a fortress that overlooked the mouth of the river at the north edge of the city. And there were more ships by that fortress—hundreds of them. It was an armada. She had not realized so many ships could even exist, let alone be anchored together in a single massive harbor.

She stared at the docks, the bridges, the abbeys, trying to puzzle the pieces together. It was all new construction, not broken remnants from the past. There were shipyards everywhere. Why so many? What would these ships be used for?

The answer came to her—clear and undeniable. Invasion. These were warships, not fishing vessels. They intended to wage war. Her heart panged with dread. These were new. They would be sailing for Comoros to humble her father for expelling the Dochte Mandar from his realm. Her mind filled with the possibility of every kingdom attacking Comoros, just as Comoros had humbled Pry-Ree in the distant past.

She squeezed the pole of the scaffold, wishing she could somehow warn her father. Wishing there were a way she could prevent it.

"Ach stounzen! Bick trot lam! Ach stouzen!"

Someone was shouting at her from below. She looked down to see that a small work crew had slowly been assembling in the courtyard below. One of the men had noticed her and was pointing up at her and shouting.

She knew where the harbor was, and though it would be near impossible to find a single Dahomeyjan ship amidst such madness, she was convinced that she was in Rostick, where she had heard the Myriad One inside her order the man to take her. It still troubled her that the being clearly approved of the decisions she was making, but she dared not stray from her path—not when it was her only chance to be free. She needed to find the *Argiver*, the ship Collier had sent.

Quickly, she descended the scaffolding. A small crowd of workers had gathered to the base. They wore scruffy clothes pale with stone dust. Many held hammers and chisels.

"*Doch nasten iffen. Tuzza breeg. Stounzen,*" said the man who had shouted at her as she reached the bottom. She did not understand Hautlander, but his scolding tone transcended language. She shoved past him and started walking in the direction of a bridge she had seen that would take her to the river.

"*Bick nuffen!*" the man sneered at her. "*Ick nuffen dorr!*"

Her cheeks flamed with embarrassment, but the feeling subsided after she had left the onlookers behind. A tower bell sounded, and suddenly it seemed as if the entire city had been summoned to the streets en masse. Doors opened and Maia watched as men and women dressed in gray skirts and white aprons emerged from homes and shops. The wardrobe was fairly uniform and she noticed the women wore padded round circlets and veils and wimples.

Maia soon realized that people were staring at her with as much interest as she was looking at them. She was not veiled, nor was anyone else wearing such a long cloak. The color of her gown was conspicuous when compared to the monotones the other women wore. All of the looks made her nervous, though it was nothing compared to the shame she had endured at Lady Deorwynn's hands. It made her realize that she was being perceived as an outsider, someone who did not belong in Rostick. People pointed at her, making comments in their throaty language.

Her cheeks were burning once again, but though the streets were teeming with life, this was not a crowd she could vanish into. She pressed on, fighting down the terrible feeling of being mocked and jeered at. Some of the women scolded her roughly as she passed. She did not know why, but Maia could tell that this was how the people of Rostick treated a woman who refused to conform.

She found the bridge she sought and crossed it. She was surprised to see the water was not fetid or reeking of dead fish, given the cramped conditions of the city. The water was as immaculately clean as the cobblestone streets . . . but how was it all kept that way? After crossing the bridge, she began searching the ships for any markings of Dahomey or Comoros. She needed to find someone who could guide her.

"*Bick nuffen*," someone said at her sleeve, tugging her. She whirled and saw four young men dressed in wharf garb with dark scarves around their necks. "*Bick nuffen trollen?*"

Most of them laughed. One of them began fishing in his purse for coins. "*Septem? Goch, drillow!*" One of the other young men butted his comrade in the belly with his elbow and leered at her.

Maia understood. They thought she was a girl who sold herself for money.

"No," Maia said firmly, her eyes blazing with anger and loathing. Her mouth firmed into a frown and she shook her head and stormed away.

"*Doch! Bick nuffen, doch!*"

She heard them following her, so she marched faster, her eyes scanning the wharf for a sign. There were only men around her, and she realized, belatedly, that she was violating another tradition in Hautland.

The men continued to follow her. She glanced back once and discovered the group had grown from four to six. Onlookers continued to gaze at her with open contempt and murmur to one another. There were different expectations of women in this kingdom and she was clearly violating them on every level. She hugged herself as she walked, trying to ignore her pursuers in the hopes they would relent.

So many ships. Most were facing upriver and moored to the wharf, but some of them were being turned about by long poles and ropes, their bulks facing outward as they prepared to set sail. The amount of traffic and congestion was baffling, but there was a certain order and rhythm to it. Commands were barked and then promptly obeyed. Men worked in unison, in small crews. Again, there were no women anywhere.

"*Bick nuffen!*" Someone grabbed her arm from behind. She spun around and raised her hand, but the man caught her wrist and squeezed hard. It hurt, but she ignored the pain. A group of men had gathered around her and she could feel them crowding her away from the wharf and toward the wall. It was like an unstoppable tide. There were so many bodies pressing around her that when a hand reached down to squeeze her rump she did not know whose it was.

The man holding her wrist leered at her. "*Cozzen, bick nuffen. Cozzen sprout.*"

She spit in his face.

That shocked them. He released her in surprise to wipe the spittle from his cheek, and a look of murder filled his eyes. "*Cozzen freegin!*" he shouted at her and backhanded her sharply across the face. Her head rocked back, but she had been struck before and harder. She did not lose her balance or cry out in pain. Instead, she stared at him defiantly.

Again, she surprised them with her brazen resistance. Several more backed away nervously, leaving an open space around her.

"No," she said, dreading what was to come. The kystrel's power began to rise inside her. The dark part of her burned to life with the anger she felt. She could quench their lust and their anger and leave them lying in the gutter. She should not. She knew she should not.

"*Ick dirk?*" the man said contemptuously, gazing down at her blade. Then he drew a sword from his belt.

Someone fell down next to the man who threatened Maia. A bloom of blood stained the fallen man's shoulder and he howled with pain. Then there was another cry of pain. The wall of men surrounding Maia parted, backing out of the way of a man wielding a bloodied sword.

"*Mein bick nuffen,*" the man said with a deadly voice. A voice she recognized. A voice that cut through the conflicting noise in her head.

It was Feint Collier.

That was all Collier said before slicing the wrist of the man who held the sword, smashing his nose with an elbow, and kneeing him hard in the groin. As the man crumpled to the cobblestones, Collier went after the next one.

Maia heard the sound of blades clearing sheathes all around her.

In all the kingdoms, the Aldermastons are empowered to teach mastons their oaths. But there must always be one Aldermaston who has the Gift of Seering. This Aldermaston, male or female, is chosen as the High Seer. When the High Seer dies or is slain, the Aldermastons from all the abbeys assemble and the Medium chooses, through a secret Leering, who the new High Seer will be. To serve as the High Seer is a heavy burden, great-granddaughter. It is a heavy burden indeed. It will be your burden, and it will be heaviest on you in the land of the darkest night.

—Lia Demont, Aldermaston of Muirwood Abbey

CHAPTER THIRTY

Queen of Dahomey

Collier moved like a serpent. That was the only way to describe it. He was all supple grace, rippling away from blows with ease before stinging with his fangs. He did not wait for the others to strike first. They were surrounded by over a dozen men with blades, and he took the fight to their cheekbones, their eyes, their wrists, their bowels. Stab, swish, parry—lunge. Maia had seen Paeizian fencing masters before. In her former life, she had even trained under one in her father's court. But this was not a controlled ritual. This was a fight to the death.

Someone's eye was pierced and she winced at the sound of it, the impact followed by a yelp and shriek of pain. Blood bloomed like flower petals from her attackers' shoulders, arms, and waists. She could see why the King of Dahomey had earned the nickname of *Feint*. His moves were completely unpredictable and utterly savage. Several of the men tried to rush him from behind, but he swept low, parrying multiple blades with a single stroke before flicking out his own blade like a serpent's tongue, meticulously stabbing his opponents in vulnerable locations, dropping them with graceful ease and debilitating wounds.

One of the victims lost his blade at Maia's feet, and she swept it up by the hilt. It had been years since she had handled such a blade, but she knew what to do. The foes were thinning quickly, but she sliced the arm of one of the men lunging at Collier's back. The man growled in pain, scowled at her, and without further ado, fled into the crowd. They had attracted the eyes of everyone on the wharf and sailors hung from the rigging of their boats to get a better view of the fight.

Maia watched as a man in a black jeweled tunic approached them from the wharf with an ornate blade in his hand. He had a trim goatee and an earring in one ear. Sweeping back his cloak, he shouted out a challenge that sent several of their opponents scurrying away.

The man did not look to be a Hautlander and when he shouted again, Maia recognized his tongue as Paeizian. He was challenging Collier to a duel.

Using the distraction, another man slowly slipped up behind Collier with a dagger, and Maia kicked him in the ribs, knocking him down, winning her chuckles of approval from the gathering crowd. She stood near Collier, blade held defensively in a bell guard stance, and positioned herself to protect his back.

Collier's voice was sardonic. "Thank you for making it so easy to find you."

"Are you going to fight him?" she asked, watching the black-clothed man approach.

"Not many other options at the moment."

The two men faced off, swishing their blades down in an informal salute. Maia felt the power of the Medium radiating out from Collier, sending tendrils of oily fear into the air. The two engaged without another word, their blades flashing in the morning light and clashing sharply against each other. Both men were masters, Maia could see, and the simple blows that had disarmed or set down Collier's previous opponents would not work the same way against this man.

The two traded parries and lunges, their weapons whistling death. The newcomer, who was older and more worldly, frowned in concentration as he deflected the blows Collier aimed at him, then riposted ruthlessly. Their blades clashed and the feeling of fear in the air darkened and intensified. Maia could see that emotion in the eyes of the other observers, who backed away from the combatants for fear of their lives.

"He is good," Collier said, sweat dripping from his nose. "*Melle bene.*"

The man with the goatee dipped his chin to acknowledge the praise.

Maia looked down the street and saw a retinue of Dochte Mandar marching toward them.

"They are coming," she warned. "He is only here to stall us."

"Give me a *moment* more," Collier said, his voice strained as he arched his back and twisted away from his opponent's thrust, but not quickly enough to escape a shallow cut that sliced open his shirt, exposing the kystrel beneath it and sending a rivulet of blood down his front. When Maia saw the kystrel, her thoughts went black and she struggled to keep her own mind.

No! No! Not now!

Collier slammed his elbow down on the man's wrist, then punched his pommel guard into the man's lip so hard his head tossed back. He twirled his body around and clipped the man's boot, knocking him on his back. The blade clattered from the

Paeizian's hand. Collier poised over him and the man's eyes went wide with terror as the blade jabbed at his chest. There was a chink of metal as the tip of Collier's sword was deflected off something under the man's shirt.

"Thought so," Collier said angrily. "A Victus." Then he adjusted his aim and plunged his blade into the man's forearm, impaling it. There was a howl of pain and agony.

Collier's face was flushed, his breathing heavy, but in a fluid series of movements he jerked his blade loose, grabbed Maia's arm, and pulled her after him. "Run," he ordered.

They charged away from the advancing Dochte Mandar, who struggled through the disintegrating crowds. Shouts and warnings threatened them from behind, but the crowds parted as they made their way through it. The naked swords they wielded ensured it.

"The *Argiver*!" Collier shouted, jutting his blade to point the way. The boat he indicated was already facing the right direction, making ready to sail. Cries of alarm filled Maia's ears, and they ran as hard as they could, rushing along the wharf toward the vessel.

"Drop it," he yelled. "Drop the sword!"

She watched him sheathe his own weapon as he ran, but—deciding to trust him—she cast hers away, hearing the metal thump against the wood of the docks.

The shouts and screams from behind them were getting louder.

Collier's hand gripped hers. His fingers were hot and she clung to them tightly, feeling her stomach begin to bubble as she realized what he intended to do. They were going to jump off the pier.

"Are we—?"

She could not finish the words. He leaped off the edge of the wharf, pulling her with him, and she barely had time to gulp in a breath of air before they struck the chill waters and plummeted into the depths. Her gown felt like an anchor pulling her down through the churning waters. She felt Collier's arm around her waist and he was swimming, pulling her after him. All was tumultuous and wet, but his grip was firm and strong as he clutched her to him and stroked toward the ship. She kicked in rhythm with him, giddy with the thrill of their escape.

A lurching feeling.

Somehow, he was clinging to a rope and the men aboard the ship were hoisting them up. His arm still pinned her safely to his chest as they were dragged free from the waters.

***

Maia huddled under a wool blanket and sipped from a mug of warm broth, her hair dripping water into her eyes. She sat on a stool in the captain's chamber, which was well furnished and tidy. A single bed was crammed against one wall, stuffed with a pallet and warm fur blankets. There was a window at the rear of the ship, but the curtains were drawn and a lantern swinging from a hook provided the only light.

Collier, who was wrapped up in a blanket himself, conversed with the captain in the open doorway.

"Are they blocking the harbor gate?" Collier asked.

"No, my lord. There is so much confusion on the wharf still. The Dochte Mandar cannot get past the crowd to warn them. My lad in the crow's nest says there are three ships in front of us, but they are not halting anyone from leaving the river."

"Excellent," Collier said with a smile. "Watch the armada when we pass it, and let me know if any ships follow us. We are bound for Naess, are we not, my lady?"

"Yes," Maia said, shivering.

"Well done, Stavanger. See my treasurer when we are done. A thousand marks, as I promised you."

"You are quite welcome, my lord," the captain said with a grin. His weathered face was covered in splits and crags and his head was topped with a thick ruff of graying hair. "I am quite comfortable in my second's quarters. These are yours as long as you need them. Welcome aboard the *Argiver*, my lady. My queen. My apologies for the rough conditions, but this is a trading ship." He smiled at her and ducked out of the room.

The boat swayed as it picked up speed. The current of the river sent it toward the sea, but first they would need to get past the harbor gate and its massive towers.

Collier shut the door and bolted it. He turned and gave her an enigmatic look. She saw the angry welt on his chest, still bleeding.

"You are hurt," she said, rising from the bed. "Let me help you."

"I have a healer on board," he said. "But if you insist."

"Sit down," she said, motioning to the bed, and then rummaging through the captain's things until she found some linen napkins. She fetched some woad from her pack and quickly made some paste from it. Collier lay down on the bed, one arm behind his head, and gazed at her curiously. He looked very comfortable and self-confident. She found her fingers trembling.

"Let me see it," she said, scooting the stool over to the bedside. He undid the lacing of his vest and then opened the buttons of his ruined shirt. The new slash would leave a scar to join the others on his skin from dozens of little nicks and cuts. She had the sudden desire to ask how he had come by them, but the kystrel gleamed in the lantern light and caught her eye. She felt it draw at her mind—the force of it making her dizzy.

"Are you all right?" he asked her.

"Yes, quite well," she replied, struggling to control her thoughts. "You looked at the medallion and swooned."

"I am a little dizzy, that is all." She blinked quickly. There was a shadowstain on his chest—just a small one, with the familiar whorl pattern. "You used the kystrel during the fight."

"Of course I did," he said. "The odds were uneven enough. But the man at the end—the Paeizian—he had one as well. He tried to shove his way into my thoughts and fill me with fear. I was not about to let him win, particularly not that way."

Maia dabbed some of the woad against the wound. He winced, but did not flinch.

"That was brave of you," she said softly. "Facing so many."

A smirk twisted his mouth. "You could have scattered them easily enough yourself. Though not with a blade."

She paused, looking down at him. Was he serving her or the Myriad One inside her? Where was his allegiance? She believed, deep down, that his understanding of her was flawed. If he believed she was a hetaera deliberately, and it was part of the reason he wanted her as a partner, what would he think when he learned that she wanted more than anything to be rid of the creature haunting her? Would he cast her aside? Did she want him to?

"What a grave expression," he said shrewdly.

"I suppose it is," she replied. "I was not expecting to see you in Rostick."

"Are you *grieved* to see me in Rostick?" he asked teasingly.

Rather than answer the question, she said, "You took a great risk coming here. If the Hautlanders knew . . ."

He nodded. "Exactly. If they knew who either of us were. Hmmm. The ransom they would charge would cripple my kingdom. And I think even your father would ransom you." He reached up and rubbed her chin with his thumb. "But if he did not, I would."

"You enjoy taking such risks," she said. "I should think you would be more cautious."

"Life is risk," he answered. "I thrill at the opportunity. Yes, that fencing master could have killed me. He took the same risk as I did, and he lost the use of his sword arm. Maybe permanently."

"Why did you not spare him the wound?" Maia asked, smoothing ripples in the salve she had applied to the scar.

"You *never* spare a Paeizian the honor of sporting a vicious wound!" he said with a bark of laughter. "First of all, I was held hostage in Paeiz, so I have some natural resentment. But fencing masters are also arrogant and proud. If you best one, they will come at you again and again, trying to win back their lost honor. Give one a decent scar, and it becomes a badge of honor. Truly, it is maddening business, their sense of revenge. I have always been very capable with a sword. It comes naturally to me. When I was twelve, I defeated my first master. I was considered too young to be a target for a blood feud, but that changed when I was fourteen. They consider you man enough to die at that age."

She looked down at her handiwork and then wiped her blue fingers off on a rag. "Let me bind this." She fetched a linen wrap and he sat up and shrugged off the rest of the shirt. She tried not to look at him, for each time she saw the kystrel, it made her stomach wrench and her mind darken. She wound the wrap around his chest and tied it off with small knots.

"Thank you," he said as he lifted himself off the bed and walked over to a chest in the far corner, hidebound and tacked. He withdrew a small key from his pants pocket and fit it into the lock.

"You locked your chest?" she asked curiously.

"For good reason. I do not want anyone stealing my clothes," he said, opening the chest and rummaging until he found a padded shirt and a fine embroidered doublet. "Or yours." He pulled on the padded shirt and fastened the doublet over it, then tossed the ruined shirt in the corner and swept back his dark hair, shaking loose some water droplets. Once he was dressed, he reached into the chest and withdrew a deep voluminous gown made of cloth of gold. The fabric almost glowed in his hands.

"I see by your eyes that you like it," he said slyly. He unfolded the gown and let it drape out so she could appreciate the full effect. There was a subtle pattern of lilies, the Dahomeyjan royal flower, in the design. The fabric was immensely expensive and luxurious and Maia's heart hungered for it. She had worn gowns like that once, but not in many years. The sleeves, which were pinned to the upper arm, were long and full and trimmed with a wine-colored fabric and inset with pearls.

"Beautiful," Maia said, blinking. "It is not really suitable for traveling."

"Of course not," he said. "But I would like to see you wear it for the voyage at least. It is the gown of a queen."

She bit her lip. "I . . . while I appreciate the gesture—"

"You cannot refuse me, Maia. Your gown is soaked! You need something to wear while it dries. You must wear this. You are my queen." His voice fell to a whisper, almost haunted. "You are a great *queen*."

Maia stared down at the fabric, her cheeks growing hot. She wanted to wear it. She wanted to feel it against her skin. She sighed. "Will you give me some privacy to change?"

He looked a little disappointed. "If you prefer it that way. Let me check with the captain. I will not be gone long."

He held out the gown and she accepted it, then watched as he unlatched the door and slipped away. Maia stared down at the soft folds of fabric. A gown like this must have cost at least several thousand marks. It truly was a gown fit for a queen. Her stomach churned with conflicting emotions. There was a deep ache inside of her that she did not fully understand. In her own country, she was considered a bastard, even though her parents had been married in an abbey by irrevocare sigil.

But Collier knew who she was, and he treated her as befit her status. They had been plight trothed together when they were children. And she had agreed, albeit unwillingly, to marry him. In the eyes of the world, they were husband and wife. But in Maia's eyes, and in her heart, they were not.

As a girl, she had always dreamed of marrying a maston. She knew it was her duty to prolong the chain of mastons that had existed for centuries. Collier was charming. He was undeniably handsome. She liked being in his presence, and he had come to her rescue more than once. He treated her like an equal in station. Yet he did not share her beliefs. He considered her a pawn in his game to become the emperor of all the kingdoms. She set the beautiful dress down on the bed and covered her mouth, struggling with herself.

She needed to tell Collier the full truth.

A shiver of despair and fear pulsed through her. How long had she been away from her mind the last time the Myriad One took over? She had no idea. Had it been days? Even longer? No matter what it took, she needed to root out the evil being inside her and banish it forever. She had to reclaim her tainted mind.

Maia took a deep breath. She would tell him. She would confess her secret. Maybe he would reject her and refuse to offer his continued help. She had to accept that possibility. Her heart burned with fear and worry.

Fighting the feelings, she reached back and began unfastening the buttons of her sodden bodice.

CHAPTER THIRTY-ONE

Betrayal

The door hinges squeaked and a rush of salty air entered the captain's quarters. The boat swayed as it glided along the water. Maia was perched on the small stool by the captain's desk, fidgeting with one of the cuffs of the gown, wishing she had a mirror to examine herself. She turned her head and saw Collier securing the door behind him. Her stomach twisted cruelly. She was so nervous, her hands trembled.

"We passed the gatehouse without . . . problem," he announced and then stumbled a bit. He stared at her. "The gown . . . it enhances your beauty. I clearly have good taste." He smiled at her and approached. "We will feel the boat jostle when we reach the sea, but it should not be enough to alarm you."

"I thought they might try to stop us," Maia said, only partially relieved.

"The armada is positioned to prevent attack on Rostick, not to block ships from leaving. In situations like this, it has been my experience that word travels slowly and messages can be confused. Blocking a major seaport like this would be difficult. With all the ships bringing cargo, it is a bit of a jumble."

Maia nodded and turned the stool to face him, resting her jittery hands in her lap. "We need to talk, Collier."

"Such a grave look," he said, a smile quirking his mouth. "On such a pretty face. I like how the gold contrasts with your hair." He gestured toward her, but then folded his arms and shook his head, a thoughtful expression on his face. "But it does not match your eyes. I have something that might."

Looking eager, he stooped over the chest again and rummaged through the contents. She waited patiently, squirming inside.

"Ah, here we are," he said, fishing out a leather-bound box with gold fasteners. He brought the box to the table and set it beside her. Flipping open the little hasps, he opened it. On a bed of black velvet lay an array of butter-gold jewelry embedded with clear turquoise gemstones. The workmanship of each piece was exquisite, with delicate weavings of metal and stone. There were two necklaces, several sets of earrings, as well as bracelets, rings, and even filigreed hairpins bedecked with dazzling gems. She stared at the treasures, understanding how much they must have cost.

"When did you purchase these?" she asked, dazed.

"They were commissioned as wedding presents," he said. "I had heard your eyes were a mixture of blue and green. The stones don't do them justice, but they were chosen for their unique color. I think they came from Avinion. Quite expensive, but a queen must have her jewels."

Maia stared down at her hands, feeling guilty. This was evidence that his interest in her was premeditated and not limited to his suspicion that she was a hetaera. "Collier—"

"No, not yet. Let me see them on you first. I would have had a bath drawn for you, considering we just plunged into a murky river, but we cannot have such luxuries aboard. Your hair is still damp. Let me comb it for you."

"I can manage that," Maia said, flushing. "I saw a comb on the table . . ."

"It is right there. Here, allow me." He raced her to it and snatched it from the table. The comb had a decorative carving along the spine. There were wider bristles on one side and narrower ones on the other.

"I can do that myself, if you give me a moment."

"But how many moments have already been stolen from us?" he asked in a conspiring voice, putting his hand on her shoulder and nudging her to turn back toward the table. "I have often thought on that, Maia. Imagine if your father had not broken off our plight troth." The teeth of the comb slid into her dark hair. He started low, at the tips, and gently began teasing the comb through some of the knots. He was very gentle and, she discovered, quite confident. She could tell he knew what he was doing as his fingers began separating and smoothing locks of hair. "We may have been wed two or three years ago. Formally, that is. When I consider those stolen years we might have known each other, I begrudge your father for stealing them from me."

There was a little tug at her scalp when the comb encountered a thicker tangle, and he muttered an apology and worked it loose. Slowly, he began to move higher up her hair. Her cheeks were warm and she was grateful he was behind her and could not see her blush.

She said, "I believe your father promised you to someone else as well. We were quite young when the deal was abandoned . . . I was seven . . . eight years old? You were younger. And you are quite skilled with a comb. How is that?"

"I have older sisters, of course," he said, and she could hear the smile in his voice. "Older sisters teach you many important lessons about dealing with other women. I could tell you stories about them. However, you distract me from my confessions. My sisters both married well. As Family, we are all pawns in a game of power. What if the Dochte Mandar are the true religion after all, Maia?" He combed more vigorously now that the majority of tangles were gone. He smoothed his hand over her scalp and she felt tingles of heat in her stomach and the threat of a shiver. She tried to focus on his words and not his touch. "How familiar are you with the teachings? You were a favorite of one of them, if I recall. A chancellor?"

"Chancellor Walraven," Maia answered. "But he never tried to persuade me of their teachings."

"No, they tend not to be preachy. Unlike *mastons*," he added with a barb in his voice. "The Dochte Mandar believe that souls are born and then reborn. Sometimes they point to the mastons' words about this *second* life as an example of their philosophy. That one can die, depart, and then come back again in another life, hundreds of years later."

"Yes, I have heard of that," Maia said. "But it is not true."

"How are we to know what is true and what not?" he said dismissively. "Have you not sometimes felt that you have been somewhere before? When I came to Rostick, it seemed . . . familiar to me. And sometimes when I travel to foreign lands and come upon an ancient Leering, it feels as if I should know it. Does that ever happen to you?"

Maia thought about it and said, "Yes, but I always supposed it to be the Medium. I have often . . . heard little whispers in my mind. Guiding me."

"Hmmm," he said, smoothing her hair with his hand. He seemed to be enjoying himself. "It may well be. As I told you before,

335

I took the maston test, but I never took the oaths. I learned some of the teachings that are not shared outside the abbeys. It is all rather confusing. I tend to go with my heart and follow where it leads me."

Maia looked over her shoulder at him. "Our hearts can be deceived, though. We should not make decisions solely based on feelings."

"Of course not!" he agreed. "But feelings are a delicious spice. I am enjoying mine very much at the moment. There is a lot of pleasure to be had in looking at a beautiful woman. Maia, you *are* beautiful. Yet timid too . . . almost as if you are not aware of it or you pretend not to be. Modesty *personified*," he said it playfully as he set the comb down on the table and placed his hands on her shoulders. "We cannot trust our feelings always, can we? I am more than half tempted to kiss you, which would be utterly foolish. While I may not believe in all the sorcerous ways of the Medium, my head does warn me that kissing you would be very dangerous. I am not sure it would kill me with some horrid disease. But you just might destroy my heart."

He let go of her shoulders and his tone became more brisk. "Now for the jewels. Lift up your hair."

Maia bit her lip, trying to understand the seasick feeling rising inside her. The boat was starting to rock a bit more. But any queasiness caused by that was eclipsed by the burning in her heart and the twisting of her stomach. Why was her mouth so dry?

With gentle hands, he lifted the jeweled necklace and draped it around her neck. "The clasps are so tiny," he said with a wince. "I think they were meant for smaller fingers, but I will do my best." His fingers grazed the skin of her neck and she felt gooseflesh tingle across her back. It was a sweet agony. "There we are. It was difficult, but I rose to the challenge. The earrings next. Which do you prefer from the set?"

"Those," Maia whispered hoarsely, pointing with a trembling hand.

"I like them as well," he said, reaching for the dangling ones. "If I kneel, it will help me see better. It is rather dark in here." She could feel his breath brush against her cheek as he knelt next to her. She prepared herself for his touch again and tried not to flinch when his finger traced the shape of her earlobe. "I think they go like so," he said carefully, but she could see him now, could see the earnestness in his face. His hands were trembling too. His voice was confident and proud, but she could see an unsettled look in his eyes—almost worry.

The pin of the earring poked her and she flinched.

"Forgive me," he muttered darkly, trying again. "I see the scar, but it is closed."

Maia nodded. "Let me." She took the earring from him and quickly brought it to the right spot. It took a little force to push the pin through. Since her father had reclaimed all of her jewels, she had not worn earrings in a long while. There was a pinch of pain as she fastened it shut. Then she quickly did the other one, gritting her teeth against the prick, and they were done.

His face was still level with hers. He was such a handsome man, his hair even darker than hers, his shoulders full and strong. She remembered how ruthlessly and bravely he had faced off against the men who had accosted her on the docks. He had stood up to Corriveaux for her. He wanted to dethrone her father because of her. So different from her father, who betrayed her at every turn.

"I *could* almost kiss you," he whispered. "Why am I so tempted?" He chuckled to himself and stood, shaking his head as if to clear it.

She had seen the look in his eyes—the struggle. As she swallowed, she realized that she had been tempted as well. There was something very powerful in a kiss, she realized. It was a mark of intimacy. It was a claiming and a surrendering. And she realized darkly that with the brand on her shoulder, it was a boon she could never give. To anyone. Not even her own children.

"One more thing," he murmured softly. He returned again to the crate and withdrew another box made of sandalwood. It had a rich smell. It was about the size of a plate, tall enough for him to use both hands. When he opened it, her heart thrilled at the sight of the gold coronet inside. Delicately, he set down the box and settled the coronet on her head, pressing it gently until it stayed.

"Now you look like a queen."

He knelt down in front of her, as if he were a knight paying homage, and grasped her hands in his. "You wished to tell me something, Maia. But before you do, I must tell you something first."

Her heart hammered violently in her chest. "What is it?" Her throat was so tight it hurt.

"I must confess something. You are not at all as I imagined you would be. I have . . . how can I say this without it sounding strange? You have probably realized this by now, but I have thought of you for many years. We were destined to be together, you and I." He swallowed. "First, we were trothed as infants to bring unity to our two kingdoms—Comoros and Dahomey. My real name, as you know, is Gideon, which I abhor and always have. Who wishes to be named after an ancient Aldermaston? You *must* call me Collier. Always. Promise me."

"I will," Maia said, smiling shyly.

"Thank you. Not in front of the nobles of the court, of course. You can address me with any endearment that suits you in that case. Second, when I was hostage to the Paeizians, I had a lot of time to think. Often I thought of you. I secretly hoped that your father would . . . well, that he would intervene. That he would help pay the ransom for me. It was a foolish hope, I know. I am ashamed to admit it. I *hoped* you would rescue me." His mouth contorted into a sad smile. "I was disappointed. Heartbroken, actually. But my father finally paid the ransom and my brother and I were freed. Maia, there is nothing more important to me. My new name, Feint Collier, means freedom to me. Please keep the secret."

Maia reached out and touched his shoulder. "I will."

"That said, I must have freedom to ride, to explore, to wander off. I give you that same freedom. I will not control you. Not that I could! All I ask is that you offer me the same troth and do not bind me to pastures or plows or pillows. I must be free."

Maia put her hands in her lap. "I do not have any problem with that. Though I do like to ride as well. I also like to hawk and hunt and practice archery."

"And wander across deadly mountains," he said, smiling wryly. "I envy your adventures. I would welcome your companionship. We are bound together in so many ways, Maia. Your name. My blood."

"What do you mean?"

"I told you that I read the tome of the Earl of Dieyre. He was a powerful man and a great soldier and swordsman. I have a Gift for making war, I think. My mind is always devising new tactics and stratagems. The one thing he failed to achieve in his life was winning the hand of his true love. Marciana was your namesake. Do you not feel that some . . . tug of destiny has drawn us both together? I am the descendent of the Earl of Dieyre. You are a descendent, albeit in a bit of a twisted fashion, of Marciana Price." He looked at her earnestly. "Now I must ask you one more favor."

Maia was not sure what to say. "What is it?"

He looked down at the floor. The vessel was rocking more violently now. There was a sudden dip and Maia felt herself flung out of the chair. They collided together, which startled them both, and Maia flushed with embarrassment. Once the initial surprise had passed, she started laughing, and he joined her.

"The sea is powerful," Collier said, touching her waist to help her sit.

Maia found her seat again, still laughing at their forced embrace. She put a hand over her heart, feeling dizzy.

"I am almost afraid to tell you now," Collier said, smiling. He reached out and took her shoulder, putting his hand on the brand. His touch sent feelings of blackness shooting through her heart. Her mind began to fog. Dizziness. Disorientation. Her heart sank and internally she screamed, *No, not now! Not now!*

"Collier," she whispered, panting and trying to shrug his hand away, but he would not release her. His grip was firm, and she felt his touch draw out the creature inside her.

"Just one more thing, please. I must tell you. Maia, in all the tomes I have read about the Myriad Ones and the Dochte Mandar and the hetaera, even my ancestor's tome, there is one thing they all agree on. One trait." His grip on her shoulder tightened and she felt the mark burning, as if it had been set on fire. Fear and sickness battled in her stomach. She saw the edges of her vision begin to close, as if she were sinking into a dark hole. She clung on to the precipice of blackness.

No! No! Maia shrieked inside her mind. *You cannot hurt him! You cannot have him! He is mine! He is* my *husband!*

"What is it?" Collier asked. "You grow pale. Are you sick?"

Please no! Please not now! No!

She felt the power roil through her.

"Maia, do not betray me. Forget my other promises. I should have asked for this one first, but I was too afraid. The hetaera *always* betray those they love. Do not love me then. I could not bear it if you betrayed me . . ."

Maia heard his words in a garbled slur. Finally she managed to fling his hand off her burning shoulder, but it was too late. She was losing herself, slipping away bit by bit. Her mind was tumbling, like a cask falling down a hill after being jostled loose from a wagon. She could feel a sense of glee in her heart, a savage delight in seeing Collier so vulnerable.

With a last burst of energy, she clutched the front of his tunic, seized him violently, and pulled him close. His eyes were wide with frenzied fear.

"You must hit me. Now! Strike me hard, knock me unconscious. Bind and gag me. Please, Collier! I cannot hold her off. I beg you!"

"Her?" he whispered, trying to pull away from her. "Why would I—?"

"Please!" she said desperately. A powerful hand gripped her awareness and pried her mind loose from her body.

He is mine. The voice in her mind was exultant.

No! I banish you! You cannot have him!

You cannot banish me. You are my daughter. Be still, little mouse. My will must be fulfilled.

"Please," Maia groaned, her face twisting with anguish.

Blackness filled her.

Cruix Abbey has fallen. The Naestors have assembled a fleet of ships, an armada in one of the ports of Hautland, a city that will be built in the image of what Dochte Abbey was in my day, a city on an island. What you must understand, great-granddaughter, is that the fleet has not been assembled to wage war on the kingdoms. The Naestors have learned about the land the Cruciger orb led us to—the land of Assinica. They have been spying on it and preparing to invade and destroy the mastons who were left behind. You see, not all the mastons returned to the seven kingdoms. A host remained behind to perpetuate the abbeys and sire the new kingdom we built to create a land of refuge, peace, and safety. By the time you read this in my tome, the mastons of Assinica will have forgotten the ways of war. They are peaceful and harmless and they will be enslaved and butchered by the Naestors if they are given their way. Ereshkigal will have her revenge. When your fore-fathers returned to Pry-Ree, Comoros, and Dahomey, they were to rebuild the abbeys and fulfill the Covenant of Muirwood. In order to fulfill it, the rites of the Apse Veil must be restored in Muirwood, and from there, to all the other abbeys. Because there have been no fully functioning abbeys in your realm for several generations, none of my progeny are strong enough in the Medium to cross the Apse Veil. Your generation will not have the ability. But look to your granddaughter. Look to save her when she comes to kill you.

—Lia Demont, Aldermaston of Muirwood Abbey

CHAPTER THIRTY-TWO

Kishion

The bed was soft, the brazier shimmered with heat, and Maia felt strong enough to sit. The shift beneath the servant's gown was soaked with sweat and her hair felt sticky against her scalp. She looked down at the gray-green sleeve and examined the fabric of the cuff, her eyes coming in and out of focus. Her memories were jumbled. It felt like a dream. Was it one?

It was the noise of boot steps marching up the stairs to the attic that had started the dream. *This is a memory. This is not real.* Maia felt foggy, disoriented. She moved off the bed and went to the door, listening. It sounded like multiple men were approaching and their heavy footfalls shook the walls. Fear twisted in her stomach and she wrung her hands as she watched the door. There was a firm rap and then it opened. She wanted to wake up. She had to wake up. Something was happening. Something she could not control. She felt like a withered leaf blown into a stream, carried along by the current.

A grizzled soldier wearing the tunic of the king's guard stood in the doorway, his jaw lined with a salty beard. "Beg your pardon, my lady. I am Rawlt. I was sent this morn by river from the palace with orders to escort you there."

Maia blinked at him, aware of how disheveled she looked. "I do not recognize you," she said warily. *Wake up!*

Rawlt shrugged. "I showed Lady Shilton the orders bearing the king's seal. Come with me."

She rubbed her arm. "What should I bring with me?" She heard her voice repeating the words she had said long ago. This was like being stuck in a play, on a stage full of actors.

"Just your person, my lady. I have a boat ready for us. Come along."

"Can I brush my hair, at least? It is early."

He frowned at her, but she ignored him and hurried to comb the tangles out of her hair. The motion brought sparks of another memory. A young man, combing her hair with such gentleness. She felt his hands smoothing through her tresses. Who was he? She did not know, but she felt an urgent need to protect him. The dread and worry that seeped around the edges of her consciousness like sticky honey was baffling. Why did she have a memory of a man touching her hair, anyway? It was her ladies-in-waiting who combed her hair. No, she had no ladies-in-waiting anymore. She was a bastard. She was banished from court.

"Are you done?" Rawlt said impatiently, then coughed into his hand.

Maia realized she had frozen. Was that part of her memory? What was real and what not? She began combing through her hair again, trying to tease out the tangles. The sky was still black outside. It was very early.

The dream carried her along, though she never lost the awareness that it *was* a dream. In the past, the dreams had subsumed her completely, but now part of her knew something was amiss. A nagging feeling told her she was in danger in the waking world, that someone she cared about would be hurt if she did not awaken, yet she could not shake herself from the fog.

She finished combing through her hair and then followed the soldier and his retinue down the steps. At the bottom, Lady Shilton stood waiting, wearing a nightrobe and holding a candelabra. There was a gaunt, worried look on her face. As Maia entered the hall, Lady Shilton nodded to the soldier.

"Lady Shilton?" Maia asked worriedly, hoping for more of an explanation.

"Your father summoned you in the middle of the night," Lady Shilton said. "He has ordered for me to pretend you are still here, but . . . I think you are leaving us."

Maia just looked at her, too surprised to say anything.

Lady Shilton bit her bottom lip. "I hope, Lady Maia, that you have enjoyed the privileges of late. The archery. The boat rides." She swallowed, her expression very sallow and nervous. She was almost cowering. "I . . . hope you . . ." She stopped, unable to speak.

"What is it?" Maia pressed in concern. "Am I to be sent to Pent Tower?" She had an ugly vision of a headsman's axe and felt as if a shadow had fallen over her shoulders.

"No!" Lady Shilton said soothingly. "I think . . . well, your father will want to tell you himself. Go, child. Go at once. Remember me . . . with mercy." She shuddered and motioned for Rawlt to follow her. The three of them walked to the rear of the house, the wet grass soaking Maia's slippers. The anxiety in her stomach was almost unbearable.

Moored alongside the river was a small skiff that could have belonged to any local fisherman. Seven soldiers had joined her and Rawlt and a ninth man was waiting at the skiff. As they approached by moonlight, she saw that there were no torches.

"Good-bye, Lady Maia," Lady Shilton said ominously. She headed back to the manor house without a backward look and Maia followed the escort to the ship.

The man at the tiller was standing, a sturdy-looking fellow wearing dark, rugged clothing. His hands were clenched around a long mooring pole and he was leaning forward to watch them approach. When she was close enough for the moonlight to reveal his face, she saw a bluff chin, chiseled features, and a countenance etched with nicks and scars. Part of one ear was missing beneath the thatch of dark unruly hair. His eyes were light, piercing in intensity, and they were regarding her with a knowing look. Part of his mouth quirked, as if he were chuckling to himself about something.

It was the kishion.

She recognized him instantly and her heart lurched with memories. They were like cobwebs spun around one another in her mind. In the tangled skein, it was almost impossible to discern where one started and another ended. He was her protector. He would escort her to the cursed shores of Dahomey.

This has already happened! Maia wanted to shriek out loud, but her tongue was swollen and she was helpless against the tide of time that drew her ever onward. Someone she cared for was in danger. She fought against the current that continued to move her through the memory, but was helpless to stop it. She sat down on the low wooden bench and the soldiers filled in around her, protecting her on each side and in front and behind.

"Shove off," Rawlt said.

The kishion obeyed, using the pole to push away from the pier. Oars were slid into place quickly and the men began to row. With so many men on board, the vessel rode very low in the river, and water slopped against the side of the hull.

Maia glanced over her shoulder, looking at the kishion in the back of the skiff. She was afraid of him. She remembered that fear, but it was different now . . . her feelings were allayed by all the experiences they had shared. He gazed at her, his expression a subtle blend of defiance and cruelty. Memories of all that had happened since that long-ago boat ride wove in and out, meshing with the sounds of slapping water, the dip and churn of the oarsmen.

Stars glittered in the dark sky above her.

Her senses blurred and she felt a queasy sort of feeling. Then she blinked and found herself on a different skiff. Looking down at her lap, she saw cloth of gold that shimmered like honey. She had rings on her fingers. She lifted her hand and felt the jeweled necklace around her neck, where the kystrel used to lie. Turning her head, she discovered that the soldiers had been replaced with men in black cassocks with silver eyes and gaunt determined faces. When she peered over her shoulder, she saw Corriveaux at the tiller, not the kishion. He was staring at her, his expression haughty with triumph, his eyes burned with lust and silver fire.

Maia felt something jolt and jostle her seat. The skiff had struck a dock post. The memories were merged somehow—she felt trapped between both worlds simultaneously.

"Up with you, lass," Rawlt growled, seizing her arm with a strong hand. The boat swayed as she was led toward the pier, where two soldiers wearing her father's livery stood waiting. The soldiers hoisted her up from the boat and onto the pier. Looking up, she saw Pent Tower rising above her. Torches hung from some of the walls, painting the stones with orange shadows. The smell of burning pitch stung her nose.

She stared up at the castle. It had been years since she had been there. Years since she had seen her father. He had summoned her in the middle of the night to send her to find the lost abbey in Dahomey. She had already lived this! She was prey to some vicious spider who could spin out her memories and tangle her in them.

Yes, this was a memory, she reminded herself. When she was asleep, when the Myriad One took over, she dreamed of the past. This moment was not that far in the past however. Not long after, she had boarded a ship with Captain Rawlt and the kishion—the *Blessing of Burntisland*. She could remember the look of the ship. It had sailed that very morning as soon as the tide came in.

They started walking down the pier toward the castle.

Again, Maia's vision blurred. Now, she saw that she was on a different dock. It appeared to be morning, yet there was no sun. The sky was a pall of shadows and low-hanging clouds. The city that lay before her was small and squat, a fishing village. The dwellings were all made of timber, not stone. But what caught her gaze was the monolithic mountain that rose like a king behind the city, with cliffs so high that the clouds scudded against them. Only a small flat reef and a few rolling hills were lower down—the cliffs were massive and jagged and they reminded her of a giant, forbidding Leering. A Leering bigger than a city.

She was under the sway of the Myriad One and only barely conscious of her reality, but she knew this was Naess, where the Dochte Mandar ruled omnipotently. She knew it deep down, beneath the webs that confounded and confused her. The craggy mountain loomed over the city, a bier stone. It made her cower with fear to see how tiny the homes and fortresses were beneath it.

Then she noticed the light. She wondered how she could see the city so well with the sun hidden away. As the Dochte Mandar escorted her off the boat and led her down the pier, she noticed that the streets were full of cracked Leerings, giving off the colors of dawn. It was only the light from the Leerings that made it seem like daytime. The differences of this place fascinated her, even through the thrall of the Myriad One. The air was cool and frosty and the people were bundled up for it in fur-lined vests and fur caps. The men wore boots with pointed toes that curled up. The women's hair was braided on each side, and they were only seen accompanied by men. There were carts and stands, trading and selling. The Dochte Mandar guided her past it all.

Maia blinked and found herself in the dream again. A soldier led her through the postern door of Pent Tower. The halls were illuminated with torches, and rushes crackled under her feet as she trod on them. The memory was sticky and clinging, and it masked the sights and sounds of Naess. She struggled to free herself. *Wake up! Wake up!* The current bubbled and crested, carrying her along effortlessly. She struggled to swim against the current of memory, to break loose of the clinging webs.

I am myself! I am me! Let me go!

Part of her vision wavered, and she could feel a sense of annoyance. But she was not strong enough to burst the bonds that entrapped her mind. They were walking toward the solar, her father's favorite chamber. For her, it had become a room of painful memories. She squeezed her hands into fists and glanced back. The kishion was shadowing the soldiers who escorted her, and his icy-cold gray-blue eyes gazed at her with ruthless intensity.

"Here we are," Rawlt said, stopping in front of the solar door. He bowed to her. "Your father waits for you within."

She did not want to see her father. He had caused so much suffering in her life, so much anguish. Yet her heart still hoped that he would soften toward her.

She remembered what happened next all too well, but she watched it unfold in the queer way of dreams. He was pacing in the solar when she arrived, agitated.

"Maia," he breathed with true warmth, and opened his arms to her. She ran to him, overjoyed by his embrace, by the still-familiar smell of him. She had been unprepared for the damage the years of absence had done to him. He was thicker around the middle, his hair more silver, his gaze more careworn and concerned. His left eye twitched uncontrollably. He kissed her head and squeezed her hard, crushing her ribs. "Look at you. Look at you!" He held her apart, holding her by the shoulders.

Her left shoulder.

The mark was not there yet.

She felt a burning sensation on her skin. *This is not real!* She had to wake herself before it was too late. She heard a muffled voice in her ears, but the speaker was not her father. Her hazy senses recognized Corriveaux.

". . . arrangements are nearly finished, my lady. There will be a feast on the morrow, after the coronation. Then a celebration. A celebration unlike any before. You are most welcome here. You are to be the first Empress of Naess since the days of our ancestors. The people are superstitious by nature. They will worship you truly . . ."

Though she heard Corriveaux's voice, Maia still saw her father's face, sensed his deep worry and concern. His hand gripped her shoulder. "You would not believe what has happened since the Dochte Mandar were expelled. The people are murdering each other, Maia! Every day there are new reports of some atrocity. The Dochte Mandar unleashed something in this kingdom before they left. Walraven did, I know it! We never found his kystrel after he died. I think he gave it to someone. Maia, did he . . . give it to *you*?"

Maia's throat was dry. She stared at her father. He knew. Somehow he knew. Yet he was not angry. He was . . . hopeful. His eyes were bright with intensity.

"You have it," he whispered hoarsely, his eyes blinding with joy. "The chain you wear around your neck, I can see it. The chain. You wear it?"

Maia nodded, terrified. Her emotions wavered between exaltation and sorrow and terror. She had never told anyone her secret. Now her father knew. He could execute her. He could destroy her without trial or witnesses . . . the shadowstain on her chest was all the proof he would need.

He gripped her shoulders, his voice low and cautious. "I will not tell anyone, Maia. No one need know. In Walraven's tome, there is mention of an abbey. A lost abbey. It was in Dahomey. Not Dochte . . . not the one the Blight destroyed. There was another abbey. It has been lost in the cursed lands for generations, but the Dochte Mandar know where it is and how to find it. Only someone equipped with a kystrel can follow the waymarkers to it. There is knowledge there, Maia, knowledge that I seek. The Dochte Mandar say the abbey is protected by Leerings that only a woman can pass. Yet they do not allow women to study, do they? There is knowledge there that will *destroy* the Dochte Mandar. Maia, it will save our kingdom. It is the only way." His look was frantic, his voice quivering with intensity. "My spies tell me things. They whisper warnings of invasion. All the other kingdoms have fallen under the sway of the Dochte Mandar and cannot be trusted. The Dochte Mandar are a cult, Maia, with ways of divining the future. When they left, our kingdom began to suffer gross tortures, and they will not relent until we are all under their thrall. You must go to Dahomey. You speak their language fluently, and can speak many more tongues besides. I know Walraven trained you to write as well. I permitted it, Maia. I knew that someday I would need you for an errand like this one. I will send protectors with you. Trusted men who will guard you and protect you at the cost of their own lives. Will you do this for me, Maia? Will you leave aboard a ship and sail to the cursed shores? Will you do it? Will you obey your king? Will you honor your father's wishes?"

Maia stared into his pleading eyes. He was desperate to save his kingdom from falling into the hands of the Dochte Mandar. If she accepted this quest, would she gain the advantage she sought? Would she finally be allowed to study at an abbey and face the maston test?

"When I return," Maia had said forcefully. "Father, when I return, will you allow me to study at an abbey? Will you please allow it?"

His look hardened, but he did not release her shoulders. His mouth twisted into a sneer. "You seek to be a maston?" He coughed a chuckle. She could see the look in his eyes, the disdain of a man who had broken every vow.

Maia knew what would happen next. She knew what she was going to say. There was one abbey she longed to visit, the abbey where her mother was banished. Muirwood Abbey.

A dream, it is a dream! This was a trick, a deceit. She clenched her teeth together. A force bubbled up inside her and a spike of anger and rage seared her mind. She had to save Collier. She had to wake up.

Say it! Say it!

"No!" Maia shouted.

CHAPTER
THIRTY-THREE

Assinica

I t was like cracking a mirror.

The shattered slivers slid away from Maia's mind and she could finally see again, breathe again, feel again. She was awake, fully alert, and herself, and she discovered that she was walking down a corridor on a velvet rug with golden tassels on the fringe, surrounded by Dochte Mandar. The air was heavy with the scent of an ancient incense. Leerings lit the corridor, several different kinds, each resting on a plinth of marble. The men who surrounded her were armed with swords fixed with rubies in the pommels, but they were not guarding her. She was being escorted in a royal manner, Corriveaux at her side, her golden dress making a gentle whispering sound as it dragged along the carpet.

"Excuse me?" Corriveaux said, his eyebrows knotting in confusion. "You mean you wish to delay the coronation? It was my understanding that the titles would be vested immediately upon your arrival in Naess. Word must go out before the storms of the season begin and communication ends with the other kingdoms."

Maia had no idea what he was talking about. She had no context for his words, but she realized that the being inside of her had been fully participating in the discussion just moments before.

He put his hand on her shoulder, her left shoulder, to help brace her. As soon as his palm pressed the mark, fire seared from the brand and her mind began to blacken again.

She shook off his touch and halted, her head swimming. "I need to sit down," she said with rising panic in her voice.

"Of course," Corriveaux offered. "Your suite is this way. I had hoped for people to see you in the audience chamber. It will get tongues wagging if we delay the coronation, of course. Do you need some refreshment? I can have wine or cider brought . . . ?"

Maia shook her head forcefully. "The suite. Please." The sides of her vision were fraying, sloughing off like ashes from a smoking log. She pressed her mouth, her stomach suddenly nauseous, and followed Corriveaux as he escorted her down another branch of the hallway.

The walls were all made of dark-stained wood. The edges had been carved and polished into strange rune-like patterns that she had never seen before. The door handles were forged of polished silver, each one meticulously crafted by master metalsmiths, the edges supple and curved and designed with the symbols of serpents. They walked for a brief while longer and Maia struggled to control her thoughts, to keep her mind her own.

Leave me be! she ordered in her mind.

We are bound together, daughter. We share one flesh. I have great need of you.

"Here we are," Corriveaux said unctuously. He fit a key into the door and twisted the lock. Then he motioned for the escort to remain where they were in the hall.

She glanced at him, at his polished boots, his trim black vest with a golden collar embedded with an absolutely massive sapphire. A frilly white ruff was at his throat, and his beard had been neatly cropped and trimmed. He gestured for Maia to enter.

"After you, Empress Marciana."

She looked at him sternly, her eyes flashing, her heart pounding in her chest, and then walked into the room. What was she going to do? It felt as if she were on a runaway boat with no oars. She could only clutch the edges and endure the ride through the rapids.

The room was easily twice her height and there was a magnificent dome in the center, supported by enormous wooden stays. There were three hearths, and Corriveaux used his kystrel to light the Leerings inside each of them. The elegant polished table in the center of the room had huge squat legs carved like pillars. It could easily seat sixteen, and was surrounded by gilded chairs. Near the windows was a huge canopied bed—monstrous in size, and covered with heavy veils and trappings—as well as chests, pedestals topped with fruit and flowers, hooks and pegs, and enormous rugs and blankets.

The sky was dark outside the windows, the black ebony of night. This was when the powers of her inner demon were the strongest. She remembered in despair that the kingdom of Naess was known for its few sunrises and shortened days. It was so far north, the sun seemed to hide most of the year. Winters were cold and frostbitten, the moon and stars the only light.

This was a perfect land for the Myriad Ones. She felt them all around her, their panting, their nuzzling, their obedience to her as their mistress and ruler. Her heart shuddered at the feelings that began flooding through her. Retribution. Revenge. Murder. The sensations were so powerful, she felt as if there were nothing left of her but a gentle spark—a spark that could be snuffed out in an instant.

"Your look has . . . altered," Corriveaux said, tapping his lip.

He gestured to a large stuffed chair, but Maia knew that if she sat down, lay down, or even stopped moving, she would lose her mind again. There were icy waters beneath her and she was moving on fragile ice.

She did not know how long she would be able to keep her mind, so she had to move quickly. "Where is the High Seer?" Maia asked, trying to summon an imperious tone.

Corriveaux's mouth twitched. "You wish to kill her already? I am not surprised. It will cause a backlash from the mastons, of course. But I know we can keep it quiet for the entire winter at least. You wish her brought . . . here? I thought you may perhaps wish to use the dungeon."

"Bring her to me," Maia said, trying to breathe.

"Very well," Corriveaux said. He walked to the door, opened it, and gave the order.

Maia could feel a thrill of victory churning in her chest. She squeezed her hands, trying to tame her feelings.

"Are you quite yourself, Your Majesty?" Corriveaux asked. "Your expression is troubled. Your hands are nervous. Pardon my noticing such things, but that is what I do. Is she still . . . *struggling*?"

Maia rubbed her hands together, pacing through the room, looking at every detail to distract her mind. The luxuriousness of this chamber was beyond Maia's experience, even within her father's court in Comoros. Every dish and spoon, every cut of cloth was exceptional and costly. The room was immaculately clean. The wealth of the Dochte Mandar was both gaudy and proud. A door led to a veranda outside. She walked over to the glass of the inset window and stared outside, seeing stone sculptures in the gardens beyond and rugged shrubs that could somehow endure bitter cold.

"Do you wish to see it?" Corriveaux said at her ear. She felt the pulse of the Medium again, and the Leerings throughout the garden suddenly exploded with light. Maia needed to shield her eyes against the glare. The blackness of the night had been completely driven away. It could have been a spring morning, just before dawn. The gardens were beautifully and intricately designed, one area leading to the next with steps and rotundas and benches and statuary that was mismatched yet fashionable.

"The Victus have spent years assembling these pieces," Corriveaux said. "Gathered from fallen abbeys throughout all the seven kingdoms. While we lack the artisans to fashion our own, I think the effect is sufficiently grand. We are your humble servants, Empress." He smiled at her—like a wolf. "I cannot tell you how long we have searched for a woman sufficiently strong and young to house your ancient spirit. I tell you, these plans have been underway for quite some time. You chose an acceptable consort, the King of Dahomey. But I think he may be too young and impetuous. Chaining him with a kystrel was brilliant, of course, but he will soon lose his usefulness to our plans, will he not? He is pining for you in one of the guest rooms."

Maia looked at him, her heart pounding with fear and desperation, but she was relieved to know Collier had not been harmed. She had ruined Cruix Abbey through her ignorance, destroying its Aldermaston with a kiss. But the one who lived inside her had much bigger and bleaker plans for her.

His expression changed, hardening. "Ahh, you are not her," Corriveaux said with a brief chuckle. "I can see the difference plainly. Good evening, Lady Maia." He bowed at his waist. "Welcome to Naess."

"Why am I here?" she asked, trying to swallow the lump of tears in her throat.

"You are here," he said with a tinge of malice, approaching her. "But not for very long. After your coronation as ruler of the Dochtenian Empire, you will be sailing the seas once more. We found them, you see. We found the land the mastons fled to. We knew that not all of them had returned to build abbeys, but the mastons would not reveal where their ships had sailed from. It has been a most closely guarded secret. Despite our best spies and efforts, from the use of kishions to torture, we could not learn about that hidden land. Until they revealed themselves by looking for their lost *cousins*."

He sneered at the word and pinched her chin smugly. "Our way of life is well-balanced, you see. Pitting each kingdom against the other. Fomenting wars and strife, but only enough to keep the people's small minds fixed on glory and gain. You have read the tomes, Lady Maia. You know that *mastons* were the ones who caused the plague that destroyed the seven kingdoms. A single, reckless young girl, over a century ago." His face contorted with anger. "Such power cannot be trusted to mortals. No one should be allowed to choose the fate of an entire generation."

Corriveaux wandered to a nearby table and traced his finger on the polished surface. "After many years of searching, we found the land they call Assinica. There is a great host living there, enough to tip the scales of power. They cannot be allowed to return and upset the balance. We have learned through the tomes, you see, that when mastons rule, the people die. We will not be trampled so easily."

Maia stared at him hard. "I do not know about any of this. I was banished from my father's court—"

"Of course you were!" Corriveaux said with a gleeful look. "Woman, we *made* you! You were chosen as a young girl by us, the Victus. You were our secret. You were our sign. We chose *you* to bring back the hetaera." He smiled with delight at her shocked expression. "Oh, Maia, please understand! Your feelings have been manipulated since you were a small child. So have your father's. So have your mother's. Lady Deorwynn has been our tool since she studied in Dahomey to become a courtier. It was her duty to seduce your father and destroy his marriage. You were banished because *she* requested it. Men are the greatest of all fools, you see." He smirked. "Men are corrupted by women, just as women are corrupted by gold. It has always been thus. It shall always be thus. The Victus do not *fear* the hetaera. We do not *fear* women learning how to read and engrave. On the contrary, it is a sign of great courage to go against ancient traditions. Was it not Ovidius who said that we are ever striving after what is forbidden, and coveting what is denied us? That while what is allowed us is disagreeable, what is denied us causes us intense desire? Maia, you have been crafted like the handle of this cheese knife." He picked it up and turned it over in his hands admiringly. "You were *born* to become a hetaera."

Maia shook her head and backed away from him. "I will not do it," she said strongly, though her voice quavered.

He snorted. "We do not need your permission. Or your willingness. You, foolish girl, allowed a Myriad One to inhabit your body. You have been in the thrall of a most ancient being who desires revenge against the mastons for destroying her order. Our interests are quite aligned. We make you queen . . . empress . . . goddess of the world. The abbeys will be destroyed again, just as you destroyed Cruix Abbey. They are so much easier to burn than to build." He smiled. "We will send you to Assinica first, however, to unleash you upon the mastons. We have a fleet of ships, a veritable armada, which will then collect the Leerings and jewels and art from that vanquished people. A treasure greater than the one we stole from the other kingdoms."

Maia's heart was pounding in her ears. She could feel the rejoicing of the being trapped inside her.

"You think you can *tame* her?" Maia said, aghast. "She will destroy you."

"I think not," Corriveaux said. "She needs us, just as we need her."

"You are mistaken," Maia said, shaking her head. "It would be wiser to simply kill me. She will destroy all that you have built. There will be no empire left for her to rule. She only knows how to destroy."

Corriveaux scratched the edge of his mouth. "I think I am done speaking with you, Lady Maia. I see you are still struggling with her. It is only the light from the Leerings that has kept her from reclaiming you thus far. Let me quench them."

Maia felt his mental command to tame the garden Leerings. As they dimmed, she felt a wall of despair slam down on her. Her thoughts struggled under the pressure. Her vision blackened. Yes, the darkness gave power to the being inside her.

Maia reached out to the Leerings in her mind and lit them again, washing the gardens with brightness once more. She felt a hiss in her mind, a scalding pain that continued to intensify, crushing against her will.

"Enough," Corriveaux said. He darkened the Leerings again, but their light did not go out fully. Maia struggled to cling to her connection. She was drowning in darkness. The gardens were pale, the light wavering in the Leerings as her will and Corriveaux's contested for them.

Help me, Maia begged in her mind. She pleaded with the Medium. *I would rather die than accept this fate. Give me the strength to keep the light!*

"You are strong," Corriveaux grunted, impressed. She saw sweat glisten on his brow. "But given your heritage, you would be. It was crucial to our cause that you were never allowed to train in an abbey. I feel your will bending. You cannot defeat me. I have trained for too long. Of course, you were trained as well. One of the best Victus of all was assigned to tutor you. To *groom* you for your role as the empress who will destroy the mastons. Walraven did his job admirably."

Maia licked her lips, her stomach wrenching, her mind pounding with pain. "I do not believe you," she gasped.

"You doubt my words?" Corriveaux said. "You were sent to the lost abbey to become a hetaera. Not, as you may suppose, so that your father could divorce your mother. All has been part of our design. The Victus have fashioned you. You do not even begin to comprehend our subtlety, but then, we were trained by the best minds. Our ancestors could not read. They could not scribe until they were taught by your husband's ancestor, the last Earl of Dieyre. What treasures of wisdom we learned from the tomes. You were made by Walraven, like a carving from a master sculptor. And he is here to appreciate and marvel at his creation."

Maia stared at him. "What are you saying? He is dead!"

Corriveaux smirked. "There is a certain venom from a certain serpent in Dahomey, you see. A poison, if you will, which will render its victim lifeless for three days." He spread his hands wide. "No one has opened his ossuary in your cursed kingdom. They would consider it sacrilege. Enter please, my friend Walraven. I think more than enough time has passed since you last saw your protégée."

As his voice boomed out beside her, one of the wooden panels on the wall opened silently, revealing a secret door and tunnel.

Her childhood mentor stood before her. His wild silver hair was as unkempt as it had ever been, and he wore a royal dress similar to Corriveaux's, including the scabbard and ruby-pommeled sword. His face was stern and serious, his eyes flat and free of compassion.

"Ah," Walraven said, his voice croaking with age. "Thank you, my friend," he said, addressing Corriveaux. "I told you she was destined to be a queen. Queen of the Unborn. Is she not magnificent?"

He bowed slowly to Maia, his wrinkled face full of crags. "Your humble servant."

One of the hard lessons I have learned in my life is to seek the will of the Medium amidst my suffering. If I did not get what I wanted, I suffered; if I got what I did not want, I suffered; even when I got exactly what I wanted, I still suffered because you cannot hold on to anything in the physical world forever. Time is like water. Please understand this, great-granddaughter, and teach it to your posterity. Your mind is your predicament. It wants to be free of change. Free of pain, free of the obligations of life and death. But change is law and no amount of pretending will alter that reality. The Medium always brings change.

—Lia Demont, Aldermaston of Muirwood Abbey

CHAPTER THIRTY-FOUR

Ereshkigal

With the words *your humble servant*, Walraven might as well have stabbed Maia in the ribs with a dagger. She stared at him, shock stricken, incredulous, but she recognized his face, the tone of his voice. It was a voice she had longed to hear. She had treasured those words he had scribbled on a piece of paper for her. Memorized them. That he would cast himself down so that she might rise up someday had been the crutch that carried her through many difficult days.

But he had raised her up for this? To become queen of the hetaera? Her stomach shriveled with disappointment and anguish, and a shroud of weariness fell on her.

"You have been prepared for this very moment," Corriveaux said archly, gripping the ornate chair and stroking the polished wood. "You will reign supreme across all the kingdoms. The finest gowns. The most dazzling jewels. You will have lovers, wine, and coin in abundance. The world is yours for the plucking, my dear."

He walked toward her. "You will be the most beautiful woman of them all. Every fashion you wear, every tress of your hair will be envied. They will bow to you and simper for a glance, a look of approval, a compliment offered freely. And the men . . . they will *worship* you."

Maia stared into Walraven's eyes as Corriveaux spoke, her look accusing and full of daggers. "You did this to me," she whispered. "You turned my parents away from each other. You . . . you *spoiled* their lives to create mine." Her jaw trembled as a burning fury erupted inside her heart.

"I did," Walraven said, stepping closer. His eyes were deep and piercing. A light flush came to his cheeks. "For this moment, I did it. So that you could claim your destiny. So that you could *become*."

Maia stared down at the floor, at the rich carpets. The enormity of what these men were offering her rose like the dawn sun. She could have carriages and pets, servants and gowns, jewels and treats. At her word, men or women would be sent to the gallows. With her kiss on his knuckles, a man would die. The freedom they offered her was more vast than oceans and continents. She would rule them all. The thought of so much power and influence made her dizzy.

Her heart crumpled in pain and despair. She was weary of running. Her endurance was spent. Instead of a cage, her prison would be made of silk, gold, and damask. Instead of an iron collar, a golden tiara. She felt the blackness swelling inside her. Perhaps it was time to accept the future these men had built for her. Now, at least, she would have unlimited powers of revenge. All she needed to do was claim them.

For this moment. You were born for this moment.

Maia stared at Corriveaux, her vision blurring with blackness. It was like standing in the waves of the sea and getting dragged out by the surf. The sands at her feet were shifting away, urging her out into deeper waters. Wave after wave of the hetaera's blackest thoughts pounded against her—*hatred, revenge, hatred, revenge.* It was vast and relentless. She realized she would live her life in dreams, while her body was used to commit atrocities. Better to bury her face in a pillow and never breathe again.

"If I will not?" Maia asked weakly, her voice coming out in a gasp.

Corriveaux chuckled coldly. "I think you will, my dear. We have invested so much in preparing you. The Victus are patient. So very patient. It would amaze you how patient we can be." His voice was thick with meaning.

"But *if* I refuse?" Maia said, growing stronger, clenching her hands into fists.

"In the past, the Dochte Mandar would use poison to force a hetaera to accept her calling. Serpent venom. You will die to be reborn. There are rare cases when the poison does not work, of course. You seem naturally resistant to poison." There was something in his voice she did not comprehend. "You would rather be a hostage than empress? You and your *husband* both? We could extort quite a ransom from your kingdoms. And if you think you are the only girl we have been preparing for this privilege, you are mistaken." He took a step toward her, his face greedy and delighted. "But why make this so difficult? *Claim* your birthright."

She backed away from him, her mind panicking. He was going to touch her shoulder. She could sense his intent. He was going to invoke the spirit inside of her. Images crashed inside her mind, like a thousand dishes shattering.

She would not submit, no matter how gilded the prison. She would *never* submit. She was the daughter of mastons. This was not her destiny.

"Do not touch me," Maia said, holding her ground. She stopped retreating and stared at Corriveaux with defiance.

His face was livid with rage at being disobeyed. "You will submit, Lady Maia. I assure you. You will."

She felt his will crushing against hers, filling her with terror and weakness and despair. His eyes glowed silver.

The feelings were not real, she told herself. They were as false as the dreams that had haunted her these past weeks. She gritted her teeth and pushed against them. He was very strong, but she did not summon her own magic. She did not invoke the kystrel's power to defend herself. To do so in this moment would be to summon *her*. Iron bands wrapped around her thoughts, clenching against her, imprisoning her. She fell to her knees, her skirts rustling, and she bowed her head. Darkness swarmed her vision. She wanted to speak, to defy him, but her tongue was swollen in her mouth. She felt death whisper in her ear that if she did not submit, her soul would be wrenched from her body. Pain ignited across her skin; anger raged inside her.

I submit to the Medium's will, she thought, unable to utter a single word. *Use me as you will. If I must live in chains for the rest of my life, I will. If I must starve in a dungeon, I will. I will not willingly serve the Myriad Ones. I will only submit to the Medium.*

It was as if a door opened inside her mind. Many times she had felt the power of the kystrel. This new feeling dwarfed it like a lake would a puddle. She felt the bands against her mind grow hot.

Walraven! Corriveaux thought, panicking. *Join my thoughts! I cannot hold her!*

Maia felt the rending of the bands, and she started to stand, feeling as if she had an enormous beam of wood across her shoulders weighing her down. Sweat stung her eyes as she pushed herself to her feet.

"No!" Corriveaux snarled. He grabbed her shoulder, the one with the hetaera's brand. Her skin burned with fire and she felt as if furnace doors were closing around her soul. She was hot enough inside to melt metal, the power of the Medium fighting to save her.

Maia thrust the edge of her hand into Corriveaux's throat and pried his hand off her shoulder with her other hand. He gurgled and bent double, choking at the blow. She stood taller, heaving against the doors closing on her mind, but they were too heavy.

You are mine, seethed a voice in her head. *You wear my brand. You are my tabernacle.*

I serve the Medium's will. Not yours.

You will serve me!

Maia crumpled to her knees, straining against the weight. *I will fight you,* Maia vowed. *You may as well destroy me. You cannot claim me. I never consented.*

Did you not? the voice laughed. *In the tunnels beneath the lost abbey, you vowed to give me your life! You made that covenant when you were asked what you offered in exchange for the knowledge of how to save your kingdom. I hold you to it.*

Maia huddled inside herself, bent double with the struggle. *Never willingly. You forced me. I am not your daughter.* In Maia's mind, she conjured the image of her own mother. *Save me!*

She cannot save you, foolish child. Even now, my servant ministers her death. Death by poison. Poison that was meant to kill you. She is too weak, too sick to survive as you do. He drips it on her lips whilst she sleeps.

Maia's mind opened and she saw a small room, dark as night. There was a woman on a bed, whimpering in her sleep, her hair both dark and silver. A man stood over her, a small vial in his fingers. She recognized his scars, the coldness in his eyes. It was the kishion.

Serve me, and she lives. Serve me, and I spare her.

Maia saw the glimmer of moonlight through the veil of curtains. But she already knew the truth. She already knew her mother would die.

I serve the Medium's will.

As Maia bowed her head, the furnace door slammed shut against her mind. Blackness. Isolation. Gibbering terror.

You chose foolishly, the voice smirked.

And suddenly, in the midst of the impenetrable darkness, there was a prick of light and a voice. A woman's voice. Her mother's voice.

"You are Ereshkigal, the Unborn. You will depart."

The prick of light widened, growing brighter and brighter. A groan of pain wrenched from Maia's lips. She heard another voice, spewing Dahomeyjan. It was her own voice, and the most vile curses blasted from her lips.

Patiently. Calmly. The voice repeated, "You are Ereshkigal, the Unborn. You will depart."

Maia shuddered with violent tremors. She felt something jar loose inside her. It was her soul. She was going to die. The pain was horrible. White light blinded her, as if every Leering in the garden had conjured the sun. She was going to vomit. She was going to explode.

In the light, Maia saw someone, but the light was painful to look at. The voice was her mother's, but the face was not.

"You are Ereshkigal, the Unborn. You will depart!"

The shredding feeling of her soul being ripped out eased, the force of it such that Maia collapsed on the rug, panting. She blinked, still blind, and breathed deeply. The air was unburdening. She took another huge swallow of air and suddenly her chest heaved and she sobbed. The feelings of taint and blackness were gone. The creature's grip on her mind had finally been broken.

She felt arms wrap around her. "I am here, Maia. I am here."

Maia could not see through her tears. She looked up and felt a thumb wipe away the moisture from her cheek. "Mother?" she whispered faintly.

"No, Maia. I am your grandmother." The woman cupped Maia's face between her palms and stared at her with blue-green eyes the same color as her own. The woman was slight and her wrinkled skin showed her age, but she looked so much like Maia's mother it was startling. "I am Sabine Demont, High Seer of Pry-Ree." She smiled with such warmth and love that Maia began to choke again on her tears. Her language switched to Pry-rian. "You are my lost one. My little girl. The Medium forbade me to see you until now. Until you made your choice. I have been holding vigil these last three days to summon enough strength to drive the spirit of Ereshkigal out of you. She is the Queen of the Myriad Ones, and she seeks revenge against our Family. You are my granddaughter." Tears trickled down the wizened cheeks framed by crinkled gray-gold hair. Then she turned, gazing up at Walraven. "I told you, did I not? I told you she would not falter."

Walraven's expression had completely transformed. He came and knelt down by Maia, his face twisting with grief. "I am and always will be your most humble servant, Lady Maia," he whispered hoarsely. He put his hand on her grandmother's shoulder. "Forgive my many deceptions. I have secretly served the mastons since I met your grandmother in Muirwood Abbey. I am a traitor to the Victus, but hopefully my treachery has saved lives. Including yours." He smiled wanly and then stood and addressed Sabine. "Lady Demont, you must flee Naess. The Dochte Mandar will kill you . . . they are already planning it. I have a ship waiting at the dock. You know the straits are heavily guarded, but I believe you may slip away . . ."

Maia's grandmother stood and shook her head. "That would compromise you further, dear friend. There is no need; I have made other arrangements." She looked down at the prostrate Corriveaux. "He will sleep under the Medium's weight for a while. You must pretend to have been overcome by it as well. Your friendship is still needed. So is your loyalty. Thank you for all you have done."

Walraven looked concerned. "Lady Demont, how will you escape?"

She smiled and tugged open a pouch hanging from her simple girdle. She plunged her hand inside and withdrew a glimmering golden orb that was the most intricate thing Maia had ever seen. It had strange golden stays and a middle that whirred and spun.

"The Cruciger orb!" Maia gasped, recognizing what it was from the legends she had read.

"But the island . . . the armada," Walraven said, shaking his head.

"My ship is waiting for us," she said, touching his arm and patting it patiently. "We will take the *Holk* to Muirwood, as agreed. Maia will be safe there. You must give us time, Chancellor. You must stall the armada from striking Assinica. Maia is not yet ready to take the maston test. She needs time." She looked down at the orb. Maia stared at the determination and emotion in her grandmother's eyes.

"Find Jon Tayt Evnissyen," Sabine said.

The spindles began to whirl.

CHAPTER THIRTY-FIVE

Ransom

The gardens were dark, the Leerings tamed to provide shadows and concealment. Maia heard the rustle of her own skirts, felt the cool touch of the wind through her hair as they passed the Leerings, one by one, a maze of tortured faces depicting every emotion known. *The Garden of Leerings.* The thought flitted through her mind and then fled.

"Grandmother," Maia said, suddenly clutching her companion's arm. Her heart thudded in her chest. "There is someone else here, someone I cannot leave behind. The King of Dahomey . . . it was his ship that brought me here." What would the Dochte Mandar do to him if Maia fled? She knew it instantly. He would be held hostage once again, kept prisoner until they had bled his kingdom of coin to punish him for Maia's betrayal. The money Collier had gathered to fund his invasion would be stripped away. She pressed her temples, remembering his last words to her.

"We cannot go back," Sabine said, her look clouding with sadness. "Maia, he is not a maston. You cannot marry him."

Her heart shuddered with pain. The truth came bubbling from her lips. "I already have. We were"—she gulped, swallowed—"wed in Dahomey a fortnight ago. I was his prisoner."

The look her grandmother gave her was full of pity. She could still see the strong resemblance to her mother, but now it was more obvious they were different people. Sabine had gray-blond hair that was crinkled slightly, whereas her mother's was more straight. Their smiles were similar. She cupped Maia's cheek. "You were not yourself, were you?"

Maia shook her head, ashamed. "I wanted to tell him. Grandmother, he wears my kystrel. I am such a fool. I have been deceived all the while."

"Shush, child," Sabine said. "The Myriad Ones are cunning. Their queen is known as Ereshkigal. You will learn all of this when you take your maston vows. You could not have known, Maia, because you were not permitted to study. Let us keep walking, the orb bids us onward."

"I cannot leave him behind!" Maia pleaded into her ear. "He will think I betrayed him. He is just as deceived as I was."

Maia's grandmother gently squeezed Maia's neck. "He had more choice in the matter than you did. The two of you were promised when you were both very little." She released Maia from the hug and pulled back to stroke her cheek. "The Dahomeyjan are known for their craftiness and subtlety. It is no coincidence that the hetaera spawn from their kingdom." She sighed sympathetically. "Let me consult the orb."

Sabine cupped it in her hands, staring at it thoughtfully. "Is there a safe way to rescue King Gideon from the Victus?"

The spindle on the orb did not turn, but writing appeared on the lower half of the orb. It was Pry-rian script, elegant and slanting.

The king's collier must be ransomed.

Maia stared at the writing, unveiled in golden aurichalcum. Her pulse quickened. The Medium knew his name.

Sabine stared at the words, then glanced at Maia.

"I understand it," Maia said, touching her arm. Her heart trembled with sadness. *Forgive me, Collier. Forgive me.*

She did not hear any echo in her mind. His thoughts were silent, which made her feel sadness and guilt. The emotions wrestled mercilessly inside her.

"Come," Sabine said. She hugged Maia again, and then the orb guided them into the thick gorse of the gardens and the hedge mazes beyond. They continued walking until a bark sounded and Argus came padding up, wagging his tail frantically.

"Oh, Argus," Maia said, dropping to her knees and letting the boarhound lick her face. She nuzzled his fur, stifling her tears of joy and regret. Stomping through the grass after the dog came Jon Tayt, who looked at her with a wise, knowing smile.

"By Cheshu, you do look like a queen," he said, coming up and mussing her hair. He turned to Sabine and bowed. "I brought her here as best I could, Aldermaston. Down, Argus, stop licking the lass's face." He shook his head, then gave a meaningful look to Sabine Demont. "Is my banishment over?"

"Not yet, Jon Tayt Evnissyen," Sabine said. She looked at Maia. "The Evnissyen are the protectors and advisers of the royal Family of Pry-Ree."

"I know of the Evnissyen," Maia said. "I met them myself when I was in Pry-Ree. I did not know you were one of them."

"That is when I asked Jon Tayt to protect you. I sent him far away, very far away, to wait in the mountains of Dahomey until you emerged. He has been patient and faithful. Jon, your duty is not fulfilled. You must protect her in an ancient land where she will study to take the maston test. There is much we must speak on, but not amidst so many Leerings. They have eyes and faces, yes, but they also have ears. Did you bring the gown from the ship?"

Jon Tayt nodded and unslung his pack. "Yes, the captain bade me to bring it," he said, rummaging through to the bottom. There were small pots, sieves, knives, spoons—a veritable kitchen crammed inside. Sabine began to help Maia unfasten her kirtle. The rich golden fabric peeled away and Maia felt her heart sadden. She wanted to rip away everything that reminded her of what she had unwittingly become. How curious then, that she would be loath to give up the splendid gown and the jewels Collier had put on her. But she kept the earrings in her ears, wanting them as a keepsake to remind her of her husband. Her arms shivered in the cold air as the dress slumped to her ankles. She wore only her shift, and her teeth began chattering.

Maia noticed her grandmother staring at her shoulder, an inscrutable look on her face. Her skin was wrinkled and aged, her beauty faded but not lost. There was something almost angelic about her, an inner peace and calmness that made her lovely to Maia's eyes. Though Sabine's eyes were narrow, they did not judge. Her small hand rested near the brand on Maia's shoulder blade, warm against her frigid skin.

"I am sorry, Grandmother," Maia whispered, feeling the shame like a yawning chasm.

Sabine shook her head slowly. "You did not do it willingly, I know that. But you did it nonetheless. We often suffer the consequences of the choices of others. But our own are the most painful." The fingers gripped her skin tightly. "There is a tome I must show you. The tome of my great-grandmother, Lia Demont.

She is the one who cursed the Leering that branded your shoulder. The curse she laid on it was done by irrevocare sigil. It *cannot* be undone." The grip firmed even more, Sabine's eyes were deadly earnest. "Maia, because of the curse, you cannot kiss anyone. Ever. Not your husband. Not your children, if the Medium blesses you with them someday. This you must *never* do. The plague it can unleash is terrible. The Medium is strong with our Family. You must find a husband and pass along our connection with the Medium, just as you were born with it. That husband must be a maston. He must know the truth about you. But no one else can know. Only we few." She paused, letting her words sink in. "Ereshkigal will not cease trying to destroy you. She wants revenge because of what Lia Demont did to the hetaera. You will always be hunted. You will always be persecuted. But you will be strong enough not to succumb. Your great-great-great-grandmother Lia saw you in visions, Maia. She told me about you in her tome. There is something you must do, something only a maston can do. Do you have it, Jon Tayt?"

Jon Tayt withdrew an oilskin bundle from his pack and began untying it. He loosed the strands and unrolled it. Maia caught the glimpse of pale fabric. It was a peasant's gown and girdle, pale in color—she could not tell if it was blue or green in the dim light of the stars.

"It is a wretched's gown," Sabine Demont said, stroking the fabric. "A gown much like Lia wore growing up. Being a wretched taught her humility and meekness. Your experiences have taught you similar lessons. I think the Medium tests us. It tries our patience. You were not swayed by jewels or riches or any of the promises of vanity. Wear this as your disguise for now, Maia. Where we are going, girls are taught to read and scribe. Even the wretcheds. This is done in secret, at night, to protect them from the Dochte Mandar. These girls are called the Ciphers. You will become one of them."

Her stomach thrilled. She would be among other girls who knew how to read? "Thank you, Grandmother," Maia said. She took the simple gown and hurriedly put it on and then tied the girdle around her waist. The fabric was wool and it was warm. The sleeves were long and drooping.

Argus's ears pointed up and he snuffled a growl.

"Best we leave," Jon Tayt said. "We have a mountain to cross before we reach the *Holk*."

***

The dinghy bobbed and pitched in the turbulent waters. Maia was soaked through from the spume and spray, and she huddled alongside Argus, who growled at the bucking sensation. It was morning, but there was no sun, only a pale sky—like the promise of sunrise except without the glorious rays of light and striations of color. The rocks were jagged like decaying teeth and the oarsmen pulled hard to crest the swells. She clung to the gunwale, watching as the oarsmen fought the pounding surf.

"Row man! Row!" the man at the helm barked in Pry-rian. "Pull hard, lads, it is a way off yet. Row man, row!"

Maia stared back at the craggy alcove, the enormous black basalt cliffs that rose from the churning foam and spray like a decaying monster. Sea creatures speckled the rock with a variety of muted colors, creating a queer beauty that thrilled her heart.

You cannot escape me, daughter of Ereshkigal. The voice sneered in her mind. *I am the Queen of Storms.*

Maia gritted her teeth, afraid of the voices in her mind.

You will all drown. If you will not serve me, you will drown.

"Maia?" Sabine's hand touched her arm. The fabric of her sleeve was soaked and her grandmother was equally drenched. "You look fearful. Do you hear her again?"

Maia nodded, shivering and shuddering. The brand on her shoulder was hot.

Another huge wave picked up the dinghy, and for a moment, Maia feared it would capsize. She clung to the hull, terrified.

"She cannot harm you," Sabine said soothingly. "You hear her many voices because you trained yourself to listen for them. Now you must learn to ignore her thoughts and begin coaxing the Medium to speak with you. It begins with a thought, Maia." Another swell made Sabine totter a bit. "That was thrilling!" she said, beaming. "It begins with a thought. Think of a safe place, of a time when you were happy. With the memory will come the feeling. You can choose what you remember, and thus the feelings those memories instill. You *must* choose wisely. Everything hinges on our thoughts."

Maia frowned as she realized something. The dreams she had experienced since her visit to the lost abbey had returned her to her most haunting memories, summoning all the dark emotions she had buried deep within her. Ereshkigal had not just devised the dreams as an empty distraction—the Myriad One had feasted on her hatred, her fear, and her resentment.

"I do not have many *memories* of peaceful times," she said, her voice rising in pitch as the next swell hit them. Her stomach bubbled and seethed. It was exhilarating, but terrifying.

She remembered the dinghy that had brought her to the shores of Dahomey. Faces and images flashed through her mind. The ruins of Dochte Abbey, a blackened skeleton of rubble that would never rise again. The kishion gripping her hand, helping her climb down a rope despite the bob of the waves. Leerings.

Blinding lightning. So many of the memories were tainted. Maia had known such little peace in her life, and anxiety flooded her heart at the reminder.

Then a memory struck her like a hammer blow. It was a small inn in the hinterlands of Dahomey. There was pretty music, clapping, and dancing. As she closed her eyes, she could hear the stamp of boots, the cheers, the thrill of the various instruments. She longed to make music again, to strum a lute with her fingers.

In her mind, she saw Collier approaching her.

"A dance," he said, extending his hand to her. "If you must go tonight, then give me this memory to take with me. Please, my lady. Dance with me."

Her raging heart began to quell as she lived again in the memory. Before she knew who he truly was. Before the illusions of her life were shattered. She could still hear the labored breathing of the sailors as they rowed, but their words were slurred, as if heard from beneath water. She felt one of Sabine's hands gripping hers, her other arm wrapped tightly around her shoulders as she stroked Maia's damp hair. But in her mind, she was in that small village as she and Collier began to dance. He had taught her a new dance, the Volta, and she remembered how it had felt when his strong arms lifted her high and twirled her around. The simple, pure joy of it.

So much had happened since then. So many surprises. So many disappointments. But Maia savored the memory, the feel of his hand in hers. She had not kept anything of his except for the single pair of earrings. She wished she still had the crumpled lily he had left in her saddlebag. She thought of his eyes, his handsome smile that had a certain cocksureness to it. She admired his thick dark hair and wondered at the little scar on his cheek. She sank deep into the memory, reveling in every detail.

Her heart ached for what would happen to him. After being held hostage in Paeiz as a child, he valued freedom above all things. Now, because of her, he was a prisoner once more. How cruel was the past. How painful. She heard his laughter in her mind and squeezed it tightly to her bosom.

Maia—are you there?

Her heart shuddered. She could almost feel him. There was darkness and cold. It was an unlit cell. She could hear the wind whistling through the eaves. Through the bond they shared, she could feel his anguish, his misery. His accusation.

Maia, why? Why?

The dinghy butted into the hull of the *Holk*. She opened her eyes, wiped a trickle of saltwater from her cheek, and craned her neck. The ship was enormous, the wood slimed and crusted with barnacles.

"Hoy! Hoy! Up! Hoy! Hoy! Up!"

Hooks were fixed to the front and rear and suddenly the dinghy broke free of the waves' clutches. It rocked and reeled and Maia feared the winds would spill her into the deadly surf below.

"Are you all right, my child?" Sabine asked in her ear. "You look forlorn."

She turned to her grandmother and embraced her. "I hear him in my mind too," she said miserably. "I hear my husband's thoughts. I want to answer him . . . if only to tell him I am sorry."

Sabine smiled sadly. "Every choice we make that brings us closer to the Myriad Ones is a choice that alters our course. But it is your decision, Maia. I cannot make it for you."

Maia wanted desperately to respond to him. It tortured her to let him think the worst of her. But she had given herself completely to the Medium, and it had rescued her from Ereshkigal. Could she renege on her commitment so soon? The feelings nearly strangled her. Slowly and sadly, she shook her head no. "I will not," she whispered.

Sabine gave her an understanding look—one that showed she had carried heavy secrets herself. "The voices will fade in time. At Muirwood, you will not hear the whispers of the Myriad Ones or your kystrel. Ereshkigal has no dominion there. It was sealed up as a safe haven for you, as a place for refuge and peace."

"Mother is there," Maia replied eagerly, struggling to put aside thoughts of Collier. "I fear she is in danger." She remembered suddenly her vision of the kishion. She looked at her grandmother. "Is she safe?"

The look in Sabine's eyes said the words her mouth could not.

To my dear one, Marciana, I give you my love, my high regard for your courage, and my deepest wishes for your happiness. I fear that happiness is an emotion you have felt little during your life thus far. I was raised a wretched in the Aldermaston's kitchen at Muirwood Abbey instead of as a Princess of Pry-Ree as was my birthright. Yet I knew more happiness in the simplicity of that life than I have found in the burdens and cares of leading others. To be a leader is to be alone. I have counsel for you, great-great-great-granddaughter who was named after my husband's sister. Choose wise counselors to guide you. Wisdom is the Gift you need most of all, for you will face dilemmas and troubles that I never experienced. You will also endure heartaches unique to yourself. Bear these with patience, Maia. Pain passes in time and forges character. The Dochte Mandar of your day think that by depriving humanity of the awful emotions—grief, suffering, despair—they can prevent the recurrence of the Blight. It is not true. Depriving your father and mother of the chance to let their private grief teach them love and compassion sowed the seeds of their marriage's failure. If these sad emotions are endured—and accepted—patiently, they teach us wisdom and compassion. You have struggled all your life to contain your tears because your father once praised you that you did not weep as a babe. Maia, there is healing in weeping. There is balm in tears. An Aldermaston once said: Tears at times have the weight of speech. I weep for you as I scribe these words. Though I have never met you, I love you, Maia.

I know you have a brand on your shoulder. You will live with the grief of the consequences of that all your life. But there is a sacred duty you must fulfill. When the abbeys were destroyed in my era, I made a Covenant that Muirwood would be rebuilt, that the gates of Idumea would be opened anew that the dead may pass on from this second life. This is the rite of the Apse Veil. It also allows mastons to travel great distances between abbeys. The longer the Veil remains closed, the more unrest will occur in the kingdoms. The dead wander among us. They grow impatient in their banishment. They speak to the living through the Dark Pools. You must open the Apse Veil. I give you this charge. By Idumea's hand, make it so. Remember—sometimes even to live is an act of courage.

—Lia Demont, Aldermaston of Muirwood Abbey

CHAPTER THIRTY-SIX

Muirwood

Maia's eyes were wet with tears and she wiped them on her gown sleeve, then ran her palm over the smooth aurichalcum page. The *Holk* swayed, its mighty beams creaking and groaning like an ancient man feeling his age. The tome was heavy in her lap, the words illuminated by light streaming in from the round window of the cabin.

"There is no shame in tears," Sabine Demont said softly, reaching out and caressing Maia's hand.

Maia felt the little tremors bubbling up inside her. "How well she knew me," Maia said faintly, her eyes swimming. "As if she had walked alongside me in silence all these years." She swallowed. "Lia had the Gift of Seering. It amazes me."

Sabine stroked her arm. "Her father had it. It does not always pass from one generation to the next. Without the full powers of the abbeys, it is an increasingly rare Gift. So many powers of the Medium have not been manifested since her generation."

"Why is that?" Maia asked, dabbing away the moisture from her eyes.

"I do not know," Sabine said, her voice fading. "When you read the tomes, you will discern that some generations are more flush with the Medium than others. There are individuals, like Lia Demont, who rise up to do great things. Then several generations pass with little notice. Occasionally a generation comes that burdens the world with evil. History is like a river, I think. There are seasons that occur over and over. Sometimes the waters are swollen and violent. Sometimes placid." She smiled at Maia and hugged her. "We live in turbulent waters, Maia. When your father abandoned his oaths, he issued a new season. We must all endure the rapids now."

Maia looked down at her hands. "Are you . . . disappointed in me, Grandmother?"

There was silence, and Maia felt her cheeks begin to burn with shame.

"Do not mistake my quiet, Maia," Sabine said, her voice choked with emotion. Tenderly, she traced her fingers through Maia's long hair. "You have never had children, so you cannot understand. Someday you will. There is nothing you could do that would make me stop loving you. I wish with all my heart that every parent felt this way. Unfortunately, you had a father whose love was conditional on obedience. I think he inherited that from his father. So many choose to bind themselves to the traditions of their fathers. Even if those traditions are wrong and harmful. But I know . . ." Her voice broke with emotion. "I know how your *mother* felt about you. There is no stronger love than a mother's love. Except perhaps a *grandmother's*." She smiled and hugged Maia again, who hugged her fiercely in return. Tears spilled down both their cheeks.

Maia swallowed, feeling the anxious churn of her emotions. She *knew* her mother was dead, that they had parted until the second life was over. She wept with that knowledge, wishing she could have at least said good-bye. Thanked her for sending her a message through the wanderer Maderos. She let herself feel the emotions, even though they were painful. She let herself cry.

"Do you know what will happen next, Grandmother?" Maia asked. "Lia's tome is blank after that last part."

Sabine wiped her own eyes and gave Maia a thoughtful look. "No, I do not know. As you said, the rest of her tome is empty. My Gift of Seering is focused on the past. That is what I can see most clearly, the time that happened just prior to the Scourging. I know what the abbeys used to look like, so I have visited the various kingdoms to help with the rebuilding. But I am blind as to the future."

Maia closed the tome and set it on the table. "The tome was not as long as I thought it would be. How long did she live?"

"We know she was a grandmother," Sabine said in a small voice. "She mentions her granddaughter in her tome. This was the granddaughter who sailed back to Comoros and began to rebuild Muirwood. It was when her granddaughter was born that she began having visions of us specifically, I think. There is something about the birth of children that makes the whispers of the Medium particularly powerful. She saw our future and began to scribe that tome for us. She gave the tome to her granddaughter to take with her when she sailed across the sea. It was then given to me. That was *my* mother." She sighed. "Lia foresaw that if the mastons did not return, the Naestors would completely overrun the land and make returning impossible. Lia saw something else in the future she only hints at. She foresaw that because of the hetaera, women would be forbidden to read."

"Yes, yet you learned to read," Maia said. "You mentioned the Ciphers."

"Yes. As you saw in the tome, Lia was the Aldermaston of Muirwood before she left. She instructed that *anyone* would always be permitted to read and engrave at Muirwood Abbey. Even the wretcheds. To keep this hidden from the Dochte Mandar, the girls' lessons are given in the cloisters at night, after all the male students are abed. During the day, they are taught languages and other skills. But their instruction in the Medium and the tomes is done in secret. In the past, all the children of the rulers were sent to Dochte Abbey to study. Now that instruction happens at the chief abbey in every realm. For Comoros, it is Muirwood. You were *meant* to study there, Maia. You were supposed to go there when you were twelve, but your father refused to send you after your mother took sanctuary there. You have missed the opportunity to learn there in your youth, but you were tutored by Walraven to read. Now you must learn the art of engraving. It will not be difficult for you."

"Tell me," Maia said. "Can Chancellor Walraven truly be trusted? My heart is unsure. I feel . . . betrayed by him, yet I also believe he is on our side. I am sorely conflicted."

"Of course you are," Sabine said, patting her arm. "You have every reason to be distrustful. He is a senior member of the Victus. They are the ones who control the politics between the kingdoms. They scheme and plot amongst themselves to choose which kingdoms will go to war against each other and to provoke the outcome they desire. They broker the truces and arrange for the payment of ransoms and the murder of rivals. They are superstitiously hostile against the mastons, fearing any power that they cannot manipulate or control.

"You see, Maia, when the first ships returned, the Naestors laid a cunning trap. They welcomed the mastons as the rightful rulers of the land. They had learned a great deal from the artifacts left behind . . . and developed some small, distorted understanding of the rituals and customs. They revered knowledge and hoarded these artifacts, like the Leerings we passed when we left. The jewelry you were wearing, the necklaces and rings and bracelets. That was melted aurichalcum, Maia—the melted tomes from the ancient generations, fashioned by goldsmiths into jewelry. The Dochte Mandar believe that those jewels have great power because of what they were made from. But the power of the Medium is not transmitted that way." She shook her head and chuckled.

"It was the intent of the Naestors all along," Sabine continued, "to enslave the mastons. They suspected, because of the Earl of Dieyre's writings, that they would return someday, and they feared losing the abandoned kingdoms they had claimed. When the mastons returned, they greeted them with celebrations and festivals and honors. The Naestors acceded the lands and abandoned cities to the mastons with the intent of re-creating the kingdoms of the past and restoring the fallen realms to their previous glory. You see, they lacked so much of the knowledge the mastons possessed—how to build, how to make music, how to restore the ruins that were left behind. Their only request was for their own religion—that of the Dochte Mandar—to remain among the populace, allowing the people to decide between it and the maston ways. The goal of the Dochte Mandar was to learn the crafts they did not know, corrupt the mastons through generosity, and then turn on the mastons and enslave them before the abbeys were finished. They suspected, and rightly so, that not *all* the mastons had returned. They began seeking Assinica, knowing it existed, and sent multiple expeditions into the sea from Naess to hunt for it. They were not willing to risk that the balance would be destroyed and the mastons would conquer them."

Maia stared at her grandmother. It was difficult to keep up with so much information, but it meshed well with what she had learned in Lia's tome and from her predictions of the future and with what Corriveaux had said to her.

"But according to Lia's tome, your mother kept it secret," Maia said, "that the Apse Veils were still closed. She knew that if the abbeys were rebuilt, not only would the doorway to Idumea open, but also the doorways that connected the various abbeys . . . including Assinica."

"Exactly! The Dochte Mandar have efficient spies and can move information quickly between the kingdoms, but never as quickly as the mastons could move when the abbeys were fully functioning. They fear this most of all, that they will lose their power over the populace once the Veils open. They would rather destroy the abbeys again than relinquish the power and wealth they have accumulated. They are so desperate to prevent this, Maia, that they were willing to unleash the hetaera in order to stop it." Her face was grave and serious. "I was able to persuade Chancellor Walraven of this finally. You see, I was at Muirwood when your father and mother's marriage was on trial. I was there in secret, or your father would *never* have come. As the High Seer, I would never sanction the divorce."

"I did not even *know* you were the High Seer," Maia said, shaking her head. "It has been a great secret. I knew very little of my mother's Family in Pry-Ree except for a few cousins I met when I was younger. And I heard you were an Aldermaston."

Sabine smiled. "There is a great deal of resentment because the High Seership has remained in Pry-Ree. It was held in Avinion during Lia's time. Hautland aspires for it. They are building a grand city, as you know. But as you also know, coin corrupts the heart. Riches are an illusion. I do not tarry in one kingdom for very long, so the petitions must follow me where I roam. I was lured to Naess recently . . . This is grim news, but I must share it with you." She took Maia's hands and stroked them. "Our brothers and sisters in Assinica grew worried since our long absence. They were expecting that the Apse Veils would be opened by now, that our kingdoms would rejoin. They feared we were enslaved to the Naestors, so they sent a ship to seek after us." She shook her head. "That ship was blown by a storm and discovered by the Naestors, who abducted and murdered them when they learned who they were. There was a tome on board the vessel, which they brought back. They could not read it, for the language was written in a cipher—a code. Only someone with the right Gift could read it. They invited me, as the High Seer, to come to Naess and read a curious tome they said they had discovered. Their intent, as you know, was to get me to read and translate it before using you to murder me." She smiled sadly. "What they did not know was that Lia had forewarned me about your condition. And Lia knew, as I did, that you would not succumb to their offer of power, just as Lia did not succumb when they tried to win her favor."

There was a firm pounding on the door of the cabin. Sabine Demont rose from the bedside and walked to the door. When she opened it, Argus squeezed through and padded up to Maia for his ears to be scratched. His tongue wagged faithfully.

"By Cheshu, lass," Jon Tayt muttered, "get your own hound!"

"What is it, Jon?" Sabine asked.

"Yesterday you wanted to know when we sailed past Pry-Ree. It was glorious seeing the Myniths again, even from the ship. I long to hunt in those woods again. But you asked this morning that I tell you when we reached the coast of Comoros and the Belgeneck River leading to Muirwood. And so we have."

"Thank you. Well done. Come, Maia. Come see your new home."

Maia rose from the bed, wearing her wretched's dress, and joined Jon Tayt and Sabine on the deck of the *Holk*. The huge ship lumbered up the thick chasm of the river. The air was brackish and musty, but the aching chill of the dark lands of the Naestors lay far behind them. The forest on each side of the river reminded her of the cursed lands of Dahomey. It was not what she had expected, and it conflicted with her memories of her kingdom. The trees were a maze of twisting, black oaks, thick with lichen and moss and overhung by creeping mist. The ship creaked and yawed, and she could hear the waves lapping against the hull as it advanced into the river's mouth.

"Now where is there a more sick and twisted wood, I ask you?" Jon Tayt said with a scowl. "And this is where I am to be banished next, my lady?" He coughed in his fist. "Ach, this is not a forest, but a swamp."

Maia could hear the buzz of mosquitoes and the clack of insects. A heron swept overhead, gliding on the breeze. She rested her arms on the railing, feeling the breeze ruffle her hair as she watched the river expectantly.

"It is the Bearden Muir," Sabine said, her mouth pursed in a dream-like smile. "It rains a great deal in this Hundred. And the rivers swell and flood. It has its own beauty."

Jon Tayt sniffed. "Well, I hope there is wild boar in these woods. With all those oak trees, there are bound to be acorns."

"Plenty of wild pig," Sabine said. Maia could see she was lost in a vision, her eyes seeing something the others could not.

Maia touched her grandmother's shoulder. "What do you see?"

Sabine sighed, her voice soft and thick with tears. "I can see them in my mind's eye, child. Lia and Colvin. Marciana and Kieran Ven. I see them leaving these shores on a ship like this one." She swallowed thickly. "There she is on the deck. So young. Like you. She has wild hair, like my mother's. There she is, Maia." Tears flicked down from Sabine's lashes. "She is looking right at us. Oh, by the *Medium*! I see her waving. She is waving to us."

Maia felt tears sting her eyes. She put her arm around her grandmother's shoulders and hugged her close. She wanted to kiss her, as a child to a mother. She wanted it so badly that the desire began to burn inside of her. There was a tingle of heat on her shoulder and a sizzle of pain. A feeling of anger and rage and blackness churned inside her heart.

Maia wondered if that feeling would ever abandon her fully. "I feel her again," she whispered in her grandmother's ear.

"Use your thoughts to tame your feelings," Sabine whispered back. "Remember, Maia, it begins with a thought." She lifted her hand to the river, waving to someone whom none of them could see.

Maia swallowed and began to focus her attention, crushing the evil brooding inside her soul. "How did Lia die?" she asked, staring at the river waters.

"No one knows," Sabine said, wiping away her tears. She turned to face her granddaughter. "She disappeared after my mother's name-day ceremony, leaving behind her tome and the Cruciger orb. She was never seen again. I think the Medium took her to Idumea to see her father and her mother at last." She sniffled. "Ah, there—you can just see the abbey through the mist! There is Muirwood!"

Maia gripped the edge of the rail as the mist began to part and dissolve. She saw the abbey grounds, the tall but humble spires. Sunlight momentarily blinded her. A feeling of warmth and safety settled across her shoulders like a blanket. The anger inside her heart was quenched, and the heaviness she had lived with all her life faded away. Her heart thrilled at the sight.

Welcome, it whispered.

EPILOGUE

Lady Deorwynn stared at her husband's sleeping face. She saw the lines and grooves, the wrinkles that marred his countenance. He was aging before her eyes, the strength of his body beginning to fail. She stared down at him, feeling a familiar sense of loathing and disgust. It was exactly how she had come to feel about her first husband before she had arranged to become a widow. She smoothed the front of her nightclothes, feeling the bulge in her middle and the quickening butterflies dancing in her womb. She blinked, wondering abstractedly whether the child was even his. His arm was sprawled across the pillow and he murmured something unimportant—gibberish.

She stepped away from the bedstead and strode over the plush fur rugs toward the anteroom. There, at his desk, was a stack of scrolls and missives, the most important of the day, left by Chancellor Crabwell. She broke the seals and quickly began reading the messages. She did not fear being discovered by her husband. He did not know she could read. She perused each one, scanning the contents quickly, memorizing the important details. Rumors were spreading across the other kingdoms. Rumors of an abbey burning in Mon. Rumors of Dahomey preparing to invade. Rumors of the hetaera returning. She frowned, her beautiful lips straining into a snarl. Where *was* that girl? Why had she not returned to Comoros?

Lady Deorwynn set the last of the missives down, and her thoughts turned dark and anxious. What if Marciana failed to become one? Would that cause the Victus to change their plans? Would they seek another to take her place? Her thoughts went to her own daughter, Murer. She could become the empress. She was in the succession, a Princess of Comoros now. Could that be arranged? Her stomach was giddy with both excitement and fear. So many things could go wrong.

She reached for the cup of wine on her husband's table, her thirst suddenly fiery in her throat as she lifted it to her lips.

"You may not want to drink that," said a voice from the shadows.

Lady Deorwynn's hand shook with a spasm of fear, sloshing the wine on her wrist and the table, staining some of the letters.

"By the Rood!" she hissed angrily. She knew the voice.

Her eyes distinguished him in the shadows of the antechamber, sitting in one of her husband's chairs, lounging like a cat. The kishion. It was so dark she could not see his face. Not that she wanted to. He was riven with scars and had a contemptible manner.

"Is it poisoned?" she whispered harshly, setting down the wine cup with a trembling hand.

"Not this time," the kishion murmured. There was something in his voice. Something dangerous.

"What do you mean by that?" she asked, annoyed. This time the fear started in her stomach and shot down to her ankles. "Have you been there this whole time?" She tried to sound outraged, but she was trembling violently.

"I did not wish to disturb you, madame," the kishion said, rising languidly from the chair. "So I waited."

"How dare you!" Lady Deorwynn spat at him.

"I dare much," the kishion said, walking toward her. His boots made no sound. Her heart spasmed with dread. She never should have arranged for such a man to enter the kingdom. She had held second thoughts from the start, especially when his poison failed to kill Maia in her mother's manor house. Careless. He was recklessly careless.

She saw his face as he reached the rim of the candle's light. He was smiling in a crooked way. He looked . . . drunk.

"Why are you here?" Lady Deorwynn demanded. "Where is Marciana? Did you bring her back, or do the Naestors want to keep her?"

"I do not know where she is," he said with a shrug. "But she is the one who burned Cruix Abbey. She razed it to ashes. She has *become*." He scratched the edge of his mouth with a finger. Then he looked at the scrolls and papers scattered about the desk. He took one of them up and then tossed it aside. "Another will arrive in the morning," he said. "Your enemy is finally dead. She gasped her last yesterday after struggling with a terrible fever. A few drops of poison on her lips."

Lady Deorwynn's eyes widened with shock. "Who ordered you to kill her?"

"No one," the kishion replied. Again, that half smile that mocked her. "She needed to be . . . removed. You must persuade your *husband* to give the lands and manor houses and castles to his firstborn. Maia is to inherit."

Lady Deorwynn's trembling increased. A pit of fear stabbed inside of her. "Her estates were already confiscated and given to the new Earl of Forshee and three other men. They will revolt if stripped of those incomes. You are mad."

"Quite possibly," the kishion replied, chuckling. Then his eyes turned deadly earnest. "See it done, Lady Deorwynn. You never know when your next drink will be your last." He picked up her husband's goblet, saluted her with it, and drained it in a single swallow.

AUTHOR'S NOTE

The origin of this story goes back to December 1998. I was a night-shift supervisor at Intel's R&D factory in Santa Clara, California. After getting home from working a twelve-hour shift, I would promptly go to bed and sleep for a few hours. One day, I had a very vivid dream about an evil father, his daughter, and a skilled protector who was assigned to guard the girl. I awoke from the dream with the thoughts bubbling inside and hurriedly scribbled notes on some paper near my bed and then fell back asleep. When I woke up to my alarm later, I could hardly remember anything about the dream until I looked at the notes. This was the origin of Maia's tale.

What struck me about the story as I pondered it was that the evil man's daughter was the heroine *and* the villain—only she did not know that she was the villain. Her actions and intentions along the way were to help solve a problem, restore an ancient magic, but she seemed to cause havoc and destruction wherever she went.

In 2002, my friends and I started publishing *Deep Magic*, a fantasy e-zine. We needed stories, so I wrote a novella called *Maia* for one of the earlier issues. The novella was intended to be the villain's backstory, and I had planned to write the novel from Jon

Tayt's point of view. I even tried a few chapters with that in mind, many years ago. Later, I came up with the idea for *The Wretched of Muirwood* and decided to use that as the history to Maia's story. So even though I wrote the novels about Lia and Colvin first, I already had the novella *Maia* in hand. That novella became the source material for my graphic novel, *The Lost Abbey*, which Jet City Comics published, and are the events that precede *Banished*.

I enjoyed writing from Maia's point of view, and the story certainly took some twists that I did not expect. One of my all-time favorite books is *A Little Princess* by Frances Hodgson Burnett. I love the story of Sara Crewe and how she goes from being a rich man's only child to a destitute pauper and that, even though she lives in squalor in the attic of Miss Minchin's school, she overcomes by focusing on her thoughts and using her imagination. In *The Banished of Muirwood*, Maia actually is a princess who loses her station. As you will discover in Book Two, *The Ciphers of Muirwood*, her troubles have not ended.

I am glad I slept next to a drawer with paper and could capture the raw seeds of this story. You never know when a random dream will blossom into a novel.

ACKNOWLEDGMENTS

Many thanks to all the staff at 47North and Amazon Publishing for the continuous excellent partnership and collaboration. It has been a life-changing journey for me that led to leaving my twenty-two-year career at Intel to write full time. Also thanks to my early readers for their feedback, input, and encouragement: Gina, Emily, Karen, Robin, Shannon, and Rachelle. I also would like to thank the fabulous Angela Polidoro, whose input and enthusiasm improved the book and made it better. And finally, a shout out to Lisa from Vermont for driving to New York City for my first author signing at Comic Con 2014!

ABOUT THE AUTHOR

Photo © Kim Bills

Jeff Wheeler took an early retirement from his career at Intel in 2014 to become a full-time author. He is, most importantly, a husband and father, and a devout member of his church. He is occasionally spotted roaming hills with oak trees and granite boulders in California or in any number of the state's majestic redwood groves.

Visit the author's website: www.jeff-wheeler.com

More ways to be enchanted by
Jeff Wheeler's
Muirwood

LEGENDS OF MUIRWOOD

The Wretched of Muirwood
The Blight of Muirwood
The Scourge of Muirwood

COVENANT OF MUIRWOOD

The Banished of Muirwood
The Ciphers of Muirwood (cover forthcoming)
The Void of Muirwood (cover forthcoming)

MUIRWOOD: THE LOST ABBEY

GRAPHIC NOVEL